LOVE ON ASSIGNMENT

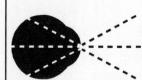

This Large Print Book carries the
Seal of Approval of N.A.V.H.

A LADIES OF SUMMERHILL NOVEL,
BOOK 2

LOVE ON ASSIGNMENT

CARA LYNN JAMES

THORNDIKE PRESS
A part of Gale, Cengage Learning

GALE
CENGAGE Learning

Detroit • New York • San Francisco • New Haven, Conn • Waterville, Maine • London

GALE
CENGAGE Learning™

LIBRARY OF CONGRESS CATALOGING-IN-PUBLICATION DATA

James, Cara Lynn, 1949–
    Love on assignment : a ladies of Summerhill novel / by Cara Lynn James.
        p. cm. — (Thorndike Press large print Christian romance)
    ISBN-13: 978-1-4104-3537-8 (hardcover)
    ISBN-10: 1-4104-3537-7 (hardcover)
    1. Secretaries—Fiction. 2. Newspaper editors—Fiction. 3. Governesses—Fiction. 4. College teachers—Fiction. 5. Newport (R.I.)—Fiction. 6. Large type books. I. Title.
    PS3610.A4284L683 2011b
    813'.6—dc22   2011003361

Published in 2011 by arrangement with Thomas Nelson, Inc.

To my two adult children,
Justin and Alicia Slaughter,
with all my love

ONE

Newport, Rhode Island
July 1900
Charlotte Hale's legs, hidden beneath her long serge skirt, wobbled like a newborn colt's. But she pinned on a confident smile and gazed directly into her boss's dark granite eyes.

"Please be seated, Miss Hale. We have something important to discuss." He gave her a curt nod as he loomed behind his polished mahogany desk, an engraved nameplate resting on the edge. *Arnold Phifer, Editor*

Dressed in his well-tailored navy suit and silk vest, he stared at her as if assessing her value. A cherrywood pipe protruded beneath a white handlebar mustache, waxed to stiff perfection.

She slid into the chair across from the middle-aged editor of the *Rhode Island Reporter,* stenography pad in hand. In the three years she'd worked at the newspaper, Mr. Phifer had never once summoned her to his private office which overlooked the bustling Thames Street, except for dictation.

He pulled the pipe from his mouth and placed it in an ashtray beside a ceramic jar of tobacco. "Miss Hale" — his bushy brows drew together across his pink forehead — "I'm impressed with your work."

She raised her eyebrows. Impressed with her typing or shorthand skills? What exactly singled her out? Accurate spelling, perfect grammar? Surely not. He'd always taken her for granted, never once praising her.

"Thank you, sir." The man seldom handed out compliments to anyone, especially unmerited ones.

"I have a choice assignment for you, Miss Hale." He spoke with a soft slur, easy on the ears. "You still want to be a reporter, don't you?"

Every nerve in her body tingled. "Yes, I most definitely do. I've always wanted to become a journalist." To date, Mr. Phifer had never allowed any woman at his newspaper rise to a position higher than secretary.

"I figured you hadn't changed your mind. You've certainly pestered me enough about giving you a chance. And now I have just

8

the opportunity you've been waiting for."

"Thank you so much, Mr. Phifer."

He smoothed a few errant strands of hair that were combed over his balding pate. "I presume you've heard of Daniel Wilmont."

Charlotte nodded. "Of course. He's the Bible professor at Aquidneck College who writes a religion column for the *Newport Gazette*. I understand he's quite controversial."

Mr. Phifer glared at the competition's newspaper lying open on his desk. If his eyes could burn holes, the *Newport Gazette* would burst into flames.

He pointed to Professor Wilmont's column and then slammed his index finger against the newsprint. "Do you read his propaganda?"

"Sometimes, sir. I like to keep up with all the news."

His eyes narrowed. Was he considering her with a tinge more respect? "Then you know the man's a menace to every hardworking entrepreneur in New England. He misuses Scripture to condemn tried-and-true business practices that benefit everyone, employer and employee alike. He's a fire-breathing rabble-rouser."

Charlotte suppressed a nervous giggle at Mr. Phifer's hyperbole. She knew little about the Bible, or standard business practices, so she accepted Mr. Phifer's words as basically true, even if inflamed.

"I want to stop him from spreading his lies across this great state. He's an agitator bent on destroying democracy and free enterprise."

Charlotte squirmed on the wooden chair as her boss built up a head of steam. Perhaps she should read the professor's column more carefully to better understand the basis for Mr. Phifer's fury. The articles she'd read sounded more like sermons than diatribes, but Mr. Phifer, as a seasoned newspaperman, was certainly the expert.

"I want you, Miss Hale, to help cut the professor down to size. Show the world he's not the savior people think he is."

"Me?" she murmured. She shifted forward, every muscle taut.

"Yes, Miss Hale. I have a plan and you're a vital part of it." He leaned his palms against the desk and thrust his head toward her. His suit coat flared at the lapels, revealing suspenders that hoisted up perfectly pressed trousers. "One of my professor friends at the college mentioned that Wilmont needs a temporary governess for his two children. His mother has taken ill."

Charlotte felt her eyes widen as she lis-

10

tened, not understanding where this was leading.

He paused, probably for dramatic effect. "I want you to fill the position and then investigate Wilmont, from the inside, for improprieties. You have an interview set for this afternoon. Are you up to the task?"

Charlotte's throat went dry. The man had hinted for some time that he might give a girl a chance. *"But she'd have to show exceptional talent and industry,"* he'd said. *"Yes ma'am, exceptional talent and industry. You hear me?"*

She shook her head, forcing herself back to the present. The time was now. He was giving her a chance! "Yes, of course, sir. I'm ready, willing, and able." And humbled that her boss considered her experienced enough for such a plum assignment. Of course she held the dubious title of senior secretary, so she was the likely pick. She imagined the new hire, Edith Ann Wengle, would give her eye teeth, and possibly every other tooth, too, for this assignment. Most of the other typists were content to work at their machines all day, but not Edith Ann, Charlotte's only serious competitor for advancement to the ranks of the reporters.

He nodded. "Good. I'm glad to hear you will consider it."

But even as he said it, Charlotte wondered if she really wanted a clandestine mission. She'd never attempted anything on the cloak-and-dagger front. Was she suited for such high adventure? She'd always assumed she'd be a levelheaded, straight shooter of a reporter. And to be less than honest with the professor didn't seem quite right.

Yet if his ideas were as harmful as Mr. Phifer claimed, then her efforts would serve the community.

With overwhelming debts to pay, she couldn't possibly refuse Mr. Phifer's offer.

"But what shall I do — exactly — once I'm hired?" *If I'm hired.*

Mr. Phifer lowered his voice to a whisper. "You're to search for evidence against Daniel Wilmont. Look for his weaknesses and vices. Find his Achilles' heel. Do you understand what I'm asking?"

He wanted her to spy on a religious fanatic, an enemy of the American way of life. This was indeed a worthy endeavor for herself and for the publication. If she could pull it off, she would make an instant name for herself. She'd have a career. A future. As one of the first female journalists anywhere. But as appealing as a journalism career might be, it didn't compare to the importance of paying off bills. She needed that peace of mind.

Mr. Phifer waited for her answer, his head thrust forward.

"I understand and I accept the assignment, sir."

"Well done, young woman. Together, we'll discredit Professor Wilmont and put a halt to his despicable blather." He slammed his fist against his desktop, his eyes nearly popping out of his head.

Taken aback by his sudden ferocity, Charlotte swallowed hard and kept silent as he went on with his plans.

Her boss wanted to force Professor Wilmont to quit his column in disgrace. An unsavory taste coated her tongue, but she couldn't form the words to decline the mission she'd just accepted. Mr. Phifer would toss her out the door if she ever gave voice to her moral scruples.

With her sister's disability requiring expensive doctor visits for which she struggled to pay, she needed her job. At this very moment, a stack of unpaid bills lay in the top drawer of her dresser where Aunt Amelia and Becky wouldn't see them. There was no need for anyone else to fret. She did enough worrying for all of them.

And even more pressing, she owed a small fortune for the new roof on their old house.

Patching had sufficed for only so long before rain finally leaked through the ceiling into the upstairs bedrooms. And Mr. Knowles, the roofer, possessed little patience with her extended payment plan. She didn't blame him, but she couldn't hand over money she didn't have.

Mr. Phifer flashed a satisfied grin. "You'll be generously rewarded for your success, young woman. I see a bright future in store for you at the *Rhode Island Reporter.*"

"Thank you, Mr. Phifer. I appreciate the opportunity to help — and to advance at the newspaper."

"A career in journalism is entirely possible, Miss Hale, *if* you find the evidence I need."

Despite reservations that nibbled on the edge of her conscience, Charlotte beamed, unable to contain her excitement. She liked her job well enough, though pounding keys on a typing machine didn't stimulate her intellect. Eventually she hoped to write substantive articles on important subjects, but to do that, she'd have to please her boss first. Mr. Phifer dangled a once-in-a-lifetime opportunity to distinguish herself and shine. And he'd practically promised a better salary would accompany a promotion.

Somehow she'd treat Professor Wilmont

in a fair and unbiased manner. She would ferret out the facts and report the truth like a competent reporter.

A niggling fear gripped her mind. Would he appreciate her efforts no matter what the results? Or would he fire the person who brought him news he didn't wish to hear? "But what if I don't find anything untoward?"

Charlotte winced as Mr. Phifer's face shook with a nasty laugh.

"You'll find something damaging, I assure you. Daniel Wilmont has plenty to hide. Report to me every few days, if possible, or as soon as you find any incriminating evidence. I know you'll make me proud."

"I shall do my very best. You can count on me, sir." Charlotte forced enthusiasm into her voice, hoping this assignment would prove as advantageous as she expected.

"Excellent. I have another lead I'm pursuing, but at the present time, I'm not at liberty to divulge anything more. Mum's the word." But then he leaned closer and lowered his voice to a theatrical whisper. "I can tell you this much, I've heard a rumor about the professor and a young female student. This could be scandalous! If this information pans out, I'll inform you of all the details and you can verify the facts."

"Of course." This was the most concrete lead her boss had given her. "He must be a dishonorable man," she murmured.

"He is, indeed. Keep your eyes peeled for shameful behavior."

Charlotte nodded, uneasy about putting so much stock in unconfirmed rumors. "I shall. About how long will this investigation take, Mr. Phifer?"

His eyes squeezed to a narrow glint. "The sooner you finish, the better. I anticipate you'll be done in a week or two at the most. Remember, I want frequent updates on your progress — every few days if you can manage it."

Charlotte gulped. She hoped to succeed within a matter of days. She'd sweep in and out like a whirlwind — that was her plan. "How shall I get time away from the child — or children — to look around, if I'm to be a governess?"

"You'll find a way, I'm sure. Use your ingenuity." Mr. Phifer nodded his dismissal.

"Sir, there's one more thing." She clutched her hands to keep them from shaking. "Would you be able to increase my salary by a few dollars every week — at least while I'm on this assignment? I'm afraid I've accumulated some bills of late. I need to pay them as soon as possible." He'd probably

16

think her impertinent to ask, but she needed to just the same.

He emitted a chuckle. "So you've spent too much on trifles, have you? Pretty ribbons and trinkets, I presume. Well, I'll tell you what, Miss Hale. If you find the evidence I expect, then I'll give you a mighty fine raise."

Even if he didn't agree to a specific amount and mischaracterized her need as personal indulgence, gratitude for her new assignment filled her heart. "Thank you, Mr. Phifer."

"I've set up an interview for an hour from now and I've hired a hack cab to drive you to Summerhill, the Wilmonts' cottage on Ocean Drive. Good luck. Don't let me down."

"I assure you, I'll do my very best."

Mr. Phifer snapped a nod and a smile. "Good. Now, let's write you some references. Whom do you suggest?"

"My Aunt Amelia, and possibly Mr. Stapleton, my former English teacher. In fact, he wrote one for me when I applied for this job. Should I contact him?"

"No, there's not enough time. I'll check and see if we still have his recommendation on file." He quickly located Mr. Stapleton's letter and then frowned. "This will do nicely except for the date. 1895. Hmm. That's hard to change to 1900, so I'll just turn the five into an eight." He took a fountain pen and carefully altered the number. "If the professor questions the date, tell him Mr. Stapleton wrote it two years ago, and you didn't wish to bother him for a newer version."

"Yes, sir."

"We need one more reference. I'll have Miss Wengle write one up."

Within minutes Charlotte left on her first assignment toward a new, fascinating career in journalism.

Ten minutes later Charlotte climbed aboard the hired carriage for the ride to Summerhill. They drove out of town toward Ocean Drive, the winding road that hugged the coast for ten scenic miles. The buggy swayed past showy mansions set among the lonely stretches of road edged by jagged rocks. Surf crashed against the boulders and burst into a spray of liquid gems. Although she'd lived in Newport for all of her twenty-two years, she'd never before seen the famed Ocean Drive. It was far too expensive to hire a hack cab just to sightsee on a Sunday afternoon.

Of course, she'd heard countless tales

about the estates and their fabled owners. These showplace mansions, always called cottages by their owners, were occupied only for the summer and designed specifically for lavish entertainment — and truth be told, mainly to impress other millionaires. Charlotte didn't know what the wealthy thought of them, but the magnificent homes certainly impressed her.

The horse slowed his pace, turned down a pebbled drive, and the carriage rolled toward a white-shingled mansion rising upon a gentle knoll. Charlotte drew in a deep breath, held it for a long moment, then let it seep out. Though smaller and probably older than many of the more ostentatious residences lining Bellevue Avenue, Summerhill conveyed a hominess that set her slightly more at ease. Striped awnings with scalloped edges flapped in the breeze and seemed to wave a welcome.

Charlotte blinked. What was she thinking? She was sent here on an assignment to spy, not to hobnob with millionaires or drink tea in hand-painted china cups with gold rims out on the veranda. She couldn't let down her guard, even for a moment.

The carriage halted before the wraparound porch. Lined with blue hydrangeas, it boasted a swing and white wicker chairs with floral cushions. The driver helped her down. "I'd been told to wait for you, miss."

"Thank you. I'll not be long — I hope."

A warm breeze blew from the sea and swept across the grassy landscape rising above the shoreline. It whispered in her ears and cooled her cheeks which were rapidly overheating from mounting tension.

Charlotte squared her slumped shoulders and strode up the steps of Summerhill, pretending confidence. But the knot in her stomach tightened. Was it really ethical to investigate an unsuspecting man, even for an admirable cause? Perhaps. Or perhaps not. But if the professor was truly bent on destroying people's prosperity, then examining his background wasn't so terrible, even under false pretenses. Yet the guilt pressing against her chest gave her pause. She'd have to think this through further.

Standing at the door, she tried to compose her thoughts, but to no avail. She steadied her breathing and uncurled her fists. *Better.* She rang the doorbell, smoothed her plain gray skirt, and waited with a lump blocking her throat.

Through the oval glass of the front door, she glimpsed a butler, followed by a towering figure with a couple of half-pint children in tow. When the door flew open, she looked past the butler to the man who scarcely resembled the dignified, almost stern photograph in the *Newport Gazette.*

"Professor Wilmont?" she asked in a small voice. She cleared her throat and flicked a tentative smile.

"I am he."

In person, sandy-colored hair fell over his forehead and blue-green eyes sparkled like a tropical sea. A pair of gold-rimmed spectacles rested on the tip of his nose, adding a professorial tone to his casual appearance. Instead of the dark suit and celluloid collar he wore in his newspaper photograph, he sported tan trousers, a rather wrinkled white shirt with sleeves rolled up to his elbows, and a jaunty blue bow tie.

Was this man with the broad smile truly Mr. Phifer's enemy? The man who fought to halt mankind's progress and curb her hard-won success? But a man's character could not be judged by the width of his grin or the degree of his handsomeness. Appearances often deceived.

He stepped back from the threshold and waved her inside with a wide sweep of his muscular arm. Even with a slight stoop to his tall frame, he dwarfed her. "I'm Professor Wilmont and I expect you're Miss Hale, the applicant for the governess position."

Charlotte nodded as she followed him into the foyer, a spacious area with a large Turkish rug covering most of the parquet floor. It took all her willpower not to gawk at the luxury of her surroundings. Antique vases rested on marble side tables and a grand wooden staircase led to the upper floors. The entire downstairs of her home could fit into this one vestibule with room to spare.

She didn't trust her voice to emerge any stronger than a croak. The heat of the professor's smile radiated down upon her and she blushed at its intensity. Professor Wilmont was at least six feet two inches tall to her five feet four. She felt insignificant enough — and nervous enough — to disappear right into the blue floral wallpaper. She almost wished she could vanish, but she'd accepted this assignment and she'd carry it out as promised.

"How do you do, Miss Hale? Shall we go into my office?"

Her nerves snapped like violin strings. She glanced toward the front door, tempted to bolt. As soon as the interview started, he'd realize she was a fraud. Better to leave now before he discovered she came here on a surreptitious mission.

Sucking in a fortifying breath, she followed Professor Wilmont into the study right off the front hallway. Piles of books and magazines cluttered the space. Overloaded bookshelves of golden oak rose to the high ceiling. The room smelled of furniture wax and a faint mustiness common to old houses built by the shore.

"Children, I'd like you to meet Miss Hale." Professor Wilmont gazed down at the boy and the girl who tumbled into the room ahead of him. They pushed and shoved each other out of the way.

"You're the prettiest one so far." The rangy boy bobbed his head. His curly hair sprang up like red wire coils. "Do you think you'd like to take care of us? Grandmother says we're a handful."

Professor Wilmont grunted. "Don't let Tim discourage you. They're really quite angelic. At least that's what we tell all the applicants."

Her optimism faltered until she spotted the grin playing at the corner of the professor's mouth. She returned his smile, embarrassed she'd taken him so seriously.

"Can you tell me your names?" Charlotte bent down closer to the children's height.

The boy, dressed in a sailor suit with a red tie, nodded. "I'm Tim and I'm ten. She's twelve." He jerked his thumb toward the girl.

"I'm Ruthie and I'll be thirteen in October." She shook Charlotte's hand with lady-like poise. Her auburn braids, as thick as ropes, stretched down to her waist and were tied with silk ribbons. They coordinated with her green and rose plaid dress partially concealed by a starched white pinafore.

"Now that you've introduced yourselves, it's my turn to speak to Miss Hale. You two skedaddle for a while." Professor Wilmont jutted his chin toward the study door, but his eyes glistened with pride.

The pair trooped out, dragging their feet against the shiny floor, but they disappeared without an argument. A good sign. They knew how to behave in front of adults.

Professor Wilmont motioned Charlotte to a seat across from his desk as he settled into his sturdy chair that easily accommodated his extra size. On the desktop a coffee cup competed for space with stacks of files and enough office supplies to last a lifetime. Charlotte slipped into the broken-down easy chair that a cat must have shredded with a set of very sharp claws. A spring poked her bottom and she shifted positions, trying not to wince.

"Sorry about the chair. As soon as I find the time, I'm going to order a new one with better springs." He smiled boyishly and then

24

moved an asparagus fern off of a stack of magazines.

Charlotte laughed. "It's really quite all right if I sit to the side."

His cheer faded. "Let me tell you about why I need to hire a governess. After my wife died five years ago, my mother came to live with us. She assumed care of the children and dismissed their governess. Unfortunately, my mother recently developed serious heart problems. She's in the hospital right now and isn't likely to regain her health for at least eight weeks. I need someone to watch over the children while she's recuperating."

"I get along quite well with children. In fact, I find young people very interesting. They're full of fun and mischief." A glimmer of confidence relaxed the tight muscles in her neck and shoulders.

He nodded. "Since you'll only be here for the summer, you need not know French or German. But are you able to teach arithmetic, English grammar, geography, and history? Do you play an instrument?"

Charlotte grinned. "I was a good student at Rogers High School, but a poor musician — though I took years of piano lessons. If the children have a music teacher, I promise they'll practice faithfully."

25

He returned her smile. "That's all right with me. Can you tell me a little bit about your past employment?"

Charlotte paused. This was the part she'd gloss over, though Mr. Phifer had carefully briefed her just before she'd left the newspaper. "I live at home with my aunt and sister, and I often care for neighbor children." She did occasionally watch the two little boys next door. And she'd been like a mother to her thirteen-year-old sister, Becky, ever since their mama died years before . . .

"Were you ever employed on a full-time basis?" As he leaned closer, she caught a whiff of woodsy aftershave mixed with the clean smell of starch.

She resisted the urge to tilt forward and inhale more deeply. "I worked for the gas company typing correspondence for several months." No need to mention she quit to accept a better job at the *Rhode Island Reporter*. He certainly wouldn't want to hire someone connected to his adversary, Arnie Phifer, even a lowly secretary.

"And now you're searching for a job as a governess?" he asked, hiking an eyebrow as if he didn't quite believe her story was credible. Even secretarial work at the gas company paid a higher wage than watching youngsters. Though a governess was a step above the other servants, she would be neither part of the family nor part of the staff.

"Yes. I enjoy children, so a temporary position as governess is ideal until I decide what I wish to do permanently."

He nodded, apparently satisfied. "I'll pray that the Holy Ghost will guide you."

What was that about the Holy Ghost?

He stared at her and gently tapped his fingers on the desktop.

"Is something wrong?" Her neck and shoulder muscles tensed.

"No. It's just that you look rather familiar. But I can't place where I've seen you before."

She swallowed hard. "I've lived on the Point all my life, so you might have spotted me in town," Charlotte suggested, struggling to keep her voice light.

She could almost hear Mr. Phifer whisper in her ear. *"Distract him before he figures out who you are and why you're there."*

Professor Wilmont gave an easy shrug. "Well, no matter. It will come to me eventually."

She shivered at the thought.

For the next ten minutes she answered routine questions about her background, filled in a short informational sheet, and handed him references concocted by Mr. Phifer. The professor scanned them before putting them aside. He smiled and Charlotte relaxed.

"I think you might be a good fit for my children's needs, Miss Hale. There's just one more thing." Professor Wilmont leaned forward and folded his hands on the ink-stained blotter. "I should have asked you before — are you a Christian?"

Anxiety rushed through her. Where had that question come from? For a moment her mind went blank. "Yes, of course I am." She didn't attend church or obey all the petty rules of religion, but she believed in God. Definitely. That should qualify her as a religious woman, shouldn't it?

Their eyes met and his sparkled.

"When did you become a Christian, or have you always believed?"

This was getting trickier. Beads of sweat bubbled across her forehead and moistened her upper lip. The July afternoon grew hotter, more humid. "I guess I've believed in God for my entire life." A reasonable answer to a question she didn't quite understand.

"I'd love to hear about your spiritual journey."

Charlotte looked down at her hands

folded in her lap, unable to meet his intense gaze. "Um, of course. Anytime."

A "spiritual journey"? Should she admit she didn't have a clue what that meant? Was it something every Christian had or at least knew about?

"We can talk about this later." He grinned and flashed even white teeth.

"I'd be delighted." Charlotte smiled weakly, her hands perspiring.

They settled on a salary and reasonable working hours. "If you want the job, Miss Hale, it's yours."

Relief surged through her. "Yes, thank you so much, Professor. I accept your offer."

"When can you begin work?" he asked.

"I can start today, sir." Even as she said it, she wished she could rise and flee the house. She forced a smile and allowed him to take her hand again, shaking it in friendly agreement, even as her heart screamed at her to stop.

She'd expected something objectionable in the man, something on which she could focus and build into a report for Mr. Phifer. Professor Wilmont's charm and amicability were . . . unsettling.

TWO

The warmth of the afternoon beckoned Daniel to the front veranda for a quiet time with the Lord. He opened his Bible, but as much as he tried to concentrate on Paul's epistle to the Romans, his mind wandered back to his new employee. A burden had lifted with the appearance of Charlotte Hale, the only applicant with a brain as bright as her smile. Attracted by her warmth, he looked forward to getting to know this young woman with intelligent brown eyes, a turned-up nose, and masses of dark brown hair piled loosely on her head. Her infectious smile made him grin even now as he relaxed on the rocker and gently pushed back and forth in the fresh sea air.

Certainly Miss Hale promised to bring cheer to his household. She exuded an optimistic attitude and the hint of playfulness — qualities, he hated to admit, his mother sorely lacked. His mother dispensed discipline and a heavy dose of criticism toward the children, just as she had when he and his brother, Edgar, were young. Granted, she kept the house and family organized and running efficiently but with an iron hand and a chilly heart. He hoped Miss Hale might add a dose of laughter to Summerhill during the next several weeks. And with her help, he'd soon have ample time to write his newspaper column. He checked himself. He would have more time if the household help would cease running to him with every trifle.

Daniel sighed as he looked up from his Bible, removed his spectacles, and rubbed his tired eyes. He would've been satisfied with a smaller home run by a housekeeper and a few maids. Instead, his mother insisted they retain a complete staff that squabbled more often than they got along.

At the sound of a carriage crunching down the drive, Daniel glanced up and recognized the driver. "Ah, Melissa Le-Beau," he muttered. Her uniformed maid sat beside her. What was one of his summer students doing here at Summerhill? Miss LeBeau waved and then flashed a broad smile that looked more practiced than genuine. Garbed in a frilly blue dress, she halted the gig, descended gracefully, and approached the veranda. Peering up at him through the longest fringe of eyelashes he'd ever seen, she adjusted her big straw hat covered with fruit and flowers and tucked a stray piece of blond hair behind her ear. Daniel dragged his feet down the shallow steps to meet his uninvited guest before she had a chance to plant herself in the wicker chair beside him. His polite smile probably came across more like a grimace, but he couldn't pretend.

"Good afternoon, Miss LeBeau. What can I do for you? Or are you merely out for a drive?"

"Hello, Professor. Lovely day, isn't it?" Before he could answer, she plowed ahead. "I have a favor to ask of you."

Her whispery voice assaulted his ears. She sounded breathless as if she'd just played a strenuous game of lawn tennis or run a mile in her high-heeled boots.

He suppressed a groan and the impulse to disappear inside his home without a word of explanation. "Yes, Miss LeBeau. Ask away." He clasped his hands behind his back and leaned forward. He hoped his reserve would persuade the problematic student to get to the point.

She paused and then drew out a dramatic

sigh. "I need to talk to you about my term paper. I'm having a dreadful time understanding St. Paul. Maybe you can assist me —"

"Of course. My office hours are between two and four Monday, Wednesday, and Friday."

"I'm afraid I can't come then. I have club get-togethers every afternoon."

"In that case, why don't you meet me at the Student Center on Wednesday evening? I'm usually free on weekday evenings. Please ask Miss Brownington to come along too. She might be helpful."

He didn't know if the prim and proper Agnes Brownington, Miss LeBeau's classmate, could really offer any insight, but two young women were better than one. He liked to avoid any appearance of impropriety, especially since women were fairly new to campus and, like many other professors, he was still figuring it out. "Treat them with kid gloves," Mrs. Finnegan, the housekeeper, had once advised with a sage nod. She didn't approve of women studying on the same campus with men, but Aquidneck College, a nominally Christian institution, took pride in its progressive stance.

Miss LeBeau pouted. "I'd rather speak to you today, but I suppose I can make that time next week. I'll ask Miss Brownington if she wishes to come."

Daniel noticed the seductive look she leveled between half closed eyes and his chest constricted. The young lady, called Missy by the other students, looked like a lioness on the prowl.

"Normally my schedule is quite booked," she said with a sniff, letting her eyelashes slowly lift as she looked up at him, "but I don't have a suitor anymore."

Daniel stifled a chuckle behind a cough. His male students made fools of themselves vying to catch Missy's eye. But despite the attention they showered on her, she seldom gave any of them a second glance. Who had maneuvered close enough to be deemed a "suitor"?

He startled, shocked at his train of thought. "Good day, Miss LeBeau. I'll see you in class."

Lifting her chin, she turned and casually sashayed back to her buggy while Daniel retreated to the seclusion of the front veranda.

Charlotte stopped at the offices of the *Rhode Island Reporter,* anxious to announce she'd secured the position at Summerhill.

Mr. Phifer ushered her into his office and

paid close attention to her every word. When she'd finished, he allowed a jubilant smile to turn up the corners of his mouth. "Good work. I expect you'll succeed without a hitch."

"I shall try my best, sir."

"I'll arrange for another carriage to pick you up at your home in about an hour. Would you like a ride there now?" he asked.

Receiving the royal treatment certainly came as a pleasant surprise, but she shook her head. "An hour will give me plenty of time to pack, but right now I'd enjoy a walk. Thank you all the same."

Mr. Phifer nodded. "Suit yourself."

Charlotte strode toward her small clapboard home on Bridge Street, part of Newport's old colonial neighborhood by the waterfront and only blocks away from the newspaper office. The two-story gray house, sadly in need of a good scraping and a coat of paint, sat directly on the sidewalk and cheek-by-jowl with its neighbors. She waved to friends as she strode but didn't stop to chat. Entering the saltbox house, she found her aunt and sister in the kitchen at the end of the unlit hallway.

Aunt Amelia stopped sweeping the wide pine floor. "Why on earth are you home so early? Are you feeling poorly?" A frown darkened her long, sallow face.

"No, I'm fine, thank you. In fact, I'm in the best of health."

The muscles that tightened Amelia's thin face into deep lines and wrinkles relaxed. "That's a relief."

Her sister, Becky, sat in her wheelchair by the table and quartered potatoes. Charlotte's heart never failed to squeeze at the sight of her once athletic sister now unable to move her legs. Four years had passed since Becky's accident, but the horror still was fresh to Charlotte. She remembered vividly how their uncle's horse had thrown her sister and hurled her into a fence, paralyzing her from the waist down. Becky's injuries still pained her.

Becky's eyes moved from her task to her sister. "Do tell us why you're home! I'm dying of suspense."

Charlotte hung her straw boater on the hat tree by the kitchen door and sat down across from her sister. "Mr. Phifer called me to his office this morning," she said, taking a deep breath, "and gave me a *journalism* assignment that could boost my career right up to the moon. Or at least start me on the road to a real journalism career."

"Oh my, that's splendid," Becky gasped.

But Aunt Amelia looked worried as she

rested her back against the wooden icebox. "Are you saying he bypassed all the men and chose you out of the whole bunch?" She raised a skeptical brow arched over a pair of hooded, dark eyes.

Charlotte nodded. "I'm saying just that. I know it sounds unlikely, even preposterous, but he picked me not because I'm a reporter, but because I'm a woman."

Aunt Amelia tossed back her head and chuckled. "Now that's a switch. The man has held you down and made no bones about it for the very reason that you are a woman. What caused his sudden change of heart?"

"He needs me to take a job that only a woman can do."

Her aunt's eyes widened to the size of wagon wheels. "Mercy me, does he expect you to do something immoral? I hope you refused in no uncertain terms."

Charlotte grinned. "Really, Aunt Amelia, you should know me better than that. The assignment isn't immoral in any way."

Investigating surely wasn't immoral, though perhaps in this particular case, a bit on the shady side. No, she'd merely perform her assignment like all the other reporters. And what was the point of mulling over the ethical issue of misleading Professor Wilmont when she didn't have a choice? What was done, was done.

"I know you're a decent young lady, but I don't quite trust Arnie Phifer. Back in grammar school, he used to dip the girls' braids in his ink well and then laugh his fool head off. He was nobody's favorite, I can assure you."

Aunt Amelia poured Charlotte a cup of tea. "Would you like something to eat?"

"No, thank you, I'm not a bit hungry. My excitement stole my appetite."

Becky reached for another potato. "Tell us all about your assignment."

Charlotte hesitated. If either her aunt or sister inadvertently let the details slip to one of their many gossipy friends, Professor Wilmont might discover she worked for the *Rhode Island Reporter* and that revelation would spoil the entire plan. Aquidneck College and the millionaires summering around the Ocean Drive and Bellevue Avenue occupied another part of town from the fishermen, carpenters, and shipbuilders of the Point, yet the two worlds could conceivably overlap. No reason to tempt fate.

"I'm taking the job of governess for a week or two at most. And that's all I should reveal."

Becky's shoulders sagged as she frowned.

"Oh, I do so wish you'd tell us more. Will you still be in Newport?"

"Yes, I'll not be far away, though I do have to live with my employer's family for the time being. Listen you two, I wish I could tell the whole of Mr. Phifer's plan, but he wouldn't want me to confide any of the particulars. I'm thrilled by the opportunity to get ahead, but I'm obliged to accept the assignment — on his terms."

Neither Aunt Amelia nor Becky responded, though her aunt's frown deepened.

"No woman at the newspaper has ever been sent out on a real assignment *to actually report a story*. I'm the first one. And if I botch this, Edith Ann Wengle would swoop right in to take my place."

Aunt Amelia drew out a long sigh and commenced sweeping the pantry, her tall frame bent over the broom. "If you're sure this assignment is on the up-and-up, then you'll hear no complaints from me. Yet I worry about you competing in a man's world, especially Arnie Phifer's world."

Charlotte softened. "I know." She sipped her tea. "But I'm perfectly capable of watching out for myself. I'll go right in, do my job, and come home before you even miss me."

"But you'll let us know you're getting along all right?" Becky asked.

"I shall come home as often as I can. If you need me in an emergency, call on Mr. Phifer. I'll stay in close contact with him." Charlotte rose and squeezed her aunt's rough hand, calloused and misshapen from arthritis. Her condition had worsened over the last few years, crippling her knees and her back.

Before Aunt Amelia tried to talk her out of the grandest opportunity of her fledgling career, Charlotte packed her valise with her clothing and two novels she'd recently purchased. She found Becky had moved to the parlor and was now bending over her knitting. A pair of blue booties and a matching infant's cap lay on the side table. Becky's lightning fast fingers kept flying as she looked up.

"I'll finish this baby sweater within the hour and then Aunt Amelia can bring the set to the shop." One of the exclusive stores on Bellevue Avenue sold her knitted infant wear to the socialites, which earned Becky a small income. Her fingers came to an abrupt halt and she let the knitting fall to her lap. "I'll miss you terribly, Charlotte, but this assignment seems like a grand opportunity."

"I'll miss you too. But it's not for long."

"At night when Aunt Amelia falls asleep in her chair, I'll truly be bored without you to keep me company. I do so wish I had a book to read."

"I have one you might like." Charlotte opened her valise and removed a copy of *Jane Eyre.* "Or would you prefer *Sense and Sensibility*?"

"Jane Austen, if you please. Thank you so much. If I can't have you around for a game of checkers, at least I'll have a good read." Becky smiled. "What would I ever do without you?"

Charlotte handed her the novel. "Don't worry, you won't have to. Now I must go." She hugged her sister and retreated to the hallway.

On her way out the door, Aunt Amelia handed her a letter. "It's from Mr. Knowles's attorney. Not good news, I'm sure."

Charlotte stuffed it into her reticule. "I'll read it later. It's probably not important. But if it is, I'll take care of it."

As soon as the carriage rounded the corner of Bridge Street, Charlotte ripped open the envelope with a trembling hand. She skimmed the contents of the letter and groaned. If she didn't make full payment for the new roof by the first of September, Mr. Knowles would sue.

Much as she dreaded an encounter with the crusty old codger, she knew she had to confront the problem head-on. "Driver, please stop at Knowles Roofing on Thames Street. I'll only be a few moments."

When the cab halted before the storefront, she sucked in a deep breath. She stepped inside the office. Mr. Knowles stood behind the counter discussing the qualities of different roofing materials with a customer. They chattered endlessly about the advantages of wooden shingles coated with boiled fish oil versus slate. She practiced patience and held her tongue as she rehearsed what she'd say.

If she were a praying woman, this would be an excellent time to invoke the Almighty, but she wasn't.

When the customer departed, Mr. Knowles glared down at her with eyes deeply set beneath bushy black brows. "So, Miss Hale, you've come to pay your bill. I've waited long enough. I'm running a roofing business, not a charity." He cocked a head too large for his skinny neck and body. "You got my letter, did you? I thought that might catch your attention."

Charlotte bit back a sharp retort because

he *was* right. She was delinquent and more regretful than he could ever imagine. "I'm sorry your payment is late." There was no point in explaining about Becky's medical bills because her sad story wouldn't soften his heart of rock or put food on his table or pay his rent. "In two weeks I'll give you every last cent I owe. And I do appreciate your understanding. I'm dreadfully sorry I couldn't pay on time."

"Apologies are meaningless. Settle up, or you and your aunt will find yourselves in court."

Heat crept up her neck into her face. "Don't you worry, Mr. Knowles, I'll bring your money as soon as possible. And again, I apologize for the delay. Good day." She left with her head held high, but her lower lip quivered.

The drive to Summerhill took only twenty or twenty-five minutes, even with the traffic on Thames Street. Yet it was long enough for her nerves to jangle from the problem temporarily left behind and the challenge that lay ahead.

The driver unloaded her baggage and carried it to the veranda. Charlotte followed on his heels, anxious to accomplish her mission before she succumbed to second thoughts. From the side yard, she heard boys shouting. Shielding her eyes from the sun, she spotted Tim and his friends climbing a sturdy apple tree. Ruthie and another girl in pigtails and pinafore read books under the shade of a nearby maple, while pretending to serve tea and cake. Charlotte waved to the children and left them to their fun.

She found the professor on the veranda, half hidden behind a jungle of ferns and deeply absorbed in his newspaper. The gold frames of his spectacles glinted in the afternoon sunshine as he glanced up.

Charlotte's breath escaped in one *whoosh*. Professor Wilmont's skin glowed with a light tan, accentuating the turquoise of his eyes as he squinted against the light. He leaned back in the wicker chair to avoid the brightness that slanted between the low roof and the spindle railing.

A warm breeze rustled his newspaper and she caught the name *Rhode Island Reporter* on page one. She swallowed the fear lodged in her throat.

The professor grimaced. "Confound Arnold Phifer and his vile newspaper. This is the most deceitful rag ever published. I hope you've never had the misfortune of reading it."

Charlotte gulped. "Oh, is it untrustworthy? I thought it was one of the state's finest dailies." She looked down, afraid Professor Wilmont would see guilt written all over her face as dark and as bold as the newsprint.

"It's disgraceful." Though his voice was controlled, his tone sent apprehension spiraling through her heart.

She shifted from one foot to the other. "Sir, I only wanted to tell you I've arrived and I'm ready to work. Does the housekeeper have the key to my room?" If she didn't conquer her apprehension, he'd notice her lack of poise and flushed complexion. He might become suspicious and fire her before she could even begin her assignment.

She relaxed the grip of her mouth and raised her lips in a small smile.

"Yes, Mrs. Finnegan has all the keys." Miss Hale's face radiated a rosy pink, like mild sunburn. Very becoming. "I'm sorry I forgot to mention it earlier. My children tell me I'm absentminded. I'm afraid they're right. I also apologize for my outburst against Mr. Phifer."

Miss Hale glanced toward the front door. "It's quite all right, sir. If you'll excuse me, I'll go unpack and then come right back down to begin my duties." She hesitated.

Daniel lifted his hand. "Look, I apologize for my rant. I'm usually not such an angry fellow." He smiled as he pulled off his spectacles. "Would you like a tour of the grounds before you get settled?"

"Yes, thank you. I'd like that."

They strolled around the side of the house to the kitchen garden and then across the grass toward the boulders that touched the lawn and reached into the roaring surf. "I often wander down to the rocks to think or pray. Nature turns my mind toward the Lord." Daniel relished the solitude of the sea, especially during the early morning hours when the mist shrouded the landscape and moistened the grass and air.

Miss Hale glanced at him sideways. "Do you and Tim come here to fish?" The sleeves of her high-collared shirtwaist billowed in the warm wind and the hem of her skirt swept around her legs.

"Fish? No, I'm afraid not. Never have."

"Ah, then you've missed out. My father used to take me fishing every Saturday. My older brother died young, so I was the substitute son."

Daniel paused. "You were blessed to have so much attention. My father spent his spare time away from home, so I entertained myself. I haunted our library and developed a great love of books. My son, however, prefers falling out of trees and sliding down the staircase on silver trays." Whenever he tried to interest his children in chess or a trip to a museum, they countered with pleas for a bicycle ride or tennis match. They usually ended up all going their separate ways.

"Are you close to your father now, Professor?"

He shook his head. "He passed on several years ago. Unfortunately, we always had a distant relationship." What was the point of discussing a sad and difficult period in his life, especially with a stranger? Yet Miss Hale seemed easy to talk to and more like an old friend than a new acquaintance — certainly not a servant.

She walked a few steps to his side. "Well, we learn from our past, don't we? I'm sure you're not making the same mistakes as your father."

Her question touched a raw spot in his heart. His mother had taken charge of Tim and Ruthie until her recent illness, and he hadn't yet hit upon common ground with his children. Perhaps when they matured, their interests would merge. Yet the distance among the three of them bothered him more than he liked to admit.

47

"I do my best. And I'm sure my father did as well. I forgave him for his shortcomings years ago. There was no point in holding a grudge." A dusting of salt coated his spectacles. With a clean handkerchief he rubbed the glass until it smeared. "I enjoy my children, but my work demands my undivided attention. That's why I hired you, Miss Hale — so I can catch up while you watch over them."

"Yes, of course, sir. Could you tell me something about their daily routine?"

"Daily routine? Yes, they have one, of course, though we've not kept to it since my mother became ill. Let me see. They arise at seven or eight o'clock, eat breakfast and . . . Actually, I'm not quite sure what my mother does with them all morning. At any rate, they have lessons in the afternoon — a Bible story, piano practice for at least an hour, and then silent reading. They also write short essays and work a few arithmetic problems."

"They have lessons all afternoon? What about play time?" Miss Hale asked as the gentle breeze loosened strands of mahogany brown hair from beneath her plain straw hat.

Wasn't reading their favorite books the best type of play? "As soon as my mother comes home from the hospital, you might ask her how she schedules their activities and chores. Child care is her bailiwick."

"Yes, sir. But may I suggest we add a large dose of outdoor activity so they won't be tempted to slide down the staircase on silver trays?"

He gave a sheepish smile. "As long as the children aren't too noisy. I don't want their enthusiasm to turn into rowdiness. I insist they act in a decorous manner." He winced at the noise of boys running around the lawn. He tried to keep order, but he really needed his mother to take charge. "Or at least I try to."

Miss Hale's eyes twinkled. "But they must have some fun as well. They're only children once. Why not let them frolic to their hearts' content?"

"A solid afternoon constitution is good for a child's health, but it cannot impede upon progress with their studies."

"Even while it's summer and school is out? Shouldn't the children be free to do as they please? At least to some extent?"

She stopped by the rocks, jammed her hands onto her tiny waist, and held his gaze. He doubted Miss Hale realized how bossy she sounded. And looked. Her apple cheeks blushed red and those chocolate eyes snapped with conviction. She'd make an excellent governess as soon as she understood he was the employer, not the child to direct and correct. Daniel snuffed out a chuckle.

"Children should always be supervised and guided. Too much freedom leads to bad behavior and a chaotic household — which is exactly what I had before I hired you. I expect things will run smoothly and quietly now that you're here." He quirked a brow and tightened his lips with mock sternness. "I'm not mistaken, am I?"

Doubt flickered across her face. "No, sir." She colored an even deeper shade of red and turned back toward the house. "Perhaps I should collect the children and begin."

"Excellent. My children will be glad to show you around the cottage and help you find Mrs. Finnegan for your key."

As soon as she disappeared inside the cottage, the children buzzing about her, he let out a hearty laugh. Charlotte Hale brought on a grin and lifted his spirits, though only time would tell if she was up to the challenge of managing the children.

THREE

Charlotte fled from Professor Wilmont, her face ablaze. Why didn't she say, "Yes, sir" and "No, sir" and stop injecting her views on raising children? Her scant experience minding the neighbor boys — or raising her little sister — counted for little. In the newspaper office with Mr. Phifer close at hand, she never dared to voice her opinion. No one asked her questions and she didn't volunteer any suggestions. That attitude earned her a reputation as a cooperative employee, a strong enough endorsement to secure her first assignment.

So why wasn't she as tactful with the professor? Nerves, no doubt. But if she failed to hold her tongue, Professor Wilmont might send her home in disgrace. From now on, she'd act like the ideal governess — seen, not heard. This was her job, right? On two different levels. She merely had to imagine herself at the newspaper office

51

rather than "at home."

Charlotte took a breath and entered the foyer behind the children. She jumped as an elderly woman bustled toward her, a snowman come to life — three balls sitting atop each other. The sash of her starched apron pulled tight at her expansive waist right below a round, ample bosom. Above, a circular face as white as pastry flour grinned broadly with blue button eyes and an oval mouth full of crooked teeth. Her head was crowned with an off-center silver-white bun tucked beneath a hair net and a small cap that resembled a doily with streamers trailing from the back. Promptly, the woman sent the children off to wash up.

"I'm Mrs. Finnegan just back from my sister's funeral, God rest her soul. And I'd wager you're Charlotte Hale, new governess to my dear little ones." Her brogue sounded musical and friendly.

Encouraged, Charlotte smiled. "Yes, I am. I'm pleased to meet you."

"Well, I'm delighted to meet you as well. I can certainly use help with the rascals. I'm not old by any means, but I'm not a spring chicken, either. I've been watching over them while their grandmother convalesces. Then my dearest sister passed on, God rest her soul."

52

"Who has been watching over the children in your absence?" Charlotte asked.

"Simone, Mrs. Wilmont's maid, helped out with Ruthie and Tim while I was gone. And thank the good Lord she was willing. It's a fine job she did, but they need their own governess, not someone to fill in."

Mrs. Finnegan looked close to seventy, but she was as spry as a forty-year-old. And as chatty as a little girl.

"I wasn't planning on staying away, but families need a lot of looking after. My sister Minnie left six good and two good-for-nothing children. 'Tis well they're all grown and on their own, but still very sad for them. And for me."

"I'm sorry for your loss."

"Thank you, dearie. Now you're probably looking for your room key. Come with me."

She followed Mrs. Finnegan to the children's wing on the second floor. Her key ring jangled at her waist. They strode into a cheerful playroom — bookshelves and toy chests resting against bright yellow walls, and an elaborate train set in the middle of the floor.

"This is your room, Miss Hale, right next to Ruthie's and across the playroom from Tim's. You'll take all your meals with the children up here." Mrs. Finnegan pointed to a small table in the corner of the play-room. "Sometimes they eat with their father in the dining room. Then you'll come down to the servants' hall off the kitchen unless you're invited to stay with them. It's fine food they serve in this house, even to the staff."

Charlotte nodded as she entered the bedroom she'd call her own for the next week or two. "This is lovely."

A breeze stirred the muslin curtains in the small, sunny chamber facing the sea. She inhaled the salty air laden with humidity. An oak bureau with a mirror, a washstand, a small wardrobe, and a white iron bedstead provided everything she needed. A rag rug gave a burst of color to the floor while an easy chair by the window added comfort. Charlotte opened her valise and hung one frock and three skirts in the wardrobe.

"Here's the key to the drawers. Always keep them locked. We've no thieves in this household, but it's always better to be safe than sorry. That's what I always say." Mrs. Finnegan chugged toward the door. "I'll be back in two shakes with your uniforms."

"Uniforms? I assumed I'd wear my own clothes."

"Then you weren't counting on Mrs. Wilmont. She insists everyone wear uniforms."

Mrs. Finnegan hesitated. "But maybe with you being a governess she'll allow a plain white shirtwaist and black skirt. As long as you don't look like a fine society lady, she probably won't object too loudly. But just in case she makes a fuss, I'll get the uniforms."

Charlotte nodded and looked to the window, watching wave after wave wash up on shore. Why did wearing a uniform make her feel more like an imposter than ever? Dragging her gaze from the view, she turned to finish unpacking her valise, placing clothes she would apparently not need, in the drawers.

The housekeeper returned with an armful of light blue uniforms for morning and black ones for the afternoon and doily caps with streamers. "Here you go, dearie."

She ran her fingers over the rough stitching of the doily cap and placed the pile of clothing on the bed. She'd never wear such an ugly thing. Would they notice?

"Thank you. As soon as I change my clothes I'd like to meet with the children."

"I sent them to the kitchen for a snack. You will find them there."

Soon after, Charlotte came across the youngsters munching cookies in the kitchen. It was tucked away in the basement so the cooking odors and heat from the ranges would be confined. Dressed as a governess in a black uniform dress with white collar and cuffs, Charlotte grinned with feigned confidence.

"Good afternoon, children. Your father said you'd show me around the house. Would one of you like to lead the way after you finish your cookies?"

"I shall." Ruthie wiped her hands on a linen napkin and put her plate into the sink. "I'm the only one who knows where everything is kept."

"Shall we start right here in the kitchen?" Charlotte glanced around the enormous room that boasted two stoves, two large iceboxes, a pie safe, and food preparation tables. Countless pans with shiny copper bottoms hung from a ceiling rack. She glimpsed the chef and kitchen maids retrieving items from the pantry.

Now was the perfect time to begin her investigation. Though she didn't expect to find anything of significance in the kitchen, it would be the perfect setup to explore the entirety of the cottage.

"I'm ready to begin." Ruthie kept up a running stream of conversation to the annoyance of her brother who tried to chime in without success. The young girl gave a complete tour of the area, spouting far more information than Charlotte would ever need. With Ruthie in charge and obviously enjoying the attention, the tour proceeded slowly, which was fine by Charlotte.

She followed Ruthie through the first floor rooms, peeking into every nook and cranny. Obviously bored, Tim ran ahead and hid, attempting to startle them in each new room. They passed marble fireplaces, antique French furniture, and enormous gilt-framed mirrors that startled Charlotte each time she caught a glimpse of her prim reflection. A mouth seamed shut, a frown at her brow — she certainly looked tense. She tried to relax, but she couldn't pretend composure when her nerves sizzled. They toured a morning room, drawing room, game room, library, back parlor, and dining room.

Professor Wilmont saluted the three of them with a wave as they trooped by his study.

"I'm showing Miss Hale around, Papa."

"Me too," Tim chimed in.

Daniel looked over a stack of papers. "Thank you, children. I'd come along, but I have tests to correct."

Ruthie's mouth drooped. "That's all right, Papa. I know you're busy."

But she quickly brightened as she gave Charlotte a tour of the second floor bedrooms.

"Summerhill has twenty-two rooms," Ruthie said proudly. "Would you like to see all of them?"

Charlotte laughed. "Goodness, no. That would take all day. Tell me, why do you need such an enormous house?"

Ruthie shrugged. "I don't know, but I believe it's Grandmother's idea to keep Summerhill. And it's convenient for Papa to walk to his classes. He only needs his bedroom and office, but Grandmother wants a lot of room to entertain her friends when she's not sick."

They worked their way down the hall, stopping by several of Ruthie's favorite guest bedrooms, now empty. "When Grandmother is well we have a house full of guests — but not very many this summer. Let's go to the playroom." At the far end of the hallway, Ruthie turned into the children's room. She pointed out every game, book, and toy in the spacious area. "Why don't we play dominoes?" For the next hour Ruthie beat Charlotte at the game, and when they finally arose, Ruthie had a satisfied look on her face.

They returned to the hallway, and Charlotte glanced up at a steep, narrow staircase leading to the third floor. "Is there anything up there besides the attic?"

"The servants' quarters." Tim answered. "The attic is on one side and the servants' rooms are on the other."

"What do you think about exploring the attic?" Excitement spun through Charlotte's chest. The attic was the perfect spot to unearth hidden letters or some other hidden evidence of Daniel Wilmont's shadows.

"The attic? I don't think so." Ruthie shuddered.

"No? And why is that?" An attic conjured up images of brass-bound trunks and boxes, a real treasure trove of rags and riches. Who knew what might be buried under old blankets and out-of-date clothing. Some information pertinent to her investigation might lurk just a short distance away. Or was she allowing her active imagination to take over?

"It's just a lot of junk." Ruthie scrunched up her nose. "And it's probably dusty."

"Perhaps we could clean it up a bit."

The girl mulled it over and then gave a vigorous nod. "We could, but that sounds awfully boring."

"Shall we go up? We might find some toys up there. Let's take a good look."

Ruthie shrugged.

"I think I'll play with my trains," Tim said, returning to the playroom.

Ruthie tromped up the stairs and shoved open the squeaky door to the left of the stairs. Charlotte glanced to the right and spotted a green baize door closing off the servants' quarters. The male servants would occupy part of the area, the female help the other, as they did in most other homes. Charlotte followed Ruthie into the attic. Except for light filtering through a few windows, the space lay shrouded in dimness. Charlotte waited for her eyes to adjust as Ruthie stepped aside.

"You go first." Ruthie gave a sly grin.

"Would you mind fetching a light?" Charlotte asked.

A few minutes later Ruthie returned with a flickering oil lamp. But even with its glow, most of the area still hung in the shadows. Charlotte hesitated. Would the floorboards splinter and crack, then plunge her to her death? Her heart sputtered. No, of course not. This floor was rock solid. She took a deep breath, mustered her courage, and stepped into the gloom. Hand shaking, she shuffled toward the center of the room where she could better view the entire area.

Sagging sofas and rickety end tables littered the cavern. Probably the decrepit chair in Professor Wilmont's study would end up in this furniture graveyard. It ought to be here already. A few steamer trunks resting against the opposite wall might hold some promise. It could hide old letters of a scandalous nature or family secrets from the past.

"My goodness. You're right, this place is dusty. It needs cleaning out. Badly." Charlotte ventured forward, tripping over a footstool. Off balance, she slammed to the floor, smashing her side against the corner of a table. Yelping with pain, she lay still, breathing hard as tears stung the back of her eyes.

"Are you all right?" Ruthie ran in from the doorway.

"No, but I will be in a moment," Charlotte muttered.

She waited until the searing pain subsided in her shoulder and her breathing steadied before hoisting herself to her feet. Gingerly she plodded on until she reached an old wooden trunk. Bending down, she dusted off the lid and lifted it slowly. *Creak.* A musty odor assailed her nostrils. Inside, a face, dead white and porcelain, stared up at her with wide-open crystal blue eyes.

Her hands covered her mouth in horror.

Every ounce of bravery drained from her body. Pressing her hands to her heart, she tried to calm the wild beat, but an eternity passed before its rhythm slowed to normal. Goodness, what was wrong with her? She was as jumpy as a cat with a dog about.

She stared at an old doll, no doubt discarded by a child of another generation. It lay prone on its coffin of rich satin that looked like the skirt of an old ball gown. Slowly she slid her fingers into the trunk, touching layer upon layer of woolen blankets and cotton quilts. Only fabric brushed her hand. Charlotte breathed deeply to steady her shredded nerves.

"It's too old to play with," Ruthie said.

"What are you looking for?" A deep voice caught her off guard.

Startled, Charlotte jumped up. More pain engulfed her. Professor Wilmont loomed in the doorway, filling the space. His brows drew together in puzzlement. Should she run right past him, down the stairs, and out the front door?

She gulped and gave a weak smile.

"I saw Ruthie run by with a lamp, and I wondered what she was up to."

Ruthie giggled. "Miss Hale wants to tidy up. She thinks the attic is one horrid mess. And I agree."

"So now you've seen our messy attic. I suppose you've noticed we seldom throw anything out." He looked rueful but not in the least bit sorry.

That should increase the odds of her discovering something pertinent to her investigation. Charlotte smiled. "Perhaps the children and I could give it a good cleaning out."

A grin spread across Professor Wilmont's face. "But this is where I keep my treasures."

His steady gaze melted Charlotte's legs to jelly. He'd caught her in the act of spying, but thankfully he didn't realize it. "Most of this stuff should be thrown in the trash or given to the poor," she said. *No, the destitute.*

The professor threw back his head and chuckled. "It's too big a job to tackle alone. Anyway, I like my things and I don't want to part with any of them just yet. Don't you keep souvenirs and memorabilia?"

Charlotte nodded. "Well naturally I do, but I strive to stay organized as well. I'd enjoy arranging your *treasures.* I wouldn't mind at all."

Professor Wilmont ran his hand through his blond hair and pulled a frown. "All my paraphernalia could use a heavy dose of organization, but please leave it to Mrs. Finnegan and the maids. Your only job is to watch the children."

Hands on her hips, Ruthie grinned at her father. "Now Papa, you know I'm quite grown up. Maybe Tim is an unruly child, but I'm not."

The professor laughed. "I beg your pardon, young miss. I came upstairs to join the house tour, but it looks like you're finished. Shall we go downstairs?"

"Yes, sir." Charlotte gritted her teeth as her shoulder continued to throb.

"Is something the matter, Miss Hale?" he asked as they headed to the hallway.

She sighed. "I stumbled and fell and wrenched my shoulder. But I'm better now, sir, at least slightly better."

"Shall I send for the doctor?"

Charlotte shook her head, surprised by his concern. "That's not necessary. But thank you all the same."

"Might I pray for you?" he suggested.

Pray? Before she could decline, the professor and Ruthie grabbed her hands and bowed their heads. Amazed that someone would think to pray over something as inconsequential as a hurting shoulder, Charlotte closed her eyes and listened to words that were unfamiliar but slowly brought back vague memories of the few times she'd attended worship services as a child. Her parents had never been consistent churchgoers and neither was her aunt.

"Heavenly Father, we love You and praise Your holy name. I ask You to please use Your awesome power to quickly heal Miss Hale's shoulder and make it good as new."

For what seemed like several minutes, Professor Wilmont spoke to God like He was a friend. His words blended in a soothing cadence that brought a strange rush of peace. Charlotte basked in the warmth, letting her mind focus on God as she'd seldom done before. Was she missing something that the Wilmonts possessed? Charlotte blinked to clear away her odd thoughts, then listened to Ruthie add a prayer of her own.

"Dear Lord, please make my new governess feel better so she can help my family and play with my brother and me."

Tears welled up behind Charlotte's eyes. What was going on? Maybe the strain of deceiving this family was already taking its toll. *Get a grip on yourself, Charlotte. You're a professional journalist — almost — doing a job. Don't let the pressure throw you off balance.*

Silence hung in the air. Her eyes opened like blinds at half-mast. Professor Wilmont and Ruthie looked nearly in a trance and still grasped her hands. They must be silently praying. Or maybe she was supposed to follow their lead and pray aloud. Her hands perspired. What could she say that would end this session?

"Thank you, Almighty God," she mumbled. She didn't think He'd look down from His heavenly perch and miraculously heal her shoulder, but anything was worth a try.

Professor Wilmont and Ruthie opened their eyes and dropped their hands. Charlotte breathed easier. "Well, thank you. I'm sure that will help."

What if he took this opportunity to ask about her relationship with the Lord? As they descended the stairs, she chattered about the weather, the architectural features of the house, anything to keep his mind off of her spiritual condition. When she ran out of topics, she said, "Actually, my shoulder feels ever so much better. It must be the prayer." *Or perhaps not.* But the pain had diminished, for whatever reason.

"Let's go down to the kitchen. I'd like an apple before dinner," Ruthie said.

"I think I'll have one as well. How about you, Miss Hale?" the professor asked.

"No, thank you," Charlotte said as she followed the Wilmonts down to the basement kitchen again. An apple would settle like a cannon ball in the pit of her stomach.

A short, rotund man in a tall toque and immaculate white apron staggered about the room and with grand flair sprawled onto a hard, ladder-back chair. The chef's Gallic face paled, and his features pulled downward like the droop of his luxuriant black mustache. Several servants hovered in the doorway, watching the drama unfold. "Ah, Mr. Wilmont. My supper for the staff was marvelous and up to my usual standards. But now I fear I've taken ill." He gulped air as his body went limp. "Call for the doctor, Simone. What shall I do about the family's dinner?" He groaned and rolled his head from side to side and cradled his stomach and chest with soft, manicured hands.

Chaos ensued while the staff swarmed the kitchen and fussed over the chef. Simone, a dark little woman with worry lines around her eyes, muttered something in French and then scurried off to telephone for a physician. Two giant footmen helped the sick chef stumble off to his bedroom.

"Poor man," Mrs. Finnegan murmured. Then she noticed Charlotte. She stepped closer and whispered, "It's probably dyspepsia. He overeats his own good cooking and every once in a while it doesn't agree with him."

She took her by the arm and introduced her to the staff before they dispersed. More than a dozen uniformed servants greeted her with polite, but minimal, interest. It was just as well. They soon disappeared, chattering about Chef Jacques, leaving Charlotte alone with the Wilmonts, and the kitchen maids busy at the sink washing the staff's supper dishes.

The professor lowered his voice. "I'm sure the kitchen help is capable of preparing a simple dinner for my children and me, but they'll probably need some supervision." He rubbed the small cleft in his chin. "Hmm. I don't know if they actually *can* cook or merely assist with the food preparation."

"Might I be of some assistance?" Charlotte asked, hoping he'd decline her offer.

Relief crossed his face. "Yes, if you wouldn't mind. I know you were not hired to cook, but undoubtedly the kitchen maids would appreciate your assistance or direction — if you think you're up to it."

"I'll be glad to pitch in," Charlotte said with feigned cheer.

"Excellent. Something simple and easy would suit us."

Charlotte hid a smile. She hoped simple and easy wasn't beyond her capability. And did his notion of a simple meal match her own?

Suddenly she regretted she hadn't learned to cook. Aunt Amelia always made all their meals, and given their funds, it was hardly anything fancy. But she was resourceful, wasn't she? She could read and follow directions. All she needed was a recipe and a few ingredients. There was no reason to alert the professor to her deficiencies.

She grabbed a tattered cookbook from an open shelf. Searching the tome for an appropriate recipe, she soon realized she didn't know an easy one from a hard one. With a sigh, she laid the book aside and glanced through the pantry. She looked up to discover Professor Wilmont watching her.

He reddened like a boy caught with his fist in the cookie jar. "I don't mean to stare at you. You just seem so intent. What were you thinking about, if I may ask?"

"Food. Is there anything you'd especially like?" she asked without considering the consequences. What if he expected a dinner with fancy cream sauces and all those other buttery concoctions French chefs were famous for? He might think the hardest of recipes were simple cuisine and easy to prepare.

"I'm partial to chicken, mashed potatoes

and gravy, and biscuits. Uncomplicated fare."

Her laugh twittered. "I like that too." *But I can't cook anything except oatmeal.* "Why don't I look around and see what I can find?" There must be something edible in the large iceboxes on the far wall or in the well-stocked storage rooms.

Professor Wilmont slouched against the black coal stove as she tried to focus on her task. With the man staring at her, she couldn't concentrate — except on his kindly smile. Or was it a quizzical smile? Surely she looked like a complete incompetent. She took in a gulp of hot air and slowly exhaled.

"Are you all right?" he asked.

He regarded her with warmth. Blinded by his concern, she averted her gaze. "I'm fine, just a little uncertain about finding my way around a strange kitchen."

"You do look a bit bewildered."

Panicky said it best.

"I'll get out from underfoot. I'll be in the library."

She wanted him to stay for moral support, yet she wanted him to go.

The professor strolled off obviously confident he'd have his dinner. With the kitchen help in tow, Ruthie introduced the pair to Charlotte. She judged Fiona, the bigger one, to be around eighteen or so. Her bold stare stripped Charlotte of all confidence.

"So Fiona, what shall we cook for the Wilmonts' dinner this evening?" Charlotte asked in a chipper voice.

The hefty girl shrugged. "The chef won't let me near his stove, so I can hardly boil water. And Ellie, she does less than me. We scrub vegetables and cut'em up, but we don't even put'em in a pot." Her mouth pressed with stubbornness.

"Mostly we scour pots and pans." Ellie raised red, rough hands as proof. Tiny and hunched, she might have reached fifteen years, certainly no more.

Fiona thrust her beefy arm into an icebox and pulled out a whole fish. "Maybe you can cook this fresh cod. We also have potatoes and summer squash. The professor likes plain food, not the fancy foreign stuff that his mother wants."

"Good. How does Professor Wilmont like his fish cooked?" Charlotte asked.

Fiona shrugged. "We don't pay any mind to how Chef Jacques does things. That's his business, not ours. And I don't think he wants us to learn his secrets."

"All right. I'll do the cooking," Charlotte said, pretending self-assurance.

Aunt Amelia usually fried or baked cod

and so would she — if she remembered how. Although the fish must have been cleaned at the market, some scales remained. She regarded it with trepidation. Cautiously she drew a knife over the top, starting at the tail and then proceeding toward the head. But the scales flew up in her face like fragments of glass. The kitchen maids snickered. Charlotte grabbed a dish towel, wiped off the mess, and glared at the dead specimen that would no doubt do her in. Drawing in a deep breath, she lopped off the head and tail of her nemesis, skinned and boned it. Only shreds remained, but at least no one would catch a bone in their throat. She sprinkled the little devil with cornmeal. Satisfaction coursed through her like balm. She'd managed to prepare the fish without assistance. Aunt Amelia would be proud.

Ellie dumped the potatoes in the sink and washed and peeled them while Fiona returned to the pantry.

Ruthie piped up, "Would you like help, Miss Hale? I can't cook, but maybe you can give me a quick lesson."

Charlotte shook out a laugh. "Why would you *want* to cook? You'll always have a chef."

Ruthie shrugged, her face downcast. "I'll watch you then, if you don't mind."

Charlotte did mind, but she couldn't explain that she didn't relish an audience while she fumbled around. Thankfully, Ruthie soon grew tired of Charlotte scurrying about and wandered off. Twenty minutes later potatoes boiled and bits of cod sizzled in the black cast-iron pan. Fiona lumbered off to help Ellie wash the dishes from the servants' meal.

Supper in progress, Charlotte dropped into a chair to read dessert recipes. Chocolate pudding with whipped cream was her favorite, so she examined the directions. Butterscotch also looked delicious. Perhaps when she returned home, she'd surprise Aunt Amelia and try these out.

"Can I help?"

Startled, Charlotte looked up at Professor Wilmont. She tossed him a big smile. "No thank you, sir. I have everything under control."

"Are you sure you don't need a hand?" he asked again. "I smell smoke."

FOUR

Charlotte gasped. "The fish is burning!" She ran to the stove and grabbed the skillet. She jerked her hand away and shrieked. A muscular arm wrapped around her waist and pulled her back from the range. With one hand, Professor Wilmont slapped on the faucet. With the other, he caught her wrist and thrust her fingers under cold tap water.

"Is it painful?" He leaned close.

"It hurts quite a bit, but no sign of blisters."

He heaved a sigh of relief. "Keep your hand under there. I'll take care of the food."

He rushed to the stove. Smoke billowed upward. The kitchen filled with a thick black stinking cloud from what was supposed to be the family's dinner. Charlotte gasped in dismay and sucked in a lungful of the acrid fog. It clogged her throat and stung her eyes. She pulled her fingers out of the streaming water and shook them dry. But they immediately began to burn again.

Two screeching children burst into the room followed by Mr. Grimes, the butler, and the kitchen maids.

"Fire! Fire!" Tim rushed toward the coal stove, thrilled at the bliss of unexpected chaos.

Professor Wilmont threw open the back door. A blast of cool air freshened the kitchen and dissipated the smoke. The kitchen maids stood by the icebox, useless.

"I am so sorry. I didn't pay attention. I can't believe my carelessness. Can you ever forgive me? Never mind, don't answer that." Charlotte babbled, unable to control herself. "But we still have potatoes. I'll mash them and they'll taste delicious. You'll see. And squash. I see the squash is all cut up and ready to cook. I'll boil it." In her haste to read about puddings and pies, she'd forgotten all about the vegetables. She ignored the amused looks on the servants' faces. And the laughter scarcely hidden behind their hands. The butler shoed them away.

"Do calm down, Miss Hale. It's all right," Professor Wilmont said soothingly.

Charlotte collapsed onto a chair. Overwhelmed by her disgrace, she cupped her cheeks in her hands and leaned her elbows on a small side table.

Why had she thought she could cook a meal without any practice? What foolish pride! She should admit defeat, apologize, and slink away. Forget her career and her future at the *Rhode Island Reporter*. The professor would soon be showing her the door. *I may as well grab my reticule and disappear, never to be heard from again.*

Yet she wasn't a quitter. She had two bosses, Mr. Phifer and Professor Wilmont, and she would serve them both to the best of her ability, which admittedly wasn't much. She'd stay and take the ridicule. Or until either of them fired her.

"Something else is burning." Ruthie sniffed and pointed to the potatoes.

Professor Wilmont strode to the range once more and pulled the pot off the stove top and looked inside. He laughed heartily.

"Miss Hale, please come here."

She hesitated. Now was the right time to bolt for the back door. But she followed his direction and peered into the pot. A mess of potato mush, thick like cooked oatmeal, clung to the bottom.

"How did that happen?" she murmured.

"You overcooked the potatoes," Fiona chirped.

"I'm so sorry I ruined dinner. I know

you're all famished." Charlotte's voice rang loud and shrill. She blinked back tears, but they slipped to the corners of her eyes. She couldn't remember the last time she'd made a spectacle of herself in public.

"Don't worry. We can go to a restaurant for dinner," Ruthie suggested, casting a longing look toward her father.

"Or better yet, eat cookies," Tim added.

"No need." Chef Jacques shuffled into the kitchen, leaning on Simone's arm, his toque tilted precariously. His eyes dropped, his shoulders slumped. He sniffed the lingering smoke with a long, pointed nose and took charge. "What happened here? Who destroyed my kitchen?"

"I ruined supper," Charlotte admitted. "I'm afraid I really can't cook."

"You don't say," Tim snorted.

"That's enough." Professor Wilmont placed a firm hand on his son's shoulder and steered him toward the staircase. "She's not familiar with our kitchen, Tim."

The chef's face reddened. "I shall cook. She will never again burn good food in my kitchen." He glared and pointed an accusing finger at Charlotte. "No one else has the skill or imagination to take my place, least of all this *governess*. I rose out of my sickbed, for my duty to this family comes before my health. When the doctor arrives, tell him I'll be with him as soon as I concoct something simple but elegant for the family's dinner."

"Thank you, Chef, but we can go out to dine, as my daughter suggested. You need to recover," Professor Wilmont said.

The Frenchman held up his hand. "No, sir. It shall never be said that Chef Jacques was in residence while the Wilmonts were forced to dine out. I shall rally once again."

The professor shrugged. "As you wish. Don't go to any trouble, however. Anything will do."

Ruthie looked at Charlotte. "Papa, can Miss Hale eat with us, please?"

Professor Wilmont waved Charlotte toward the staircase. "We'd be delighted if you'd join us."

"Are you certain, sir?" Head down, Charlotte followed the Wilmonts upstairs. She'd join them tonight because her empty stomach rumbled like thunder, but she'd almost prefer to go to bed hungry. Still, the sooner she got to know Professor Wilmont, the faster she'd gather information for Mr. Phifer.

"Yes, I'm certain. Please join us." The professor grinned sheepishly. "This dinner debacle is really my fault, not yours."

"Oh?" Charlotte sent him a grateful smile for taking responsibility when the blame was hers alone. She so wanted to reach over and plant a big kiss on his cheek, but naturally she wouldn't dare to even give his hand a squeeze.

Dinner was served by a footman in the large dining room lit by crystal chandeliers and candles in tall silver holders. Throughout the meal, the children laughed and teased her. The red-faced Professor Wilmont tried to quiet them, but he failed to curb their high spirits and good-natured jibes. They were simply kids having fun at her expense, but Charlotte had to keep reminding herself of that.

Chef Jacques worked a culinary miracle. Clearly it was concocted from leftovers, but it was the best meal Charlotte had ever tasted. She ate a small portion of tender beef bathed in rich onion gravy, but the shock of destroying dinner had robbed her of her normally robust appetite. A Parker House roll sunk to the bottom of her stomach and she couldn't swallow another bite.

She'd destroyed tonight's supper. Would she fail at her other duties as well?

The professor leaned back in his chair and tilted his head. Early evening sunlight filtered through the sheer curtains behind him and streaked his light hair to pure gold. "Don't look so upset, Miss Hale. Our meal turned out fine."

His cheerful manner brought sunshine to her anxious heart. "No thanks to me, I'm afraid. But I'm grateful for your tolerance. I promise you I'll be much better at taking care of the children than at cooking."

"That's all I ask," he said, lifting a silver forkful of blackberry pie.

Still, she wondered if she were up to all her duties. The professor was compassionate, but would his mother be as understanding? Ladies tended to expect more from the help. Charlotte pushed that disturbing question out of her mind; with any luck she'd return to the newspaper long before Mrs. Wilmont came home from the hospital.

After dessert, the professor excused Ruthie and Tim to retreat to the veranda for a game of checkers.

"Miss Hale, you should have told me you were uncomfortable in the kitchen." The professor's words carried more censure than his voice, but his tone held an earnest appeal she couldn't ignore.

Her voice trembled. "I — I was afraid you'd dismiss me if I wouldn't pitch in." Heat spread from her tightly collared neck up to her cheeks. "And I wanted to please you. I apologize, sir. I thought I could manage well enough even though I seldom cook at home. Actually, I never cook at home. My Aunt Amelia prepares all our meals." She lowered her eyes and hoped the flames in her cheeks would quickly fade. "I never darken the kitchen except to eat." *Be quiet, Charlotte. You're making a fool of yourself.*

He didn't crack a smile. "You should have explained your inexperience. I would've understood."

"You're right, of course. But I truly wanted to help."

She held her breath, hoping he wouldn't ask any more questions.

"I appreciate your good intentions and all your hard work."

"But not my cooking." She tossed him a shy smile as she rose and began to carry the dishes to the dumbwaiter.

"That's not necessary. The footman will clear the table."

She put her hands on the back of a chair. "I'm very grateful for your understanding. I took on more than I could handle."

He steadied his gaze. "Always be honest with me, Miss Hale. Please. I value the truth and I cannot abide lying."

"I understand." She averted his appraising stare. This assignment was becoming more complicated than she'd anticipated. What terrible fury she'd provoke if he learned of her underhanded work.

His smile broke the tension. "You look frightened to death. Don't give your dinner attempt another thought. And please don't cry. I don't handle tears well at all."

Charlotte giggled nervously before her trembling lips slowly curled in a tentative smile. "I promise you, sir, I never cry in public." Well, she'd shed a few tears in the kitchen, but perhaps he hadn't noticed.

"Nor in private, I hope. You applied for the position of governess, not cook. Chef Jacques' duties were thrust upon you. So don't fret about tonight." He pushed his spectacles to the bridge of his nose. "Please excuse me. I have piles of work to attend to. Enjoy your evening."

"What about the children? Shouldn't I attend to them?"

The professor shook his head. "No, Miss Hale, I can do that myself. You've done enough for one day."

Her mouth twisted in a wry smile. "You're quite right, sir. My day was rather eventful." More than he could ever imagine.

Charlotte returned to the basement and found Mrs. Finnegan alone in the servant's hall reading a newspaper. The elderly woman looked over her frameless spectacles. "Do come in, dearie, and have a seat. Would you like to look through the *Newport Gazette* when I'm finished?"

"Yes, I would. Thank you. I like to keep up with what's going on in the world."

"Well good for you. I try to as well, but often I'm too weary at the end of the day to do more than drink me tea and put me feet up. They tend to swell if I'm on them too long." She sighed. "I know you're feeling bad about the supper, but truly there's not a thing wrong with trying to help out when help's needed. I applaud you for pitching in. So put it all out of your mind."

"I shall try."

"We're so happy you're here and ready to take the children in hand. A firm but gentle hand is needed with those two, to be sure. The professor tries his best, but sometimes he doesn't know what to do with them. His head's so far up in the clouds, way above everyone else's, he can't find his way back down to earth. But you seem earthy enough to me." Mrs. Finnegan tilted her head and chuckled. "Oh, he can talk to them about the things of God and even of life, but those children need a good dose of fun too. You look like a girl who can mix right in with them and play. The professor and his mother aren't much for playing. But it's what the tykes need."

"I do agree with you, Mrs. Finnegan. We'll start tomorrow."

Daniel strolled to his study to correct several sets of homework assignments, but his thoughts remained on the poor young woman who had suffered such humiliation tonight. She'd obviously tried her best to put together a decent meal. How unfortunate she'd burned the cod, one of his favorite dishes.

But if she could keep the children quiet while he worked, she'd indeed prove to be a blessing. He hoped her lovely face and form hadn't influenced him to hire her when he should have searched for a woman with more experience. No, he felt sure he wouldn't regret his decision.

"Papa, will you help me with my jigsaw puzzle, please? Ruthie's tired of losing at checkers and wants to read a book," Tim said as he and his sister peeked inside his office.

Daniel sighed. He'd wasted several minutes daydreaming about Charlotte Hale when he should have been grading papers. And now his son wanted him to fritter away more precious time. He instantly regretted his selfishness. Tim deserved to spend time with his only parent. "I'll play for ten minutes and then it's off to bed. I have student essays to read."

After assisting Tim, he herded the duo upstairs. Without his mother's help, he felt totally out of his element, like a codfish in the forest — or Miss Hale in the kitchen. His mother prodded the children to do her bidding, but he'd neither inherited nor developed the same talent for intimidation.

Half an hour passed before Daniel settled the boy down. Perhaps he should've asked Miss Hale to put the children to bed, but he'd discovered he really enjoyed the evening ritual. He suspected she'd approve of his hands-on involvement.

Unlike Tim, Ruthie slid right between her sheets.

"Papa, can we have a heart-to-heart talk?"

He coughed back a chuckle. "Of course, pumpkin."

"I've been thinking. Grandmother is getting old and won't be around forever. Of course, we'd like her to live to be one hundred. But in case she doesn't, it might be good to have a stepmother. A really nice lady, someone like Miss Hale. Sometimes I get so lonely for a mama, I cry."

He pressed his daughter in a gentle hug

and buried his head in her auburn hair flowing loosely down her back. Ruthie squeezed him tight before he sat back on the edge of her bed. "Sometimes I get lonely too," he admitted.

Desolation surged through him with a familiar ache. He missed not having a woman to love, to wrap in his arms and hold close. Not that Sarah was one to ever really care about the important events in his life or even the trivialities. He tried to look ahead, not back to a past he couldn't rewrite. And sometimes he succeeded.

"Are you ever going to marry again, Papa?" Ruthie clutched her stuffed bunny to her chest, a last remnant of childhood.

Pinned by his daughter's sincere eyes and straightforward question, Daniel squirmed on the pink and green satin bedspread. "I honestly don't know."

"I'm sure God wants you to. You need a wife and I need a mama." The children deserved a mother who adored them and spent time with them, but he was quite sure he didn't need a wife. Or want one. He'd already been down that road . . .

Daniel pulled her light summer blanket up to her chin. "If the Lord wants me to remarry, He'll let me know who she is when He's good and ready. We can pray about it, but remember, we must wait for the Lord."

Ruthie groaned as she thrust the covers back down. "Grandmother wasn't waiting for the Lord's timing when she made you meet all her friends' daughters."

Daniel grinned. "But it didn't work, now did it?" During the last few years his mother had badgered him to court her current favorite — the Belle of the Month, as he'd come to call them. They were all upstanding Christian women from good families, but not one caused an ember to flare. Or even flicker.

He kissed Ruthie good night, turned off her bedside lamp, and retreated to his bedroom. This was the first time Ruthie mentioned wanting a stepmother. He wondered if she still mourned Sarah, though now that he thought of it, Ruthie hadn't spoken of her in ages. Five years was a long time for a child to remember. Her image of Sarah had probably faded just as his had.

Heavenly Father, please fill Ruthie with your love and take away her loneliness. Send her a helper to guide her as she grows up — but not necessarily a stepmother — unless this is Your will for me.

She'd reach young womanhood in a few short years and need someone besides an old-fashioned grandmother or an awkward papa to steer her in the right direction and teach her the feminine things he didn't know anything about. He shuddered at the idea of tackling the task by himself.

As he climbed into his four-poster bed, a picture of Charlotte filled his mind. The gleam in her dark eyes and the thick brown hair swept up into a topknot stirred his imagination. She certainly added a fresh spirit to the household.

If he ever remarried he'd like a wife like Charlotte Hale — playful, not coy, and totally natural. After years of Sarah's indifference, all he wanted in a wife was honesty and a desire to share his life. A woman who loved him and loved the Lord. A woman he could trust.

He sighed in the hushed night air. Was that too much to request? Probably so. He knew from experience if a woman demanded all of his time and attention, then the relationship veered toward disaster.

He couldn't tolerate emotional storms complete with accusations and tears, so he ought to avoid the fuss and never chance another marital failure. With a weary sigh Daniel took Sarah's journal from the drawer of his nightstand and paged through it. After her death he read it cover to cover, absorbing her pain, wallowing in it, belatedly understanding he caused so many of their problems. Even though she betrayed him, he knew he shouldered part of the blame. Yet when he replayed the events of their marriage, he still didn't understand exactly why their love had died so abruptly and completely.

The memory of their unhappiness still anchored him to the past. Snapping the journal shut, he padded over to the wardrobe, retrieved a hatbox where he'd stored odds and ends, and shoved it inside.

It was time to shake off sad memories and concentrate on his children.

The future.

Life.

FIVE

Charlotte burrowed under the covers and tried to relax and let the day fade into oblivion. Tomorrow she'd redeem herself. She wouldn't give the professor even the remotest reason to regret his decision to hire her. Rolling to her side, she pulled the light blanket up to her chin and hoped for a peaceful sleep. It wouldn't come.

In the distance waves crashed against the rocks, and below her bedroom window crickets hummed softly in the warm night air. But nothing soothed her restlessness. On her own, she'd have to depend solely upon her wits for the next week or so.

Maybe she wasn't suited for spying, even for a worthwhile cause. Her heart sputtered as she recalled the unpaid roofer's and doctor's invoices. Charlotte groaned as she sat up and turned on the bedside lamp.

She picked up the Bible lying conspicuously on the nightstand. Perhaps the professor had left the book for her. He seemed to put a lot of stock in his religious beliefs and no doubt expected she did as well. She wasn't particularly interested in learning more about Jesus. But she was interested in Professor Wilmont, and he seemed interested in Jesus.

What did he find so fascinating about a man who lived two thousand years ago? She couldn't imagine. But maybe Scripture held the key to understanding the professor. And that might help her investigation. It was worth a look.

She opened the Scriptures at random. The gospel of St. John. She skimmed the first few chapters with some interest. Then verses nineteen through twenty-one in chapter three grabbed her full attention.

"And this is the condemnation, that light is come into the world, and men loved darkness rather than light, because their deeds were evil. For every one that doeth evil hateth the light, neither cometh to the light, lest his deeds should be reproved. But he that doeth truth cometh to the light, that his deeds may be made manifest, that they are wrought in God."

Were her deeds really evil or was she merely doing her job? She certainly feared being exposed for what she was — a reporter and a snoop. Not one bit comforting. Maybe she'd ponder this another time.

Closing the book, she tried to sleep. After a long while her mind slowed. She drifted off just as dawn seeped through the off-white curtains.

Charlotte awoke with a start and sprang out of bed. Her pocket watch read six o'clock. Time to help out in the kitchen — if they wanted her. Thoughts of those Bible verses came to mind. That men loved darkness rather than light because their deeds were evil. This rubbed her conscience raw, but she pushed it aside as she checked on the sleeping children.

Charlotte dressed quickly in the light blue uniform and hurried down the backstairs to the basement. When she entered the kitchen, she found Fiona whisking eggs in a bowl while Ellie carried dishes into the servants' hall.

Stirring a pot of oatmeal, the French woman glanced at Charlotte with eyes nearly as dark as the coal stove. "We didn't formally meet yesterday. I am Simone, Mrs. Wilmont's maid. My husband is Chef Jacques." She lifted her chin up, as if she expected the utmost respect for her exalted position.

"I'm pleased to meet you," Charlotte said. "How is the chef feeling this morning? I hope he's better."

Simone shrugged one sloping shoulder. "He'll recover, but right now he fears he'll be gone by nightfall. He's not used to feeling poorly and he's taking it like a man." The maid twitched her first hint of a smile.

"Do you need my help with breakfast?" Charlotte asked, ignoring Fiona and Ellie's snickering.

The little woman shook her head. "That's not necessary. With Mrs. Wilmont in the hospital, I have little to do. So I'll cook in place of my husband. But Miss Hale, you need not fill in for another member of the staff. We each have our own duties. They are not interchangeable."

Charlotte blushed. "Of course." She hadn't known.

Simone waved Charlotte away. "You go off now and eat in the nursery with the children. They'll be waiting for you."

Charlotte nodded before she climbed the steep backstairs to the second floor.

At the top of the staircase she nearly collided with a plump, chestnut-haired maid she instantly recognized. "Grace Thompson! I never expected to find you here. How nice to see you again." But Charlotte feared

her voice held more trepidation than pleasure.

Childhood friends and neighbors, a few
years back Grace had suddenly stopped
speaking to her for no reason. And then
Grace's parents had died from diphtheria.
She had gone to live with her aunt and
uncle on their farm in Portsmouth, several
miles from Newport and on the opposite
end of Aquidneck Island. Charlotte hadn't
seen her since her move.

"You're not still angry with me, are you?
I'm not exactly sure what I did to offend
you, but I am sorry our friendship ended so
abruptly." Charlotte stared into a pair of
bright hazel eyes that added sparkle to her
small, even features.

Grace grasped Charlotte's hands in her
own and squeezed. "I apologize to you for
getting mad before I learned the truth. I do
hope you'll forgive me."

"Forgive you for what? I really don't know
what you're talking about, Grace."

The pretty girl glanced down the staircase.
"I need to get back to work, but maybe we
can talk later tonight and I'll explain."

"Yes, I'd like that. My bedroom is directly
off the children's playroom."

Grace smiled. "I'll come by after I'm
finished for the day."

She hurried away leaving Charlotte to wonder if her old friend knew she worked for the *Rhode Island Reporter*. She'd have to find out and beg her not to tell. But what if she gossiped to the other maids first? Charlotte sighed then pushed worry to the back of her mind. What she couldn't control she wouldn't dwell upon, at least not right now.

Charlotte found Tim and Ruthie in the playroom. The children sat at the table as the dumbwaiter delivered their breakfast. Charlotte served the oatmeal, eggs, and toast.

"Would you two enjoy a bicycle ride this morning?" Charlotte asked. She nibbled cinnamon toast and sipped strong coffee doctored with a generous dose of cream and two spoons of sugar.

Tim's eyes sparked. "You mean we won't have lessons?"

She'd forgotten about their schoolwork. "We'll read later today. But let's have a bit of fun first."

Ruthie clapped her hands with delight. "Thank you, Miss Hale."

Mrs. Finnegan located a split skirt for Charlotte to wear, and with a belt to tighten the waist, it fit fine. For most of the morning Charlotte and the children rode bicycles on the Ocean Drive. Spectacular views of the rugged coast and cottages as big as palaces appeared as they rounded bends and conquered gentle inclines. Charlotte perspired from pumping hard, but the ocean breeze cooled her off. They returned to Summerhill windblown and slightly sunburned, despite their sleeves and hats.

"That was such fun. May we play a game of croquet or tennis now?" Ruthie asked as she adjusted the bow on her middy blouse.

"Maybe later, but reading comes first. Would you prefer to read on the veranda or in the nursery?"

Ruthie rolled her eyes. "Please don't call our playroom a nursery. That sounds so babyish."

"Yes, you're absolutely right. Pardon my mistake," Charlotte said with a smile.

"I choose the veranda. And I think I'll get a cookie or two first," Tim said.

"All right, but no dawdling in the kitchen," Charlotte warned. "I'll meet you on the back veranda in about half an hour. And remember to bring your books."

She watched the pair head to the kitchen before she slipped into Professor Wilmont's study to search for evidence. The possibility of someone catching her in the act of snooping loomed large. Her every nerve vibrated, pulsing unease through her chest. But it was better to start now before the professor returned from his morning classes.

With shaking hands she rifled through papers on his desk and opened cabinets and desk drawers. She scanned notes and writings but discovered nothing except a few dust bunnies in the far corners.

She wasn't surprised. A smart man, Professor Wilmont would surely lock up incriminating information to thwart a nosey person such as herself. She hastened upstairs to check his bedroom. She took a deep breath and stepped inside the large, expensively furnished room flooded with light and the ever-present salty smell of the sea. She spotted few personal items except for a gilt-framed wedding photograph displayed on the wall.

She drew closer to examine the picture of a young Daniel Wilmont gazing adoringly at his lovely bride. The lady, who looked no more than eighteen or nineteen, had wavy hair topped with a crown of orange blossoms and a lace veil. Delicate features set in a heart-shaped face seemed to caress the unseen camera with half-closed, sensuous eyes. Charlotte was caught in the enigmatic gaze of the young woman, long dead.

What was Mrs. Wilmont like? Smooth and sophisticated?

Charlotte shook the musings from her mind and pulled her attention back to her task before someone discovered her in a room where she had no business. She needed to hurry. Rummaging through the bureau and chest of drawers, she found only clothes stuffed inside all in a jumble. On the far side of the room she looked through a cedar chest containing winter blankets and handmade quilts. The nightstand yielded nothing either. Peering under the bed, she noted a lone dust ball.

In the wardrobe, vests and woolen scarves spilled over the top shelf, crowding a stack of books, scrapbooks, and photograph albums. And a hatbox. She kept listening for voices or footsteps in the hallway. Satisfied she was still alone, Charlotte pulled down the hatbox and lifted the cover. A small book labeled *Prayer Journal* lay on top of several dime novels and books of poetry. She opened the journal and found the name *Sarah Wilmont* written on the inside cover. Had she discovered gold? She took a peek.

With no time to read now, she'd have to borrow the book. Most likely the professor wouldn't notice its absence. She shoved the hatbox back in place, tucked the journal under her arm, and then hesitated. Was it right to read someone else's personal account? Certainly not, but this was for a good cause, indirectly for the betterment of society. She'd return it to its proper place as soon as she glanced through it — and before the professor had a chance to notice its absence.

Charlotte flew to her bedroom and locked the book safely inside her bureau. She collapsed in a chair and tossed back her head and breathed slowly. For several seconds she sat perfectly still, relieved and exhilarated that she might have found something promising. She'd read it tonight before bed, when her time was her own. Glancing at her pocket watch, it confirmed she still had a few more minutes to search. But only a few, so she'd have to hurry.

Taking a kerosene lamp from her bureau she hurried upstairs to the attic. A lump in her throat grew to the size of a cannon ball as she plunged through the shadows and into the depths of the unlit space.

Charlotte shivered in the hot semidarkness, but she pushed onward. Brushing dust off old boxes and trunks, she coughed and sneezed and sent mice scurrying across the attic floorboards. She again rummaged through the trunk with the old doll, but no old letters turned up as she hoped. Quite disappointing. Cobwebs stuck to her disheveled hair and apron.

She closed the attic door and ran smack into Simone.

"Excuse me," Charlotte muttered.

"What are you doing in the attic? You job is to mind the children."

Charlotte paused. "Yesterday Ruthie and I found an old doll tucked away in a trunk, and I thought she might like to play with it. But on second look I realized the doll was too shabby." Charlotte flinched at the lie that came so easily to her lips. Would this assignment change her into a woman she could never again respect?

Simone shook her finger. "You must stay out of places where you have no business. The attic is a storage area for junk the professor can't bear to dispose of, nothing more."

Charlotte nodded, feeling duly reprimanded once again. "Yes, of course."

Simone surveyed her with obvious disgust. "You're covered in dust. Go change your clothing so you don't disgrace the family."

Once in her room Charlotte brushed and re-pinned her hair then beat the dust off her skirt. She hurried downstairs, still smarting from Simone's rebuke. Mr. Phifer felt sure she'd ferret out information in his campaign to ruin his adversary. She'd examined most every nook and cranny in the household, but she hadn't uncovered even one shred of evidence against the professor. If such discrediting data existed, it was probably in the professor's college office, a place she'd never be able to search. Only his wife's chronicle brought her a glimmer of hope.

If she failed at her once-in-a-lifetime opportunity, she'd never receive another chance. Mr. Phifer would see to that. But she couldn't conjure up facts that didn't exist, could she?

Unfortunately, her boss demanded results, not excuses.

That afternoon, after returning from the college, Daniel accepted his bowler and umbrella from Mr. Grimes and waited for the butler to open the front door.

"Papa, where are you going?" Ruthie called.

Daniel turned around as she clattered down the staircase with Tim at her heels. Their governess followed close behind.

"I'm off to buy your grandmother a welcome home present."

"May we come too?" Ruthie pouted her plea, but her eyes shone with mischief.

If the children accompanied him, the

short trip would take twice as long since Tim couldn't resist begging for the over-priced toys on display in the shop windows.

"I'm afraid I'm in a hurry. I have to finish my column this afternoon. Perhaps another time." He flashed an apologetic smile that he hoped would end the conversation.

"Please, Papa." Ruthie clasped her hands at her chest in such a sweet and childish manner that he weakened and had to recon-sider.

He glanced toward Miss Hale. "Would you mind coming along?"

"I'd be glad to, Professor."

"Yes, Papa, please." Ruthie reached for her straw boater dangling from the foyer hat rack and plopped it on her head. Miss Hale came forward, straightened the tilted hat, and retied the sash on his daughter's dress.

So the decision was made for him. He raised his hands in mock surrender. "All right, you win. But we must be quick about it and not waste time."

They hastened outside and all piled into the surrey bound for Bellevue Avenue. As he grasped the reins, Miss Hale helped the children into the backseat. When she slid onto the tan leather seat beside him, his heart inexplicably jumped. Glancing side-ways, he noticed her perfect profile, creamy complexion, and long, slender neck rising above the plain white collar of her black uniform. Her shiny hair framed her face and disappeared beneath the crown of her straw hat. She was far lovelier than the beauties of Newport who sported Worth gowns and extravagant jewels. He dragged his attention away before he steered the horses off the winding road.

The matched pair trotted around the Ocean Drive and up Bellevue Avenue past magnificent summer cottages secluded behind hedges or high stone walls. Daniel seldom rode down millionaires' row, socialized with the other cottagers, or shopped at the exclusive stores. His life revolved around Aquidneck College and Summerhill, though his mother often entertained friends from the highest social circle and tried her hardest to include him in her activities.

The air weighed heavy with dampness and wilted his starched white shirt. He noted the gunmetal gray sky punctuated with thunderclouds. If he didn't rush they'd get caught in the rain. The horses picked up their pace as they drew closer to the small shopping area. Breathing in Miss Hale's light floral scent, Daniel fought the urge to move closer to her on the front seat. He gave his head a slight shake to release such an unexpected and unwelcome impulse.

He halted the carriage by the shingled-style Newport Casino. This was the club where the nation's richest set gathered to play tennis, view plays, dance, and impress one another. Branch stores from New York's finest shops and boutiques fronted the Casino on the wide Bellevue Avenue sidewalk. On occasion, he watched a tennis match or a play in the small theatre, but usually his work kept him too busy to indulge in idle entertainment.

Daniel stepped down from the carriage, glad to be released from Miss Hale's odd effect. Several other equipages with coachmen garbed in top hats and impeccable livery lined the street as their employers enjoyed leisure time and vast fortunes.

"Shall I help you choose a gift for Grandmother?" Ruthie asked as she climbed down. "A bracelet or necklace might be nice."

Daniel chuckled then patted his daughter on her auburn head. "A pair of kid gloves is more like it."

"But gloves are so boring. How about a book? I love stories," Ruthie said. "And a ring also. She adores sapphires. They're her birthstone."

Tim peered in the window of a bakery.

"How about an éclair while you decide? Maybe we could buy a dozen and save one for Grandmother."

Daniel noted the tempting confections and couldn't resist either. "I'll buy each of us a treat before we leave, but you know your grandmother doesn't have a sweet tooth except for bon bons and —"

"Oatmeal raisin cookies," Ruthie finished.

They mingled with the fashionably dressed ladies who swept down the sidewalk and wove in and out of the shops like a school of fish. Then Daniel spotted his old suite mate from Yale pushing a pram with a lovely young woman Daniel assumed was his wife.

"Jackson Grail. How are you?" he called as the trio approached.

His friend halted and shook Daniel's outstretched hand. Tall, black haired, and looking prosperous in a well-tailored suit, Jack was not the poor but brilliant scholarship student Daniel remembered from Yale. In college he wore threadbare trousers and patched jackets that singled him out among the sons of privilege.

"Good to see you. The last I heard you were mining for gold in the Klondike and finding it by the ton."

Jack let out a hearty laugh. "I came back to New York more than a year ago, married

105

Miss Lillian Westbrook, George's sister. As you can see, we now have a baby son named Thomas Jackson Grail. Daniel, I'd like to present my wife, Lilly."

Daniel bowed to the tall young woman with a warm smile. Jack had done well for himself. A lovely wife, an infant son. The look of joy tempered by contentment shown on Jack's face. For a long moment Daniel felt a pang of envy.

"It's a pleasure to meet a friend of Jack's. And the owner of the lovely Summerhill," Lilly said, sending a small smile toward her husband. "We have such fond memories of renting your fine home." She turned toward Charlotte. "And you must be . . ."

"Miss Hale, our new governess," Daniel said before she asked if Charlotte Hale was his wife. Even in her plain clothing Miss Hale didn't resemble a matronly governess most might expect him to hire.

"How do you do, Mrs. Grail?"

Lilly looked to the storefronts. "While the gentlemen talk, why don't we glance in the window of the millinery shop? That hat catches my eye." So the two women and Ruthie strolled over to the shop to critique the outlandish headgear. Tim discovered a wooden train set beckoning from another store close by.

Daniel and Jack sidestepped a pair of silver-haired matrons and tipped their hats.

"I'm a publisher now," Jack said. "I bought Jones and Jarman along with a small New York newspaper and magazine. We struggled last summer, but business has steadily improved."

"I'm pleased to hear of your success." Daniel leaned against the window of the Newport branch of Tiffany's. The edges of its striped awning beat back and forth in the increasing breeze.

He glanced toward Jack's tall, slender wife who vaguely resembled her brother, George, another college classmate. But apparently Lilly received the best of the family's good looks. "I understand your wife is the authoress Fannie Cole."

Through Mrs. Finnegan's connections with other Newport servants, he'd learned the new Mrs. Grail had created a tempest-in-a-teapot among their social circle by penning romance dime novels some mistakenly considered scandalous. Actually, her books extolled the highest Christian virtues and encouraged readers to avoid the temptations of the world. During the past year his mother had read a few Fannie Cole novels and she'd come to appreciate them. From the happy appearance of the couple, they'd weathered the publicity well.

"She is indeed Fannie Cole." Pride shone in Jack's dark eyes.

"Congratulations on your marriage, Jack. I'm very happy for you."

Jack nodded contentedly. "I'm truly blessed."

"I believe I shall purchase one of her novels for my mother. She and my house-keeper both enjoy Fannie Cole books. They speak highly of her writing." So a novel, along with gloves and roses from the garden might warm his mother's heart. And maybe a small sapphire pin.

"I'm sure Lilly would be happy to sign it for her."

"Wonderful. How long are you here in Newport?"

"We just arrived yesterday for a short vacation," Jack said. "We're staying at the Coastal Inn for two weeks, then it's back to New York. I can't neglect my businesses for long."

Daniel nodded. "I understand." They moved away from the crowd.

"Did you know I visited Lilly's family at Summerhill last July? That's where we became engaged and married." Jack's grin spread from one corner of his face to the other. "As she mentioned, we both have fond memories of the cottage."

Daniel had rented Summerhill to the Westbrooks the previous summer when he'd traveled to Europe with his mother and children. "It's a wonderful place to spend the summer." Though expensive to maintain for a professor with only a small salary and an even smaller inheritance.

Jack's voice softened. "I was so sorry to hear your wife passed away, Daniel."

Daniel nodded. "Yes, Sarah's death was a terrible blow to my whole family, but we're muddling through, thanks to my mother and now a new governess."

Jack's glance strayed toward Miss Hale who was pointing out a hat displayed in the shop window to Ruthie and Lilly Grail. Daniel grinned. The hat boasted more feathers than a peacock and was just as colorful. He thought it suited Miss Hale's cheerful personality to a *T*. But even if she could afford it, he doubted she'd wear something so gaudy.

"Your governess seems to enjoy the children." Jack lifted an eyebrow. Curiosity shined in his eyes.

Daniel wondered why, though he felt his face flush. "She's a very agreeable young woman. I was fortunate to hire her."

Jack's gaze returned to Daniel. His old

friend didn't pry, though from his quizzical look, he clearly wanted to. Daniel sighed inwardly. Why was Jack reading something into mere — interest? He found Miss Hale easy to talk to about the children, nothing more.

"Let me congratulate you on your religion column, Daniel. I subscribe to the *Newport Gazette* and look forward to reading your views each week. Your opponents are buzzing like a hive of hornets. They're a greedy bunch more interested in profits than their workers." Jack chuckled. "Keep up the good work." He lightly slapped Daniel on the back.

"Thank you. I intend to continue my ministry."

"Good for you." Jack cocked his head. "Perhaps you'd like to write for the *Manhattan Sentinel* as well. Would you consider it?"

Taken by surprise, Daniel hesitated. "Thank you for the offer. I'll certainly keep it in mind, though at the moment I'm doing as much as I can handle."

Promising to spend more time with Ruthie and Tim precluded adding another newspaper column to his work schedule. But writing was his favorite ministry, even more than teaching students, many of whom were disinterested in learning more than the minimum necessary for a passing grade. Still, the Lord called him to write and instruct, so he'd do both. Maybe accepting Jack's offer was part of God's plan. He'd give it serious thought.

"Perhaps you can join us for dinner at Summerhill and we can talk it over," Jack suggested. "Can you come sometime next week?"

"We'd be delighted."

They set a date. "I'll look forward to it," Daniel said.

SIX

On the trip back to Summerhill, a stiff breeze gusted across the rocks and whipped around Charlotte's shoulders. She pulled her shawl tighter.

A crash of thunder drowned out the low whistle of the wind. Sheets of rain pelted down from a blackened sky in large, cold drops. The surrey's roof offered little protection from the streaming torrents. Charlotte angled her hat to keep the water out of her eyes and face. She glanced back at Tim and Ruthie. The girl's yellow pique dress was too light to keep her warm. Charlotte whipped off her knitted shawl and handed it to Ruthie who rewarded her with a big grin and a thank-you. The children huddled inside the shawl's soft folds. Professor Wilmont shed his navy blue jacket and flung it around Charlotte shoulders.

"Wear it," he insisted.

Too wet and miserable to object to his

chivalry, Charlotte slid into the coat. He handed her his umbrella, and she popped it open and raised it above both their heads, forcing them terribly near. Charlotte inadvertently shivered. As they rounded a curve in the road, he leaned into her. When his shirt brushed against her arm, Charlotte felt a small jolt of pleasure.

It reminded her of what she'd once felt for Paul Seaton — before he left her for a woman without encumbrances. She never wanted to feel that way again, especially about a man she had to discredit. She'd taken great care to never let her heart weaken again — not that there was any real danger of her succumbing to the frivolities of romance. She tilted her head toward the edge of the umbrella, as far from the professor as she could possibly get. The idea that a scion of a rich family would ever fall for her, a lowly secretary and townie, made her smile at herself. *Perhaps I should be a fiction writer like Fannie Cole rather than an aspiring journalist.*

When they arrived at Summerhill, the professor said, "Let's all change into dry clothes and meet in the library for a story and perhaps some hot chocolate."

"Yes, Papa!" Tim called as he dashed up the stairs two at a time.

Ten minutes later all four crowded on the soft leather sofa near the fireplace and watched the flames blaze and the wood crackle. In a dramatic voice the professor read *The Legend of Sleepy Hollow* until the children's piano teacher arrived half an hour later. The two finished the last sips of their hot chocolate and left the library, dragging their feet across the Oriental carpet.

From the doorway, Tim asked, "Must we go, Papa?"

"Yes. Please don't keep your teacher waiting."

"Tim doesn't seem to enjoy playing the piano," Charlotte said, after the children were out of earshot.

The professor's eyebrows furrowed. "Perhaps not. Yet music lessons are worthwhile."

Charlotte shrugged. "I'm sure they are for some. But I remember my mother and then my aunt forcing me to practice the piano. I detested every moment I had to pound those keys. It was a waste of their hard-earned money. And I never learned to keep time to the music — or even carry a tune. Some of us are hopeless and don't enjoy looking like incompetents."

"So you believe I ought to allow Tim to quit his lessons?"

"Maybe he'd prefer some other instrument. Or perhaps he'd rather listen to music than make it."

"I shall mull it over, Miss Hale. Thank you for your advice." His blue-green eyes sparkled. But he looked more amused than grateful.

Eager to change the subject, Charlotte said, "The children were so engrossed in *The Legend of Sleepy Hollow*. Do you read to them often?"

Professor Wilmont shook his head. "Not often enough, I'm afraid. I'm normally too busy, but I suppose that's an excuse, not a reason."

"My parents read to my brother and sister and me every night before bedtime. We couldn't afford many books, but we treasured the ones we had. I miss those happy times. They ended all too soon."

"I'm so sorry. May I ask, did your parents pass away when you were young?" He folded his long, slender hands on his lap.

"Yes, they did. I was only twelve. My brother too. Influenza."

"That must have been very hard."

"It was and it still is. The pain doesn't quite go away, even after ten years."

"How are you and your sister doing now?"

She smiled. "Becky and I live with our dear Aunt Amelia. We have food and clothes and a roof over our heads, although it's not paid for yet. Aside from that problem, I have no reason to complain. What more could I want?"

"Nothing, I suppose." He glanced around the enormous library with richly paneled walls, floor to ceiling books, and alabaster busts on marble tables.

Charlotte grinned. "Well, of course I could wish for more. I live in a tiny house with the bare necessities. But it's sufficient. Sometimes I'd like a few luxuries, but they're not necessary for my happiness. I always search for the positive in every situation." Though the entire length of the sofa separated them, their gazes drew them close. A jolt of fear ran through her. "Sir, I — I'm not minimizing the beauty of Summerhill. It's the most impressive house I've ever been in. But I'm content to live without the elegance and wealth I shall never have."

"I see," was all he said, maddeningly brief. His long face, with a wave of light hair flopping over his forehead, was without pretense or guile. And she could stare, mesmerized, into the depths of those eyes forever.

Charlotte pulled herself back to reality. "If you'll excuse me, sir, I should tidy up the playroom."

"Very well," he said. Was there a tinge of

reluctance in his voice? *What an unusual gentleman,* she thought as she picked up wooden soldiers from the playroom floor and placed them back on the shelf. He actually seemed to care about what she thought and felt.

Charlotte shook her head. This assignment was most definitely softening her brain. The professor seemed to be such a good man, but he had no idea how difficult grubbing out a living could be for a woman with a family. If she had a real choice, she wouldn't be here now pretending to be a governess. He'd never understand how sheer survival influenced all her decisions.

Later that night she ate supper with the children in the playroom, and at eight thirty Charlotte tucked them in bed. She retreated to her bedroom, eager to read Sarah Wilmont's prayer journal. Dropping into her easy chair by the screened window, her hand shook as she opened to the first page. A fresh breeze blew in from the sea, curling around her skin and sending shivers up and down her spine.

Throughout the day she'd resisted the urge to run upstairs and skim through the pages during her short breaks. But her good judgment prevailed and she waited until evening.

She hesitated for only a moment before delving in; once again curiosity muffled the hushed voice of her conscience. She inhaled a deep breath, and by the dim lamplight she deciphered the tiny handwriting.

After several paragraphs she grew accustomed to the ink blots and abbreviations, but the narrative confused her. She laid the book in her lap, a cold sweat coating her skin like a sodden garment. Would Mr. Phifer really care about the musings of Daniel's departed wife? Without a doubt. She squirmed to find a comfortable position on the chair, but it was more an internal than external discomfort she felt. Did she have any right to read Sarah's personal thoughts? Of course, if she followed that line of reasoning, should she investigate Professor Wilmont at all? Fighting down unpleasant pangs of guilt, Charlotte read more. She'd wrestle her conscience later.

Without any mention of God, the misnamed *Prayer Journal* sounded more like a diary filled with the intimate details of a restless wife suffering from acute loneliness. On page after page, Sarah's rant about her dull, tedious life grew more strident. And desperate. Her mind and spirit screamed for help — and deteriorated day by day as her marriage disintegrated.

A few paragraphs later a sentence grabbed Charlotte by the throat.

My dear friend invited me for tea after our meeting today. I agreed without a second thought for anyone but myself. What a change that was! How freeing to do exactly as I pleased on a pure whim. He has flirted with me for weeks, but never once ventured beyond a sweet, beguiling smile. I've waited so long, wondering, hoping for more.

This explosive revelation far surpassed Charlotte's expectations. Professor Wilmont never once hinted at marital trouble or his wife's unhappiness. But then again, why would he confide in his children's governess whom he scarcely knew? And perhaps he hadn't even realized how distressed Sarah had become.

Charlotte's hands trembled as she continued. On the following pages Sarah detailed a clandestine weekend with her male friend, racy enough to burn a hole in the carpet. Charlotte gulped a big breath of damp air. Had the professor ever discovered his wife's dalliance? She hoped not.

Her heart tapped a faster beat. This was exactly the sort of scandal Mr. Phifer coveted. Sarah's affair could provide enough damaging information to reward Charlotte with a substantial promotion, possibly to junior reporter — if she turned the prayer journal over to him. Sarah Wilmont had confessed enough in those dozen pages to condemn herself and damage the professor's reputation beyond repair. He might garner sympathy from his supporters, but his enemies would snicker and ridicule. Mr. Phifer might convince the professor to drop his column in exchange for keeping the humiliating information out of his newspaper.

Yet this scandal belonged to Sarah, not her husband. Using it against him was unethical. Not that Mr. Phifer would hesitate. As an employee of the *Rhode Island Reporter,* she ought not to hesitate either.

With a sigh, she snapped the journal shut. She didn't know quite how far Mr. Phifer would go to ruin the professor, or how far she ought to go to further her career. She'd have to think carefully how this would affect everyone involved, including the professor and his innocent children.

A tentative knock startled her.

"It's me, Grace," came the whispered voice.

Charlotte shoved Sarah's journal into a

bureau drawer, then opened the door and invited her old friend into the room. She motioned to the cushioned chair covered in faded chintz. "Do sit down, Grace." Charlotte plopped on the bed. "It's so good to see a familiar face at Summerhill. I didn't know you were in service. Last I heard you were living in the country."

Grace nodded. "I was until my aunt passed away and my uncle moved in with his daughter. With both my parents gone, I had no home, so I took this job as chamber maid. The Wilmonts and Mrs. Finnegan treat me very well. I'm truly blessed."

Charlotte smiled. "I missed you, Grace. We were such close friends growing up. I often wondered why you left Bridge Street so suddenly and without saying good-bye." She recalled how hurt she felt from her friend's indifference.

Grace sighed as she shifted her position in the chair. "I hate to admit this, but I was so jealous of you I couldn't abide living nearby any longer."

Charlotte pressed her hand to her chest. "You were jealous of me? I can't imagine such a thing."

Grace eased onto the bed next to Charlotte. "It was all because of Paul Seaton."

Charlotte's heart shrank at the mention of

Paul's name. "I don't understand what you mean."

Grace spoke quietly. "I thought you stole him away from me — on purpose. I was so fond of him. He was ever so handsome and attentive. I even fancied we were in love, though he never said so exactly. I didn't tell you about him and me because I wasn't quite sure of his feelings. And we were both so busy working that year we didn't see each other nearly as often as when we were younger. The next thing I knew you were stepping out with him. He left me high and dry. I was furious with both of you."

Charlotte grasped Grace's hand. "I had no idea you cared for Paul or he for you. I never even saw you together, so I hadn't suspected a thing. If I had known, I never would have given him the time of day."

"He was quite the lady's man and fickle as they come." Grace's voice softened. "I heard he left you as well."

Charlotte bit her lip. "He did. And he broke my heart."

"You two were engaged . . ."

"Yes, for a short while — until he realized I supported Becky and Aunt Amelia. He wanted me to forget my responsibilities. But of course I refused. Neither one of them can work, so who would support them if I

122

didn't?"

Grace's full lips tightened. "That sounds just like Paul. He's an awful, selfish lout. We're well rid of him." She raised her eyes toward the ceiling, or was it toward heaven? "Thank You, Lord, for protecting us from the likes of Paul Seaton."

"I vowed never to fall in love again," Charlotte said with a small smile. She hoped she didn't look as sad as she felt at the memory of a lost dream.

Grace looked askance. "Oh no, surely you don't mean that. When the right man comes along, you'll change your mind." Her round face colored to a pretty shade of pink. "I have."

"Oh?"

"I have a beau. His name is Martin Vance and he's a footman here at Summerhill. It's a secret, so please don't tell anyone. Mrs. Wilmont doesn't allow us to have followers. If she found out, she'd dismiss me."

"Of course, I won't breathe a word."

"And you, Charlotte — surely you have lots of suitors."

She gave a dry smile. "As I said, I'm not interested in men. I'm involved in my career. This is just a temporary position until Mrs. Wilmont recovers." Charlotte stopped short. Would Grace believe becoming a governess was her career choice?

"You always wanted to become a newspaperwoman like Nellie Bly."

"Well, yes I did, at one time."

"Then what happened to change your mind?"

Should she risk confiding in Grace? The girl looked trustworthy. Still . . . "It's difficult for a woman to become a reporter. It would be better if we didn't discuss my years at the *Rhode Island Reporter.* Professor Wilmont would never approve. The newspaper has criticized him and he might fire me if he knew I once worked there." *Or continue to.* Another lie to weigh upon her conscience. "Of course I was only a secretary, but he might not like the connection."

"Indeed, that paper has attacked him unmercifully. The whole staff follows the story. The poor man. He's as honest and fair-minded as anyone I've ever met. For that newspaper to harass him is nothing less than criminal."

"Yes, I suppose so." Charlotte looked down at her hands clutched in her lap. "I'm afraid I'm getting rather tired. It's been a long day."

Grace rose. "It's time for me to turn in as well. I'm so glad you're here at Summerhill now."

"So am I." As long as Grace didn't continue to associate her with the *Rhode Island Reporter,* she'd be all right.

Grace glanced toward the nightstand. "I see you have a Bible. Did the Wilmonts leave it for you? They give Bibles to all the staff."

"Yes, I suppose so. It's not mine."

Grace's hazel eyes lit up. "You must read it, Charlotte. It's made such a wonderful difference in my life."

Charlotte nodded as she followed Grace to the door. "Yes, I read some last night." And didn't like what she'd read one little bit.

"It's well worth studying cover to cover."

"I'm sure I shall, as soon as I find the time."

Grace squeezed Charlotte's hands. "Will you forgive me for my envy? It's such a sin. I'm truly sorry."

"Of course I forgive you. I hope we will see a lot of each other while I'm here." Charlotte swallowed hard. What would Grace think of her dishonest behavior?

Long after her friend returned to the third floor servants' quarters, Charlotte felt the heat of shame branding her cheeks. On a whim, or maybe because of Grace's encouragement, Charlotte opened her Bible. She continued reading St. John's gospel, amazed that Jesus spoke of things she'd never heard before. *He is the Bread of Life and the Living Water that quenches thirst. He's giving Himself to us and pouring out His love.* She'd never pictured God as love. Somehow He seemed more real and closer than she'd ever thought possible.

Charlotte rose early. A gray mist blew in from the sea, swirling damp air through the screens. In the distance came the mournful wail of a foghorn. Closing the window against the dreary morning, Charlotte peered into the dense curtain of gray. She knew the sun would take its time to burn away the clouds that dipped to the ground, but in a few hours the coast would awaken with color.

She wrapped a shawl around her shoulders and retrieved Sarah's journal from her bureau. For a long moment she hesitated to open it again. She ought not to read any further since she'd already uncovered plenty of damaging information. But no matter how unethical, she couldn't resist peeking into the secret life of Sarah Wilmont.

Charlotte opened the book to the page where she had left off the previous night.

Our marriage is a sham but Daniel doesn't notice. He acts as he always does — polite, solicitous, yet absorbed in his own world, a world no one else can enter. As long as he has his books he's content. If I screamed the cottage was on fire, he'd ask me to repeat what I said. How can we salvage a marriage between such dissimilar partners? We're joined in name only. We have the children in common, but they're certainly not enough to hold us together.

I want a man to love me, to cherish me. Someone to fit into my world. If I must continue as a professor's wife, I shall go mad.

Often I wonder why I ever married Daniel. At the time I assumed we had everything necessary to make a marriage thrive. Our families are friends, we've known each other all our lives, we were brought up with the same values. Or so I thought. But he loves the Lord first and his studies second. They interest him far more than I do. And I can't change that. No matter how fashionably I dress or fix my hair, or smile sweetly or seductively, I can't capture him for longer than a brief compliment. Once I yearned for his heart, now I want nothing except my freedom.

Charlotte stared out into the gray, swirling mist. It was tragic, really, being privy to the disintegration of a marriage on a most intimate level. Had the professor been aware? Had he deliberately ignored his wife? Intended to hurt her? Drive her away?

Charlotte placed the journal in her bureau and locked the drawer.

Late the next afternoon Daniel searched for the children and Miss Hale. When he couldn't find them in their usual haunts, he ventured down to the kitchen. Just as he suspected, they were there. But why were they hovering over an open picnic basket?

He swiped a gingersnap from the cookie jar and stepped behind the children's governess, close enough to smell her clean scent. She had the unmistakable fragrance of Pears soap and maybe a touch of toilette water. He peered over her shoulder into the woven basket. "Golden fried chicken, potato salad, and string bean salad. It looks delicious."

Charlotte stepped to the side. "It's picnic food! We're taking our supper down to the beach. The children requested an outing."

He imagined she relished time out in the great outdoors. "A splendid idea."

"Would you like to join us, sir? Chef

Jacques prepared plenty of food."

Summerhill had a small curve of sandy beach right on the edge of the property. How delightful to relax at the coastline secluded by rock and a tangle of wild roses.

Daniel frowned. "I set aside tonight to catch up on my work. I'm afraid I can't take time for a picnic."

Tim grumbled and Ruthie pouted. "Please, Papa."

Daniel wiped his spectacles on a clean handkerchief and pushed them to the bridge of his nose. He noted the clear disappointment etched in his daughter's face. And also in Miss Hale's. Her stubborn little chin jutted and pink lips curved downward.

"A picnic sounds like great fun, but I'm afraid I have an enormous amount of work to accomplish. Perhaps another time."

He averted her steady gaze as he grabbed another cookie. This one didn't taste quite as good as the first.

Miss Hale cocked a brow. "If I may say so, Professor, you have to take at least some time away from work to eat. You might as well enjoy a picnic with Ruthie and Tim."

He cleared his throat. "I'm certain I would, but work comes first. If I have the time, I will take a late supper in my den."

"*Without* the children."

She spoke so softly he wondered if he'd heard her correctly. Her apple cheeks burned as red as a MacIntosh — as well they should. Yes, the impertinent young woman did indeed question his parental decisions. He ought to fire her on the spot, but she merely pointed out the truth — though with far less tact than he expected. It wasn't her place to criticize him, especially in front of his children.

"I cherish my two children more than you can imagine. They're all I have. I like teaching and writing, but nothing compares to Ruthie and Tim. However, to support them I must work hard. Sometimes it's a pleasure, but often it's a duty I can't shirk." His head of steam evaporated. He seldom disclosed his feelings, especially to someone he hardly knew. But it felt surprisingly cathartic.

Her voice seemed to hitch in her throat. "I apologize. I shouldn't question your priorities. And I certainly understand the need to work."

She hung her head, yet he suspected she hadn't changed her mind. Such a pretty head with mounds of shiny dark hair pulled up in a pompadour, he thought they called it.

He sighed. "Perhaps I can take a half hour to join the children." *And Miss Hale as well.*

Despite her penchant for blunt speech, she was easy to talk to, amusing. To say nothing of being easy on the eyes . . .

The children squealed in delight and Miss Hale's face lit up. "Splendid. Clearly, Ruthie and Tim are quite pleased."

Ruthie and Tim, he mused. But what about her? Was she glad he was coming too?

He didn't take to society ladies, especially the debutantes who were too young or even the widows who tried so hard to please. But Miss Hale was different; she was utterly fresh, new, unique. No one would ever think to pair them up, so he need not worry about elderly biddies gossiping behind their open fans. But why was he himself imagining such a thing?

Despite the plain white shirtwaist and black skirt, she shined like a beautiful young lady summering on Bellevue Avenue, Newport's premier neighborhood. Her natural grace and willowy figure enhanced her femininity, a trait he couldn't help but notice.

She carried a faded old quilt, and he hoisted the picnic basket laden with more food than the four of them could possibly eat. All together they strolled across the wide stretch of back lawn. They picked their way across the piles of rock, down a few wooden steps, and onto the smooth strip of silvery beach that slowly thinned as the tide washed ashore then receded with a gentle yet steady roar.

In short order they devoured a hamper-full of delicious food. The fresh, briny air gave Daniel a huge appetite, and the children and Miss Hale ate with relish as well. Ruthie and Tim kept up their constant chatter, and Daniel realized they were vying for his attention. Sad to think how little time he allocated for these two, but he did his best to focus completely on them and keep his eyes off his pocket watch. Finally full, the children wandered barefoot to the water's edge. The rising tide lapped at their toes and they laughed and splashed and searched for clamshells.

Miss Hale stuffed the remains of supper into the basket and leaned back on her arms, her legs stretched across the sand, covered by her long skirt. A gentle breeze ruffled the hem and Daniel forced himself not to watch for a glimpse of her trim ankle encased in black stockings. The late afternoon heat cooled him as he relaxed for the first time in . . . maybe months.

"Your idea for a picnic was grand, Miss Hale," he admitted. He raked his fingers through the warm sand.

She cocked her head. "Why do you call me Miss Hale? I should think you'd call me Charlotte. After all, I'm only a servant."

Taken aback, Daniel took his time in answering. "A servant deserves to be treated with respect and appreciation. That's how I try to treat everyone regardless of their station in life."

She nodded. "Well, I must say you're unusual."

"Thank you," he mumbled. "I try to put my beliefs into action. The Bible directs us to love" — he colored at the word *love* — "which means to treat one another as we wish to be treated. It's a clear and simple command, though often inconvenient to follow."

"Your newspaper columns are based on that idea, aren't they?"

"Yes, most definitely. Jesus also tells us to pay a just wage. Exploitation is a sin. I'm afraid many employers take advantage of their workers. They get rich on the backs of the poor by demanding long hours of work, low pay, and unsafe conditions." He stopped short. "But as a Christian, I'm sure you know this." Much as he believed his words, he feared he sounded preachy and perhaps a bit pompous. He was far from perfect and always hesitated to criticize others.

Miss Hale hesitated but then nodded. "Of course, I agree with you. But most of the workers I know are at the mercy of their bosses. If they do not like it, there is always someone else ready to take their position. What is worse? A job with poor conditions or no job at all?" The thought made her visibly shudder.

"Exactly," Daniel said. "That is why I feel compelled to write about the plight of the poor and the responsibility of the upper class. Do you by any chance read my column?"

"I do. I confess I don't read about politics — or religion — as often as I should, but I find it fascinating how you connect the two." A gust of wind fluttered the ribbon streamers on the back of her hat. "I imagine not everyone approves of your reformist views."

He laughed. "That is certainly an understatement. I merely point out that the factory owners have an obligation to treat their workers fairly. I'm not instigating rebellion. If I tweak a conscience or two, then I'm succeeding in my mission. I'm trying to show the gospel as the living, breathing word of God. It's meant for every aspect of our lives, not just Sunday morning. But not everyone agrees."

Miss Hale nodded. The breeze loosened the hair framing her face and curls broke free from hairpins. She let the strands blow gently. "So you think many of these millionaires are hypocrites."

"*Hypocrite* is a harsh word, but I think some are failing to live their Christian beliefs and many people are suffering because of it. I try not to rant, because we're all sinners. Jesus talks about the plank in one's own eye."

Miss Hale nodded. "The rumor around town says you've angered the upper crust. They resent your criticism. And I know you've caused a stir among the workers. Your ideas make them feel . . . heard. But it doesn't change their situation. It only makes them feel more . . . agitated." He shifted his weight in the soft sand. "Sir, why do you write such things when they cause such a sensation?"

He leaned closer to Miss Hale. "Not because I enjoy the attention. My column is a ministry. I believe God has called me to point out the evil, not with self-righteous indignation, but with love. It's a difficult balance to maintain, but I strive to be tactful and avoid invective. I'll continue to write until the Lord directs me to stop."

"But sir, if I may ask, what first prompted

you to champion the cause of the common worker? You're a rich man; surely your interests conflict with the welfare of the working class."

The wind ruffled his hair and he tried to smooth it down. "I've been steeped in the Bible for as long as I can remember. But it didn't mean much until the summer I worked at the Wilmont Enterprises. Are you sure you want to hear this story?"

"Yes, I do. Please continue."

He shrugged. "My father wanted my brother Edgar and me to learn the business from the ground up. He thought our training should start at an early age. Before then I hadn't considered anything besides my books. But when I was sixteen, I decided I'd give the business my best try. My father assigned me to the bookkeeping department where I poured over numbers all day from eight to seven and half a day on Saturday."

"Now that must have been tedious. Or did you enjoy it?"

The professor laughed, but Charlotte didn't detect any humor. "I was bored with facts and figures, so I explored the factory. I'm afraid I found the mechanics of stove building just as tiresome as accounting."

Miss Hale smiled. "Did you stay with it for the summer or quit?"

"My father didn't give me a choice. But each day I escaped for a while by wandering through the factory and talking to the workers."

"I bet they were rather suspicious."

"Of course, given that I was the owner's son. They assumed he sent me to spy on them. But once they realized I was truly interested in their welfare, they opened up. One of the young men invited me to his home. I was shocked at how little he could afford on his salary. A cramped apartment with no running water, barely enough food, ragged clothes."

Miss Hale nodded and glanced off to the distance. "That's the way most people live."

"I'd seldom seen poverty, so I had never given it much thought. Finally I mustered my courage and asked my father to raise the workers' pay. But he ranted like a lunatic and called me a radical. When he realized I'd continue to badger him about the lax safety conditions, he banished me from the factory. Later Edgar inherited the business. He has treated the workers the same way my father did."

Miss Hale studied him. Was that shock in her eyes? Perhaps she assumed he had inherited half the family fortune. "And later you decided to write about it in the column?" she finally asked.

"Yes. My faith demanded I speak out against injustices. During the summer I worked at the factory, I came to know the Lord in a personal way for the first time. I felt He was directing me and I had to obey."

She paused for several seconds. "But how do you know when He's . . . speaking to you?"

Her earnest expression nearly made him chuckle. Although she was a believer, perhaps she didn't have a close enough relationship with God to recognize His voice. "I pray about it. The Lord answers my prayers not verbally, but in my spirit. Do you understand what I'm saying?"

She fussed with the pocket watch pinned to her blouse and avoided his gaze. "Yes, of course I do." But she looked and sounded unconvinced. "My goodness, it's already eight o'clock."

"It's time we returned home. Thank you for inviting me on your picnic."

She gave a merry smile as she rose. "I'm so glad you could leave your work behind for a while. I'm sorry I kept you longer than your half hour." Turning toward Ruthie and Tim, who were tossing a rubber ball, she called for them to gather their belongings.

"Papa, please play a short game of ball

with us." Ruthie clasped her hands to her chest and pleaded. His determination to leave weakened.

"Just for a few more minutes," Tim said.

"We need to go, you two." The children's groans assailed Daniel's ears as they trudged across the beach kicking sand, heads down. "Come on. We can toss the ball as we walk."

"Schedules are all well and good, but flexibility is the key to any happy relationship," Miss Hale said lowly, but with conviction.

Daniel let out a breathy chuckle. "Throw me the ball, Tim." He raised his hands in a catcher's stance.

Tim tossed him the ball and sped ahead to catch Ruthie, who was now waiting for Daniel's toss. He loved the joy in the children's sun-warmed faces.

When was the last time he'd played with Ruthie and Tim for more than a few minutes? He couldn't recall. Work stole his attention. It forced the children into second place while they begged for top priority. He sighed. There wasn't enough of him to go around.

He hired Miss Hale to occupy them and shift the burden of child care away from him. So far she'd coaxed him from his work and pinched his conscience as a parent. But he was glad she did. Yet his newspaper column wouldn't write itself. Further behind than ever, he needed to refuse Miss Hale's future entreaties when he ought to bury himself in his study and work without interruption.

She caught Ruthie's ball and tossed it to him. "Sir, I enjoyed our talk about putting your beliefs into practice. I'd like to read more of your columns. Do you have any I may borrow?"

"Of course," Daniel said, pleased. "In fact I have several I'm trying to put together for a book, but I have to organize them first. And that's quite a task."

"Perhaps I can help. Organization is one of my strengths — at least I think it is. I can do it at night or when Ruthie and Tim are working on their lessons."

"Why, thank you. Are you sure you don't mind?"

"Not a bit."

"Of course, I shall pay you extra. I don't expect you to do this in your spare time." He named a generous sum. Obviously the professor practiced what he preached.

Charlotte's eyes widened. "Sir, that's much too much for the task." But it would pay for Becky's doctor bills. How could she turn it down? "I accept. Thank you."

She called Tim and Ruthie. When they

came she surged ahead, chasing and tickling them as if she were still a child herself. But as engaging as the children were, it was Miss Hale whom Daniel found he studied.

SEVEN

In the quiet of her room that night, Charlotte sorted through the stack of columns Professor Wilmont had given her after their picnic. Many of them seemed similar to sermons since they were peppered with Bible verses. Well, what did she expect from a religion column? She picked the top one from the pile on her bed and settled into the comfortable chair by the window. She began reading.

Saints Mattthew, Mark, and Luke all tell the story of Jesus answering questions posed by learned men who were trying to entrap him. In Chapter 22 verses 34–40, St. Matthew says, "But when the Pharisees had heard that he had put the Sadducees to silence, they were gathered together. Then one of them, which was a lawyer, asked him a question, tempting him, and saying, Master, which is the greatest commandment in the law? Jesus said unto him, Thou shalt love the Lord thy God with all thy heart, and with all thy soul, and with all thy mind. This is the first and great commandment. And the second is like unto it, Thou shalt love thy neighbour as thyself. On these two commandments hang all the law and the prophets."

Jesus was clear as He could possibly be, repeating what these men would have already known. For in Deuteronomy 6:5 God says to His people, "And thou shalt love the Lord thy God with all thine heart, and with all thy soul, and with all thy might." God directs them and us, as well, to give all our love to Him. We must totally commit ourselves in every conceivable way. He doesn't leave us any other option.

But Jesus doesn't stop there. Out of our love for God comes the second commandment, which initially comes from Leviticus Chapter 19, verse 18. "Thou shalt not avenge, nor bear any grudge against the children of thy people, but thou shalt love thy neighbour as thyself: I am the Lord."

God made man in His own image, which elevates man above all other creatures. Loving God makes it possible for us to love our neighbor. Now we must ask: Who exactly is our neighbor? The answer is obvious. Our neighbor includes everyone, not just the man who lives next door! He's the worker in our shipyard, the woman who rides on the trolley with her children in tow, our boss, and our servant. He's the man who needs a few coins for a bowl of soup, the family without shelter. Our neighbor is anyone who requires our assistance. Can we look the other way or pass them by and still call ourselves God-fearing Christians? We demonstrate our love for the Lord through our actions toward others.

Charlotte lowered the paper to her lap. No wonder Mr. Phifer detested the professor. When the paper had made record profits last year, he had begrudgingly given every employee a small raise — but then demanded that every employee work an extra couple of hours a week "to be worth their keep." He obviously held little love in his heart for any of them, thinking only of the bottom line.

To be honest, she herself had never thought much about loving either the Lord or her neighbor, though she did lend a hand from time to time. Maybe when the next opportunity came along she'd volunteer to help, not wait for someone to ask.

She admired the professor for writing about a commandment that pricked the conscience. He wouldn't make many friends reminding people of their responsibilities, but he'd certainly make a slew of enemies.

Mr. Edwards, Daniel's editor at the *Newport Gazette*, snatched away the paper in his hand. The gray-haired, gray-suited stick of a man glanced at the office clock.

"Your deadline passed half an hour ago, Wilmont. You've always been on time. I require punctuality from my people. No excuses accepted. Do you understand?"

"Yes, of course. It won't happen again."

"See that it doesn't."

Daniel exited the office in a hurry, disgusted he'd allowed a picnic to interfere with timely delivery of his column. Up late last night polishing his writing, he'd overslept. Now he suffered from the fuzziness of too little sleep.

Never before had he neglected his work. But yesterday he readily tagged along on Miss Hale's outing, content to idle away precious time he should have spent with pen and paper. He seldom allowed pleasant distractions to interfere with his responsibilities. Never again would he indulge himself. Unfortunately, Miss Hale possessed the uncanny ability to dissolve him like a sugar cube in hot tea.

As he drove off in his buggy, duly chastened, he vowed to keep his mind off the governess and concentrate on his columns and classes. Pointing out the wrongs of the world and connecting them to biblical truths sounded insignificant to many people. But to his mind, trumpeting the Word of God was equally as important as teaching his students. And he reached a larger audience through the newspaper.

Lord, I pray I haven't jeopardized my column through negligence. And please don't let a bright smile and dancing brown eyes distract me from the tasks You've given me.

Eager to forget his lapse and Mr. Edward's rebuke, Daniel returned to his college office ready to begin the day anew. Miss Gregory, his matronly secretary, waylaid him before he reached his desk.

"You have a message from President Ralston, Professor."

Every fiber in Daniel's tired body tensed. "Thank you. I'll see him right away." The knot in his gut twisted. What did the president of Aquidneck College want? Nothing came to mind as he headed down the long, empty corridor. He'd only spoken a word or two to the man during the entire summer term.

Professor Ralston's assistant ushered Daniel into the president's large office, paneled in dark walnut and carpeted with a fine Turkish rug that muffled the sound of his footsteps. Portraits of two predecessors hung on the wall in gilt frames. Narrow faces stared down at Daniel with cold, arrogant eyes.

He rapidly examined his conscience and it came up clear. No dissatisfaction in the ranks of students that he could recall, and he hadn't failed any pupil recently who might have complained. He got along well with his colleagues and even with the administration, which oftentimes irritated him for straying from the Aquidneck's Christian heritage. But for the most part he kept his opinions to his columns, not the halls.

Then Miss Melissa LeBeau popped into his mind. Could she have reported he'd put off a meeting when she'd requested assistance in her studies? Maybe her family wielded influence and power with the college administration. Perhaps her father contributed to the building fund or sponsored a scholarship or endowed a chair. Daniel sighed. He didn't keep track of trivial things that others considered crucial.

Frowning, President Ralston directed Daniel to take a seat. He dropped to the edge of the brown leather chair and waited. His heart raced with uncharacteristic anxiety. Clifford Ralston stood behind his massive desk. His lips thinned and his square face compressed like an accordion into an expression of pain. Feigned, Daniel suspected.

President Ralston avoided Daniel's steady gaze and cleared his throat. "Professor Wilmont, I called you here because of a problem that's recently come to my attention."

"Yes, sir." Daniel shifted in his chair as the man began to pace in front of the windows behind his desk, his head bowed in thought.

"I'll get directly to the point. Some of our generous benefactors have criticized your newspaper column. To be perfectly frank, they feel your writing is unseemly for an esteemed professor."

"Oh?" Daniel frowned.

"Whipping up the masses against their benevolent employers is hardly a suitable undertaking for one in your position. Our students look to you as an example, as well they should. But if you're unwilling to represent the highest values of this college, then I'm afraid I must step in and warn you of the consequences." He leveled a glare as deadly as a bullet.

"I see," Daniel murmured. The blood in his veins froze. "I'm sorry these men are pressuring you, sir, but I can assure you my viewpoint is entirely Christian and in accordance with the gospel, as well as the highest values of this college — at least those of the founder's. And I am a professor of biblical studies. Does it not make perfect sense for me to write about my views as a Christian?"

"Professor, I'm merely asking you to remove *politics* from your religion column. It is not a matter of *faith* that incites our benefactors. Indeed, these men are fine, Christian men who all regularly attend church. It is how you choose to *apply* your theological views to the day to day of our lives. It becomes rather . . . personal."

"But faith is a personal matter," Daniel sputtered. "For everyone."

President Ralston's lips clamped together. He held out a hand toward Daniel. "Listen to me. You are clever enough, Professor, to seek a more conciliatory method to convey your views. If you do not at least attempt to do so, I shall have no choice but to insist upon your resignation from this institution."

Choked by President Ralston's threat, Daniel rose. "I understand the dilemma you're facing, but those who complain mischaracterize my writing."

"That's immaterial."

Daniel blew out a sigh. He was getting nowhere with the man. "I shall, of course, mull over your advice," he said, choking over the words.

"Then I expect you'll heed my words. Excellent." His expression eased for the first time. "You're a fine teacher and we'd hate to lose you, Professor. Your reasonable attitude is commendable."

Daniel shook his head. "No, I didn't mean to suggest I'd alter the direction of my column. But I shall consider all the ramifications."

Ralston's wrinkles in his forehead returned. "You have only one viable option. Please accept it without further delay."

"I'll convey my decision as soon as possible." Daniel turned on his heel and left the president's office before he sputtered some self-righteous cliché he'd regret.

Only the Lord could command him to quit heralding the truth. He didn't preach and he didn't condemn. He merely illuminated the horrifying effects of greed and indifference toward the plight of those less fortunate. It mattered not who wanted his opinions silenced because as long as deplorable conditions continued among the poor, the problem would flare up again and again.

But Daniel knew that many of the country's great industrialists, including his own brother, Edgar, supported the college and held tight reign over the administration. Was he prepared to battle with them over his column? David would undoubtedly fall to Goliath this time around unless the Lord intervened. A negotiator by nature, he couldn't imagine raising his fists in even a metaphorical fight — unless he utilized his pen for a sword.

Returning to his department, Daniel smiled gamely at Miss Gregory. He disappeared into his office and closed the door. He'd expected to encounter resistance to his writing at some point, but he hadn't truly prepared himself.

From the beginning of his stint as columnist he'd known powerful men might try to silence him. But God nudged him at first and then shoved until he started to write. The Lord had expected obedience and He still did. Daniel buried his head in his hands and let the rhythmic tick of the wall clock pound into his ears. President Ralston was forcing him to decide sooner rather than later.

A knock sounded at the door and then opened. "Ruthie, Tim. Miss Hale. Is everything all right?" His mother kept them from visiting during the day, but apparently the governess didn't know the unwritten rule. Or maybe she was ignoring it.

"Oh yes," Miss Hale said. "We're quite all right."

"Children, you know perfectly well you must not disturb me at my office during the day. The college doesn't welcome professor's children running around the campus."

Miss Hale's face reddened. "Sir, it's my fault. They explained the policy, but I thought just this once we could break the rule." Her words were apologetic and the tone of her voice calm, yet her eyes flashed.

Daniel shook his head. "No, Miss Hale, rules are made to keep, even when you don't agree with them."

Ruthie tentatively held out a box. "Miss Hale and I baked sugar cookies for you. They're scrumptious." He hated the look of fear in his daughter's eyes. She'd brought him cookies and all he could do was preach rules and regulations. Where was the love and grace in his own heart?

Miss Hale's full lips tilted upward in a small, sheepish grin as if *she'd* already forgiven *him* for his outburst. "We learned together. I burned the first dozen, but the second batch turned out perfectly. Do try one."

He reluctantly took a lopsided cookie and bit into it, expecting the worst. Instead, the buttery confection melted in his mouth. "Delicious. Thank you." But they still shouldn't disregard the rules. And Miss Hale ought not to condone it either.

Ruthie clapped her hands in delight. "They are good, aren't they? Tim ate half a dozen all by himself." Tim stuck his tongue out at his sister and then picked up two cookies and crammed one in his mouth. Miss Hale abstained.

"No one wanted us near the kitchen, especially Chef Jacques, but Miss Hale volunteered to clean up the mess after we baked. And we did. All three of us," Ruthie said.

"You can be proud of them, Professor."

Ruthie glanced toward the door. "Do you mind if we go outside and roll our hoops? We left them in Miss Gregory's office."

Perhaps outside they would not bring

down the ire of the other faculty. "Go ahead, but be certain you don't bother anyone. And keep the noise down, please," Daniel said.

He motioned Miss Hale to take a seat as the children tore out of the room. She slid gracefully into a chair and glanced up at him expectantly.

"Is everything all right, Professor? I mean besides my mistake in coming here with the children. You do look a bit down this morning and I suspect it's not from a surprise visit."

Taken aback by her perceptiveness — and informality — Daniel didn't know how to respond. He'd never confided in a servant before, but Miss Hale seemed more like family, and as a governess, she wasn't exactly a part of the regular staff.

"I ran into a problem. But since everything is in God's hands, I'm sure all will be fine — eventually." Maintaining a positive attitude wasn't easy, yet the Lord would work things out as He always did. In the meantime — well, he wouldn't dwell on future difficulties. And he certainly wouldn't share his troubles.

Miss Hale's eyes filled with concern and her perfectly shaped mouth turned downward. She leaned forward across the desk, her hands folded together. He inhaled the fragrance of her hair, and her freshly starched and pressed white shirt. Her straw boater adorned with only a band of black ribbon tilted down over her creamy forehead. She removed it and laid it on her lap, obviously unaware her hairpins had loosened. Her topknot seemed in danger of cascading down her back. Wispy dark curls spiraled around the curve of her cheeks, giving her a girlish look — so young and carefree, not prim and proper as her attire would suggest.

Those eyes set beneath arching brows radiated more compassion than he'd ever felt from a woman before. Certainly more than his mother or Sarah had ever shown. Before he knew it, he found himself spilling the whole story.

Charlotte listened carefully to Professor Wilmont as he confided the misery of his morning. She wanted to rush around the desk and nestle her arm around his shoulder and tell him she was so sorry for his predicament. And how he had every right to feel anger toward the ungrateful President Ralston, a man who should defend him against the wicked men who wanted him fired. The professor lived his convictions to the point of putting his job on the line. She wished she could do the same.

But instead of offering a consoling hug or at least a squeeze of the hand, Charlotte sat on the opposite side of the desk, her palms folded rigidly in her lap. Her voice shook. "I'm not a bit surprised your writing would raise the ire of such people. But it's so unfair they expect you to give up your column or lose your position here."

And how hypocritical of her to take his part when she was sent to Summerhill to ruin him. The stifling air made her perspire. She ran her finger beneath her tight collar to loosen it.

Yet his misfortune might turn the tide for her. Her heart thudded. She considered herself a loyal employee of the *Rhode Island Reporter,* though her conscience called her a snitch, traitor, betrayer. Perhaps if he was forced to quit his column, Mr. Phifer would be appeased and she could take her leave of Summerhill. She'd find another way to prove herself as a journalist and pay her bills. But what other way?

There was no other way.

"Thank you for your sympathy, Miss Hale." He smiled sheepishly.

She looked down at her hands. She was hardly his friend. A spy — that's what she was. A quick glance revealed a man struggling against anger and despair. Warring emotions marched across his face. And the worst of it was he trusted her enough to pour out his fears. He had far more faith in her than she deserved.

So how in good conscience could she possibly betray the professor?

She tried to shake away her doubts. She had to place her own survival first and not let a soft heart weaken her. She'd fail at her assignment if she worried about Daniel Wilmont's job as much as her own. A few days at Summerhill made her troubles fade like a distant memory. But her creditors awaited payment. How could she forget Mr. Knowles's threatening letter for even a moment? He'd toss Aunt Amelia and Becky out on the streets, without a moment's hesitation. But the professor looked like he had been served with his own papers.

"I'm so very sorry about your troubles, Professor. Have you decided what to do?" She couldn't keep empathy out of her voice.

"I'm leaving it in God's hands," he said.

"As well you should." Leaning closer, she gave the professor's hand a reassuring pat despite her better judgment. Horrified, she snatched her fingers back. "Sir, I'm sorry. Please forgive my audacity."

"Don't apologize for offering a kind gesture. And it's I who should apologize. I have no right to impose my problems upon you." His shook his head. "I don't know what got into me. Normally I keep my trials to myself."

"I'm honored you confided in me." Though she couldn't imagine why he'd tell such personal things to a servant.

"I don't want to worry my family, so I won't mention it until I carefully think things over."

Her voice shook. "I suppose you have no choice but to give up your column now."

Professor Wilmont let out a sigh. "It goes against my principles to cave in to pressure."

Her optimism faded. "That's brave of you, sir." *And foolhardy too.* "I'm afraid if I were in your position, I could never do that. I'm not equipped to fight the forces of the world."

Professor Wilmont dragged a wry smile to the corner of his mouth. "Neither am I. But the Lord will provide me with everything I need, including His guidance. I put all my trust in Him."

"What would be worse?" she dared to ask him as she fiddled with the hem of her blouse. "Losing your column or losing your position here at the college?"

He paused for a few seconds before he smiled. "I need funds to support myself and my children and maintain the cottage. Teaching gives me a livelihood and more important, a purpose. But so does my column. They're both ministries and equally important."

"I understand, sir," Charlotte murmured, though she suspected the loss of the job he loved would be far worse than the loss of his salary. He had no inkling of what real poverty entailed. "Might you sell Summerhill to tide you over for a time, if you must go? There are so many New York millionaires looking for ocean property these days."

The professor nodded. "I've thought about selling the cottage more than once, since it is so expensive to maintain. But my mother loves it. And so do the children. Their only memories of their mother are at Summerhill. Truth be told, I'm fond of the place myself. I've spent most every summer there."

Charlotte found the financial arrangements of the rich quite strange, but she couldn't say that to the professor. In fact, she found most of their habits odd. Did a family of four truly need a twenty-two-room mansion with fifteen or more servants? He might not consider himself wealthy, but she certainly did. She'd wager he could survive quite comfortably without his teaching position as long as the family economized. And to hold on to an impractical, money-sucking mansion for sentimental reasons seemed nonsensical. But then again she'd lived on the edge of poverty all her life.

"I must keep doing the work the Lord set aside for me. I hate to be idle. I need to contribute something to society," he said.

"Might you consider a break from the column, then? Just a temporary interval until the criticism dies down." That would benefit both of them.

But Professor Wilmont shook his head. Charlotte bit her lip to keep from blurting out that he was an idealist who ought to back away from trouble before it crushed him.

He leaned forward in his chair, his eyes earnest. "As soon as I resumed writing, the objections would start again. I need a permanent solution."

Again Charlotte hesitated. She had to say it. "If your intent is to keep Summerhill, should you not find a way to compromise?" Heat blazed through her face.

From his grimace, she knew Professor Wilmont disagreed.

"My duty to God comes first before anyone or anything else. And He has asked me to stand, not bend."

Charlotte forced her gaping mouth shut. Didn't he understand that sometimes you had to put the well-being of your family above your own interests? And sometimes you had to reorder your values just to survive?

"You look shocked, Miss Hale. Do you disagree with my logic?"

Logic? It sounded more like a *lack* of logic. "Sir, I'm afraid I can't begin to fathom your reasoning." How could he trust so blindly? "I also support my family — an aunt and a sister. And I can't envision putting my religious convictions ahead of them." *If I had any religious convictions.* But maybe that was the problem. She and the professor viewed the world very differently.

Professor Wilmont blanched. She tensed and waited for his verbal reaction. He'd accuse her of lying about her Christian faith. But he didn't say a word as he stared at her, obviously bewildered.

"I must be going, sir. Please excuse me. As usual, I spoke with too much candor." Charlotte leaped up to exit the room before she uttered something else she'd regret. She

could barely force herself to pause at the
doorway to say good-bye.

EIGHT

Daniel shook his head as the small, feisty woman swept out of his office. She paused at the threshold and glanced over her shoulder, her face resuming a mask of politeness.

"I'll be back by suppertime, if that's all right, sir." Her calm voice held an edge. "This is my afternoon off. The children are going to visit their friends, the Hopkins children, on Cove Road. I'll fetch them before dinnertime."

He'd forgotten. "That will be fine."

As soon as she departed, Daniel opened his Bible to prepare for tomorrow's lesson, but his mind detoured from St. Paul to Miss Hale. Charlotte. Her reliance on her own power rather than the Lord's signaled caution. She claimed to follow Christ, and Daniel believed she had no reason to lie about her faith. Yet apparently she didn't understand how God helped those who trusted Him. How could she have missed such a crucial principle? He'd try to explain later, but would she understand or merely pretend to? Her instinct for self-preservation seemed so strong she might not want to relinquish the power she thought she had. Better to pray about it first and seek the Lord's direction.

A twinge of disappointment about her faith unsettled him. Was it as shallow as it seemed or had he just hoped for more?

Daniel gathered his books and left for the day. Just off campus, he glimpsed Ruthie and Tim rolling hoops in front of the Hopkins', at the end of Cove Road, the official name for Faculty Row, the housing area for many of the professors. Even from a distance, the children's hoots and hollers carried on the breeze. He'd spent years attempting to quiet them down to no avail. In a few short days their irrepressible governess had stirred them up and encouraged their exuberance. Yet his heart warmed at the sight of his children romping with gusto and shouting to the rafters along with the Hopkins children. He watched Charlotte follow along far behind, her skirt swaying slightly, head held high, arms swinging at her side. Whatever fears that drove her didn't seem to rob her of her spirit and her joy.

He'd walked only a few yards when footsteps sounded at his heels. Glancing over his shoulder, he spotted Miss LeBeau striding to catch up. Her chest rose and fell from labored breathing and perspiration coated her face with a slight sheen. As usual, she wore a fancy dress decorated like a wedding cake and a hat, undoubtedly the latest fashion, chock-full of fake fruit and greenery.

"Good afternoon, Miss LeBeau. Out for a walk?"

He didn't relish strolling down Cove Road with his young, beautiful student for all the faculty wives to see. A widower, even one with half-grown children, always snagged the interest of matchmakers. He disliked being the center of female attention with speculation either from faculty wives or from students, but their interest was difficult to avoid.

"Professor, I saw you leaving your office, so on a whim I decided to speak to you." She giggled for no discernable reason. "Do you have a few moments?"

"Of course, Miss LeBeau. What can I do for you? This isn't the day we're supposed to meet, is it?"

She sidled so close her arm brushed against his side. He stepped back onto the dean of students' grass.

"No, that's not today, sir. I decided to join the Ladies Prayer Circle. They have meetings and devotions and even weekends away for deeper contemplation. I want to improve my spiritual life and learn a bit more about the Lord. Even beyond what I'm gaining in your class." She gazed up at him with innocent eyes, yet somehow they looked oddly calculating.

"That's splendid. I'm sure you'll gain much from the group."

"I do hope so, Professor. I don't want you to think badly of me."

"Of course not. Why should I?" he asked as they strolled down the dirt lane. Cove Road ended at the edge of his property and provided a shortcut to Summerhill.

"Because I'm so unschooled in Scripture."

But why did Miss LeBeau care about his opinion? He merely taught her one required course; he didn't advise her about her studies. Her flirtatious attitude struck him as not quite genuine, her manner a little too bright and brittle. She prattled on and he only half listened to her high-pitched, breathy voice.

"The Prayer Circle scheduled a spiritual

get-together in August, and I'm planning to attend. Aren't you proud of me, Professor?"

Her white-gloved hand lightly touched the sleeve of his jacket, yet it struck like a burning coal. When he sidestepped, she lowered her arm, apparently unfazed by his movement. How could she find so many words to spout?

"Yes, I'm glad you're seeking the Lord in such a tangible way."

She chatted on about her new interest in spiritual things, and when she finally took a breath, he excused himself and hurried off, relieved to escape her capture.

Charlotte left the children with the Hopkins' governess, strode to the end of the road, and then crossed acres of freshly cut lawn to Summerhill. Once in the drawing room she found the housekeeper running a white-gloved hand across the polished surface of a side table.

"Mrs. Finnegan, it's my afternoon off and I'd like to go into town. Do you know if anyone is headed in that direction?"

Inspecting her dust-free fingers, the older woman smiled with satisfaction. "It so happens I'm sending Grace on an errand. She'll be taking the buggy. If you hurry you can catch her at the stable before she leaves."

"Thank you." Charlotte hastened back outside into the warm afternoon filled with humidity and birdsong. The buggy, pulled by a spirited black horse, rolled down the lane between the stable and the cottage. She waved at Grace, who halted the carriage by her side.

"Mrs. Finnegan said I might catch a ride with you. Are you going anywhere near Thames Street?"

"Indeed, I am. Hop in."

For a while they chattered amiably about friends from the Point, the neighborhood where they'd both grown up. Then Grace turned toward her and cocked her head. "Charlotte, I've been wondering why you left the *Rhode Island Reporter* to work for the professor. He's so hated by the newspaper. It seems a bit strange."

Grace was connecting the dots, just as Charlotte feared she might. "I needed a job and the position of governess was available."

"Did Mr. Phifer fire you?"

Charlotte shook her head. "No, he didn't." It was bad enough to deceive her old friend without lying.

"Hmm. Well, I'm glad you left there. Did you apply at the *Newport Gazette*? Surely they'd hire you."

"Perhaps as a secretary, but certainly not

as a reporter. While I decide about my future, I'm perfectly content to be a governess."

Fortunately the traffic thickened and made conversation difficult. Grace stopped talking as she drove, though she looked deep in thought. And her brow creased with unasked questions. Charlotte clutched her hands in her lap until they reached Thames Street.

Stretched along the harbor, the narrow street boasted lunchrooms, taverns, and shops catering to the needs of the town folks who lived close by in cramped houses locked in crowded neighborhoods. Behind the stores closest to the waterfront, fishing boats and steamships rode through the waves and clogged the wharfs. The smell of fish and low tide filled her nostrils with a familiar and not unpleasant odor. Seagulls shrieked overhead and soared through an azure sky.

"You can let me off here, Grace. Thank you for the ride."

As soon as the buggy halted, Charlotte hopped down. They agreed to meet at the same place in two hours. She waited for the carriage to disappear into the stream of traffic before she climbed the stairs to the offices of the *Rhode Island Reporter*. Unfortunately she'd have to stay away from Grace as much as possible to avoid her inquiries — unless she decided to confide in her old friend. That would bring her such comfort, yet it was a terrible gamble.

Right now she'd think only of her visit with Mr. Phifer. Dread wound up her spine and wrapped around her bones. If she let her nerves seize control, she'd never find her voice to rationally explain why she returned without a shred of damaging evidence. Just a few days ago she'd held high hopes of quickly discrediting Daniel Wilmont, but she'd found no proof or even suggestion of wrongdoing. Yet Mr. Phifer would most definitely appreciate and gloat over the news about President Ralston's ultimatum. Perhaps that would be enough to appease her boss.

She passed through the newsroom on her way to Mr. Phifer's office. Just as she raised her hand to knock on his door she heard voices from inside.

"See here, Arnold, you've got to stop Wilmont from writing anything further about the so-called rights of the worker. My employees are threatening to strike and close down the mills. If I can't stop them, we'll be forced to shut down. Do you have any idea how much money we'll lose?"

Charlotte held her breath.

"I'm doing the best I can," Mr. Phifer said. "I sent a girl to investigate the professor. She'll uncover something we can use against him. There's no doubt."

"Make sure that she does. We can't allow him to continue that column of his. He's dangerous. I won't stand for his interference."

"I'll take care of it, Sam."

A big man, older and balder than Mr. Phifer, stormed into the corridor. When he was gone, the editor looked toward Charlotte. "That was my brother. Do come into my office, Miss Hale."

"Yes, sir." She gulped a big breath of stifling air. The rumble of carriage wheels floated through the open windows that overlooked the street.

"What have you got to report, Miss Hale?" His eyes gleamed with anticipation.

Apprehension sucked her throat dry, but Mr. Phifer awaited her account. Lifting her chin, she cleared her throat. She'd convey the good news first. She didn't consider it good, not in the least, but Mr. Phifer would.

"Sir, Aquidneck College gave Professor Wilmont an ultimatum — either he quit his column or his teaching position." The moment the words fell loose from her tongue, she wished they'd stuck to the roof of her mouth. Her stomach flipped and she feared she'd lose her breakfast. She should've let Mr. Phifer find out all on his own.

"Splendid. And what did he decide to do?" He rubbed his hands together in delight.

"I don't believe he's made a firm decision."

She hadn't personally contributed to the professor's downfall, but she'd tattled like a gossipmonger. Even this small slice of success felt worse than a Quinsy sore throat. But at least she'd concluded her mission without really betraying the professor, at least not directly. His dilemma would soon become public knowledge whether or not she delivered the news first.

"What else did you learn, Miss Hale?" Mr. Phifer's frown dragged her back to reality.

"Why, nothing else about the professor. Isn't that enough, sir?"

"Certainly not. I need something that will stop him for good."

Charlotte stared at her boss, surprised at his vindictiveness. "Sir, I searched Summerhill as well as I could." She swallowed. "I looked through cabinets and boxes and —"

His mouth pursed. "Yes, yes, but what exactly did you discover?"

"Just dust and junk. Nothing unfavorable. If there's any evidence against the professor, it's most assuredly not in his home. Perhaps it's hidden at his college office, but I'm afraid I have no access."

His face turned as red as a tomato. Charlotte held her breath and waited for Mr. Phifer's infamous temper.

His voice remained surprisingly steady. "I am distressed by your investigation, young woman. You obviously didn't dig deep enough. Don't just look with your eyes. Search with your nose and your hands."

Who was she fooling? Surely Mr. Phifer coveted every bit of information. He'd want to decide what was pertinent. Now was the time to tell him about the journal if she was ever going to. But her tongue refused to form the words.

Of course her career might very well depend upon divulging that juicy tidbit. But she couldn't bring herself to hand the journal over to Mr. Phifer and betray Professor Wilmont, a man who'd shown her nothing but kindness and patience. Any other boss would've sent her packing from her repeated impertinence. So far she'd only borrowed the book with the intention of returning it as soon as possible. She'd keep it to that.

Mr. Phifer frowned. "No, Miss Hale. I'm not satisfied with your efforts. Not at all."

Here it comes. Charlotte braced herself. A future of grinding poverty flashed through her mind. She blinked back an onslaught of tears and straightened her spine. If she had to go, she'd leave with dignity.

He leaned forward, grasping his pipe in his teeth. "I expect much more from you, Miss Hale." He glowered, causing her to flinch. "But fortunately I've recently received news that will set you on the right track."

"Oh?" Was this a blessing or a curse?

Round eyes gleamed in a jowly face carved with lines that displayed every one of his fifty-plus years. "When you accepted this assignment, I mentioned I was following a lead about Professor Wilmont and a student. Do you remember?"

"Yes, sir." Her voice rattled like a sack of marbles. Was he providing a reprieve? She dare not hope for such luck.

"That lead has brought me explosive new information." He leaned down and whispered close to her ear, exhaling a strong tobacco smell. "Last week I received an anonymous letter concerning Daniel Wilmont's behavior."

Charlotte's heart lurched.

"Today I received another note." His face lit with joyful animation as he picked up a piece of quality stationary and waved it in front of her. She caught a glimpse of the short message written with a bold, back-handed slant. "The writer claims Professor Wilmont is involved in an — improper relationship with a student." His voice dropped to a confidential whisper. "Her name is Melissa LeBeau. They call her Missy. She's a summer student in his New Testament Bible class."

"That's quite a tip," Charlotte mumbled, her stomach tumbling.

"Yes, it surely is. Apparently the person doesn't like the professor's behavior any better than I do." He stuck his thumb into a red suspender and thumped his fingers against his shirt. "This gives us a lot more to go on."

"I wonder how the informant knows her name."

Mr. Phifer shrugged. "I don't know how the person obtained his information and I don't much care as long as it's accurate. That's your job — to find out if he speaks the truth. You can do it, Miss Hale."

"Yes, of course. I intend to. And thank you for the vote of confidence." Relief washed though her, though she felt sure this second chance wouldn't pan out either. If the professor was guilty, he deserved to be denounced, but she felt quite sure he was innocent.

"If you obtain the goods on Wilmont, your career will advance. There's no telling where you'll end up." His eyes glinted. "But you must find some useful information."

He was playing her. She knew it, but she couldn't help glowing from his acclaim and the possibility of promotion along with a bigger paycheck. "I'll do everything in my power, sir."

His eyes squinted. "I expect you to follow him every time he's with Missy LeBeau. Sooner or later you'll find them in a 'compromising' position. I guarantee it."

His self-assurance irked her. "How can you be so sure, sir?"

Mr. Phifer's mouth twisted in a sneer. "He's a man, isn't he?" He challenged her with a raised eyebrow. "And reportedly, this Missy LeBeau is a beauty."

A blast of heat scalded her cheeks. Although the professor didn't seem the type to succumb to illicit passion, she didn't know him well enough to predict his weaknesses. He was a Christian to the core. Didn't his faith influence his conduct? Or were Christians just as quick to fall into sin as everyone else?

"Don't worry, sir. I'll keep my eye out for the young lady."

"Do what it takes to catch them together. Question him about his students. Act interested. He's bound to open up. And search Summerhill again with more care this time. I'll wager he has a skeleton in at least one closet."

"I'll be sure to look under the beds too," she said with a touch more sarcasm than she intended.

He glared at her. "What's the matter? You look uneasy."

She hesitated. "I'm as anxious as you are to discover the facts, Mr. Phifer, but I'm not comfortable using deceptive tactics." There — she'd spewed what nibbled on her conscience.

"Miss Hale, you're most definitely not deceiving anyone. You're merely undercover. You're a journalist on an investigation."

She nodded. "Yes, sir. But my journalistic intuition tells me this new rumor is false. From what I've seen so far, the professor is too straight-laced to fall for a student. I believe you might be headed in the wrong direction." She held her breath for his reaction. No doubt she'd gone too far.

Arnie Phifer snorted derision. "You're the

one who's mistaken. My hunch tells me there's hanky-panky going on and I'm seldom wrong about the weaknesses of human nature. You listen to me. I don't care if it's Missy LeBeau or something else, but you find me the method to stop Daniel Wilmont from writing another column — or something that will force him to move to California to escape the shame. Understood?"

"Yes, sir," she said, hoping he didn't hear the quiver in her voice.

"Good." He puffed on his pipe. "We don't have a lot of time. Professor Wilmont's preposterous ideas are sweeping through the region like wildfire. He's stirring up the rabble. If we can stop him before this whole thing gets out of hand and becomes an actual movement, then we have an obligation to do it."

"The power of the press," Charlotte murmured.

"Yes, my dear Miss Hale. The power of the press is formidable. We'll find something to silence Wilmont forever. A scandal will do the trick. And we must report it before this beautiful state of ours turns into a theocracy."

Exasperated at Mr. Phifer's penchant for exaggeration, Charlotte dropped her gaze.

"If there's really a story here, I'll find it."

"What do you mean, 'If there's really a story'? Of course there's a story. You just have to dig it out."

"If he's behaving improperly with a student, then we have something to print. If he's not, then we have nothing." How much clearer could she be? But how far could she push him before he sacked her?

"The romance angle is only part of what I want you to look into. You have the opportunity to examine every aspect of his life. He might be concealing something else. Go through his belongings, especially his papers, once more. Talk to people in his church and at the college."

"I shall." She managed to keep the skepticism out of her voice.

He rose. Six feet tall and rotund, Arnie Phifer made a formidable figure. "As soon as you have something, tell me about it. Anything at all."

"What if he's innocent?" Her voice shook.

Arnie let out a grunt. "Nobody's completely innocent."

"No, I suppose not." But Professor Wilmont was too moral to take unfair advantage of a vulnerable student — or so she thought. She'd have to prove it to Mr. Phifer or she'd find herself investigating the professor from now until doomsday — or until the editor fired her.

Mr. Phifer ushered her to the door.

On the walk home to Bridge Street, Charlotte tried to quiet the queasiness that rumbled through her stomach. Despite his certainty about the professor's guilt, the esteemed and feared Arnie Phifer might not be correct. How reliable was his anonymous source? He placed all his trust in a stranger without questioning the man's facts or motive. An enemy of the professor might spread a rumor for reasons of his own.

Her every instinct screamed Professor Wilmont's innocence, but only a thorough investigation would prove her right or wrong. She owed it to both men to uncover the truth, no matter where it led.

But all through her visit with Aunt Amelia and Becky, she wondered if she'd made a dreadful mistake accepting her assignment. If she pleaded her unsuitability for investigative work, Mr. Phifer would send the new reporter, Edith Ann Wengle, in her place. Now *she* would definitely appreciate the opportunity to shine. And snap up the promotion Charlotte needed so badly. And who knew how far Edith Ann would go in destroying Professor Wilmont's reputation? She suspected the woman would even lie to give Mr. Phifer what he wanted.

"We miss you, Charlotte," her aunt said as she served her a bowl of steaming clam chowder and oyster crackers in their cramped kitchen.

"I miss you both. I hope to finish up soon and come home."

Becky wheeled herself to the table. Pain distorted her lovely facial features as she braced her back with her arm. Charlotte took a good look at her sister. When had Becky grown up? Even at thirteen, her stunning face and slender form promised future beauty. Enormous brown eyes and dark blond hair that curled around her heart-shaped face attracted attention. But being confined to a wheelchair would lessen her future opportunities for marriage. Chances were great she'd always depend upon Charlotte.

"Can you tell us who you're working for?" Becky asked. "Aunt Amelia and I can keep a secret."

Charlotte looked from her sister to her aunt. Amelia stood by the range, her arms folded across her chest. "You look troubled, Charlotte."

Charlotte paused. "Yes, a bit. I'll tell you the story if you promise not to breathe it to a soul."

"You can trust your family," Becky said. Aunt Amelia nodded as they gathered around the scarred kitchen table.

"I'm working as a governess for Professor Daniel Wilmont's two children. He writes a religion column in the *Newport Gazette*."

"And a mighty fine column it is." Aunt Amelia's surprise quickly turned into a suspicious frown.

"Mr. Phifer believes the professor is engaging in" — she looked first toward her young sister then shifted her gaze to her aunt — "inappropriate behavior with a student."

Becky frowned. "What does that mean?"

"Never you mind," Aunt Amelia said. "But make sure you don't repeat a word of this conversation."

Becky nodded, her expression wounded.

"Do you think there's any truth to Mr. Phifer's suspicions?" Aunt Amelia asked.

"None whatsoever. The professor is the most moral man I've ever met. But I can't be positive until I investigate further."

"I know you've wanted to be a reporter for years, but are you quite sure this is the right way to prove yourself?" Aunt Amelia's bony fingers gently pressed Charlotte's hand. "What I mean is: you're not being aboveboard with the professor. That's not right. You know, I read his newspaper column every once in a while and I most often agree with him. He thinks the rich people should treat their workers right because it's what the Bible says. Now I don't know much about the Bible except for the stories I learned at my mama's knee, but what he says makes sense. Rich people have no right to cheat poor folk out of what belongs to them fair and square."

Charlotte bit her lip. "Do you think Mr. Phifer defends abusive employers?"

Aunt Amelia bobbed her head. "Yes. And your Professor Wilmont has shown a great deal of courage, addressing their abuse."

For some strange reason Charlotte's chest filled with pride for the professor.

Aunt Amelia leaned forward. "Did you know that Arnie Phifer and his brothers own a woolen mill in Fall River? They pay no more than a pittance, I hear. And they practically let their workers starve while they live in their fancy mansions with servants and fine carriages parading around town." Aunt Amelia inhaled a deep breath and poured more tea. "I get carried away when I think of all the people I know who slave away and never get ahead. Look at you. At that newspaper for years now, working sixty hours a week. For what? A pittance, considering what the paper earns."

"It's far from working in a mill, Aunt Amelia."

"Different than a mill. But I'd wager it's not as different as you think."

Charlotte took a sip of the strong, hot brew, then spooned in more sugar."

Aunt Amelia rose to wash the luncheon dishes. "Arnie's family always had money, but they weren't millionaires like they are now."

"They have a good reason for wanting Professor Wilmont silenced," Charlotte said.

Aunt Amelia snorted. "The strongest reason you can have — pure greed." Aunt Amelia uncovered a pie plate sitting on the counter. "Would you care for some cherry pie? I made it this morning."

Charlotte shook her head. "No thank you." She'd lost her appetite. Aunt Amelia cut a generous piece for Becky. "I have some hard thinking to do. I'm afraid this assignment could bring me more trouble than it's worth."

"Before you leave, Becky and I have birthday gifts for you." Aunt Amelia retrieved a parcel tied with ribbon and handed it to Charlotte.

"Thank you so much." Charlotte pressed her wiry aunt into a hug, careful not to squeeze too tightly and hurt her arthritic back. And then she leaned over to kiss her sister on the cheek. She'd forgotten about her upcoming birthday — the first one she'd spend by herself. But a birthday without a celebration was the last thing on her mind. "Shall I open them now?"

Aunt Amelia shook her head. "Why don't you wait?"

"All right." Presents would make an ordinary day much more special.

"If you'll excuse me, girls, I have to work in the garden."

Once Aunt Amelia left, Charlotte turned all her attention to her sister.

"What's it like living in a mansion?" Becky asked as she finished her pie.

"It's very different from Bridge Street, I'll tell you that. Summerhill is a rambling old house with big, airy rooms. Twenty-two of them, in fact. It's got wide, shady porches that catch the sea breezes, lush green lawns, and even a beach of its own."

Becky's face shone. "It sounds lovely. I hear the cottages need a staff the size of an army. And they all eat roast beef and fancy chocolate éclairs and tortes. I'd love to try one of their fancy desserts."

"The food is delicious, and Chef Jacques cooks simple dishes for the staff as well as fancier meals for the family. And there's always plenty. So much food, Becky! I don't think all the millionaires treat their servants so nicely."

Becky sighed. "It must be grand living at Summerhill — especially if you're the lady of the house. I'd so like to see the mansion someday."

"I wish you could. But I won't be there much longer. And after I leave I won't be invited back."

She choked on her last words. No, once he knew the truth, Daniel Wilmont would never want to see her again.

NINE

The following morning Charlotte met the children in their playroom just before breakfast arrived on the dumbwaiter. She served them their toast, soft-boiled eggs, and juice.

"Are you coming to worship with us, Miss Hale?" Ruthie asked between bites of toast.

Church? That was the last place she wished to go. She still hadn't reconciled her unsettled conscience, and she certainly didn't want quiet time to listen to its nagging voice.

"I'm afraid I have a slight headache, so maybe next Sunday would be better."

Ruthie nodded. "I do hope you feel well soon."

"I'll put a cold compress on my forehead and I'll be fine."

Later, when the family returned from services, Charlotte helped the Wilmont children wrap welcome-home gifts for their grandmother. With Charlotte's assistance, Ruthie added a red satin ribbon and a great big, lopsided bow.

"Lovely," Charlotte proclaimed.

Ruthie shook her head and the sausage curls Charlotte had created with a curling iron bounced behind the girl's ears. "Why did you fix my hair like a doll's?" she asked as she wrapped a corkscrew around her index finger.

Charlotte spun Ruthie around and retied the loose sash on her dress. "I'd like to please your grandmother and make a good first impression."

Ruthie snorted. "She's dreadfully hard to please, but you'll find that out soon enough."

"Do stop smirking at me. I'll try my best to make friends with her."

"Miss Hale" — Ruthie gave an exaggerated sigh — "Grandmother has friends. What she wants is another servant she can boss around." She covered her mouth with her hand and giggled. "That wasn't kind, was it? I shall try to keep my opinions to myself."

"Go find a clean pinafore, if you please. You've gone and spilled cranberry juice all over this one." She pointed to a small stain that a sharp eye would spot instantly. "I want you to look clean and fresh for your grandmother."

Ruthie rolled her eyes and trooped to her bedroom, dragging her feet across the parquet floor and pulling on her curls to straighten them. Charlotte sighed. Maybe she shouldn't try so hard to impress Mrs. Wilmont. From all accounts, she was a tyrant. Yet, if she wanted to stay at Summerhill until she discovered the truth, Charlotte suspected she'd better bend over backward to satisfy her.

When Ruthie returned, she carefully carried a fancy pink dress with ruffles and lace. Holding it in front of her, she grinned. "I'm to be a bridesmaid for my cousin Eloise. Isn't this the loveliest gown you've ever seen?"

Charlotte touched the delicate fabric. "Indeed, it is. You'll look like a grown-up young lady when you wear it."

Ruthie grinned. "I can't wait for the wedding."

"I'm sure you'll have a splendid time and look like a princess. But right now we should pick some flowers for your grandmother's homecoming." Ruthie returned the costume to her wardrobe. Together they hurried to the garden and chose the most perfect red roses and placed them in a crystal vase.

"Beautiful." Charlotte sniffed the delicate fragrance. "Would you please put them on your grandmother's chiffonier? I'm going to find Tim and choose some nice clean clothes so he won't look like a ragamuffin."

Within ten minutes she'd scrubbed Tim's freckled face and found short navy blue pants and a starched white shirt in his wardrobe. Once he dressed properly, she stood back and examined her charge.

"Much better." Charlotte brushed the boy's mop of red curls as he squirmed. "I know you want to look like a young gentleman for your grandmother. No playing outdoors before she arrives."

He shrugged. "I don't understand why neatness is so important." But he looked so genuinely puzzled she couldn't help but smile.

"Shall we go downstairs and wait for your papa and grandmother to return from the hospital?" Charlotte asked as she led the way.

Once on the front veranda, Charlotte settled in a wicker chair. Ruthie pushed back and forth on a rocker while she waited, and Tim played jacks in the corner.

The *clip-clop* of a horse's hooves and the grinding of carriage wheels soon caught their attention. The enclosed brougham halted in front of Summerhill. The professor alighted and the uniformed coachman in a silk top hat assisted the older woman down from the carriage. The professor and his mother slowly made their way up the shallow porch steps.

Heading toward the door opened by Mr. Grimes, Vivian Wilmont clung to her son's arm and leaned into him. Tall, angular, and strong featured, she tilted her chin upward.

"Welcome home, Grandmother," Ruthie and Tim said, almost in unison, before the regal lady bent down to receive their awkward pecks to the cheek.

Mrs. Wilmont ignored Charlotte as she passed her and then shuffled through the foyer and into the drawing room. Everyone followed. With a grateful sigh Mrs. Wilmont sank into the white brocade sofa patterned with gold thread and edged with gold fringe. She looked in need of a nap, though she arrived home dressed for visitors. She wore a silk blouse, lacy ecru skirt, and a single strand of pearls. Charlotte thought she retained a vestige of beauty, and despite her sixty-odd years and her frailty, she obviously liked to keep up appearances. Blue eyes held the same intelligence as Professor Wilmont's, but hers glittered like ice chips without a drop of warmth. They swept a chill over Charlotte.

"How do you do?" Mrs. Wilmont's grimace cracked her alabaster face into a web of fine lines.

Charlotte braced herself as the woman muttered to her son, "I expected an older woman, Daniel, one with more experience. Definitely not a young girl."

"I'm really not so young, ma'am. I'm twenty-two." Charlotte squeezed out a smile. *Almost twenty-three.*

Ruthie, sitting primly on a chair near the marble fireplace, spoke up. "That's quite old, Grandmother. She's awfully nice and we like her a lot. And so does Papa."

Mrs. Wilmont arched one thin brow. "Oh?"

"Well, Papa wouldn't hire her if he didn't like her, now would he?"

"I suppose not." Vivian Wilmont frowned. She pulled a velvet and satin throw over her long legs and narrow hips. "But please watch your tone, young lady. I won't tolerate insolence."

Ruthie's head bowed, almost hiding her unrepentant face.

Charlotte caught the professor's amused look and struggled not to roll her eyes.

Tim dangled a piece of yarn at the cat.

Goldie's paws grabbed the end and pulled in a tug of war.

"Would you like some tea or coffee, Mrs. Wilmont?" Charlotte asked as pleasantly as possible through gritted teeth.

The older woman gave a curt nod. "Tea with cream and sugar will suit me fine, and a few oatmeal raisin cookies. Send for the maid, if you please." She turned toward Tim. "And remove that cat, Timothy. He doesn't belong in the cottage."

Tim scooped up Goldie and sprinted across the room.

"No running indoors. Really, Timothy, where are your manners? I've only been gone for two weeks and you're already acting like a ruffian."

Mrs. Wilmont looked pointedly at Charlotte. "You must stress impeccable manners."

Tim stopped at the French doors. "Chef Jacques made a few batches of cookies. I think they're mostly gone, except for one or two."

Charlotte had caught him earlier with a fistful, so he would undoubtedly know if the supply was depleted.

"They are my favorites." Mrs. Wilmont emphasized every word. "They're not on my new diet, of course, but one or two won't hurt."

"I'm sure we have gingersnaps and sugar cookies . . ." Charlotte offered.

Mrs. Wilmont shook her head so vigorously her steel gray pompadour almost bounced. "No, no. I'm partial to oatmeal raisin. No other kind will do.

"Where is the maid? Good help is impossible to find these days." She drew out a weary sigh. "I don't wish to wait any longer. Charlotte, go fetch my tea and cookies, if you will."

Charlotte understood an order when she heard one. "Of course," she said, anxious to leave the aging *enfant terrible.* "I shall not be long."

Please, Lord, give me an abundance of patience. She truly hoped God listened and cared enough to help because she needed extra assistance with this woman.

"I'll help her," Daniel volunteered.

His mother's jaw dropped. "Well, I never heard of such a thing. *Assisting the help.* Really, Daniel."

Professor Wilmont followed Charlotte to the stairway leading to the kitchen, an embarrassed grin crossing his face. "Don't pay attention to my mother."

"Is she always so — particular?" Charlotte whispered, then immediately regretted her impulsive remark. "I apologize. I ought not to criticize. After all, she is your mother and my employer."

He chuckled. "She's always particular. You'll get accustomed to her. Her bark is worse than her bite."

Charlotte shrugged, unconvinced. "I'll do my best to please her." But she'd try to stay clear of the lady who had a personal maid and a houseful of other servants also at her beck and call.

"Would you like something to drink, sir?" Charlotte asked as she started down the stairs.

Daniel shook his head. "My mother will keep you busy enough without the rest of us adding to it."

Charlotte smiled, certain Professor Wilmont was right. His mother promised to be a stern taskmaster. "That's kind of you."

"Well, I'd better return to Mother or she'll have my head." He smiled and didn't seem concerned about his mother's indignation.

Simone hustled into the kitchen and raised an eyebrow at Charlotte. "What are you doing here?"

"Mrs. Wilmont would like tea and oatmeal raisin cookies. I'd be glad to fetch them for her."

Simone's stern mouth softened. "Yes,

make yourself useful. I'm terribly busy, preparing her rooms. She'll be calling for me at any moment."

Charlotte nodded and fished out the last few cookies from the bottom of the ceramic jar.

With a silver tea tray in hand, she soon climbed upstairs with her offerings. When she heard her name, she stopped short in the hallway outside the drawing room.

Mrs. Wilmont spoke in a low tone, but Charlotte heard every word. "She seems like a nice enough girl, but I wish you'd waited for me to come home before hiring someone off the street."

Charlotte's pulse quickened. *Off the street?* Anger spurted through her veins and poured its heat into her face and neck. How dare Mrs. Wilmont imply she was less than respectable.

"Now Mother, I hired Miss Hale because we needed a governess right away. I'm glad I did."

"Was Miss Hale the first one who came along or was she just the most attractive?"

Professor Wilmont let out a hearty laugh. "No, there were others, but she was definitely the prettiest."

"And the nicest," Ruthie added.

"I'm sure she's a lovely girl, but she's not

appropriate for our family. We don't know anything about her, now do we? Have you checked her references?"

"I haven't had a chance, but I shall if you really want me to."

"I most certainly do."

The professor paused. "Mother, I hardly think it's necessary."

"Please do as I ask."

"All right," the professor murmured in a voice Charlotte could barely hear.

She shuddered at the mention of references. Mr. Phifer had taken care of all the details with Edith Ann's assistance. Charlotte bit her lip. Why hadn't she glanced through those recommendations before handing them over to the professor? How could she have been so careless?

Stepping closer to the open doorway, she peeked around the corner into the drawing room.

Mrs. Wilmont shook her head and raised her eyes toward the ceiling. "I'm too tired to argue, Daniel, but you should pay attention to my requests without questioning me. Consider replacing this girl with an experienced and mature woman. You'd be doing all of us a favor." Her weak voice grew more insistent.

Charlotte held her breath. How would the

professor respond? Did he like her well enough to keep her on? Time stood still as she waited for his reaction. Her feet were stuck to the hallway floor, too heavy to move. Her hands shook and a few drops of tea spilled into the saucer.

"Mother, let me pray about this. I'm convinced Miss Hale will work out if you give her half a chance. When the Lord answers me, I'll let you know."

Good response. Charlotte smirked. Maybe she'd hold on to her position after all. Without a job they'd soon lose the house and everything they owned. She carried the tea and cookies into the den and delivered them to Mrs. Wilmont with a faint smile. She wouldn't give the old bat any reason to dislike her or fire her.

The next morning his mother waved Daniel into the morning room where sun streamed through the screened windows.

"I'd appreciate it if you'd speak to the people who vouched for Miss Hale — without delay." His mother sat on an over-stuffed chair, her long fingers pushing a quilting needle in and out of the fabric stretched tight in her hoop. "It will relieve my mind to know Miss Hale is a woman of impeccable character — if indeed she is."

Pursed lips clearly stated her opinion.

Daniel knew he should have checked Miss Hale's references before he hired her, yet he'd felt sure they were as genuine as the young woman herself. But if he didn't check, his mother would pester him to death. "As soon as my classes are finished for the day, I'll be on my way."

He retreated to his home office and shuffled through papers and files, searching for the letters. Growing more and more impatient with his chronic habit of losing everything, he vowed to organize the chaos on his desk. The parlor maids straightened up every day, but somehow he wasn't able to maintain neatness. Now where could he have put those recommendations? After a thorough search, he found them beneath a stack of books.

He scanned the names and addresses and noted all three people lived in Newport. Mrs. Amelia Hillman, Miss Hale's aunt; Miss Edith Ann Wengle, a friend; and Mr. Henry Stapleton, a former teacher, now retired. Finding the trio should be a relatively simple task.

Later that day he drove the gig toward town, references in hand. He came to a stop on Spring Street and knocked on Mr. Stapleton's door, but the woman who answered insisted she'd never heard of the man. Odd, but most likely the gentleman was getting on in years and wrote down an incorrect street number.

Next he called at the boardinghouse where Miss Wengle resided. The landlady, a Mrs. Foley, claimed the young woman worked at a newspaper until six o'clock, so he could return later if he wished.

Her lips thinned. "Oftentimes she stays around the office. Or" — one eye squinted — "she goes off gallivanting with her friends. I can't say, but I have my suspicions."

"Do you happen to know which newspaper employs her?" If she worked for the *Newport Gazette,* he might stop by to speak to her. He didn't recognize her name, but she could be a new hire.

The elderly woman frowned. "Miss Wengle works for that rapscallion Arnie Phifer over at the *Rhode Island Reporter.* She's ambitious, that one is." Mrs. Foley took Daniel's measure in one sweep of her rheumy eyes. "And what would you be wanting with her?"

"Miss Wengle wrote a recommendation for my children's new governess. I'd like to ask her about it."

"I see." She had a skeptical glare in her

eye that wouldn't soften. "What's your governess's name?"

"Miss Hale. Charlotte Hale. Do you know her?"

The woman shook her head. "Never heard the name before. I'm quite sure she never comes to visit. I'd know if she did. No one gets inside my boardinghouse without my say-so."

"Perhaps she and Miss Hale are school friends," Daniel suggested.

"Not if your governess is from Newport. Edith Ann Wengle moved from Tiverton just a few months ago. May, I think it was. The only people she seems to know work with her."

Taken aback by the implication of Mrs. Foley's comment, Daniel felt his nerves tense. "No, Miss Hale wouldn't be associated with the *Rhode Island Reporter*. Definitely not."

Mrs. Foley shrugged her thick shoulders. "Then I can't tell you how they know each other. If you'll excuse me, I must be getting back to my stew."

She left him in front of her closed door. Daniel boarded the gig and started toward his next destination. Questions concerning the two young women niggled at his mind. How had they met, and why would Miss

Hale ask an employee of Arnie Phifer for a recommendation? Very peculiar. Yet he felt certain that if he questioned her, Miss Hale would offer a reasonable explanation.

He drove through town and soon arrived on the Point, his last stop. He was not surprised that the houses in this working class neighborhood needed more care than they received. Many labored as fishermen, ships carpenters, and chandlers and probably found little time or money to improve the exteriors of their century-old homes. Even Miss Hale's home sagged in the middle.

He knocked on the door. Miss Hale spoke little about her family and when he asked, she only offered a few words. A thin woman of middle years opened the door, a wary expression etched on her face. Her dark, heavy-lidded eyes looked curious, but not unfriendly.

"May I help you?"

He tipped his bowler. "I'm Professor Daniel Wilmont, Miss Charlotte Hale's new employer. She gave me a letter of recommendation written by her aunt, Mrs. Amelia Hillman. If I may, I'd like to speak to her."

Alarm flashed across the woman's face as she stepped onto the sidewalk. "There's nothing wrong with Charlotte, is there?

She's not taken ill, I hope."

Daniel gave a reassuring smile. "No, she's fine. I'd merely like to check the accuracy of the reference."

Her worried frown smoothed, though it didn't quite disappear. "Do come inside. I'm Charlotte's aunt, Mrs. Hillman."

She led him into the tiny parlor cluttered with too much furniture and inexpensive bric-a-brac. Flimsy curtains let in enough sunlight to brighten the chocolate brown chairs and sofa. He inhaled the harbor breeze faintly tinged with salt and seaweed, a pungent scent. Mrs. Hillman directed him to an overstuffed chair by the mantel as she perched on the edge of the old settee.

A girl in a wheelchair glanced up from her knitting and flashed a broad smile. Mrs. Hillman introduced her as Charlotte's sister, Becky. With wavy hair and brown eyes, Becky closely resembled Miss Hale. The girl's green dress looked worn and faded, probably a hand-me-down.

Mrs. Hillman leaned forward. "What is it you'd like to know about Charlotte?"

"I'm checking merely to ensure Miss Hale is who she says she is."

He expected the aunt to smile at his rather ridiculous statement and assure him Charlotte was indeed her beloved niece just as she claimed. Then he could return home to report to his mother her worries were unfounded. Instead, the color leeched from Mrs. Hillman's lined face, leaving a grayish-white pallor.

Becky's knitting needles clattered to the floor, distracting him from her aunt. He picked them up and handed them back to her.

"Thank you, Professor. Please excuse my clumsiness." Becky bent over her half-finished mittens, and her needles immediately resumed their *click-clack.*

"Of course." Why were they both so nervous? "Excuse me, but did I say something to upset you?" He turned his attention to Mrs. Hillman.

A tentative smile flickered across her face. "No, of course not. Now you wanted to know about my niece — yes, Charlotte Hale is my late brother's daughter. She and Becky have lived with me here for ten years, ever since their parents passed on. I can assure you Charlotte is a most respectable and responsible young woman. You can ask anyone down at the — in the neighborhood. Everyone knows her." Mrs. Hillman's fingers picked at the crocheted armrest, and her mouth twitched as if she'd said more than she ought.

"I'm sure her character is above reproach." Daniel stood to leave.

"Do you have any more questions, Professor Wilmont?" Mrs. Hillman asked as she rose and led him toward the front door.

"Why do you suppose your niece decided to take the job of governess? She graduated from high school, which is quite an accomplishment. Surely she could find a position more challenging than caring for my children this summer."

Mrs. Hillman shook her head. "I think you ought to ask her, not me. Her decisions are her own." Her mouth tightened.

"Did you approve of her accepting work outside your home?" He felt quite sure from her expression that she did not. Perhaps that was the undercurrent he was sensing.

She stared at her hands with regret. "I'm afraid I'm too arthritic to work anymore. Charlotte has supported Becky and me for several years. I don't know what we'd have done without her. She's a hardworking, generous girl."

Daniel's good opinion of Miss Hale — Charlotte — rose even higher than before. She labored diligently to support her family and never complained of her considerable responsibility. How could he not admire her loyalty and selflessness? His heart swelled with high regard for her virtues.

Yet, after he said good-bye and drove off, Daniel reviewed the visit in his mind. He wasn't completely satisfied with Mrs. Hillman's responses. Something didn't seem quite right. What was it?

TEN

Tim smashed his red croquet ball through the last two curved wires and into the stake. His arms pumped in victory. "I won! I won!"

Charlotte clapped. "Indeed, you did. But now it's time to practice piano." She watched his face fall. "Come now," she said, slipping an arm around his narrow shoulders, "there's no need to glower. You'll have it done before you know it."

Ruthie gathered the wickets, balls, and mallets and headed for the storage room.

"Miss Hale, may I speak to you for a moment?" Professor Wilmont appeared on the veranda. With hands clasped behind his back and a frown twisting the corners of his mouth, he looked like he might be preparing a lecture. For her.

"Yes, sir." She joined him beside the ferns as the children greeted their father and then disappeared inside the house.

He leveled a steady gaze. "I checked your

references today."

"Oh? Did you find everyone at home?" She flicked a weak smile.

"No, unfortunately not. Mr. Stapleton doesn't live at his old address anymore. He must have moved."

Charlotte's throat went dry. "Yes, that's the logical explanation."

Daniel shrugged. "No matter. I did find your aunt, but your third reference, Miss Wengle, was at work." He ran his fingers through his blond hair. "Miss Wengle's landlady claimed she's employed at the *Rhode Island Reporter*." He looked straight into Charlotte's eyes and she flinched. "Does she work for Arnie Phifer?"

A denial strangled in her throat. "I believe she does, sir."

"Is she a friend of yours? The landlady said she only moved to Newport a short time ago."

Charlotte's legs melted to jelly. She gripped the porch rail. "That's true." Without thinking, she blurted, "Miss Wengle is my cousin. She recently moved here from Tiverton."

Though Charlotte knew next to nothing about the woman, she did remember the name of her hometown. Edith Ann rarely talked to her, though Charlotte kept trying the friendly approach. Unsuccessfully. Right from the beginning Edith Ann let her know she'd stomp over anyone who stood in the way of her advancement.

Professor Wilmont's frown deepened. "You should explain to her that Arnie Phifer is an unmitigated scoundrel. Tell her to apply at the *Newport Gazette.* It has an excellent reputation, unlike the *Rhode Island* — well, don't get me started."

"Yes, sir. I'll be sure to tell her."

"Do that. No self-respecting young woman should work for that man."

Charlotte nodded and then hurried to the back parlor, her face burning. She dropped to the sofa as Tim pounded out more sour notes than sweet ones.

She had to consider her family, not herself. Despite the myriad of reasons she needed her position, Professor Wilmont's comments rang true. Perhaps Mr. Phifer didn't deserve her allegiance. What was she to do?

Later, when she passed by the library she heard Mrs. Wilmont mention her name. Charlotte halted by the door and strained to catch the rest of the conversation.

"Did you check Charlotte's references today?" Mrs. Wilmont, the old battleaxe, demanded in that imperious tone Charlotte had rapidly grown to hate.

"Yes, Mother. They're in order," Daniel said.

"Oh?" Mrs. Wilmont sounded skeptical. "Did you check them all?"

"Actually, only Miss Hale's aunt was at home. Her cousin, Miss Wengle, and Mr. Stapleton, a former teacher, weren't at home."

Mrs. Wilmont *harrumphed.* "You can't expect a relative to give anything but a glowing report. I'd like you to pursue Mr. Stapleton just to be on the safe side. That would bring me peace of mind."

"It's not necessary, Mother. I trust Miss Hale and so should you."

Charlotte pressed her lips in a grimace. She knew the woman wouldn't give up. What if she discovered the truth? Hopefully, she'd be long gone from Summerhill and Mrs. Wilmont's prying eyes and sharp tongue.

Sounds of the bridal procession filled the back lawn of Grassy Knoll, one of the most elaborate Bellevue Avenue mansions. Charlotte held her breath as Ruthie slowly proceeded down the path toward the gazebo where her mother's cousin, Eloise Carstairs, would soon be joined in matrimony to Harlan Santerre, a railroad man and this season's most eligible bachelor. At least that's what Mrs. Finnegan claimed, and she knew nearly everything that transpired among the elite.

Behind Ruthie came a bevy of senior bridesmaids also dressed in pale pink silk and the matron of honor, looking stylish in mauve. Eloise slowly followed, leaning on her father's arm. She looked lovely in white satin and her rather plain, flat face glowed with the joy of a happy bride. Her long lace veil, attached to a coronet of orange blossoms, streamed out behind her.

Two page boys gripped the corners so it didn't touch the path strewn with rose petals. Poor Tim. His face grew pink as he marched forward in his royal blue velvet jacket, short trousers, and round collared shirt with a white crepe de chine bow.

The bride and her attendants arrived at the gazebo decorated with masses of greenery, mums, and lily of the valley. Music from the string quartet faded into the mid-afternoon hush, and the ceremony began. Charlotte glanced at Professor Wilmont standing beside her and smiled. The children had made it down the outdoor aisle without incident. The muscles in his face relaxed and he grinned back. He'd insisted she accompany him to the wedding to take care of the children's needs.

The guests descended onto the gilded ballroom chairs set in rows on the freshly mown grass and listened to the couple declare their vows before the minister. Half an hour later Mr. and Mrs. Santerre walked arm in arm toward the hedged-in garden where they'd accept their guests' congratulations and good wishes. Charlotte and Professor Wilmont passed through the reception line and then led the children into the dining room.

"I'm starving," Tim said as he released the top button of his shirt. They all took plates from the long buffet table covered with an embroidered linen cloth and vases of pink and white roses. Charlotte spooned small amounts of ham mousse, creamed oysters, chicken a la king, and celery salad in tomato aspic onto her china plate and followed the Wilmonts out to the terrace where small tables were set up for dining.

A short time later Tim said, "I'm full for now." He patted his stomach. He'd eaten all his dinner and more than his fair share of strawberry ice cream. "I think I'll go play on the rocks."

The professor frowned. "I'm not sure that's such a good idea. Why don't you stay here with the rest of us?"

"I'll watch him," Ruthie volunteered.

Their father hesitated then looked toward Charlotte. "What do you think, Miss Hale?"

"I'm sure they'll be fine," Charlotte said. "If they stay away from the edge."

Daniel pulled a long face. "All right, but do be careful and come back soon."

They were off. Charlotte sipped her tea as music from the ballroom floated to the terrace. She softly hummed the Viennese waltz. "It's lovely, isn't it?"

"Yes, indeed. Shall we watch the dancers?"

"Yes, I'd like that. But are you sure you want to be seen with a governess? Shouldn't I disappear to the kitchen or someplace suitable for servants? I shouldn't stay with the guests."

"Nonsense. Shall we go now?"

"As you wish, sir." Charlotte trailed him into the gilded ballroom scented with roses.

"Please dance with the ladies, sir. I see several of them eying you and glaring at me." Charlotte laughed. "If they can't figure out I'm only a governess, then they must be blind. I'm certainly not dressed well for a society wedding."

She knew she looked respectable in a cream-colored skirt, ruffled blouse, and flowered hat she'd borrowed from Simone, who had great fashion sense. But she certainly didn't blend with this social set. They'd obviously spent a fortune on their fancy outfits and flashing jewels.

He tilted his head. "And I get the distinct impression you don't care about the opinion of others."

"To a fair extent." She stepped back as dancers swept past.

And the professor stepped closer. "I'm not interested in dancing with any of these ladies. I know many of them and they're quite charming, but we don't have much in common."

"Except you belong to the same set."

He shrugged. "I'm afraid all my academic and religious pursuits would bore most of these ladies — along with my introverted personality."

Charlotte rolled her eyes and laughed. "You underestimate yourself, Professor."

His face flushed. "No, I don't believe so. I've always been more comfortable in a classroom than in a ballroom. When I was young I wanted to be outgoing like my brother, but I was tongue-tied with the ladies."

"Sir, I find you quite interesting." He wasn't shallow and full of superficial charm like Paul Seaton. She appreciated the professor's sincerity and kindness. He appealed far more than any other man she'd ever met — not that it mattered.

He studied her intently for a moment. "May I have this dance, Miss Hale? Please don't say no."

Her eyes widened. "I'm honored, sir, but I don't dance. I've never had time to learn."

He chuckled. "With my two left feet I'm not the one to teach you. But if we shuffle around in the corner perhaps no one will notice we're unskilled."

"No, we can't dance in the ballroom. Everyone will start talking about the professor and the governess."

"It doesn't matter to me, Miss Hale, if it doesn't matter to you."

Her heart fluttered. "But it would matter to your mother. Perhaps if we adjourned to the terrace it might be all right. But just one dance."

He bowed and smiled. "As you wish."

They wove their way through the crowd and out to the nearly deserted terrace. Most of the guests had already wandered into the ornate cottage, leaving Charlotte and the professor practically alone. The music floated from the ballroom, muffling the distant rumble of thunder.

He drew her close. Slowly they moved

back and forth to the rhythm of the waltz, their clothes brushing together. Their shoes tapped lightly against the stone floor as he guided her expertly around the terrace. His arm pressed firmly, yet gently, against her back. He'd been joking when he claimed he had two left feet. He moved like a whisper on the wind.

"This isn't so difficult, is it, Miss Hale?"

"Not in the least." Her breath caught in the back of her throat. His aftershave blended with the fresh sea air and the perfume of flowers blooming in enormous stone urns.

A middle-aged couple appeared through the open French doors and Charlotte felt a pang of disappointment at the interruption.

"Wilmont! It's so good to see you. Where have you been keeping yourself?" The gentleman glanced toward Charlotte, then back to the professor.

Daniel broke away from her and moved to shake the man's hand. "I'm busy at the college as ever."

"And no doubt writing those incendiary articles," the man said lowly, his brow furrowed in concern. "You can't imagine the ruckus you've caused. And hard feelings as well."

Daniel nodded. "I regret so many misunderstand my words. I merely suggest Christians ought to take their faith seriously enough to apply it to their business endeavors."

The gentleman blanched when Daniel refused to back down, and Charlotte tucked a laugh into her cheek and turned away. "Excuse me, Professor. I'd like to check on the children."

He nodded. "Of course."

She was glad to escape from Professor Wilmont, who'd quickened her pulse and sent quivers of pleasure down her spine. She needed time and space to sort it all out. As she walked across the lawn, the sun slipped behind a mountain of blue-gray clouds and the breeze stiffened. She re-pinned her hat, then held on to it, afraid it might lift off like a kite. She came to the rocks, which stretched along the coast for as far as she could see, and looked for the children. Where were they?

"Ruthie! Tim! It's time to return to the cottage."

No answer.

Charlotte eyed the horizon. It looked like rain would soon be upon them. She cupped her hands and called for the children again. But her voice disappeared in the roar of the sea slapping against the rocks. She inched her way over the craggy boulders, careful not to catch her best bone-colored shoes in the wet crevices. Holding up her skirt with one hand, she stretched out her other arm to keep her balance. Around the bend, she spotted Ruthie resting on the edge of a rock high above the pounding surf, her head in her hands.

Charlotte picked her way over the rough boulders and halted by her side, but not too close to the edge. "What's wrong, Ruthie?"

Ruthie glanced up, her eyes brimming with tears. "I fell and tore my beautiful gown. Now I look a fright." She sniffed, then pouted. "Everyone will laugh at me. And Papa will never allow us out of his sight again."

"That's not true. Stand up. I'll brush off the dirt."

When she finished, Charlotte smiled. "There. That's better." She glanced around for Tim but didn't see him. "Where's your brother?"

"I don't know. I'm afraid I lost track of him when I took a tumble."

"Don't fret. I shall find him. You stay here, please." Charlotte unpinned her hat and handed it to Ruthie. "I don't want to lose this. It's not mine."

As Charlotte approached the edge of the

boulders extending into the roiling waters, she paused. Tim was far below, at the end of a trail of hops, skips, and jumps. Stranded.

"I'm coming to get you, Tim!" But the low howl of the wind swallowed her words once again. The boy didn't even glance over his narrow shoulder. "Tim!"

He looked so tiny on that small rock separated from the other boulders by at least a yard. The waves crashed against the stone and rose in a spray to slap the boy. Standing far above, Charlotte tried to find a way down to him. If she waited much longer the breakers would whip up and possibly wash him away. Her heart slammed so hard she felt it could burst through her blouse.

Lord, if You're up there in Your heavenly kingdom, please look down and help me. I can't save Tim by myself. And there's no one else around.

The professor would help, but by the time she struggled back over the rocks, Tim might already be swept off the boulder. She swallowed hard and started climbing down the pile of rocks. Step by step she descended, jamming her foot into any crevice that seemed solid. Slowly she lowered herself, scraping her hands and fingernails. Her hair pulled from her carefully coifed pompadour and swirled around her face as the wind increased. She glanced up. Yellow-white lightning streaked the sky as dark as an inkblot. Thunder boomed.

As she drew closer to the ocean, she heard Tim's sobs and cries for help. She turned her head. He was looking toward shore. Waves with white caps broke all around him.

"Stay where you are, Tim! I'll be right there."

Once she reached the lowest boulder on the water's edge she hurried toward the chain of rocks. She'd have to step across several to get to Tim. Slimy seaweed coated the surface and clung to the cracks. The angry waters broke over them and then engulfed them. She couldn't see where to step.

"Help me, Miss Hale! I'm going to drown."

Spurred on by Tim's panic, Charlotte stretched her leg to the first rock and pushed herself ahead. She teetered on the edge, barely an inch from the water, but she heaved herself forward and regained her balance. She tried another giant step and made it. "I'm coming, Tim!"

But then the leather soles of her shoes slipped on the seaweed, and she collapsed to her knees. Pain reverberated through her body and stole her breath. Then a powerful wave hit her in the face and pushed ice-cold water over her. But she gripped the rock and held on. She gasped for several seconds before she forced herself to her feet. Her legs wobbled.

Bent nearly in half, she stepped to the next rock, and then the next. Looking up, she saw Tim's hand reach toward her. The space between them seemed so far. But she leaned forward, grabbed his hands, and helped him to leap. They embraced for a long moment.

"All right, Tim," she said. "Off with you, now. You can make it. You've made it past the worst."

He leaped to the next rock and looked back at her. "Come on, Miss Hale."

It wasn't quite as easy in high-heeled shoes and a long skirt, as he'd made it seem.

Glancing over her shoulder she saw a wall of water surging toward her. She turned toward Tim but knew she'd never make it back before the waves pounded her. And possibly Tim. "*Go,* Tim!"

Oh Lord, please help me. She tried to jump to the next rock, but mid-leap the breakers knocked her down and sucked her under. Salty water poured down her throat and she sputtered and coughed while she thrashed around, trying to find the surface. The undertow tossed her like a piece of drift-wood, ramming her head against the rocks. *I'm going to die,* she thought distantly. *I'm going to drown. God, please help me.* She fought against the force of nature and gasped until her strength ebbed. Her lungs kept filling with water, and she kept coughing it out each time she surfaced, only to be dragged down again. How much longer could she fight when she had no vigor left? Yet she wanted to live. *Please, Lord. Please.*

Then she felt someone grab hold of her arm and pull her from the roiling waters. To safety. She leaned into a damp jacket and chest, coughing up seawater. Tears streamed down her already wet face.

She looked up. "Daniel."

"Charlotte," he returned tenderly. Professor Wilmont picked her up, moved several paces higher, and then carefully sat down, holding her close.

"Thank you for saving my life," she said through chattering teeth.

"Thank you for saving my son. He wouldn't have gotten back without you." The boy edged into her line of vision, staring at her with wide eyes.

She smiled and rested her head against Daniel's chest, not caring how inappropriate it might be. "I — I've never been so close to death before. I was so frightened."

"Are you alright, Miss Hale?" Ruthie asked as she scrambled over the rocks toward the trio. Tim buried his head in his father's shoulder.

"I shall be fine in a minute or two."

The professor didn't make a move to leave. "I thank the Lord I got here in time. The weather looked threatening and the three of you weren't back, so I had to search for you. I didn't expect to find you in such danger."

Lightning split the blue-black sky and another thunderclap sounded. Daniel rose, with Charlotte still in his arms. "Come, children. I'm afraid it's time to take our leave from the rest of the festivities."

As soon as Charlotte said good night to the children that evening, she returned to her own room, read her Bible for a while, and then reached for the stack of Professor Wilmont's newspaper columns. She'd already sorted them into topics. Not all pertained to politics as Mr. Phifer indicated. Many spoke of God's love and faithfulness and living the Christian life in harmony with the Lord's plan and purpose. Then she came across one with the word *truth* in bold print. Her eyes skimmed the page, but she couldn't pull her gaze away.

The Lord Jesus Christ claimed He is the Way, the Truth, and the Life. Lying is antithetical to God, to His truth, and to our Christian calling. "That by two immutable things, in which it was impossible for God to lie, we might have a strong consolation, who have fled for refuge to lay hold upon the hope set before us" (Hebrews 6:18). To follow in His footsteps we must not lie either, even when it's difficult to be honest with others or with ourselves. Falling into the sin of dishonesty will destroy our relationship to the Lord and also to the people we associate with in our daily lives. Honesty is a reflection of one's inner character. A liar must hide his lies, a deception that's often not easy.

Charlotte laid the paper down, leaned back in her overstuffed chair, and closed her eyes. *Lord, I'm just beginning to know You, and already I am failing. I understand why You'd be displeased with me when I can't even manage to tell the truth. But Lord, I have my reasons and they're good ones.* She couldn't allow her family to starve, now could she? Yet somehow she didn't feel justified. Nagging doubts corroded into her stomach like acid. If God understood her predicament and approved of her actions, then why didn't she feel some sense of peace?

Charlotte read one more verse. Proverbs 11:3, "The integrity of the upright shall guide them: but the perverseness of transgressors shall destroy them." Groaning, she put the columns back on the chest of drawers and slid into bed. *Lord, please show me what to do.*

The following evening, as the grandfather clock in the foyer struck seven, the children started upstairs to dress for the college band concert. Charlotte followed. Still weary from the trauma of the night before, she yearned for the comfort of her feather bed and light quilt, not an evening out. They were halfway up the staircase when the doorbell rang.

Charlotte stopped and looked around. She waited while Mr. Grimes answered the door in his stiff, formal manner befitting an important staff member.

The butler stepped aside for a beautiful, curvaceous young lady of medium height with the air of a *grande dame.* She tossed back platinum blond hair topped with a plumed hat that tied beneath her chin with gauzy streamers. The gaze from her light blue eyes passed over the butler and settled on Charlotte as she descended to the foyer. The girl appraised her with a cool haughtiness before she turned back to the butler.

"I'm here to see Professor Wilmont." The girl strutted into the foyer, silk skirts rustling. "My name is Miss Melissa LeBeau. Will you tell him I'm here?"

Charlotte's heart fluttered. This was Missy, the girl Mr. Phifer hoped would charm Professor Wilmont and bring about his destruction. She was the student talking to the professor on the corner of Cove Road the other day. She'd seen them!

Her heart skipped a beat. Could Mr. Phifer possibly be correct about a relationship between Missy and the professor? How could an intelligent man like the professor be hoodwinked by such an overblown and rather vulgar beauty?

Charlotte cleared her throat. She couldn't let an opportunity to question the girl go by, even if ladies weren't interested in exchanging pleasantries with servants. Perhaps a few friendly words would encourage Missy to reveal something pertinent. The quicker she learned the truth about the so-called affair between this young woman and Daniel Wilmont, the sooner she could return to the safety of home.

"How do you do, Miss LeBeau? I'm Charlotte Hale, the children's governess."

Missy gave her a curt nod.

"Are you one of Professor Wilmont's students?" Charlotte broadened her smile, hoping to put her at ease.

"Yes, I am." Missy shifted from one high-heeled shoe to the other and stared at the staircase as if her concentration would conjure up the professor.

"I imagine he's a splendid teacher."

Missy lowered her chin and looked up through glittering eyes. "Yes, he is. In fact, he's my favorite teacher ever. He's kind and caring — and uncommonly handsome." Surprisingly, Missy giggled, ruining her facade of sophistication and betraying her young age. She couldn't be much more than eighteen. "You're so fortunate to work with him every day."

She gave the girl an understanding smile. "Are you a summer student, Miss LeBeau?"

"Yes, I am."

"What are you studying?" If she kept her chattering, maybe she'd open up.

"I'm only taking Professor Wilmont's New Testament course." Missy sparked like a bonfire. "I do so enjoy his class. He makes the Bible come alive. He's such a remarkable man. He's interested in all his students, but he's taken a personal interest in me." She giggled again and then flashed a smug smile, displaying startlingly white teeth.

"How fortunate for you," Charlotte murmured. She could never believe the professor would fall for such a young woman who dabbed her cheeks with rouge.

Missy's full lips tilted upward. "He's so charming."

Charlotte chuckled inwardly at Missy's inappropriate comment. "I think you have a crush on him, Miss LeBeau," Charlotte teased, watching for a reaction.

The girl angled her head. "Well, why not? He's a widower and I'm unattached."

Charlotte's jaw dropped open. She slammed it shut and eased closer. "Has he truly taken a romantic interest in you?" Her voice cracked. Perspiration seeped from her palms. This was exactly what Mr. Phifer wanted to know.

"Perhaps." Missy's eyes gleamed like blue marbles.

Charlotte wagered the girl was capable of anything and used to getting whatever she wanted whenever she wanted it. A rich socialite, spoiled and pampered.

The professor strode into the hallway.

"Good evening, Miss LeBeau. Please follow me to my office." His features pinched with a sternness Charlotte hadn't seen before. She trailed behind by a few paces to listen in.

"We had an appointment at the Student Center tonight at six thirty," Daniel said. "I waited for half an hour, but you never came."

"I'm so sorry," Missy said with an insincere pout. "I was unavoidably detained, so I decided to come here instead. Is it a terrible inconvenience?" She leaned forward and plucked a piece of lint from his shirt and reached to straighten his tie. He took a giant step backward as his face flushed.

"There, that's better," she cooed, unperturbed.

Daniel glanced to the doorway and spotted Charlotte. "I'd like Miss Hale to sit with us."

"I'd be glad to," Charlotte said, pleased that he would ask.

But Missy shook her head. "No. I prefer to talk to you in private, Professor."

He hesitated. "Well, as you wish. But Miss Hale, would you stay close by — in case we need you?"

"Of course," she agreed.

Missy slid gracefully into the study chair

with the broken springs. From the foyer, Charlotte watched the surprise on Missy's face as her silk bottom encountered the wayward spring. The girl squirmed then moved to a more comfortable position on the edge of the chair. Charlotte squelched a laugh. The professor took a seat on the opposite side of the desk and leveled a stern gaze at his student.

Perhaps he was feigning annoyance at Missy to hide their romantic involvement. But was he really duplicitous? Charlotte doubted it.

Professor Wilmont tapped a pencil against the glass top of his desk as Missy murmured in a voice low and satin smooth. Charlotte strained to hear the conversation, catching all but a few words.

Missy licked her lips and then slowly curled them in a moist smile. Daniel's chest tightened with the pressure of a boa constrictor wrapped around it. Why was she flirting with him? He was quite a bit older, practically of another generation — and a teacher. But a glance at her narrowed eyes verified her unmistakable interest. He glanced toward the door and found comfort in Miss Hale looking in from the hallway.

Daniel tried to swallow the dryness in his

throat. "So, what can I do for you, Miss Le-Beau?" He kept the edge in his voice from cutting, but he couldn't believe she'd waltzed into his cottage without an invitation. Occasionally he'd invite an entire class over for tea, but never a female student by herself. He pushed back his spectacles as they slid to the tip of his nose.

Missy fussed with the folds of her skirt. "I'm having trouble with my assignments. I don't understand the Gospels at all. I know so very little about the Bible and if I don't get help, I'm sure to fail your course. I do enjoy it, but it's quite difficult." Her words tumbled out in a rush. "I'd truly appreciate it if you would tutor me."

Daniel shook his head. "I'm afraid my schedule won't permit it. But I can provide you the names of a few seniors who'd be glad to help." Even eager. He rifled through his grade book, searching for appropriate names.

Her arm swept across the desk and touched his hand. He snatched it away as she looked at him, eyes wide and smoldering. He arose from behind his desk. What was this young lady up to? "Miss LeBeau," he said in warning.

Missy stayed seated, one leg crossed over the other and swinging slowly beneath her skirt. "I wish you'd tutor me yourself. I really do need your personal attention."

He bent and finished scribbling the names of possible tutors, handed her the note, and strode toward the door, nearly tripping over her feet. "I'm afraid I don't have the time for tutoring anyone, Miss LeBeau. If you're afraid the material is too advanced, perhaps you should take a more basic course. Mine is designed for students who are familiar with Scripture. In fact, I'm certain you'd fare far better in a survey class with another instructor."

"But Professor Wilmont, you're the best professor at the college."

He recognized blatant flattery and choked down a laugh. "Thank you for the compliment. But you ought to learn the fundamentals of the faith before you take my classes."

Missy's stubborn chin jutted. "No, that won't do at all." Her lower lip quivered. "Don't brush me off, Professor Wilmont." Slowly she lifted from the chair and sauntered toward him, swaying her rounded hips. Moving in close she whispered in a breathy voice, "I want your help."

A whiff of sickly sweet perfume swirled around her. He rushed into the foyer, past Miss Hale, and then to the door. He flung it open before Mr. Grimes had a chance.

"I'll help by remembering you in prayer. And I'll ask one of my best students to tutor you. That's the most I can do. Have a good evening, Miss LeBeau."

Missy grimaced as she waltzed past him, saying not a word. At the door she spun around. "There's a dreadful rumor going around campus that you may not teach here next year. Is it true, sir? I'd so hate to see you leave."

"You shouldn't listen to rumors, Miss LeBeau. If and when I depart my teaching post, I shall tell my students."

"Thank you, sir. It's the talk of the campus, you know."

He watched her descend the veranda steps and glide down the walkway to her buggy. Daniel drew a deep breath of cool night air, relieved that the minx was finally gone. Now if she'd only vanish from Aquidneck College, he'd feel more comfortable.

But he knew she'd be back.

Leaning against the wall, Charlotte buried her face in her hands, shoulders heaving with what he suspected was mirth.

"I do apologize, sir," she sputtered. "I shouldn't laugh, but that girl has set her cap for you."

"And you find it amusing?" His lips twisted in a dry smile, his face heated.

"Yes, I'm afraid I do."

"Well, you're overreacting, Miss Hale. Miss LeBeau's behavior wasn't one bit humorous. Or was it my behavior you find so funny?"

ELEVEN

She'd heard most of the conversation *and* seen Missy advancing, as well as Professor Wilmont retreating. But it wasn't just amusement that set her laughing. Relief at the professor's obvious innocence brought forth a wave of giggles she couldn't control. This turn of events proved Mr. Phifer had misjudged the good professor and she couldn't wait to tell him. She felt herself gloating. She'd have to be diplomatic with her boss or he'd fire her for insubordination. Or perhaps he'd fire her for failing in her mission.

"Please excuse me, sir. I get carried away easily." In an effort to regain her dignity, Charlotte straightened her back and held her head high like the most dignified of society matrons as she stared up at the professor. But her giddiness kept the corners of her mouth curled upward.

Professor Wilmont nodded as he shoved

his hands deep into his trouser pockets. "Yes, I can see you're prone to laughter. I agree, Miss LeBeau did seem — overly familiar. I'm obliged to assist my students if I can, but —"

"That young lady doesn't want your help. She wants you." Charlotte tried to add gravity to her voice but broke into another hiccup of laughter.

Professor Wilmont's face glowed. "Utter nonsense. I'm old enough to be her — well, if not her father, at least her much older brother."

How could a man over thirty be so naive? It was enough to finally sober her. "Miss LeBeau is chasing you, sir. Forgive me for speaking bluntly, but take care she doesn't lure you into a compromising situation." *Or Mr. Phifer will take full advantage of it.*

Professor Wilmont winced. "I do believe you're exaggerating. At least I hope so." He gazed into space for several seconds before he flashed a disarming grin. "Enough of Miss LeBeau. It's time to leave for the band concert. Would you like to come along?"

Her eyebrows shot up to her hairline. She hesitated for only a split second, her exhaustion disappearing in the wake of his enthusiasm. "Why, yes. That sounds delightful. I'm glad you're taking the children. I know they will enjoy spending time with you."

And so shall I. The words rang alarm bells in her ears. Did she want her career in journalism? Or to chase the silly fantasy of the man who rescued her?

Professor Wilmont leveled a quizzical stare, then asked kindly, "Are you feeling all right, Miss Hale? You suddenly grew pale."

"I'm fine, sir, really I am. Just a moment of light-headedness. I was just thinking of yesterday, sir. Excuse me. I need to fetch my things."

"And where are you going at this time of night? It's not your evening off," Simone said as Charlotte descended the backstairs, hat and shawl in hand.

"Professor Wilmont asked me to accompany him and the children to a band concert. And I'm well aware it's not my night off." Simone's disapproval caught Charlotte off guard, but she controlled her annoyance. Of course the maid took her cue from her mistress.

"Take care, Miss Hale. It's not seemly for a servant to be out at night with her employer." Though Simone's voice emerged in a soft French accent, her meaning was clear.

"I know, but the professor wishes me to watch the children at the concert." Charlotte turned away and hurried to the foyer. Why else would he want her to attend? Certainly he took no personal interest in her.

She caught a glimpse of Tim heading out the front door with Ruthie at his heels.

"Are we ready to go, sir?" she asked the professor who waited in the hallway.

"In a moment." Professor Wilmont gestured toward the drawing room. "My mother's friend, Mr. McClintock, recently arrived. He'll keep her company until we return."

Through the panes of the French doors, Charlotte spotted the gentleman perched on the edge of the settee. His eyes, magnified by thick spectacles, fastened on Mrs. Wilmont.

The professor leaned closer and spoke softly. "Mr. McClintock has been sweet on my mother for the last several years, but he seems hesitant to take the next step."

Professor Wilmont's breath tickled Charlotte's ear and sent warm shivers down her spine. She let the feeling linger, knowing full well she ought to shake herself free from his spell.

Pulling herself back to reality, she whispered back, "I did notice how your mother perks up when Mr. McClintock arrives."

For the last few days, the natty little man strutted into the drawing room laden with a bouquet of flowers and a box of candy. Each time Mrs. Wilmont babbled her thanks like a young schoolgirl. He brought out a warmth that lay buried deep inside Mrs. Wilmont's icy exterior.

"He never comes empty handed. I'm going to wish them a good evening." Professor Wilmont pushed open the French doors and addressed the couple on the settee. "Please excuse the intrusion. Good evening, Mother, Mr. McClintock. We're going to the band concert with the children. We'll return in an hour or two."

His mother's soft smile hardened to a glare. "We? Do you mean to take Miss Hale along?" Her gaze slid to Charlotte standing in the hallway near the open door. "I might need her to fetch me something. I haven't regained my strength yet."

Mr. McClintock intervened with a soothing pat on Mrs. Wilmont's lacy wrist. "If you need anything at all, Vivian, I'd be delighted to fetch it. No need to worry. I'll take good care of you, my dear."

Mrs. Wilmont blushed and her face sweetened. "Well, I suppose it might be all right, if you don't mind, Horace."

"We also have a house full of maids and

footmen," Daniel reminded her. "Simone is always at your beck and call."

That settled, Charlotte followed the professor outside. While the children ran ahead, they strolled across Summerhill's wide lawn toward the Aquidneck College campus. When they came to the edge of the Wilmonts' property, they followed the dirt path skirting the coast that ended at Cove Road.

The professor strode beside her, much too close for propriety. If he wouldn't think it odd, she'd walk alone on the other side of the lane. His presence stripped her mind of all rational thought and conversation. First she babbled, and then her tongue tied itself in knots. Again and again, she thought back to the night before, to how close she came to death . . . and how he saved her. She needed time to sort out these strange, emerging feelings. She wasn't behaving at all like herself.

He curved over to speak, and from the look in his eyes she knew he didn't recognize her confusion. She hoped she wasn't making a spectacle of herself like Missy LeBeau. Charlotte banished her confusion and concocted an open expression.

"I hope you'll enjoy the band. The college music department sponsors weekly concerts, and I try to attend a few every summer. I thought this was a good way to incorporate more time for the children." He glanced to Tim and Ruthie ahead of them and back to her, clearly seeking her approval.

Charlotte stifled a snort. "I'm glad you took my advice, sir."

"You're hard to ignore, Miss Hale." He tossed her a crooked grin that fired heat into her neck and face.

Was he flirting? No, her imagination must be playing tricks. But, horror of horrors, she wanted to flirt with him — maybe even poke him in the ribs, though that would be much too unseemly, especially in plain view. Why were these foolish thoughts dancing through her head? No, it wasn't that she liked him in a *romantic* sort of way; she merely enjoyed a bit of fun and frivolity. But he was her boss and she dare not forget that for even a moment.

The mild air blew in gentle puffs through the trees that lined the lane and cast dark, lacy patterns across the lawns. She hoped the breeze would cool her countenance and drain the color from her face. She'd die of embarrassment if he even suspected she cherished even a twinge of fondness for him. And that's all it was — a fondness

241

she'd feel toward any kind and pleasant person.

Professor Wilmont looked at her from the side. "You're grinning like a Cheshire cat. What's so humorous, Miss Hale?"

Charlotte gave up her flimsy hold and let her smile broaden. Finding him innocent of Mr. Phifer's ugly suspicions propelled her to turn cartwheels down the center of Cove Road.

"I was picturing your student, Miss Le-Beau. I found her behavior quite outrageous. There isn't one subtle bone in her body."

Professor Wilmont nodded. "You're right. But as a Christian I can't turn my back on her, though I was sorely tempted. In order for her faith to grow stronger, she needs to read and study the Bible. And pray, of course. I'm afraid I failed to get that across. I just pushed her away without offering much assistance." His voice held a surprising amount of regret. "I wasn't as understanding as I should have been."

Charlotte shook her head. "Don't feel guilty about protecting yourself and your reputation, not even for one second. You should run away from that girl just as fast as you can. Mark my words, she'll only cause trouble."

His eyes narrowed. "Do you really think so?"

"I most certainly do." If only she could explain how Mr. Phifer counted on him to succumb to his student's charms. Yet right from the beginning Charlotte had felt sure the fine, upstanding Professor Wilmont wouldn't fall prey to a young vixen. He was too smart and too good to be snared by such overt flattery.

"I believe you're exaggerating. She's forward, but that's the extent of it, I'm sure."

"She'll use any ploy to capture your attention, even pretend an interest in religion." Charlotte uttered the truth, but Daniel's questioning gaze made her wish she'd spoken with more tact.

"You're quite cynical, Miss Hale." His face registered surprise, though he didn't sound judgmental.

"Oh no, sir, I'm not in the least bit jaded. But I am realistic. And I understand women, including Missy. I mean, Miss LeBeau."

"Then you must know Melissa LeBeau needs the Lord in her life. Somebody should help her before she takes a wrong turn."

Charlotte jerked a nod. "Yes, of course. But, sir, if you'll pardon my saying so, you're *not* the right one to guide her. She'll cling to you like a vine." She hoped she wasn't stepping out of line by voicing her opinion, but he had to take heed.

Professor Wilmont drew out a long sigh as the shadows lengthened across lawns and gaslight glowed in the windows facing Faculty Row. "Sometimes students have crushes on their professors, or so I've been told. It's just a passing fancy. Fortunately, it's never happened to me before."

Such a good-looking man was an obvious target for a girl's fantasies. "Just beware of her, sir. That's all I'm suggesting."

"Yes, I shall keep her at arm's length." He spoke in a light, dismissive tone.

His lack of concern made Charlotte groan inwardly. "Sir, you're humoring me when you should be taking my warning seriously. You're giving her the benefit of the doubt on the off chance she's sincere. And that could be a grave mistake." Charlotte glanced at him sideways and held her breath.

"I do thank you for that admonition" — he gave a wry smile — "but you needn't worry."

She tried to hide her apprehension, but she felt the muscles in her face tighten. "You're so open you leave yourself vulnerable to people with dishonorable intentions."

Professor Wilmont shrugged. "Maybe, but I won't turn my back on anyone. The Lord will protect me if necessary." He frowned. "Why do you look skeptical? Don't you believe that?"

She should say, "Yes, of course I do." But she couldn't force the words. Professor Wilmont ought to trust his own common sense, not rely on a God who was out there somewhere beyond the moon and the stars — certainly not close enough to offer personal counsel or assistance. Though lately she'd sought to communicate with Him through prayer. She thought He might be listening, but she couldn't be sure.

"God doesn't always protect us from harm," she said softly. He'd taken her parents and brother John all within weeks. Influenza had struck them, and He hadn't intervened. Sadness laced with anger ripped her heart — even now, years after they'd died.

His eyebrows arched in astonishment. "Perhaps not physically, but the Lord keeps us from spiritual peril and that's what counts in the long run." Professor Wilmont regarded her with a steady gaze that cut right through her.

She looked down at the stones and twigs scattered across the lane. "I suppose so."

She knew all about the physical harm that came from disease and pain and death, but what exactly was *spiritual* harm? She had so much to learn and experience. Her Scripture reading and feeble attempts at prayer had given her a taste, though it was hard to forgive a God who stole half her family and left her with the other half to take care of.

He gave her arm a conciliatory pat. "At any rate, I appreciate your concern. Not many governesses take such a special interest in their employers."

She scrutinized his face for sarcasm but found gratitude instead. She pushed away the sad memories, as she always did when they came to mind, and dragged her focus back to the present. Why was the professor so open and trusting of others, ignoring their less-than-honest motives, her own included? She appreciated his transparency, but she couldn't quite understand how the Lord could become such a force in one's life to direct every thought and deed. It was beyond her comprehension. Yet with her job nearly finished, it didn't matter. She'd soon go home. Whether or not she succeeded in Mr. Phifer's eyes remained to be seen.

"You look troubled, Miss Hale." He read her like a book. And that's what she was — an overblown, overdrawn character from one of Elna Price's outrageous dime novels — filled with joy, angst, remorse, and fear all rolled into one pathetic story.

Charlotte pulled on her cheerful mask and forced a smile. "I'm fine."

As they came to the ivy-covered brick buildings, the professor's penetrating gaze drew her in. "I'm always nearby if you care to talk."

"Thank you. I do have things on my mind, but nothing to burden you with, sir." She clamped her mouth shut.

They followed Ruthie and Tim to the benches set in front of the bandstand where the concertgoers were gathering in small groups. Well-dressed ladies and gentlemen crowded together on the hard seats and chatted with friends. Their conversations rose above the noise of the brass band tuning their instruments. Several children raced across the wide swath of grass while most remained under the watchful eyes of their parents. Ruthie and Tim slid into the back row and motioned to their father, but Professor Wilmont held back.

"Save us a place, please. We'll be there in a few minutes," he said.

Charlotte followed him to a corner of the lawn, bathed in early evening shadows. They settled onto a stone bench set beneath a silver maple shimmering in the pale light. Still in full view of the other concertgoers, they were several yards away and out of earshot.

Charlotte's heart thudded against her ribs. Why did he want privacy — with her? His colleagues and their wives glanced their way with obvious curiosity. What was a professor doing huddling with a servant? She wondered herself. A rich young woman who belonged to the smart set ought to stir his interest, not a governess with a hidden agenda. She must discourage his attention at once, if that's what it was. But as she edged away, the professor inched closer.

"Miss Hale, let me explain why I try to be open and accessible, even to those who may not have my best interests at heart. It's not because I'm too stupid to spot trouble."

Charlotte tossed him a droll smile. "You don't owe me an explanation."

"I know. But I feel compelled to tell you anyway."

"All right."

He looked to the horizon, as if remembering. "When Ruthie and Tim were young, I returned to Yale for an advanced degree. My wife cared for the children while I tried to study. But they shouted and cried so much, I couldn't concentrate. Sarah thought

I should quit the university and work for my father, but I couldn't see myself as a businessman. So I spent long hours at the university library to avoid the children . . . and Sarah too. She begged me to stay home more often, but I refused." He wrung his hands. "I didn't understand the extent of her melancholy. Then one night I arrived home from class, and she and the children were gone."

"Oh my," Charlotte murmured. In the approaching dusk she saw pain etched in Professor Wilmont's face. If only she dared to reach up and touch his skin and smooth away the sorrow.

"Sarah left me a note detailing all of my shortcomings." He grimaced. "She accused me of being selfish. I'm afraid she was right on target. I didn't spend enough time with her and the children. She was overwhelmed and alone. And I was to blame."

Charlotte's heart raced. "What happened then?" She touched his hand and then snatched it away, afraid someone might observe her gesture.

"Sarah moved home to her parents. I followed and apologized, but she demanded a divorce anyway." His voice broke. "That nearly destroyed me."

"But you reconciled, didn't you?" Living

apart was unusual and divorce practically unheard of. It would have caused a scandal still gossiped about to this day.

"Eventually she agreed to give our marriage another try."

"Does your story have a happy ending?" After reading the journal, she feared it didn't.

Professor Wilmont's shoulders slumped. "Not a storybook ending, I'm afraid. We worked hard to make each other happy, but we were only partially successful." Groaning, he looked past the bandstand toward the sea, his eyes clouded. "Then a year later Sarah died in a coaching accident."

"I'm so sorry," Charlotte said, touched that he'd confide his deepest failures.

He looked directly into her eyes. "So now if someone requests my assistance, I give it gladly with no questions asked. I believe Sarah turned away from the Lord because I turned away from her. I didn't realize I was running from my marriage while I was burying myself in my studies, but I was."

"And that's why you won't dismiss Miss LeBeau." Now his attitude made more sense.

"That's right. I don't want her to turn away from the Lord because I was too thoughtless to help."

Charlotte nodded. "Of course, as a Bible professor you have to set an example."

"As a decent human being and as a Christian, I need to set an example and practice what I preach."

"I understand." *To an extent.* But setting a good example was quite beside the point. "Just stay on your guard. Your student is concerned about her own best interests, not yours."

"Don't worry. I shall be careful. That's why I suggested she hire a tutor."

The professor's version of his marriage sounded so different from the stories Sarah shared in her journal, especially the ones about another man. Did Professor Wilmont learn of Sarah's infidelity? If not, he must have suspected something was amiss. But he hadn't allowed bitterness to affect his relationships with other people or with his God. He was a truly remarkable man.

She wished she were more like him.

TWELVE

They took their places beside Ruthie and Tim and listened to the brass band fill the hot summer evening with snappy military marches interspersed with a few popular waltzes. Daniel barely heard the music. Against his will and better judgment, he focused on the lovely governess by his side. Out of the corner of his eye he glimpsed the brim of her straw hat devoid of satin ribbons and bows, as charming and practical as Miss Hale herself.

His gaze swept her perfect profile — the slight tilt of her nose, her sculptured cheeks, and full, pink lips. He wanted to loop his arm around her right here amidst his students, colleagues, and their families. But he was already in more than enough trouble with the college without adding impropriety. Yet nothing could distract him from Miss Hale. Her smile brought sunshine to Summerhill, drawing him home from class with the music of her laughter and her playful chiding he'd grown to enjoy.

He leaned back on the bench and drank in the evening. Behind the bandstand the sun dipped toward the water, painting the sky with peach and rose swirls. They were the colors of his world — at least the one he imaged for his future. But gradually the brilliance faded and folded into the night sky. He couldn't hold on to the glory of the sunset. And he couldn't hold on to this moment — or to Miss Hale. Beneath her golden smile lay a young woman with darker, deeper shades to her personality than she seemed willing to share. Yet somehow it seemed so right to sit beside her as the moon rose and the stars blinked and the music played on.

When they returned to Summerhill, he said good night and retreated to his bedroom. Charlotte's determination to face life without flinching had convinced him to bury the past and look only to the future. While his head was in the clouds, her feet were rooted to the ground.

Perhaps he should glance through Sarah's journal one last time and then toss it into the fire. Reading it again and again had kept the final remnants of pain locked inside his heart. He padded over to the wardrobe and removed Sarah's old hatbox and placed it on the bed. As he opened the cover he realized how much he needed to let her hateful words burn to ash. She'd spilled all her emotions onto these pages, the last testament of their charred marriage.

Yet did he have the courage to leave it all behind? He searched the hatbox, but the journal was gone. Daniel fumbled through it again and then glanced around. Had he misplaced it, as he had so many other things?

"Everyone is talking about you and the professor going to the concert tonight," Grace said in the dim light of Charlotte's bedroom. "I told them it was your job to watch the children, so of course you went along. But they think Tim and Ruthie don't need constant care. And they say if you were old or ugly he'd have taken them by himself."

A groan escaped from Charlotte's throat. "I can't speak for Professor Wilmont, but I can speak for myself. He's my employer, nothing more. Why would the professor be interested in me? I'm just a governess. He could court any number of rich ladies. He's a fine, well-connected gentleman." *And handsome, to boot.* Still, they had a point.

The professor didn't need to take her along.

"I just wanted you to know the staff likes to gossip. Professor Wilmont hasn't shown interest in any lady since his wife passed away, so this is causing quite a stir. They believe he's interested in you romantically. They watch everything he says and does. So do take care, because they'll be watching you as well."

Charlotte nodded. "Thank you for warning me." She'd be extra vigilant from now on.

Once Grace departed, Charlotte dropped into bed, tired yet filled with nervous energy that wouldn't let her sleep. Professor Wilmont's smile filled her mind. He liked her, she felt sure of that, but of course he didn't have romance on his mind. Mrs. Wilmont would burst all her buttons if she thought her son even noticed anyone in their employ. Charlotte had heard that sometimes wealthy gentlemen paid undue and inappropriate attention to their maids, but she wasn't that kind of girl and the professor wasn't that kind of man. It was all too ridiculous.

All the next day Charlotte's mind churned as she searched for a plausible excuse to venture into town again without eliciting questions from Vivian Wilmont. She had to relay the news of the professor's innocence as soon as possible. But nothing turned up, so she spent the morning riding bicycles with Tim and Ruthie and later enjoying a few sunny hours at Bailey's Beach, the only beach set aside exclusively for the rich. In the afternoon they each took turns reading aloud *The Legend of Sleepy Hollow,* followed by arithmetic lessons and piano practice.

The following morning, Mrs. Wilmont summoned Charlotte to the drawing room. She hurried to the matron's side lest she accuse Charlotte of malingering.

"Yes, ma'am?"

The professor's mother glanced up from her needlework. Seated in the morning room on her favorite chintz-covered chair, she looked wrinkled as a prune with all the life sucked out of her. But her voice rose in a commanding tone designed to send servants scurrying.

"I want you to purchase some blue thread at Nancy's Notions on upper Thames Street. I can't continue until you return." She waved Charlotte out the door. "I have an account, so you will not need any money."

"Yes, ma'am."

"I'd send Simone, but she's adding a bit of lace to my dress for the dinner I'm hosting for the Grails. See that you buy the right shade of thread. Royal blue, not navy."

Charlotte winced at the woman's insulting manner, but how fortunate she finally needed something right away and Simone was too busy to fetch it. When Mrs. Wilmont required an item, it was always immediately, never "later, at your convenience." Her manner made Charlotte pity the legions of girls and women who endlessly toiled in the mansions of the privileged with little compensation or thanks. At least she'd return to her own home in a matter of days.

"I'll be back as soon as I can, ma'am."

"See that you don't dawdle. And ask Mrs. Finnegan to watch the children."

Charlotte bit back a retort, nodded, and left. If she sassed Mrs. Wilmont, the old gargoyle would happily dismiss her.

Within minutes she drove off in the gig, anxious to accomplish her errand before facing Mr. Phifer.

Once in town she purchased the correct shade of thread and hurried the two blocks to the *Rhode Island Reporter.* Her heartbeat clicked faster than the sound of typewriter keys that greeted her as she entered the main newsroom. Several reporters smiled and waved as they continued to work.

Mr. Phifer, dressed in a light gray suit, came out of his office and turned his attention to Charlotte.

"Ah, Miss Hale. I was wondering when I'd hear from you again." He rubbed his hands together in anticipation as he led her into his office and shut the door. "I'd like you to report more often, but I suppose that it's difficult to get away from Summerhill."

"Yes, sir, it is."

"Tell me your news."

Charlotte swallowed hard but stood straight and tall, unwilling to cower, though her news was mixed. "My investigation is progressing well." She breathed deeply. "I met Miss Melissa LeBeau."

"You did? That's splendid."

Charlotte heard the glow in his voice. He directed her to take a seat in front of his desk. Gratefully, she sat on the edge of the hard chair. She took a few seconds to calm herself before she began her report.

"Miss LeBeau is definitely enamored with Professor Wilmont, but I'm convinced the feeling isn't mutual. Not at all."

Mr. Phifer stood between the two open windows with his head down and hands clasped behind his back. His long pause signified displeasure. When he looked up, he glared with such ferocity Charlotte's breath caught in her lungs. Just as she feared — he expected her to discredit the professor. How could she have ever thought him fair and impartial?

"That doesn't sound right to me. You must have misread his reaction to the girl," he said.

Intimidated but not crushed, she squared her shoulders and lifted her chin ever so slightly. "No, sir, I assure you I did not." His frown warned her to tone down her report, yet she had to tell the truth. "I'm convinced he's not guilty of any impropriety." She met his gaze, but her throat went so dry she could hardly swallow.

Mr. Phifer gave a condescending chuckle. "He's trying to throw you off track. I'm disappointed in you, Miss Hale. I was sure you were a shrewd judge of character. That's why I sent you on this crucial assignment."

Charlotte bit back a sarcastic reply. "I'm an excellent judge of character, sir."

"I'm not so sure." He paused, drew his brows together, and inhaled the aromatic tobacco from his clenched pipe. After a while he placed it in his ashtray. "I'll tell you what. I'll give you a bit more time to redeem yourself. You stay put for a while longer and search a whole lot more thoroughly for some real evidence. Don't give me your opinion. Give me facts. Incriminating facts. I know they're ripe for the picking."

"All right, sir, as long as you realize the rumor about Professor Wilmont and Miss LeBeau isn't credible."

His snowy eyebrows met in a scowl. "Why are you so insistent? I know considerably more about human nature than you do, young woman. So keep an eagle eye on those two and don't let the man trick you into believing he's a white knight. Do you hear me?"

"I do, sir, but — I still believe you're mistaken." Charlotte trembled at her boldness and clutched her hands to keep them from shaking. Why was she provoking her boss?

He grimaced. "I don't appreciate an employee contradicting me, especially a flighty inexperienced female." His face turned brick red while his eyes bore into hers. "I expect you to report back to me in three days with information I can use. I'm depending on you."

"Yes, Mr. Phifer." She tried to sound enthusiastic and confident, but her voice faltered as she stood.

"I'll be out of the office most of the beginning of the week, but I can squeeze you in

260

at one o'clock on Monday. I'm having lunch at O'Neill's Cafe at noon, so meet me there at one sharp. You won't have trouble getting away, will you?"

She might with Mrs. Wilmont suddenly running her life, but she'd manage to conjure up a reason to come into town. "I'll be there."

Mr. Phifer nodded. "Good day, Miss Hale. I expect you'll hand me some solid news on Monday afternoon." He wagged a finger. "And remember to follow up on Missy LeBeau. I'm sure she's the key to all of this." With a wave of his hand he swatted Charlotte away as if she were a fly.

"I'll continue to search for the truth." She struggled to lace her voice with optimism.

His stare drilled into her. "And while you search make sure you find some useful evidence, Miss Hale."

"Yes, sir." Charlotte gulped.

She turned on her heel and headed out the door, stifling a sigh that arose from deep inside. Mr. Phifer chose to ignore the facts when they contradicted his opinions. Nothing she said could convince him the professor wasn't corrupt or immoral. She'd always considered Mr. Phifer to be fair-minded, but he didn't seem to be so anymore. As a secretary she hadn't been aware of his strong biases, so she'd undoubtedly given him more credit than he deserved.

Charlotte descended the staircase to the first floor. Perhaps she should quit her job on principle, though she'd never known anyone to resign because of Mr. Phifer's tactics. Given her circumstances all she could do was accept the world's injustice. She couldn't fight it alone and it was certainly easier to adjust to its flaws than confront it head on. Hardly an attitude to boast about, but common enough.

Charlotte returned to Summerhill, gave Mrs. Wilmont the thread, and found the children who were more than ready to put away their grammar lessons. Together they headed for the boulders that edged most of the back lawn. Tim and his toy soldiers fought a valiant battle on the rocks, staying distant from the sea. Charlotte and Ruthie sketched sailboats riding the surf as squawking seagulls skimmed through the bright blue sky. Charlotte's pencil flew across the paper, forming shapes created by nature itself. No, created by God. She'd never thought of it quite that way before, but it was true.

She watched Ruthie draw a rock formation with its crevices splashed with salt water and seaweed. Only a few feet away, a fiddler crab scrambled over the stone toward the damp sand. Charlotte turned around and drew Summerhill with its wide veranda and mansard roof. She'd always enjoyed drawing, though she'd seldom had time to indulge in a hobby.

"Sketching is such fun, Miss Hale. Can we do this every day? Fresh air is good for us, isn't it?"

"Yes, indeed. And since art is an academic subject, we can classify our drawing as genuine schoolwork." Charlotte flashed a smile. "Do you think your grandmother would agree?"

"I don't believe so, but she seems too busy with her friend Mr. McClintock to worry about us."

When they returned to the cottage, sun-warmed and a bit less pale despite their hats and long-sleeved clothes, Charlotte went up to the playroom while the children joined their grandmother in the drawing room. A laundress delivered several of Ruthie's dresses, washed and pressed. Charlotte hung them in the girl's wardrobe, careful not to wrinkle the fabrics.

Her mind returned to her predicament. Her prospects of a journalism career and security for her family would end soon unless she satisfied Mr. Phifer's obsession to ruin Professor Wilmont. Apprehension slithered through her, spreading tentacles of panic. No, she wouldn't let fear defeat her. Maybe God would help if she prayed — a novel idea, but worth a try.

Lord, I never bother You with my troubles, but this time they're so serious, I can't handle them myself. Please help me find a solution — by Monday. You know I can't maintain this pretense much longer. I want to go home and return to my old life. And I need to flee from the professor before I grow to care for him. A little too much.

She didn't know if the Lord listened to prayers, but she did feel somewhat better. So maybe He did care, just as the Bible said. Every night she read a few more chapters, intrigued by the possibilities of a God who loved His children with a passion she could scarcely comprehend. It pricked her already troubled mind, yet the words of Scripture also brought a growing sense of hope. She couldn't explain it, but she felt her heart slowly opening like a rose, one petal at a time.

Lord, I need to find a new job and I don't know where to look. I doubt the Newport Gazette *would hire a former employee of Arnie Phifer's, especially if they discovered I'd spied on Professor Wilmont. How shall I sup-*

port Aunt Amelia and Becky? The professor counts on You. Can I do the same?

Charlotte hung up the last of Ruthie's gingham frocks in her pink-and-white bedroom just as the professor strolled into the children's playroom.

"Have you seen Ruthie and Tim? I can't seem to find them." He leaned against the doorframe. His glasses slid down his nose, giving him a scholarly yet boyish appearance. His longish hair glinted with golden highlights and slipped down across his tanned forehead.

Charlotte cleared her throat. "They're playing dominos in the game room with your mother and Mr. McClintock, I believe."

The professor smiled. "Ah, Mr. McClintock again. My mother really enjoys his visits. And speaking of my mother, how are you two getting along?"

Charlotte tried to keep a straight face, but a sardonic smile escaped with a turn of her lips. "All right, I suppose. She doesn't seem to like me very well, but when she asks me to do something, I serve her as best I can."

"Excellent. In time she'll grow to appreciate you just as I do."

Charlotte sputtered, "Thank you, sir." She turned away as a blush scorched her face.

265

Surely she was misinterpreting his remarks and letting her imagination carry her away.

"What's troubling you, Charlotte?" he asked. "I'm sorry. Miss Hale."

"Please, sir, call me Charlotte. It's quite all right."

He nodded, looking pleased. She let his question hover in the warm summer air unanswered. A sudden urge to confess swept through her, but thank goodness, the words strangled in her throat. He seemed to have a way of disarming her, leaving her vulnerable to his empathy.

"My life is too complicated to explain, so I'll not even try. But thank you for caring enough to ask." She caught her breath.

He nodded and frowned in confusion. "I didn't mean to pry."

Charlotte looked down at the cabbage-rose carpet, which probably had less color than her cheeks. She felt his gaze rest upon her, but she couldn't look at him directly without pouring out her confusion. So much was changing in her life and in her heart.

Professor Wilmont reached toward her. For a moment she thought he'd wrap his arm around her shoulder, but instead, he dropped it to his side. A pinch of disappointment squeezed her chest, along with relief.

"I'm really easy to talk to, Charlotte."

He was her boss. Her temporary boss. Nothing more. "I'll remember that, sir. I'm going down to the kitchen for tea. Would you like me to bring you a cup?"

"Yes please, if you'll join me on the veranda."

Charlotte hesitated. "Of course, sir. If you wish."

A short time later they sat side by side on the wicker chairs, teacups in hand. A mild breeze buffeted Charlotte's flushed cheeks and hummed in her ears. It carried the scent of the sea and blended with perfume from wild roses that grew along the shore and in the garden. She breathed deeply and her heart calmed.

"Charlotte, I want to thank you for listening to me last night" — he grinned — "and giving me your opinion."

"I apologize if I spoke too forcefully, but I did — enjoy — our conversation, as well, though it wasn't altogether proper. I'm a governess, not someone you'd ordinarily confide in." She ought to excuse herself and run from his radiant gaze.

"Normally I don't confide in anyone." He hesitated for a moment. "Charlotte, I'd like to spend more time with you. As long as you don't think I'm too intrusive, I'd love to hear more about your family and your childhood —"

Charlotte stiffened her back. Her teacup and saucer rattled in her shaking hand. "Sir, I don't believe that's suitable or wise." She gulped. "And why do you want to know about me? I'll only be here for a short time and then you'll never see me again, except perhaps around town. So what is the point of learning more, sir?"

Obviously taken aback, Professor Wilmont gazed at her, his eyes soft and filled with emotion. "I've grown fond of you, Charlotte. I thought we liked each other's company. Was I wrong?"

At first her words clogged in her throat and she had to force them out. "I'm a temporary employee in your home, nothing more. You best remember that, sir. And so must I. I ought to check on the children." She stood.

The light in his eyes dimmed. "I'd hoped that in time something more might develop between us. It doesn't matter to me whether you're a governess or a great lady from one of the cottages."

"Oh, but it does matter. It matters very much." Charlotte set her cup down on the table. Tea splashed in the saucer and her spoon rattled against the china. Then he arose and his size alone overpowered her. But a man with such kind eyes could never intimidate.

"Sir, you think you want to know me better," she said, daring to look up at him, "but if you did, you'd be disappointed. I'm not the woman for you. So let's forget we ever said these things."

"Indeed, you should." A strident voice interrupted. "This is disgraceful, Daniel. Charlotte, leave me alone with my son." Mrs. Wilmont leaned against the doorway, her face parchment white. Slightly hunched, she appeared physically fragile, yet fierce in spirit. Her eyes burned bright. "Go, Charlotte. Now."

Charlotte scurried inside but lurked behind the door, poised to listen. Her heart pounded so loudly she feared she wouldn't hear Mrs. Wilmont's voice. But she did hear every angry word.

"What is the meaning of this ridiculous talk between you and the governess? What's gotten into you?"

Daniel answered in a level tone. "I'm quite fond of Charlotte and I'd like to really get to know her."

"That's out of the question. If you want a

wife, find one who is suitable, not a town girl with no money and no background. You've taken leave of your senses."

"Mother, I see no point in discussing this."

"I want her dismissed, Daniel."

A long pause ensued. Charlotte held her breath until she heard Professor Wilmont's calm voice.

"She stays."

They were coming in. Charlotte quickly retreated to the library. While the professor strode down the hallway, his mother followed at a slower pace, sputtering her objections all the way. Charlotte drew a sigh of relief when no one noticed her beside the high bookshelf.

Professor Wilmont's declaration of interest had startled her. She'd liked him right from the beginning, though she didn't wish to admire the man she was sent to destroy. But she had never expected *liking* might blossom into genuine *fondness*.

Under different circumstances she might allow Professor Wilmont into her life, though no matter what the conditions, she wasn't sure she *wanted* a man, and a religious one at that. Of course, all this speculation was silly. It was over before it had even begun, anyway. The notion of romance was as utterly preposterous. Charlotte sighed and left the library in search of the children.

Finding the game room empty, she headed down to the kitchen where she found them devouring cream puffs.

"Come join me for a short break while the young ones indulge," Mrs. Finnegan urged. "How about walking over to the garden? The fresh air would do us both a world of good."

"I'd like that. Ruthie, Tim, please stay put until I return."

They nodded as Tim reached for another treat.

Charlotte followed behind Mrs. Finnegan as they exited the cottage and started down the pebbled path toward the rose garden.

"I want to talk to you without big ears listening to every word. Let's sit for a spell." Mrs. Finnegan swatted a bee that buzzed around her crooked bun.

They strolled beneath the rose arbor and inhaled the fragrance of hundreds of blossoms.

"What is it? Did I do something wrong?" Charlotte asked as she dropped onto a stone bench shaded by the skirt of a leafy maple. Mrs. Finnegan lowered her considerable bulk beside her.

"No, dearie. But to be blunt, the staff is gossiping about you and Professor Wilmont.

Your friend Grace probably gave you an ear-ful already. Didn't I try to hush those wag-ging tongues, but it's near impossible when they all see how fondly he looks at you. He's not one to hide his affection."

Charlotte sighed. "I want you to know the professor behaves most honorably toward me."

Mrs. Finnegan chuckled. "O'course he does. He's a gentleman, through and through. But he's lonely." She leaned toward a prime rosebud, bent to sniff it, then looked back at Charlotte. "Let me tell you about his wife, Sarah, God rest her soul. I think it's important to know a bit o' the past, in order to engage the present."

"Of course." Charlotte shifted her weight on the uncomfortable stone.

"A society girl, Sarah was. Rich and elegant like the millionaire ladies living in those Bellevue Avenue palaces." The old lady's gaze sharpened. "I'll not be saying a word against her because it's wrong to speak ill of the dead. She was a lovely young woman with a zest for living. But not easily satisfied." Mrs. Finnegan opened her mouth as if to say something more, then clamped it shut.

Charlotte turned her face to the side, afraid to reveal her feelings for a man she had no right to care for. "The professor loved her?"

"Indeed, in his own way. He's gone without love and happiness for a long while, the poor man. And it began far before Sarah died. He is lonely." Mrs. Finnegan searched Charlotte's face with questioning eyes. Frowning, she tilted her head. "Forgive me for saying so, but it's easy for a young miss to fall for a gentleman without meaning to. When I was a lass and new in service, I tumbled head over heels in love with my employer's son. But I soon realized happiness lay with the head gardener, Mr. Finnegan. And marry him, I did. Thank the good Lord for showing me the way. We two . . . we *belonged* together."

Charlotte bit her lip from the not-too-subtle warning. Mrs. Finnegan was probably smart to marry among her own class and nationality. Charlotte knew she ought to take heed. The barriers separating her from the professor stretched far beyond even those differences. They were impossible to overcome. If he knew . . . knew the full extent of her duplicity . . . She shook her head and forced a smile.

"You're right, Mrs. Finnegan, and I thank you for your wise words. You needn't worry about the professor. I have no intention of ever being anything more to him than his children's governess."

In the last light of evening, Charlotte sat by her bedroom window, cleared her mind of the day's events, and read another newspaper column written by the professor. His columns had certainly piqued her interest in spiritual matters.

We're creatures designed by God, for God. He has a purpose and a plan for each and every one of us, which He wishes us to follow. But first we must place Him first in our lives, confess our transgressions, and ask for forgiveness. Then we must place the needs of others before our own. This is almost always a difficult and often a painful task. But with the Lord's help, it is possible, and it's what He wants from us and commands of us.

Charlotte returned the column to the others on her chest of drawers. What kind of plan or purpose did the Lord have for her life? Of course He wanted her to care for her family. But did He have something else in mind as well? If she was supposed to pursue journalism, then surely He wouldn't want her to use deceptive methods to advance. Charlotte sighed as she glanced out the window into the dusky sky. *Lord, if You have a purpose for me, please show me what it is and how I ought to go about it. This is all quite confusing. But I think You can make things clear.*

Maybe God had another plan in mind, other than a career. She'd have to wait and see and continue to pray. If she hadn't come to Summerhill, she never would've paid much attention to the professor's columns and turned toward the Lord. Was that part of God's plan too?

THIRTEEN

Two days later, Daniel feared this Sunday morning would be especially chaotic without Charlotte to haul the children out of bed and find appropriate church clothes. After breakfast all the servants had Sunday morning free for worship service. So he was on his own and unprepared. Usually his mother found Tim and Ruthie appropriate clothes, but today she was in bed sleeping, still tired and weak.

He checked on Ruthie and Tim and found them both dressed for church and waiting in their playroom.

"I'm ready to go, Papa. Miss Hale and I picked out my church clothes." Ruthie spun around in a white frock with a blue sash at her waist, her face aglow. "Do you like my new dress?"

"You look lovely."

She smoothed her auburn hair pulled back at the crown with a ribbon. "Miss Hale fixed my hair differently. No braids." Glancing in the mirror, she examined her reflection. "What do you think, Papa? Do I look older?"

Daniel laughed. He was hardly the best one to judge hairstyles. "Beautiful. And I do believe you look all of thirteen."

A minute later, Tim appeared in the playroom nearly awake and dressed in a sailor suit with a crooked navy blue tie.

"Since we're presentable, perhaps we can have a quick breakfast and leave for church." Oatmeal soon arrived via the dumbwaiter and the three ate in the playroom.

As they headed for the door after breakfast, Bibles in hand, Charlotte stepped into the room.

"Good morning, everyone." Her gaze swept by Daniel and settled on the children. Automatically she adjusted Tim's crooked blue tie and pulled down the bunched shirt of his white sailor suit.

Delight mixed with anxiety rippled through Daniel's chest. Yesterday he'd declared his feelings for her and she'd rejected his overture. *So be it.* A person couldn't force someone to care for them. He'd learned that sobering lesson from Sarah. He'd leave this in the Lord's hands and pray that He had a plan to somehow bring them together. Their friendship might appear unsuitable to many — probably most — people, but he didn't think their social differences should raise an insurmountable barrier. At least for him, they counted for little.

He twitched a smile when Charlotte entered the playroom. "We'd be pleased if you'd join us for church, Miss Hale. We're about to start off."

Bewilderment flashed across her face before she nodded. "Of course, if you'll excuse me, I'll fetch my hat."

She returned in short order dressed in a becoming light gray skirt and jacket and her unadorned straw hat. Softer and lovelier than in her uniform, Charlotte Hale was the prettiest woman he'd ever seen.

"Shall we go?" Daniel's voice scratched.

They departed Summerhill, cut across the lawn, and headed for Cove Road, the easiest route to the campus church.

"You forgot your Bible, Miss Hale." Ruthie's face scrunched in a frown as they strolled across the dewy grass.

"So I did." Charlotte smiled and continued to walk.

"We'll wait for you if you want to get it," Daniel said.

She shook her head. "It's not necessary, is it?"

"We have Bibles in church, so you really don't need your own," Daniel said.

Ruthie chimed in, "We always bring our Bibles to worship service."

"I — I'm sorry. I didn't know that."

"Don't you bring your Bible at your church?" Ruthie asked.

"I must admit I'm not a frequent church-goer. I mean, I don't go as often as I should."

Ruthie's eyes widened. "We're supposed to read Scripture every day as well."

Charlotte grinned at Daniel's cheeky daughter. "I read the one in my bedroom every night before I go to sleep."

Daniel couldn't stifle a grin. "Excellent." The Lord was most definitely working in her heart. Relief washed over him.

They strolled side by side, but not so close that anyone on Cove Road would notice. Charlotte didn't even glance at him during the entire walk to the college, though she responded politely to his feeble attempts at small talk. He found the effort tiring and soon gave up. Charlotte seemed lost in her own musings or perhaps in the memory of his intemperate admission. He usually considered his thoughts carefully before divulging them. Well, this proved to be a valuable lesson. From now on he'd guard his tongue and not be so quick to jump into the briar patch of romance.

They turned down the path leading to the fellowship hall and followed Tim and Ruthie into the building. It was designed in the same Georgian style as the rest of the college, with ivy trailing down its red brick walls, which had faded over the last thirty years.

"Where are we going?" Charlotte frowned.

"To Sunday school, of course." Tim flung open a classroom door. Inside, a gaggle of youngsters ran around while their teacher, a distraught young woman, clapped her hands in a futile attempt to impose order.

"Do behave yourself, Tim."

Daniel led Charlotte to the end of the hallway and entered a small room with a group of about twenty or thirty men and women settled in rows like a lecture hall. Daniel introduced Charlotte to some of his friends and colleagues and the Sunday school teacher. Her voice barely rose above a squeak and her gaze darted around the room as if she were searching for an escape. What happened to her friendly, confident manner? Maybe she was newer to the faith than he'd previously thought. He retrieved a Bible from the bookshelf and handed it to her. She looked uncomfortable. Or was he imagining it?

The Sunday school leader gave her a bright, welcoming grin. "Can you tell us a little about yourself, Miss Hale?"

"Um, of course." She cleared her throat. "I'm the Wilmonts' new governess. I live on the Point with my aunt and my sister." She flicked a tentative smile and sat down.

"We're so glad you joined us this morning. Where do you normally worship?"

She hesitated. "I attend different churches. But while I'm working for the Wilmonts, I'll be coming here."

She looked at Daniel for confirmation, her forehead creased. He nodded. Why was she practically whispering?

"Good to have you with us. We'll look forward to seeing you on Sundays."

Bowing her head over the Scriptures, Charlotte's mesh veil concealed most of her face. Throughout the discussion she hardly moved a muscle and never once added a comment or posed a question. Very unlike Charlotte. From time to time her fingers fanned the pages of her Bible or fidgeted in her lap. When the teacher directed everyone to turn to a particular chapter and verse, Charlotte consulted the table of contents first. This meant nothing, of course, except that she wasn't as familiar with the text as most longtime Christians. And she didn't feel comfortable among these strangers. Or did it mean something else? He shuddered to think she might have misled him about her faith.

"Did you like the class?" Daniel asked later as they headed for the sanctuary.

She quirked an odd smile. "I learned a lot."

I learned I'm mired in quicksand and I want to get out of here!

How had Mr. Phifer ever convinced her she could pull off this ridiculous charade? Pretending to be a Christian was impossible. Straightforward and direct — that was how she thought of herself. Truly, she wasn't a liar, at least not until this assignment. She didn't fool the professor. She felt quite sure of that. He stared at her with narrowed eyes every time she fumbled through her Bible, unable to locate anything past Genesis. He must know, or strongly suspect, she wasn't a genuine Christian. Perspiration coated her skin despite the cool air flowing through the open front doors of the church. She rubbed her palms against her skirt, resisting the urge to mop her brow.

Sliding into the pew between Professor Wilmont and Ruthie, Charlotte took her seat and glanced around the plain, almost stark room. People of all ages crowded shoulder to shoulder, chatting quietly.

The robed singers filed to the right of the pulpit and focused on their director. Bursting into song, they raised their voices to the rooftop, blending and harmonizing like a choir of angels. Then the congregation joined in, belting out an upbeat hymn she'd never heard before. Charlotte glanced around. No one else needed to read the lyrics from the hymnal.

Ruthie peeked sideways and whispered, "Don't you know the words?"

"I'm afraid not. We sing different hymns."

"Like what?" Ruthie insisted. Professor Wilmont frowned and the girl reluctantly turned toward the front.

The songs were so easy to sing, Charlotte joined in softly at first and then louder as a few of the melodies became familiar. The lyrics must come from Scripture. Words about the Holy Ghost, the Comforter, the Counselor. She'd certainly appreciate guidance from the Holy Ghost and confirmation that she was doing the right thing. But how could any holy personage give snooping a nod of approval?

For no discernable reason tears stung the back of her eyelids and threatened to spill down her hot skin. What had come over her? Was she disintegrating emotionally? Or was she just responding to the wonderful music?

A feeling of peace settled into her heart and then intensified, leaving her alone with . . . God?

Charlotte was surprised that the unexpected warmth lingered even after they left the sanctuary. Savoring her spiritual experience, she felt a part of a new realm she hadn't known, though after reading the Bible several times before bed, she suspected there might be something far beyond her experience and knowledge. Unable to define it, she let God's unseen presence overwhelm her with joy, quite different from the familiar happiness that appeared and disappeared so easily.

She needed to ponder the feelings the church service had stirred in her heart. "I believe I'll take a walk around the campus and enjoy the beautiful afternoon."

"Then we'll see you later," Daniel said, looking a bit disappointed. He headed down Cove Road, glanced back, and waved.

Charlotte waved back. With a light spirit, she strolled across the lawn toward the bandstand. Several young ladies, students she presumed, gathered on the benches, giggling and chatting. Missy LeBeau sat right in their midst. Charlotte dropped onto a stone bench under the shade of an elm and watched her from a discreet distance. Missy was the swan amid the ducks. Her cream-colored frock stood out among the charcoal gray and brown garments the other students wore. Even her laughter rang out above their giggles.

"May I join you?" asked a young woman dressed in a dark plum walking suit without lace or trim. It shaded a square face punctuated with plain features. Charlotte recognized her from the church. "Lovely service, wasn't it?" she asked as Charlotte motioned her to sit.

"Yes, indeed."

"I'm Agnes Brownington. I'm a freshman."

"How do you do? I'm Charlotte Hale, governess to Professor Wilmont's children."

"Yes, I noticed you sitting with him in church."

They chatted amiably before their attention drifted to the girls by the bandstand. Agnes's mouth tightened so much her lips nearly disappeared. "They're a rowdy group, especially the blonde with the cat eyes. Missy LeBeau. She's in Professor Wilmont's

New Testament class with me."

Charlotte's nerves stood on end. "Oh? I take it you're not close friends."

Agnes shook her head. "You are indeed correct. We're the only two women in the class."

"Is Miss LeBeau a good student?"

A grunt escaped Agnes's throat. "The very worst." She leaned closer while keeping her gaze fixed on Missy. "She's a disgrace to our sex."

"Truly? Why is that?" Charlotte asked.

"She's chasing Professor Wilmont all over campus. Everyone's noticed. She ought to be ashamed, but she's not. She flaunts herself like a hussy. Someone ought to report her behavior to the dean."

"And the professor, how does he react to the attention?" Charlotte leaned closer.

Agnes's eyes narrowed. "He dislikes it, I can assure you. He's a model Christian man."

"I agree. But Miss LeBeau is not a model Christian woman?"

"Not in the least. She ought to be expelled."

With nerves twitching, Charlotte pumped Agnes for details, but the girl soon rose. "If you'll excuse me I must be off to the dining hall or I'll miss my meal. It was so pleasant conversing with you, Miss Hale."

At least Agnes had confirmed Charlotte's assessment of the professor and his brazen student. Her instincts were right.

Then the young woman turned around. "I've heard a rumor that Professor Wilmont expects to leave at the end of the semester. That's not true, is it?" She wrung her hands. "He's such an excellent instructor. We'd all miss him terribly."

"You'll have to ask him, Miss Browning-ton."

"Yes, I expect you're right."

They soon parted and Charlotte returned to Summerhill. During the afternoon she sketched with Ruthie on the back veranda, while out of the corner of her eye, she watched Tim and the youngest Hopkins boy climb trees on the side lawn. No doubt Mrs. Wilmont would disapprove, but the woman was ensconced in the drawing room entertaining the dapper Mr. McClintock and anyone else who stopped by to wish her a rapid recovery. A dozen or more well-wishers had streamed into the cottage during the last few days.

Charlotte finished her drawing, satisfied she'd captured Ruthie's whimsy.

"Why, that's me," Ruthie said with a smile, looking over at Charlotte's sketch pad. "May I show the picture to Papa? He'll love it. You're a splendid artist."

Charlotte laughed, embarrassed by the praise. "Yes, of course. You may have it, if you'd like."

"Thank you, Miss Hale. I shall sketch you now."

Charlotte grinned. She laid her pencil on the wicker table set atop an Oriental carpet and glanced toward the sea, more quiet than usual in the stillness of the late afternoon.

The warm feelings she'd had in church had remained throughout the day, although they could easily fade in the light of reality. But at the moment they radiated within, like captured sunshine. The Lord loved her. Recently she'd read a verse in Proverbs: "I love them that love me; and those that seek me early shall find me." She understood that now. And it changed everything. While Ruthie silently sketched, Charlotte prayed.

Lord, I've committed so many sins and I ask for Your forgiveness. I am truly sorry.

And then the gravity of her deception smashed into her stomach. She'd lied for the vindictive Mr. Phifer who was using her shamelessly.

Should she continue to work for him? Quitting her position would mean she'd have to obtain another job quickly. Where could she apply?

The back door opened and Daniel stepped outside. Charlotte's heart lurched.

"Good afternoon, Charlotte, Ruthie. I've been searching for Sarah's prayer journal, but I can't seem to locate it. Did you happen to run across it? I can't imagine why you would've seen it, but I've asked my mother and the staff and no one has any idea where it might be. It was in a hatbox on the shelf of my wardrobe not long ago. I looked for it last night and searched for it again just now, but I'm afraid it's disappeared."

"I'm sure it will turn up soon." Charlotte's voice trembled. She should have returned the prayer journal days ago, but she'd read it cover to cover over the course of several nights. Then she'd shoved it to the back of her chest of drawers without ever finding an opportunity to return it. As soon as possible, she'd sneak the book back to its proper place.

But why did he suddenly want it?

"I'm sure it'll turn up. I have a bad habit of losing things right when I want them the most." Daniel shook his head and started for the door, still looking puzzled.

"Look at the sketch Miss Hale drew of me and the one I made of her." Ruthie beamed. "Would you like them, Papa?"

"If Miss Hale wouldn't mind, I'd love to have them both." His smile slid from one to the other.

FOURTEEN

Charlotte awoke to a dreary day punctuated by the mournful wail of a foghorn. A damp chill spread across her bedroom and raised goose bumps on her bare arms. Closing the window, she watched charcoal clouds skitter across the opal sky and darken the surf to gray. Fog veiled the lawn.

Today she'd celebrate her birthday by herself. No one at Summerhill knew of it, so of course no one would make a fuss. Twenty-three years wasn't really special. But she did miss waking up to the aroma of Aunt Amelia's devil's food cake wafting from the oven.

With a sigh, Charlotte dressed in her plain, light blue uniform with white collar and cuffs, brushed her hair into a neat pompadour, and donned the silly cap with streamers that Mrs. Wilmont insisted she wear. She looked like a parlor maid minus the apron. She glanced toward the locked bureau drawer concealing Sarah's journal. Gulping in a big breath, she steeled herself for the day's most crucial task. At the first opportunity, she'd slip the diary back into Sarah's hatbox. The professor need never know she'd pilfered it, though she really ought to confess and clear her conscience. Easier said than done.

Charlotte headed for the bedroom door. She could kick herself for accepting such a dishonorable assignment, but at least she hadn't tattled to Mr. Phifer about the journal and made matters even worse. Yet nothing excused her.

From the corner of her eye, she spotted the birthday present from Aunt Amelia and Becky. Too curious to wait for evening, she tore open the wrapping with one quick rip. She lifted a fine lawn blouse with tucks down the bodice and pearl buttons! It was by far the loveliest shirtwaist she'd ever owned. Her aunt must have toiled for hours sewing this fine garment. How thoughtful, especially since the crippling in her fingers made handwork so difficult. Several linen handkerchiefs edged with crocheted lace came from Becky.

Her spirits restored, Charlotte roused the groggy children from their beds and served them breakfast in the playroom. All morning she looked for a chance to return the journal, but Ruthie stayed by her side. Then an hour of cross-stitch, a game of chess with Tim, and lessons in arithmetic and grammar swallowed up the rest of the morning and into the early afternoon. She couldn't squeeze in even a few minutes to replace Sarah's journal until well after lunch.

The fog burned off and the grass dried by early afternoon, allowing Charlotte and her charges to enjoy the outdoors. While both children read their favorite books under a maple tree in the side yard, Charlotte excused herself.

"I shall be right back. Do stay put. That means you, Tim." The little boy's bad habit of vanishing when she wasn't looking often sent her in all directions in search for him.

"Miss Hale, may I get my book, *An Old Fashioned Girl*? It's in the playroom. I'm almost finished with *Jo's Boys*," Ruthie asked.

"I'd be glad to fetch it," she said, rising. "And I shall grab a book of my own. I'm about to begin *Life on the Mississippi*."

Charlotte hastened up the backstairs, grabbed Sarah's journal, then hurried to the professor's bedroom. Fortunately the hallway was deserted. Her heartbeat throbbed in her eardrums. With shaking hands she yanked the oval box from the wardrobe, shoved the journal inside, and pushed it back on the high shelf. Relief rushed through her. Professor Wilmont would probably find the book and assume he'd overlooked it. Heading out the door, the heels of her sturdy shoes clicked softly against the floorboards.

Thud! A crash loud enough to wake the dead assaulted her ears. She stopped short and glanced over her shoulder and back into the professor's room. A stack of textbooks lay on the floor beside the hatbox, its cover knocked off. Charlotte groaned, picked it up with shaking hands, and thrust it back in the box and onto the shelf once again. She piled the books beside it and raced toward the back staircase.

Tearing downstairs she paused at the landing, breathless.

Mrs. Wilmont looked up from the bottom of the steps, hands on her narrow hips.

"What was that noise?" the woman demanded.

Charlotte looked down, attempting to remain calm. Surely the professor's mother would notice the terror in her eyes and hear a squeak in her voice.

The cracks in Mrs. Wilmont's face hardened. "You dropped something in my son's bedroom right over the drawing room. What were you doing in there?"

"I was upstairs looking for one of Ruthie's books. I went to fetch her copy of *An Old Fashioned Girl*."

Mrs. Wilmont's eyes widened with triumph as she stared at Charlotte's empty hands. "I see you didn't find it."

Charlotte paused. "No. When I heard the noise I got distracted and forgot all about the novel."

"Are you claiming you weren't in my son's bedroom?"

Charlotte took a deep breath and willed her heart to stop thumping. "No, ma'am. I was there for a few moments. The clatter seemed to come from the wardrobe, so I looked inside and found a hatbox lying on the floor beside several books. I put everything back on the shelf and left immediately. If you'll excuse me, I'll run upstairs and fetch Ruthie's book." She tried to dash around Mrs. Wilmont, but the woman blocked her exit.

"You don't fool me, Charlotte Hale. You have no business in any bedroom except for the children's. Do I make myself clear?"

"Yes, ma'am." Charlotte hung her head so her employer wouldn't see the guilt rising to the surface of her face.

"One more misstep and I shall dismiss you."

Mrs. Wilmont's threat hovered in the stifling air. Charlotte nodded, turned on her heel, and climbed the back staircase to retrieve Ruthie's book and her own.

The afternoon slowly faded into early evening. Charlotte had a light supper with the staff while the family ate together in their spacious dining room. After the kitchen help cleared the table, Charlotte looked up at the sound of giggling on the basement stairs.

"Miss Hale, Papa would like to see you in the playroom."

Oh Lord, please don't let this be about the journal. I don't have the strength to confess — if You think that I must. I need a little more time to muster the courage.

"Miss Hale, do hurry." Ruthie's face glowed with anticipation.

Charlotte followed the children up the back staircase to the second floor and into the playroom. Brightly wrapped packages were piled beside the table holding a bucket of ice cream and a two-layer cake, iced in pink, and resting on a crystal pedestal plate.

"Happy Birthday, Miss Hale," the professor, Ruthie, and Tim shouted all together.

Charlotte's jaw popped open. "How did

you know today is my birthday?"

Daniel grinned, happily smug. "The date was on the sheet you filled out when I interviewed you."

Tears clogged her throat. "I can't believe you'd do this for me. Thank you so much." Charlotte's voice cracked. "I'm over-whelmed."

Ruthie spoke with authority. "Everyone should have a birthday party. And Miss Hale, you're practically family, so it's up to us to give you one."

Charlotte grinned with pleasure tinged with regret. What kind of woman betrayed her family?

"Chef Jacques helped me bake the cake." Ruthie gazed at her creation with unfettered pride.

Tim volunteered, "It's a little bit lopsided, but that doesn't matter. Ruthie put gobs of frosting on the top so you really can't tell."

After making an appropriate fuss, Char-lotte cut the cake and served it along with homemade vanilla ice cream. A real treat.

"Is it impolite to ask how old you are?" Tim asked between bites.

Daniel frowned. "Never ask a lady her age, even a young one."

Charlotte laughed. "I'm twenty-three."

"That's old. Shouldn't you be getting

married soon?" Tim tipped his chair back precariously. "Is that a rude question too?"

"You know it is," the professor said with mock sternness while Ruthie rolled her eyes. "Please excuse my son's bad manners. He knows better."

Tim hung his head, but a mischievous smirk belied true repentance. "I'm sorry."

Nothing could ruin Charlotte's unexpected happiness, certainly not childish curiosity. The Wilmonts' kindness meant so much. "You've made my birthday very special." A few tears escaped and rolled down her cheeks. Dabbing with a handkerchief, she smiled ruefully. "Pardon me for getting carried away."

"I've never seen a grown-up cry before," Ruthie said, apparently perplexed.

"It happens sometimes." Charlotte sniffed. "Please excuse me."

Tim shook his head, his forehead crinkled in bewilderment. "I don't understand grown-ups either."

"You shouldn't have done all this for me. I don't deserve such generosity," Charlotte murmured.

If only they knew why she'd come to Summerhill in the first place, they'd toss her right out the door.

"Nonsense," the professor objected, "of

course you deserve a birthday party."

When they'd all finished eating, Ruthie stacked the plates and silverware on the dumbwaiter while Tim spread their gifts in front of Charlotte.

"There's mine." Ruthie pointed to a package wrapped in pink floral paper and tied with a rose ribbon. "Hope you like it."

Ruthie's shining smile touched Charlotte's heart. "Of course I shall." No matter what the child gave her, she'd appreciate it.

Charlotte ripped off the paper. "A prayer journal! Thank you so much. I'll write in it every day." She hugged Ruthie and the girl squeezed back. Hers would be completely different from Sarah's.

Tim shoved his gift across the table. "It's okay if you don't hug me."

Charlotte laughed as she opened the paper sack tied with a grosgrain ribbon. "Candy! Thank you, Tim. Would anyone like a peppermint stick or a lemon drop?"

Tim reached for some, but Daniel stilled his hand. "Thank you, but we've already had more than enough cake and ice cream. Isn't that right, Tim?"

With his mouth turning down, Tim shrugged but didn't reach again.

"Do let him have a piece," Charlotte urged to the delight of the curly-haired boy.

Professor Wilmont acquiesced with a nod and a wince. He handed Charlotte a small package. "This is from my mother and me."

She'd wager Mrs. Wilmont had nothing to do with the gift. Charlotte tore off the wrapping and found a Bible edged with gold, her name engraved on the black leather cover. "Thank you so much, Professor. I never owned a Bible of my own." She wanted to throw her arms around him and kiss his cheek. But she smiled instead.

Ruthie's eyes narrowed with suspicion. "You've never owned a Bible? All Christians have Bibles."

Ruthie, Tim, and Daniel stared at her with questioning faces. Swallowing hard, Charlotte couldn't speak. What explanation could she possibly give? No one said a word. The silence thickened.

Daniel rose. "Children, please run along. And no complaining. Miss Hale and I will drink our coffee on the front veranda." His voice sounded so serious, Charlotte's pulse quickened.

The lighthearted atmosphere of the birthday celebration had vanished. With shaking hands, Charlotte carried her cup down the stairs and outside. She perched on the edge of a rocker and tried to quell the nausea rising toward her throat. Daniel leaned against

300

the porch rail, his arms folded across his chest. A frown darkened his face. Was it sadness mixed with disillusionment or just plain anger that she'd been less than honest?

She cleared her throat, but a croak emerged nevertheless. "Thank you for the party and the gifts. I certainly didn't expect anything."

He nodded. "I hope you enjoyed it. Charlotte, is there something you should tell me?"

Wiping away a thin layer of perspiration from her forehead, she hesitated. Should she confess now? Or try to finesse an answer?

"Yes, there's a lot I ought to explain." Her voice quavered. "Is it a good time?" *Oh Lord, not now.* She wanted to flee to the safety of her home and her aunt's loving arms. *You're a miserable coward, Charlotte Hale.*

"Now is the perfect time," he said softly, his grimness gone.

"All right." She placed her coffee cup on a small wicker table and rose, her back touching one of the long windows. "Would you like to know why a good Christian never owned a Bible?" Her mouth twisted in an uneasy smile.

Daniel nodded.

She gulped a deep breath. "On the day you interviewed me, you asked if I was a Christian. It seemed like an offhanded question, so I said yes, of course. And I thought I was, though not truly committed. I believed in God, so I knew I wasn't a heathen. I assumed that made me a bona fide Christian. But since you needed a governess and I needed a job, I told you what I thought you wanted to hear. At any rate, I felt guilty for deceiving you — but I didn't know how to confess." Throat dry, Charlotte paused and watched his inscrutable expression.

"Go on, please."

"I began to read the Bible you left on my nightstand and for the first time I understood God's love. He became real to me. And that's made a world of difference." Charlotte met the professor's gaze, hoping for reassurance, but she couldn't decipher his intense expression.

He leaned back against the porch rail, lost in thought. Slowly the tense lines in his face relaxed. "Have you sincerely repented?"

She nodded. "God knows my sins and, believe me, I'm so sorry I ever committed them. And I know in my heart He's forgiven me. He's lifted a heavy burden off my shoulders. Forgiveness is such a remarkable gift."

"Indeed, it is."

"Through your example you showed me the Lord was missing in my life. Thank you for helping me see that."

His smile seared her conscience. *Tell him now.* "There's more, Professor. I ought to admit something else, but it's hard to find the right words because I'm so terribly ashamed." She stumbled over the last words and paused to inhale another breath of cool evening air before she confessed what had brought her to Summerhill. A few words and he'd be lost to her forever.

He took her hand. "Charlotte, there's no need to bare your soul if you find it difficult. The Lord forgives you."

"No, you don't understand —"

Charlotte gasped as Daniel moved closer and wrapped his arms around her waist. Putting a finger to her lips, he hushed her unspoken words. "I have such strong feelings for you, Charlotte," he murmured in a ragged voice.

"No, you must not say that." But she cared for him as well. No, she couldn't let herself. Tears choked her throat. She had to confess her part in Mr. Phifer's scheme. Now. She had no right to indulge her feelings under false pretenses. She pulled back, faced him, and held his hands, wishing she would never have to let go.

Soft voices from the front hallway grew louder. Mrs. Wilmont and Mr. McClintock. Charlotte pulled away, afraid to linger, yet reluctant to leave, wanting this horror done, over with. But the voices were coming closer. "I'd better go."

She squeezed Daniel's hands and then raised the hem of her skirt and swept inside the cottage.

FIFTEEN

Charlotte vanished before he could reach out to stop her. Excitement shot through Daniel's chest as he considered a future ripe with possibilities. Loving Charlotte was sanctioned by the Lord — he felt God's approval deep within his heart and even down in the marrow of his bones. And despite her discouragement, he felt sure she loved him too. Or at least she could once she got used to the idea.

He settled into the rocking chair and listened to the evening sounds of crickets and tree frogs.

The front door creaked open and his mother and Mr. McClintock stepped onto the veranda, laughing and flirting like a young couple. Daniel held back a broad smile. Until the devoted widower had come into his mother's life, she'd seldom enjoyed much of anything except perhaps complaining. Now she looked forward to Mr. Mc-

Clintock's frequent visits, bouquets of pink and white carnations, and the always-appreciated bonbons. His mother wished her beau a good night and watched Mr. McClintock ride off in his gig before she dropped into a cushioned chair next to Daniel. Her weary sigh seemed to rise from the bottom of her lungs.

"I relish Mr. McClintock's visits, but I'm a bit tired. My heart still twinges every once in a while — thank goodness they only last a matter of seconds."

Daniel frowned. "Have you told Doctor Lowe?"

"I shall at my next appointment." She flashed a reassuring smile. "I have a lot of life in me yet, so don't look so anxious."

"I know you're improving." Daniel patted her long, thin hand. "But I am concerned about those 'little twinges.'"

Was she minimizing the chest pains so he wouldn't worry or were they really relatively minor? He couldn't tell from her words or her expression. When she felt neglected, she tended to try and garner his attention. But sometimes her eyes radiated pain and her face reflected an advanced age she hadn't yet reached chronologically. He'd keep a closer watch on her.

"Is there anything I can get you before I

turn in?" he asked, rising.

"No, thank you." Vivian furrowed her brow and gestured for him to sit back down. "There's something I need to mention — about Charlotte."

Daniel's nerves twitched. "Yes?"

Vivian lowered her brows. "I've discovered something you need to know." She leaned closer, her voice low and conspiratorial. "She's sneaky as a cat."

Daniel chuckled. "No, Mother, Charlotte's not sneaky. She's open and forthright — a blessing from the Lord."

"*Humph.*" Vivian's eyebrow arched. "I heard her snooping around your bedroom this afternoon. Now, Daniel, don't look at me like I'm a muddled old woman because I'm not. I was in the drawing room with Mr. McClintock when I heard a crash directly overhead, in your room. Charlotte was the only one upstairs." She paused to let her words sink in. "I asked her what exactly she was doing. The sly young thing, she blushed to the roots of her hairline, but she wouldn't admit anything. She claimed she heard a box tumble off the wardrobe shelf along with some books. Now you explain how a box fell *all by itself.* She must have been going through your things. But why?" Her eyes sparked with triumph.

Daniel stifled a groan. Why couldn't she appreciate Charlotte, who bent over backward trying to please her? Yet what if his mother was right? He doubted her accusations would prove true, but he ought to check.

"I don't know and furthermore, I don't care." Still, uncertainty pricked his heart.

"You ought to care, Daniel. Rest assured I'm not making a mountain out of a mole hill." Her mouth thinned and curved downward. "Ask her about it, though she's sure to lie to you as well."

"You're being very unfair."

"Daniel, I'm telling you because you value honesty so much. You like that girl, but she's crafty and not a bit truthful. You're blinded by her pretty face and . . ." Glancing at Charlotte's coffee cup resting on the wicker table, Vivian frowned. "Was she out here with you? You know I want you to stay away from her, but for some unfathomable reason she attracts you like a moth to a flame."

"Miss Hale is delightful and the children adore her."

His mother's face twitched. "She's a servant. Nothing more. You must remember that, Daniel."

He expelled a deep sigh. "Charlotte is much more than just a servant, Mother.

She's a warm, wonderful woman who loves my children. I'm quite fond of her."

His mother shook her head in obvious disdain. "Why . . ." she sputtered. "Daniel, you can't . . . She's not worthy of you!"

He gritted his teeth as he tried to cool his rising anger. "Let me help you to your bedroom, Mother. It's getting late."

"You don't want to hear any word against her, do you?"

"No, I don't." Daniel shook his head. "Please don't criticize her, Mother."

"You're deluded, blinded by her counterfeit charm." Vivian sighed and said nothing more.

Lord, please soften her heart before I lose my temper.

Despite her wealth, his mother had suffered humiliation from his father's indifference and neglect and then buried most of her anger beneath a hard exterior. She'd lost her husband and now he knew she feared losing her son as well.

As soon as he settled her for the night, Daniel trooped upstairs to his own room. His gaze strayed to the wardrobe, and almost against his will, he pulled open the door and took the hatbox down from the shelf. Lifting the cover, he spotted Sarah's missing journal.

He stared at the worn book. How could he have overlooked such a large object? Had Charlotte or one of the maids replaced it then lied? It made no sense. But according to his mother, Charlotte had admitted hearing a noise in his room, coming in, and replacing the hatbox and books.

Doubt marched through his chest. Could his mother possibly be correct about Charlotte? He let out a groan as he climbed into bed.

Lord, should I question her or let it pass? Is she duping me? Am I too taken with her to see her clearly?

Daniel turned off his bedside lamp. If he couldn't trust her, he had no business loving her. The two qualities went hand in hand. *Lord, show me the woman she really is and please don't let me be fooled again.*

Daniel headed toward his college office the next morning, glad to put his mother's accusations out of his mind. As he walked down Cove Road toward the college, he knew his feelings for Charlotte had preoccupied him lately and he'd shoved President Ralston's ultimatum into the far corner of his mind. He waited for the Lord's voice. But he'd known all along he couldn't avoid making a decision about his future at Aquidneck.

When he opened the door to the outer office, his secretary glanced up from her typewriter, a dark frown compressing her face. Miss Gregory gave a sad, sympathetic smile and he knew something was amiss.

"President Ralston wants you to stop by his office — immediately," she said.

Daniel bit his lip. "Did he mention why?" Of course he knew the reason, though he'd hoped to have more time.

"No, but he seemed unhappy. In a snit, you might say."

"I expect I shall look unhappy as well when he finishes with me," Daniel murmured.

"I do hope your meeting turns out all right. I'll say a prayer."

"Thank you, Miss Gregory. I appreciate your support."

Undoubtedly she'd heard the rumor about Ralston's ultimatum. Over the last week or so his friends and colleagues had asked discreet questions, but he'd given vague responses. God held the answer in the palm of His hand; he didn't.

Daniel's throat constricted as President Ralston's assistant ushered him into the commodious office. Standing like a sentry,

Daniel waited for the older man to look up from the papers on his desk.

"Ah yes, Professor. I'd like to have a word with you about your future employment at our great institution. I'll come right to the point." Ralston folded his hands on his desktop while Daniel stood at attention. The president flashed a pained smile. "Have you made a decision about quitting your column at the *Newport Gazette*? It's a matter of extreme import to our trustees and benefactors, since the financial stability of our fine college is at stake. I'm sure you understand our position."

"Yes, sir, I know how crucial my decision is to everyone concerned." Daniel swallowed hard. "So I've prayed and pondered this carefully." But had he correctly interpreted the Lord's direction? He felt he had.

Ralston nodded impatiently. "Of course. And your conclusion, Professor Wilmont?"

Daniel took a deep breath.

"I've decided to resign my teaching position. I'll leave Aquidneck College with great sadness and deep regret. I've taught here for eight years and I've grown quite fond of my students and my fellow professors. It appears I must leave, though I certainly don't want to."

President Ralston blanched as white as his

starched shirt. "Can you explain your decision, sir?"

Daniel shifted from one foot to the other. "This may seem naive to you, but I firmly believe I must follow God's will. I'm convinced He's guiding me to speak out through my column."

Ralston's eyes widened with disbelief. "See here, Professor, you're an outstanding instructor. You can't just leave on a whim because you mistakably think God is commanding you to martyr yourself. Consider your family and how this will affect them." His hollow cheeks caved inward. "Be reasonable. Won't you admit quitting is a selfish and self-righteous decision?"

"Sir, you're not giving me any other choice. I'd love to stay, but I won't give in to pressure."

The president groaned with frustration. "All right, if that's your last word on the subject, I reluctantly accept your decision. You will remain until the end of the term; that gives you another two weeks to reconsider your future. Good luck to you, Professor."

Daniel gulped as the import of his choice bore down upon his shoulders. He'd apply for other teaching positions immediately, although he suspected most of the jobs were already filled for the next semester. Perhaps a preparatory school for boys might hire him — if he could find one with a vacancy at this late date.

He returned to his office, explained the situation to a crestfallen Miss Gregory, taught his only class for the day, and returned home, wishing he could avoid announcing his bad news.

Odd how the sun still shone and the wind still floated puffball clouds across the blue sky. It hummed in his ear and shook through the scrub bushes along the ragged coast, competing with the roar of the sea. He couldn't afford Summerhill's maintenance without a job to supplement his small inheritance. Even with his teaching position he barely had enough funds to pay for the large staff and costly repairs on the aging cottage. He'd sorely miss living right up against the power of nature, hearing its incessant voice, smelling the pungent odor of seaweed at low tide, tasting the tang in the air. Selling seemed the only viable option. But telling the people who depended upon him tore at his conscience. *Lord, am I hearing You correctly? Please confirm my decision because I'm still in doubt.*

He dropped into the rocker on the back veranda and let his nerves unwind, thinking about his years at Summerhill. He'd summered here since he was six, and most of his happy childhood memories revolved around this old, rambling cottage.

"Professor Wilmont, you're home early," Charlotte said. She wore the split skirt she donned for bicycle rides with Ruthie and Tim.

"Would you ask my mother and the children to meet me in the library? I have some news I need to share." He drew out a long sigh. "With you, as well, Charlotte."

"Of course." She lightly touched his arm, then quickly dropped it to her side. "You spoke to President Ralston, didn't you?" Her voice seemed to choke as she looked at him with eyes filled with apprehension.

"I did."

"I'll find your mother and bring the children to you immediately."

As soon as they gathered in the library, Daniel took a fortifying breath, removed his spectacles, and rubbed his tired eyes. "President Ralston recently gave me an ultimatum. I chose to consider my options carefully before I made a decision or burdened any of you. He demanded I give up my newspaper column or my teaching job."

Seated on a wing chair before the fireplace, his mother gasped. "I don't understand. You're a popular professor. Why would he say such a ridiculous thing?"

"My writings upset some of the board of trustees."

"I told you writing that column was a mistake. You can't criticize the industrialists and expect they'll ignore it." Her eyes narrowed to slits. "Did you tell the *Newport Gazette* you won't write for them anymore?"

"No. I resigned my teaching position instead."

His mother gaped at him. "Daniel, whatever led you to such an unwise decision?"

"Mother, I followed the Holy Ghost's guidance."

She rolled her eyes. "Your idealism is sophomoric. Your duty is to support your children."

"And I shall. There's a high probability that I must sell Summerhill, because without a job, the cottage is too expensive to maintain. I know we'll all miss the place, but we don't need such luxury for a good life."

With a flick of her wrist his mother opened her fan and cooled herself off. "Where do you get such odd ideas? Certainly not from me."

Daniel stifled a laugh as he arose. "I shall search for a job at one the local schools and inquire at colleges as well. I trust the Lord will find me a new position."

His mother thrust her hand over her heart. "My dear son, please don't do this; it's not worth all the bother. You can't expect us to leave our home. We've lived here for too many years to pack up now and begin again."

She refused to consider his rationale, but that didn't surprise him. Her mouth twitched. "Think of my health. I can't absorb such a shock. And what about the children? You'll tear them from the home they love and break their little hearts."

"I'm truly sorry to disrupt your lives. Please forgive me." He looked at Tim and Ruthie, who seemed more bewildered than upset. His gaze travelled to Charlotte, standing by a glass bookcase, hands clasped at her waist, a frown cutting into her brow. What did she think about his decision?

"And Miss Hale —"

"Don't fret about her," his mother said. "She's a young woman perfectly capable of finding another job, though I can't provide a helpful recommendation." Her hostile gaze scraped Charlotte with disdain.

Charlotte flushed deep crimson. "That's exactly what I'd have expected," she muttered, then looked down, apparently shocked she'd spoken out loud.

"Please, Mother, don't say things you'll later regret."

Vivian shook her fan at Charlotte and stared at him. "Don't lecture me, Daniel. Reprimand Charlotte for her unforgivable rudeness."

"Perhaps we all need to calm down." Daniel sighed.

"Pardon me for my impertinence, Mrs. Wilmont." Charlotte stiffened her back, but her voice sounded neutral.

"Miss Hale, I'd like you to stay with us," Daniel said. He couldn't quite read her expression. Bewilderment mixed with surprise spread across her face. "The children will still need a governess."

"You can't mean that, Daniel." His mother's eyebrows shot upward.

"I most certainly do."

Charlotte's gaze shifted from him to the children. "Thank you, sir, but I'll have to give it some thought."

"Please stay, Miss Hale." Tim grabbed Goldie, the cat, before she shimmied up the heavy gold curtains and clawed the tassels.

"We need you." Ruthie touched her arm. "Don't leave us."

Daniel said, "Of course, you need time, Miss Hale. We understand. I shall begin my job search immediately. I'll inquire at all the preparatory schools in New England, though I fear all the positions will be filled for the fall semester."

His mother brightened. "Telephone your brother. Edgar will have a place for you at one of the factories."

Daniel shook his head. "I turned from that road long ago. I'm a teacher and a writer."

His mother's long hand gracefully waved away his objections. "*Pshaw.* This is the perfect opportunity to take your proper place at Wilmont Enterprises."

"No, Mother. I'm leaving this situation in the Lord's hands. He won't let us down."

SIXTEEN

At Daniel's request the staff came together in the servants' hall. Pacing back and forth, he quickly conveyed the bad news and watched their faces droop with dismay. "Right now I don't know if I'll be forced to sell Summerhill and move away or if I'll find a position locally. As soon as I have more information, I shall tell you at once. I apologize for this terrible inconvenience."

If necessary they'd all find jobs at other cottages, for good employees were highly prized and hard to come by, he'd heard. Oftentimes, new owners of cottages chose to employ the staff that was already familiar with a home. Daniel answered their questions as best he could and then departed on a search for Charlotte. According to his mother, she'd taken the children to a birthday party at Ocean Vista, one of the Bellevue Avenue cottages. Could he convince her to stay on after he'd so spontaneously declared his fondness for her, or would that very admission send her back home? Not knowing set his nerves on edge.

For the remainder of the afternoon Daniel travelled from one local school to another inquiring about teaching positions. Each one had been filled weeks before, and though the school officials seemed anxious to hire him, none could offer a job. Discouraged by his fruitless search, he returned home and wrote inquiries to several institutions in the northeast and as far west as the Mississippi River.

Moving his family, especially his mother, would cause a terrible upheaval, but, like it or not, they had to go wherever he secured a job. She might prefer to live with Edgar in Massachusetts since he owned a mansion and led the social life she enjoyed. Daniel put down his pen and let out a soft groan. His brother found their mother's temperament so difficult he wouldn't want her to live in his home. And she wouldn't be satisfied playing second fiddle to Edgar's wife.

A jolt of fear rammed his confidence.

Heavenly Father, please help me secure a job that will suit all of us.

He *did* trust God, but it wasn't often he needed to rely upon Him so completely. The Lord answered prayers, but not always in the manner one expected. God's solution might be painful. Well, he'd ask for grace to accept whatever came his way and hope the Lord would give him the strength to overcome the trials that lay ahead. It seemed easy in theory, but in practice — well, the nausea in his stomach demonstrated the difficulty of trust in the harsh face of adversity.

After eating a light supper at his desk, he continued writing until nearly eight thirty. Tired, he shoved his fountain pen and stationery into the crowded desk drawer, turned off the gaslight, and made his way to the playroom. He found Charlotte tidying up. She met his gaze with a sad smile.

He'd proceed slowly — not that he had much time to convince her. The realization that he cared deeply for her flooded him with joy and hope and despair, all at the same time. He couldn't envision his life without her bright smile and upbeat chatter. He loved that she was so *herself,* speaking her mind, how she made him laugh.

But now the uncertainty about his future career added to the problem of their relationship.

Turning to face him, her gaze held steady. "Professor, I'm so sorry about your job. I know how much you enjoy teaching and —" She blinked back tears and didn't speak for several seconds. "Perhaps if you confronted the people pressuring President Ralston, you could convince them to keep you on."

Daniel shook his head. "If it were that easy, I'd try immediately. But I believe Arnie Phifer, the editor of *Rhode Island Reporter,* is the primary instigator. He and his friends contribute a great deal of money to the college and wield a lot of influence. They want me out of journalism and gone from Newport. I guess they don't care what the Bible teaches about caring for others."

A frown hardened Charlotte's eyes. "Do you really believe Mr. Phifer is behind President Ralston's ultimatum?"

"I most certainly do, though I can't confirm it. Not that they'd be hard to convince. Most undoubtedly feel the heat of my words, given their own enterprises."

He tried to smile but feared he'd grimaced instead. "I'm feeling sorry for myself when I should count my blessings. Please excuse my sour mood." He tried to wipe the woebegone look from his face. "I promised you would have eight weeks here while my mother recuperates, but I'm afraid we'll probably be gone as soon as the semester ends. I'm sorry, Charlotte. I'll find you another position before I leave — if you decide not to stay with us."

He paused, wondering if he dared say what was ringing through his mind. "Would you . . . might you consider coming with us?"

"If you leave Newport, I definitely can't go with you. I have my sister and my aunt to watch out for. They need me here."

"Couldn't you send them money?" he asked.

Charlotte shook her head as she shelved the remaining books. "Perhaps, but I won't. Aunt Amelia is getting older and more feeble. It will become more and more difficult for her to see to Becky's needs. It's one thing to leave them and yet still be nearby. Another to move away entirely."

"I understand. I won't badger you." But he needed her as well. He rose, wanting to stay. "Please excuse me." He headed for Ruthie's bedroom.

"Sir, it'll all work out. I know the good Lord will watch over you and your family."

"You're right, of course." He'd doubted the strength of her faith, but it seemed her trust in God was deeper than his own. That came as a surprise — and a challenge.

"He won't forsake you when you need Him the most. I do believe He's helped me all along, even when I didn't recognize Him."

Daniel smiled. "Thank you for reminding me."

He wanted to lean over and gently kiss her, but with her arms wrapped around her chest, she looked pensive and guarded, hardly disposed to his affection. Abruptly, Daniel turned around. "Good night, Charlotte."

He headed for Tim's bedroom. His little boy was sound asleep and snoring lightly. Checking on Ruthie, he found her sitting up in bed with several feather pillows stuffed behind her head. She looked up from her book and grinned sheepishly.

"You snuck up on me, Papa!" She giggled. "I suppose it's past my bedtime, but I *have* to finish this chapter of *An Old Fashioned Girl.*"

"It's time for sleep. The March sisters can wait until tomorrow."

She giggled. "You've got the wrong book. That's *Little Women.*"

"No matter."

"But I'm not tired." She hugged her knees to her chest, letting the ruffled hem of her pale pink nightgown fall to her feet. Cocking her head, Ruthie's forehead puckered with a frown far too serious for a young girl. "Can we talk awhile?"

Daniel braced himself as he dropped onto

the end of the single bed. "Of course. Are you upset about moving, pumpkin?"

"Yes, but not quite as upset as Grandmother. I'll —" she began, her voice breaking, "I'll get used to the idea." But her lower lip quivered. "It's something else."

If this was about girlish things, he'd hush her up and send her to his mother or Charlotte.

"Papa, I don't want Miss Hale to leave. Please, would you ask her to stay even after Grandmother gets better — and we move?"

His muscles tightened. This would not be easy to discuss either. "I did. I'd like her to remain with us, too, but she won't leave her family alone in Newport. Besides, this is only a temporary job."

Ruthie pouted. "I think she'd stay if you asked her to marry you."

Daniel forced a hearty laugh and patted Ruthie on the head. "Oh, I doubt that." *Marriage.* He felt heat rising to his neck and up into his ears. In a moment steam might lift from his head, giving him away. "She's a beautiful young woman who'd never settle for a widower." *An unemployed widower with children.*

"I can tell you like her, Papa."

He chuckled. "I like most everyone."

"You watch everything she does even

when she's working or playing with Tim and me."

Daniel grunted. "You're too observant." He raised his hands in mock surrender. "I confess — she's a joy to be around."

"Then ask her to marry you."

His eyes widened and his breath hitched in his lungs. "Whoa, young lady."

Ruthie giggled again.

"You're putting the cart before the horse. Miss Hale and I are newly acquainted. You can't rush these things."

"Then there's a chance! She likes you too. She asks me questions about you all the time."

"What sort of questions?"

"Every kind. She's terribly nosy, but that's all right because she's in love." A mischievous smile tilted Ruthie's lips. "And you love her, too, don't you?"

Daniel rose and strolled toward the door, anxious to escape. "This is a completely inappropriate conversation, but let's pray about it and see what the Lord says."

He said a stilted prayer asking for guidance and then opened his eyes.

Ruthie cocked her head. "Papa, praying is important, but sometimes the Lord is slow in answering."

"Then we'll just have to wait for His

perfect timing."

"But Miss Hale won't be here very long. God needs to hurry up."

Daniel smiled as he stood in the doorway, silently agreeing with his daughter. "We've talked about this before. Obviously complaining about God's timing doesn't make Him act any quicker if He doesn't want to. So, with that, good night."

"Good night, Papa. I know it will all work out, somehow. I'll pray for both you and Miss Hale."

Daniel pulled the door shut, glad to escape Ruthie's scrutiny. He passed through the playroom into the hall, lost in thought. His daughter was right.

He was falling in love with Charlotte Hale.

The next morning, Charlotte entered the drawing room. "Ruthie, your voice teacher is here for your lesson."

"Thank you. Please excuse me, Grandmother." Ruthie rushed off. Unlike her brother, she enjoyed music and practiced her singing and piano without prompting.

Charlotte watched Mrs. Wilmont's lightning-fast fingers quilt a square pulled taut in a small hoop. Charlotte peered over the woman's thin shoulder at the basket of appliquéd flowers pieced in bright calicos and sewn onto muslin. Charlotte admired the tiny, neat stitches she could never manage to make. "It's beautiful."

Vivian gave a curt nod. "All my life I've quilted, but it's harder now that I'm afflicted with a touch of rheumatism." She glared at her fingers and slowly flexed them. An emerald ring surrounded by diamonds flashed in the sunlight filtering through the window. "I see you also admire my ring."

Charlotte blushed. "Yes. It's exquisite." She waited for a reprimand. A servant shouldn't comment upon anything so personal.

But Mrs. Wilmont smiled sadly and laid the hoop on her lap. "It was my mother's ring. My father gave it to her for their twentieth wedding anniversary. I was her only daughter, so Mama left me all of her fine jewelry." She looked out the window, as if remembering. "I'm grateful because my husband never gave me anything better than a cheap wedding band — not even a measly diamond chip for our engagement." She scowled as she stared at her hands. "Of course, we had very little then, but later when his business prospered, he still didn't buy me anything of value. And he knew how much I appreciated jewelry."

Charlotte nodded. How could she respond

to that unexpected revelation?

"While my husband was expanding Wilmont Enterprises," she went on, "I brought up my sons by myself. Edgar, my oldest, runs the business now. But when he and Daniel were young, their father wasn't interested in them or in me. I took care of all their needs." She spoke with pride mixed with bitterness so deep, it sent chills down Charlotte's spine.

Why was Mrs. Wilmont spilling her life's pitiful story?

Her fingers flew. "But my husband is dead now, so I've put the past behind me."

From the set of Vivian Wilmont's jaw and the press of her mouth, Charlotte suspected she hadn't even tried to forgive the man. Weren't Christians supposed to absolve those who harmed them? Of course, forgiveness never came easily, especially under such hurtful circumstances. She was shocked at the twinge of empathy she felt for the woman who treated her so shabbily.

"I wanted the best for my children, even though their father was tight with money. I wanted them to have the best educations, the best marriages. Daniel picked a splendid girl to wed. Bless her heart." Vivian drew out a long, mournful sigh. "Sarah and I were as close as mother and daughter. We were all devastated when she passed. So tragic for us all."

Charlotte shifted from one foot to the other. Why was Mrs. Wilmont telling her this? And for all of Sarah's journal entries, she had scarcely mentioned her mother-in-law.

Vivian peered through half glasses at Charlotte, her eyes as hard as gemstones. "If Daniel lives to be one hundred, he'll never get over her. I don't suppose he'll ever find such a sweet, charming girl again." She let her words sink in. "And oh my, Sarah was talented. She decorated this house, entertained — there wasn't anything she couldn't do and do well."

Charlotte suppressed a grimace. No, Daniel would never meet such a paragon again — at least not in her. "You must all miss her." Although, Mrs. Wilmont's characterization scarcely squared with what she'd read in the journal.

The elderly woman nodded. "We do. No one can ever take her place. She was a perfect wife and mother."

Though it was an obvious lie, Charlotte understood her meaning, loud and clear.

Were her warm feelings toward Daniel so obvious his mother had to warn her to keep her distance? The lady must fear she'd lose her son just as she'd lost her husband. Well, Mrs. Wilmont shouldn't worry. She wouldn't lose Daniel, at least not to her.

Charlotte plumped the pillows on the sofa. "Would you like lunch now? I can order it for you."

"I'm not hungry. I never eat before two o'clock and it's only twelve thirty," Vivian snapped. "Besides, Mr. McClintock will be joining me for luncheon later on."

"Not even a cup of coffee or tea?"

"I *said* no thank you."

Charlotte hid her annoyance behind a faint smile. "Of course, ma'am."

"I don't have much of an appetite these days. I'm still feeling poorly." Mrs. Wilmont gave a moan of self-pity and then lifted the parcel that had come in the morning post. "I believe these are the books my son has been anxiously awaiting."

"I have a few errands to run in town. I could drop them by his office, if you'd like."

"What is it you need to buy?" Vivian Wilmont's eyes narrowed with skepticism.

Charlotte had prepared an answer well in advance. "Some sheet music for Ruthie. I shall not take long."

"All right. But where is Tim? You can't expect me to watch them while I'm convalescing."

"Of course not. Mrs. Finnegan volunteered to keep an eye on him."

"Why don't you take him along instead of imposing on my housekeeper? She has her own duties to attend to."

She couldn't bring Tim to a meeting with Mr. Phifer. "As you know, the professor prefers the children not come to his office. Besides, Tim loves Mrs. Finnegan. She promised to play checkers with him."

Mrs. Wilmont sighed. "All right. You may go on your errands, but be quick about it."

Charlotte left Summerhill in the gig with the parcel of books beside her. She drove the short distance to the college and then hastened into the professor's office. She'd have just enough time to meet Mr. Phifer at O'Neill's Café at one o'clock. Dread spurted through her, but she quickly calmed her nerves.

When she peeked inside Daniel's college office, his face split in a grin. "What a nice surprise! I see you have the books I ordered. Thank you for delivering them." He cleared away a pile of papers and she set the package down. His cluttered space reminded her of his Summerhill study.

"It was no trouble at all." She stood before his desk, her hands clenched at her waist until he motioned her to take a seat. She perched on the chair across the desk. The wall clock read twelve thirty. If she didn't hurry, she'd arrive late for her appointment.

He pointed to a copy of the *Rhode Island Reporter,* opened to the editorial page. Arnold Phifer's name flashed like a fork of lightning. Perspiration erupted on her face and neck and dribbled in a clammy rivulet down her back.

Daniel read the headline out loud, " 'Radical Columnist Condemns Business Practices.' Of course I'm the so-called radical he's complaining about." A wry smile tugged at his mouth. "I think that's a bit overstated, don't you?"

Her muscles tightened. "I'm sure it is, sir."

"Arnie Phifer brings out the worst in me. I shouldn't let his ranting get under my skin, but I can't stomach distortions and lies."

A sick feeling spread through her. "Does he actually lie about you?" Stretch the truth a bit, but outright lie?

"Yes, he most certainly does. I expect him to be fair and confront my ideas point by point, but instead he uses ridicule and character assassination. I detest that, especially when I'm the target." He laughed ruefully and ran his fingers through his hair. "On one occasion, Arnie Phifer wrote such a scathing piece about me, I actually went down to his office and gave him a piece of my mind."

During her interview Daniel had mentioned she looked familiar. Now she knew why. He must have seen her that day, though bent over a typewriter, she probably wasn't memorable.

Oh Lord, please don't let him recognize me. I promise to confess my part in this awful scene, but let me prepare myself first. I'm not quite ready, Lord. Please forgive me for being such a coward.

Daniel tossed the paper into the trash can. "Every day I pray that Arnie Phifer will change his attitude. And I pray the Lord will soften my heart, too, since my thoughts about the man are far from charitable."

Charlotte bit her lip to keep from snorting a nervous laugh. Arnie could use all the prayers he could get, though he wouldn't appreciate them if he knew.

A soft knock on the door drew Charlotte's attention. Glancing over her shoulder, she saw Missy LeBeau stride into the room. Decked out in a raspberry pink outfit with ruffled parasol and plumed hat, she looked ready for a garden party. Most of the female students wore tailored skirts and shirtwaists

335

in practical colors and plain, serviceable hats.

Missy stuck her nose in the air like a spoiled debutante, looked through Charlotte, and then turned to Daniel with a broad smile. "Excuse me, Professor, may I have a word with you? Alone, if you please."

"Perhaps you can make an appointment with my secretary. As you can see, I'm rather busy at the moment." His voice was cordial but cool as he stood behind his desk. Charlotte swallowed a smile.

"I'm sorry, this won't wait." Missy waltzed over to the professor, edging so close he had to step back. "Professor Wilmont, do you remember I mentioned joining a prayer group? Well, we're having a retreat next weekend and we're in desperate need of a speaker." Missy pleaded with a smile worthy of Sarah Bernhardt. "At the last minute our guest lecturer, Miss Symington, withdrew because her father is going into the hospital. I'm in charge of finding a substitute, so I immediately thought of you. I know you'll truly inspire us."

Daniel shifted from foot to foot and rubbed the back of his neck. "I'd afraid I'm terribly busy just now. Have you asked Professor Fielding or perhaps Miss Rollins? Either one would be excellent."

Missy frowned. "No one else can come because it's such short notice. Please, Professor. You'd be doing us a tremendous favor."

"I understand your dilemma, but please try to find someone more suitable."

Missy's lower lip quivered. "I've asked everyone I could think of and all have turned me down because they didn't have enough time to prepare. You're so frightfully clever, I know you could do this without any preparation at all."

Charlotte stifled a groan and waited for Daniel to say no for good.

Daniel let out a sigh of resignation. "All right, Miss LeBeau. I'll do it."

Missy grabbed his hand and squeezed. "Thank you so much, Professor. The ladies and I will be forever grateful."

Charlotte's eyes widened in surprise. How could he have fallen for the girl's patent play?

He cleared his throat. "If that's all, I believe it's almost time for my next class. Please send me the details, including the topic I'm to speak on."

Missy nodded and sashayed out the door, her skirt rustling. Daniel turned to Charlotte.

"I'm doing Miss LeBeau a favor because —"

"She's so persuasive and you didn't know how to refuse." That was the truth, but had she spoken too plainly?

Daniel winced. "Ouch, that pinches. You're right. I do hate to let anyone down, especially when they're in a bind."

"You'll be making a dreadful mistake if you speak at Miss LeBeau's retreat. I can't explain exactly why, so I'll just say it's my womanly intuition." Mr. Phifer's "tip" about the girl rang through her mind.

"Are you still worried Miss LeBeau has a crush on me?" Daniel turned as red as a radish.

Her gaze fastened on his. "I'm more convinced than ever."

He wiped the embarrassment off his face and shrugged. "Perhaps she does, but that's beside the point. I'm gratified she's taking such an interest in spiritual things. That's a big step forward."

When he crossed his arms over his chest, Charlotte silently groaned. The subject was closed. He'd already explained his reasons and obviously he wasn't open to persuasion. "I hope you're right."

SEVENTEEN

"If you'll excuse me, Professor Wilmont, I have an errand to do in town. Ruthie needs a few items from the music store." Charlotte glanced at her pocket watch. Twelve forty-five. To meet Mr. Phifer at one o'clock, she'd have to leave at once. She headed for the door of the professor's office when he stopped her mid-step.

"Are you going to Thames Street, by any chance?"

"Thames Street?" she sputtered. "Why yes, I am."

He grabbed his gray bowler and umbrella and strode toward her. "Mind if I come along? I need to purchase some supplies at the stationery store."

How could she refuse him the use of his own carriage? "Of course, if you wish, but I may take awhile and I wouldn't want to delay you."

"That's no problem. I don't mind wait-ing."

Rats. She'd have to dash to the music store, buy the items, and then, literally, run to her meeting. What if the professor saw her entering or exiting O'Neill's Café? How would she explain that? Nothing came to mind. She'd think of a reason later, if neces-sary — though, if she were lucky, the need wouldn't arise. *Please Lord, I don't want to lie. I've already told too many lies and half-truths.*

Only confession would settle her stomach lurching with queasiness. Charlotte silently led the way outside and climbed into the buggy.

A mist swept down from thick gray clouds, dampening the early afternoon. The profes-sor pulled up the folding top of the gig to keep off the impending shower, then climbed in beside her and took the reins. He chatted about the children but avoided discussing the important things — his resignation and future plans.

"Professor, please tell me why you chose to keep your newspaper column instead of your teaching position."

He sighed. "It was a difficult decision . . . one I didn't want to make. I prayed about it and asked the Lord to show me what He wished me to do."

Charlotte nodded. "So how did He tell you? Obviously He didn't whisper in your ear or talk to you out loud."

He let out a laugh. "No. If it were only that clear I wouldn't hesitate for a moment. But I did realize that if I chose teaching it would be for the wrong reasons. The salary was the incentive, even more than the satisfaction of instructing students. I could keep Summerhill and I wouldn't disrupt my family." His mouth curved in a crooked smile. "And Arnie Phifer would leave me alone. But I knew in my heart the Lord wanted me to write my columns and continue to challenge anything that harms the defenseless or takes us away from our Christian walk. Once I accepted that as the Lord's will, I felt at peace."

It would be so much easier for her if Daniel had just quit the newspaper, but she understood why he decided to leave the college instead. "Do you know what you're going to do, besides write your column?"

The professor shook his head. "No. The Lord hasn't told me yet, but I'm listening for His voice."

By the time they arrived in town, a steady drizzle obscured their vision. But the pounding of the rain on the roof of the carriage halted their talk.

"I'll pick you up in about twenty minutes." Daniel pulled up in front of the music store, helped her down, and rode off. Opening the umbrella he insisted she borrow, Charlotte waited for the gig to vanish into the cold drizzle. She splashed through puddles on the sidewalk.

Fortunately, she found the shop nearly empty. She made her purchase just as the clock on the back wall struck one. Two blocks separated her from the restaurant. She'd never arrive on time if she didn't hustle. She wove past workers and house-wives crowding the sidewalk. The umbrella, along with her hat brim, kept her face and hair dry, but the rain poured down faster and soaked through her black uniform.

She entered O'Neill's Café, drenched and shivering like a puppy. Once her eyes adjusted to the dim light, she spotted Mr. Phifer seated by the front window finishing dessert and coffee. She slid into the chair opposite him as a gust of wind rattled the awning that covered the front of the brick building. Rain splattered against the windowpanes.

"Miserable weather," she muttered over the din of customers dining on simple luncheon fare.

Mr. Phifer grunted his agreement and then, without asking, ordered her a cup of tea. "Would you like a piece of blueberry cobbler?"

"No thank you, sir."

He requested another square for himself. "So tell me about the inestimable professor and his student. What have you learned, Miss Hale?" He leaned toward her, elbows on the checkered tablecloth. His eyes looked ravenous.

Charlotte's pulse raced. "There's really nothing new, sir." He looked askance. "Miss LeBeau asked Professor Wilmont to speak at her college retreat, but I'm quite convinced it's not any sort of tryst, though she does seem to be more than a little interested in him."

Mr. Phifer gave a nasty laugh. "And he in her?"

Charlotte tried to relax her tightened jaw. "No, definitely not. The professor is a man of integrity — and much too smart to be seduced by a student."

"Have we been wasting your time and my money investigating a saint? If he's innocent, do you think we should just give up this whole inquiry?"

Charlotte ignored the dripping sarcasm and met his glare. "I believe so. I haven't found one bit of incriminating evidence, despite a thorough search. I learned from another student that Missy is telling everyone about her crush on the professor, but he doesn't seem to reciprocate her feelings."

He grunted. "You give up too easily, Miss Hale."

As soon as the waiter deposited the tea and cobbler on the table, Mr. Phifer dug in. Charlotte stared at him, though with his head bent over the plate, he didn't notice. Would he fire her now for insubordination or incompetence — or would he wait awhile longer?

He finished the last crumb before looking up. "I was convinced you'd discover something valuable by now. But perhaps the good professor is craftier than I thought." His eyes bore into hers. "I need something to print, young woman."

"Sir," she began in a croak, "I can only do so much. I can't get rid of him for you. I can't poison his coffee or concoct evidence that's not there."

Mr. Phifer exhaled through his nose. "Your coffee would poison anyone." His hearty guffaw caused heads to turn and Charlotte to wince.

The morning coffee she brewed for the staff always ended up either too strong or too weak, never just right. It was the object of many jokes she'd learned to laugh off.

"I agree you can't poison the man. It looks like we'll have to take matters into our own hands." His face radiated optimism that chilled her. "In fact, I've already devised a plan."

She raised a shaky palm. "Sir, you wouldn't plant false evidence, would you? That's unethical and probably illegal."

He dismissed her scruples with a snort. "Miss Hale, you have a Puritan streak a mile wide. Where did that come from? Too much exposure to the high and mighty Professor Wilmont? Or was it there all along and I never noticed?"

He'd never noticed *anything* about her before. She met his gaze. "I've always had moral values, sir." She sounded so self-righteous. How could she pretend high standards when her ethics were obviously adjusted to meet the needs of the moment? She detested hypocrites and here she was, the worst offender. When she'd agreed to investigate the professor, she'd conveniently ignored the importance of honesty.

"I must return to Summerhill or Mrs. Wilmont will question why I took so long. I'll keep you informed, sir."

Mr. Phifer drew his shaggy brows in a

frown. They resembled an untrimmed hedge covered with snow. "I'm beginning to doubt your loyalty to the *Rhode Island Reporter*. You're not doing your job effectively and you don't seem to care."

A quick denial caught in the back of her throat but threatened to dislodge in a torrent of truth that would cost her everything. It was hypocritical to protest her innocence when he was correct. Her regard for Daniel Wilmont kept her from turning over Sarah's journal and performing her assignment as she was paid to do. She had no right to continue employment with either Mr. Phifer or the professor.

Yet she didn't have the gumption to quit either position. Or did she? The poison of self-disgust spewed through her chest. She jumped to her feet and opened her mouth to say her peace. "I quit" lay on the tip of her tongue. She gulped in a breath of air, finally ready to stand up for her principles.

Mr. Phifer looked up at her, one eyebrow raised. "If you can't accomplish the task, I'll send someone who can. Miss Wengle is raring to take over. She's a born journalist and chomping at the bit for a big story. Fortunately, she's not hampered with an overactive conscience."

His threat pushed the determination out

of Charlotte's lungs. Edith Ann Wengle would stop at nothing to further her advancement, even fabricate evidence. Charlotte feared the woman was as ruthless as Mr. Phifer himself. No, she couldn't possibly allow that unscrupulous toady to take over her inquiry and put Daniel in jeopardy. Charlotte dropped into her chair, deflated. "Yes, sir, I understand."

"Good."

The door flew open and Wes Dobbyns, one of the newspaper's up-and-coming reporters, rushed inside and skidded to a stop at their table. He pulled off his fedora and inadvertently spattered water in her face. Charlotte dabbed at her cheeks and eyes with a cloth napkin.

"Excuse me, Miss Hale." He bobbed his head and then faced Mr. Phifer. "And I'm sorry to disturb you, too, sir, but a fire has broken out down at one of the wharfs. Shall I cover it myself or should I send —"

"You can handle it. All this rain should extinguish it in short order." Mr. Phifer thrust himself out of his chair, tossed a dollar bill and change on the table. "Ambitious pup," he mumbled with grudging praise. "We're finished for now, Miss Hale."

Charlotte followed the reporter and editor outside. Why couldn't Phifer have assigned her to a fire story rather than the destruction of Daniel Wilmont?

Charlotte darted to the edge of the sidewalk flanked by the two newspapermen and popped open her umbrella. Waiting for a break in the traffic, she looked down Thames Street for Daniel's gig. Peering through the rain, she couldn't distinguish one equipage from another, although a steady line of carriages and wagons headed in her direction.

Mr. Phifer grumbled, "Nasty weather. Don't look so morose, Miss Hale. I've handed you the chance of a lifetime and you act as if I've condemned you to the gallows. What is the matter with you?"

Charlotte tilted her umbrella to get a better look at her boss. "Nothing, sir. I merely wish to uncover the truth."

"Grow up, Miss Hale. This isn't child's play. The professor is stirring up the rabble and I won't have it. Wilmont is a troublemaker using the cover of religion to build himself up. You seem to ignore that fact."

The urge to quit her job swelled within her chest. Angry tears burned behind her eyelids, but she blinked rapidly until she finally regained her composure and common sense. Quitting in haste would be shortsighted. She'd ponder her options first and then decide a course of action.

But what if she never found the strength to follow through on her convictions? How horrid to go through life compromising on her values just to get along with others.

The answer suddenly settled in her heart. God had heard her prayer and He'd help her. Without a doubt she'd act according to her convictions, no matter what the consequences.

But right now she needed to protect the professor from the likes of Mr. Phifer and Missy LeBeau. And Edith Ann Wengle.

"Mr. Phifer, please don't send Miss Wengle to Summerhill. I'm quite capable of completing the assignment on my own. She's not suited for minding children. If Mrs. Wilmont hired her, and I doubt she would, she'd let her go within hours. I'll uncover the truth within the next few days." Spewing false bravado, she stared directly into his scarlet face.

Mr. Phifer wagged a finger. "You haven't produced the goods, young woman. I have a mind to fire you this very minute. But I shall think it over before I decide what to do, between you and Miss Wengle. You'll be hearing from me. Good day, Miss Hale." He turned on his heel and stomped off.

The professor's gig, splashing through the

rain and mud, drew to a halt on the opposite side of the road. Charlotte stepped forward, but Wes Dobbyn's voice stopped her.

"Whew!" He swept his hand across his forehead. "I couldn't hear all Mr. Phifer said, but you certainly angered him. You'd better do as he asks and fast, or you'll be pounding the pavement looking for another position. Good jobs are hard to come by these days."

"I know, I know." Charlotte grimaced. "And thank you for your concern. Good afternoon, Mr. Dobbyns."

Grasping the umbrella with one hand and holding on to her hat with the other, Charlotte jogged through the congestion as carriage wheels splattered mud on her skirt. Wes followed close behind, called good-bye, and then headed toward the wharf. The soles of Charlotte's polished boots skidded through the slippery dirt before she reached the opposite sidewalk. She jumped into the buggy beside Professor Wilmont and folded the umbrella.

The professor eased out into the traffic and glanced sideways. "You look worried. I saw you standing with two gentlemen across the street. Did that older fellow distress you? He looked angry."

Charlotte shook her head and yanked her veil down to obscure her face.

Daniel's eyes widened as he stared at the figure striding down the sidewalk. "My goodness. That's Arnie Phifer. Why were you talking to that scoundrel?"

Charlotte gulped, speechless. Of course the professor recognized his harshest critic. And in a few seconds, he'd probably remember where he'd seen her before — in the office of the *Rhode Island Reporter*. She wished she could vanish into the rain and never be seen again.

From the questioning look in his eye, Daniel expected an explanation.

He peered at Charlotte. Her skin seemed to reflect the gray of the sky. Despite her denial, Arnie Phifer must have upset her. Daniel seldom ventured to assess anyone's feelings, especially a woman's, but her pinched lips and furrowed brow betrayed turmoil. There was no mistaking it. "Did he say something rude to you?"

She shook her head, releasing tendrils of shiny hair from beneath her hat. "No, nothing like that. He was muttering about the awful weather. Really, I scarcely paid attention."

Perhaps the man enjoyed striking up a

conversation with a young, attractive woman, though his scowl excluded any sort of flirtation. Besides, the man was well into middle age and probably married. "If he bothered you, I'll gladly go over and speak to him." He glared toward Arnie strutting down the sidewalk toward the offices of the *Rhode Island Reporter.* "I believe I'll do just that." He pulled back on the reins when Charlotte gripped his arm. Her eyes were bright with alarm.

"Thank you for your concern, but that isn't necessary." Pushing up her veil, Charlotte pinned on a smile as cold as the winter sun.

End of conversation. Yet the brief encounter had looked just like an argument, certainly not a friendly exchange of information. "Strange," Daniel murmured, "you both appeared to know each other." He couldn't help himself. The words flew out of his mouth before he had a chance to check them.

Charlotte flashed a warning with her eyes. "Professor, the man was not harassing me." She enunciated every word in a low, deliberate voice. "Please don't concern yourself."

He raised his hand, spreading his fingers wide. "I'm sorry. I have no right to question you." But why did the normally sweet-tempered girl suddenly bristle? There was so much he didn't know about her, yet that only propelled him to delve deeper and learn everything he could — her thoughts, her ideas, all the details of her life.

Charlotte tossed him a faint smile. "No need to apologize, sir."

But he couldn't control his curiosity. "Why were you outside the café? You said you needed to buy some items —" He hated himself for prying, but questions kept tumbling through his mind. Did she have plans to meet someone at the café and merely used running errands as an excuse? Who did she meet? A beau she'd never mentioned before?

"I decided to get out of the rain and have a quick cup of tea." She spoke in a breezy tone of voice as she fingered her reticule.

Perhaps the fellow who exited the café with Charlotte and Arnie Phifer was her friend — or even sweetheart. Yet the young man looked exceedingly boyish with his sparse mustache and gangly gait. Surely he was too immature to attract Charlotte. Daniel exhaled sharply. He hated his uncharitable thoughts toward a man he didn't even know. He was reacting like a lover spurned.

"Did you have tea with that young fellow?" Daniel asked casually.

Charlotte hesitated. Then her eyes widened with understanding. "Oh no. He's merely an acquaintance, not a close friend."

"I'm sorry. It's none of my business."

Charlotte raised a wry smile. "If you were wondering if I have a beau, the answer is no. I've had a few, but no one who actually suited. A few years ago a fireman proposed, but when he realized I wouldn't desert my aunt and sister, he reneged on the engagement."

"I'm sorry. That must have been quite a blow."

"To my pride, yes. But we weren't meant for each other. It worked out for the best."

Daniel's spirits rose higher than the highest cloud. Apparently he still had a chance at winning her affection. Well, possibly.

EIGHTEEN

The next morning the ring of the doorbell pierced the quiet. Mr. Grimes pulled open the front door of Summerhill and gaped as Edith Ann Wengle whirled past him into the foyer. Charlotte's stack of children's books clattered to the floor just as Daniel emerged from his office. The young woman flew directly at Charlotte with arms outstretched and sorrow etched in every feature and freckle. With a lunge forward, Edith Ann squeezed her in a tight embrace, punching the air out of Charlotte's lungs. She struggled for breath, then mustered her strength and shoved Edith Ann away. But the wretched woman clung like a wet bathing costume.

Charlotte glanced at Daniel, who stood at his office door, his eyes wide with interest.

"What are you doing here?" she mumbled. With one final push, she freed herself from Edith Ann's grip.

Her hand thumped her chest as she dragged out a theatrical sigh. "I'm afraid I have sad news. Devastating news."

Oh no, not Aunt Amelia or Becky! As Edith Ann turned toward Daniel, Charlotte spotted a gleam in her eye. Mr. Phifer's typist thrust out her hand and grabbed for Daniel's, snapping it with a fierce shake.

"I'm Penelope Smith, Charlotte's first cousin, twice removed. You must be her employer. I'm very pleased to meet you, even under such heart-wrenching circumstances." She pumped Daniel's hand. "Good to meet you, sir. My cousin has told me all about you."

"What are you talking about?" Charlotte planted her hands on her hips, irritated by the farce.

Edith Ann's face pulled down with contrived grief. "I'm so sorry, dear Charlotte, but I received a frantic message from your Uncle Wilbur this morning."

"Who?" Charlotte shook her head. She didn't have any relatives by that name.

"Your Uncle Wilbur from Portsmouth. He sent word to your Aunt Amelia who pleaded with me to come straight over and deliver the sad news." Her voice broke. "I do so hate to tell." Edith Ann sniffled and then blew her nose with a handkerchief from her reticule. Charlotte stared at her narrow, hawkish face. What was she jabbering about?

The bearer of bad news lowered her voice. "It seems your sweet Aunt Louise passed away last night of heart failure. She went to her reward in a matter of seconds without any pain. Thank the good Lord she didn't suffer." She raised her eyes toward the ceiling. "Your uncle says the funeral will take place in two days. He really needs you out in Portsmouth tomorrow to help serve the guests and feed the chickens."

Daniel wrapped his arm around Charlotte's shoulder. "I'm so sorry for your loss. Is there anything I can do?" He quickly stepped away, apparently afraid his gesture might seem too intimate, especially in front of a stranger.

"No, thank you," Charlotte murmured as she glared at Arnie Phifer's messenger. Two could act out this charade. With hands covering her face, Charlotte sniffed, as if crying. "Poor Aunt Louise. I didn't know she was ill. I do appreciate you coming here to tell me about her passing, Penelope. I'll call on Uncle Wilbur next week and offer my condolences, but I couldn't possibly get away right now."

Charlotte grabbed Edith Ann by the arm to steer her out the door, but the stubborn woman wouldn't budge.

"Your Uncle Wilbur needs you," Edith Ann insisted. "He wants you to come to him in his hour of need."

"Well, I'm so dreadfully sorry, but the Wilmonts need me too. Uncle Wilbur has dozens of relations who can take care of him, so I'm sure he can do without me."

Edith Ann's face scrunched with determination. "But he said he needed *you*. And besides, you're his favorite niece."

"You misunderstood. He hardly knows me. Besides, Uncle Wilbur has ten children who live close by the farm. They'll help him get through this."

Daniel looked surprised. "With ten children, he'd certainly appreciate your help."

"Ten *grown* children, all over the age of twenty-five." *Dear Lord, please forgive me for this falsehood. I can't tell him the truth in front of Edith Ann.*

Daniel gently patted Charlotte's shoulder. "Take a few days off anyway. We can get along if we have to. Being with your family is more important."

Charlotte groaned inwardly.

Edith Ann raised her hands as if to stop the conversation. "There's no need of that. It just so happens I'm available this week and I'd be glad to assist you, Professor Wilmont. Now don't refuse, Charlotte, it wouldn't be an imposition. I'd really be happy to help out my dearest cousin."

Charlotte's jaw nearly dropped open. This was Mr. Phifer's devious way of replacing her. "Thank you for your kindness, both of you." She glanced toward Daniel. "Before I decide, I'd like to speak to my Aunt Amelia."

"By all means," Daniel agreed in a sympathetic tone.

Heading for the door, she glanced back at Edith Ann. "Please come with me, cousin."

Without waiting for a response, Charlotte strutted out to the veranda and across the lawn to Edith Ann's hired carriage. The woman's boots ground against the pebbled drive as she fell behind Charlotte's fast pace.

Once alone, Charlotte let her anger boil over. "*Penelope,* I know what you and Mr. Phifer are trying to do and it won't work."

All pretense gone, Edith Ann shrugged. "He wants you back in the office tomorrow morning since you can't come up with anything against Professor Wilmont. He knows I can do a better job. And I shall." She stood against the carriage door, back straight and head held high. A smirk played on her lips.

Immediately, Charlotte lifted her chin. "What are you going to do that I haven't already done?" As soon as Charlotte asked the question, she knew the answer. "Mr. Phifer is planning something underhanded, isn't he?"

Edith Ann flinched for only half a second. "Not unless it's necessary."

"You'd plant evidence. I know you would." Charlotte held her breath, waiting for confirmation.

Edith Ann rolled her eyes. "Don't be such a moralist. It's so unbecoming."

"I'm ashamed my standards have already sunk so low, but I won't allow them to drop any farther." Charlotte waved back at the house. "Since you aren't needed here, I want you to leave Summerhill at once."

Edith Ann gave a disdainful shake of her head as she turned. Glancing over her shoulder, she said, "You're making a big mistake by tossing me out. Mr. Phifer won't like that one little bit. Without a reference, you'll never work in journalism."

An unexpected feeling of self-assurance erased Charlotte's apprehension. Something blossomed inside, something solid and strong. Confidence, courage, a willingness to do the right thing and pay whatever it cost — including losing her job and risking her family's finances. Charlotte suddenly understood the meaning of truth and honor.

And faith. These feelings didn't come from within herself. They came from God.

"It's a price worth paying."

Edith Ann stared at her as if she'd taken leave of her senses. Shaking her head, Edith Ann climbed into the cab. Charlotte watched the carriage disappear down the driveway in a cloud of dust. Weak-kneed, Charlotte returned to the veranda and collapsed onto a wicker chair, her bravado spent.

Mr. Phifer planned to fire her as soon as she walked into the office tomorrow. No doubt he wanted the pleasure of sacking her in person. Not that it really mattered because, in good conscience, she couldn't continue to work at the *Rhode Island Reporter.* Quitting was an enormous step that she couldn't avoid. Well, so be it.

She'd rely on her governess salary until she found some other position. With her career in shambles and no reference from Mr. Phifer, she'd have to explore something other than journalism. Apprehension crawled up her spine.

As much as she regretted the necessity of starting over, a spark of satisfaction from making the right decision fueled her confidence. *Lord, courage comes from You. Please don't let me falter.* It still felt strange to turn to God, but surprisingly, not difficult. The warmth of His presence surrounded her like a ray of sunshine on a clear summer day. *Lord, thank You for coming into my life at the very time I need you the most. I'm sorry I didn't look to You before I deceived the professor. I know now You would've guided me down the right path. I'd have resisted Mr. Phifer's offer and avoided the mess I'm in now. Please forgive me, Father.*

The future would take care of itself, with God's help. She had a powerful feeling she was in loving hands. Charlotte returned to the house and found Daniel gathering his books for his ten o'clock class. Concern deepened the fine web of lines edging his eyes.

Tell him the truth. But he was rushing off to work. Confession would have to wait awhile longer.

He took his bowler from the hat rack and then paused. "Charlotte, please take the rest of the day off and speak to your aunt. If your uncle needs your help, you ought to go to him."

"Thank you, sir. I believe I should speak to Aunt Amelia, but I'm quite certain Uncle Wilbur doesn't require my assistance."

Daniel nodded. "Feel free to use the gig."

"Thank you, sir."

She didn't deserve his generosity. She owed him the truth. "Sir, I need to speak with you privately when you're less busy."

A smile turned up the corners of his mouth. "Yes, how about late this afternoon?"

She left Summerhill before she lost her determination. As she climbed into the gig, she planned her strategy. She'd confront Mr. Phifer, say her peace, and accept the consequences of her brazen action, if not fearlessly, then at least with dignity. Swallowing the lump in her throat, she wondered if her nerve might fail her once she faced her boss's wrath.

Daniel wouldn't compromise his principles and neither would she.

Anxiety filled her chest as the gig rolled past the estates along Ocean Drive and neared town. She halted in front of the newspaper office and inhaled a deep breath of sea air that tasted dank and briny. "I'll be right back, old girl," she murmured to the horse. The mare snorted and stamped her foot. Charlotte fed her a sugar cube and patted her head. "Wish me well."

Charlotte entered the building and slowly climbed the steps to the second floor. Before she reached the landing, her legs weakened and threatened to let her fall. She gripped the stair rail and slowly made her way up the steep flight. Her boots felt as heavy as concrete. When she finally reached the door of the *Rhode Island Reporter,* she squared her hunched shoulders and marched into the newsroom, feigning bravado.

A few of the news reporters nodded, then continued their work. Smiling in reply, she strode toward her boss's office. She rapped twice on Mr. Phifer's closed door and waited.

No response. She raised her hand to knock again when a shout blasted through the door. "Come in."

Delaying the inevitable was pointless. After a moment's hesitation, Charlotte pulled the door open and stepped into the editor's inner sanctum. When she noted his belligerent glare, her heart crashed against her ribcage. He sat at his desk, pipe in hand.

"You thwarted my plan for placing Miss Wengle with the Wilmonts. I don't appreciate your insubordination, Miss Hale."

"Sir, Professor Wilmont is an upstanding citizen, and the only way Edith Ann will find something against him will be by conjuring up false evidence." She shook her head. "It is just not right."

"It is out of your hands, Miss Hale. My

decision has been made." He glared for several seconds before his expression unexpectedly softened. "Listen, if you leave Summerhill without a fuss, I'll allow you to resume your old position. You gave it a shot, but you came up dry." Then his eyes steeled. "But I will not tolerate an ounce more of your disobedience. Do you understand, Miss Hale?"

Air rushed back into Charlotte's lungs. Despite all her fears, she was still employed at the *Rhode Island Reporter*. She could scarcely believe her ears. All she had to do was to move aside and let Edith Ann complete the assignment and she'd be right back in her original position, except for this one black mark on her record.

But how could she leave the professor alone and unarmed? Especially knowing what was sure to ensue?

Mr. Phifer's voice boomed. "Return to the Wilmonts at once, adopt the excuse we gave you, and explain that Miss Wengle will take over your job. She'll begin tomorrow." He looked down at the papers on his desk, dismissing her.

Charlotte's voice quavered. "Mr. Phifer, I'm afraid I cannot." She swallowed the dust floating in the stifling air. "What you intend to do is unethical, and I cannot be a part of it."

Mr. Phifer's face blew up like a red balloon. "Excuse me, Miss Hale, but you're already part of it. I'm certain I misunderstood your last comment. You didn't accuse me of being immoral, did you?"

"Unethical, sir."

His eyes bulged. "I'm afraid we're not on the same page anymore, young woman. I won't put up with you criticizing my methods. If you disapprove of me and my newspaper, perhaps you should find yourself a new employer."

A wave of nausea rolled through Charlotte's stomach. "You're right, I should." She took a deep, steadying breath, but it didn't slow her thundering heartbeat. "In fact, as of this very instant, I quit."

Her voice wavered, but she'd said what she had to. Relief flooded through her, along with a ripple of fear that she'd ruined her career forever. At least she'd saved the professor from the likes of Mr. Phifer and Edith Ann, and that was what really mattered.

The editor bellowed, "I can't believe you'd quit the best job you'll ever get just because we disagree."

"I can and I did," Charlotte said calmly.

"Well, Miss Hale, you won't get a reference from me."

"That's all right, sir. I'm ashamed I worked for your newspaper and I'm just sorry I took the assignment at Summerhill." She exhaled a long breath. Freed from the bonds of deceit, her conscience lightened. A half smile formed on her lips. "Good day, Mr. Phifer."

She spun around and silently left the office. He followed on her heels. Charlotte quickly gathered her personal belongings from her desk and glanced up to see Mr. Phifer scowling in the doorway, hands planted on the sides of his ample waist. She exited without daring to wish her fellow employees farewell or offer them an explanation, though they glanced at her with unspoken curiosity.

As she drove the short distance to Bridge Street, fear bubbled up in her chest. She had no job prospects and no way to support her family. Her subterfuge now lay in the past, albeit the immediate past, but gone forever. Never again would she jump at the chance for success without weighing the consequences. She hurried to Bridge Street, ready to pour out her news to Aunt Amelia.

She found her aunt digging up potatoes in the back garden. A basket of yellow squash lay on the grass beside her. The poor woman straightened and braced her arthritic spine with her rough and dirty hands. Despite her pain she managed a smile.

"You're a sight for sore eyes, Charlotte. What brings you home?" Amelia piled the potatoes on top of the squash. They went inside to the cool and quiet kitchen. Her aunt dumped the food into the sink, scrubbed her hands, and exchanged her dirty apron for a clean one.

"I've lots of news."

Aunt Amelia grunted. "I do hope it's good."

"Where's Becky?" Charlotte asked, looking around the empty kitchen bathed in the golden light of afternoon.

"Next door visiting the neighbors." After pouring a glass of milk, Amelia plucked a blueberry muffin from a woven basket, then found a plate, knife, and slab of butter. "Just in case you're hungry. Becky baked them herself. She's turning into quite the good cook." She raised an eyebrow.

"Please sit down. I have something to say that affects all three of us."

The older woman obliged, her face pinched with worry. "Out with it, please."

"I quit the newspaper."

Aunt Amelia's hand thumped her chest

and her mouth gaped. "Mercy me! What happened?"

"It's quite a story." Briefly Charlotte explained the situation and waited for Amelia to absorb the news. "I'm so sorry for letting you and Becky down. I have a few more weeks at Summerhill before the Wilmonts move away. During that time, I'll search for another position." If she had the chance.

Aunt Amelia flicked a smile. "Anyone would be fortunate to hire you. You're a hard worker, reliable, and full of fun. I'll start asking around myself. You'll find something."

Charlotte nodded, though not at all confident she'd find a good position without a reference from either Mr. Phifer or the professor. "When I return to Summerhill, I'm going to confess my part in the scheme."

Aunt Amelia pressed her lips together and nodded. "Yes, I suppose you must." She leaned forward across the table. "To be perfectly honest, I'm a mite relieved you walked away from Arnie Phifer's newspaper. And I'm proud you told him why you were quitting in no uncertain terms." She squeezed Charlotte's arm. "You've always done what's right."

Charlotte shook her head. "No, I'm afraid

I haven't. I accepted the assignment when I should've turned it down, no matter how enticing. I've learned my lesson. I'll be ever so much more careful in the future."

"Of course you will." Aunt Amelia steepled her fingers. "So you're coming home soon?"

Tears threatened to spill down Charlotte's cheeks. "Yes."

"Hmm." A gleam of understanding shone in her eyes. "But I think you'd rather stay at Summerhill. You're more than a little interested in Professor Wilmont, aren't you? I can't blame you. He's a mighty handsome fellow. Don't deny it, Charlotte. I can see the truth in your face. That blush of yours gives you away."

Charlotte busied herself buttering the muffin. "All right. I admit I admire him. And he's a kind and considerate employer." And so much more.

"Does he have feelings for you as well?"

Charlotte took a bite to delay her answer. "He mentioned he'd like to get to know me better, but I don't take that as a declaration of his devotion. He's rich, though he might not think so, and I'm not. Being poor causes me no shame, but it puts an impossible barrier between us. Please don't fret. I'm not making a spectacle of myself chasing after him." She hung her head. "I've done enough to disgrace myself without adding forwardness to the list."

"Do you think his intentions are serious, despite the differences in your social standing?"

Charlotte gulped. "I don't know. But it couldn't possibly work out between us. Even if he did have feelings that could surmount our differences, I'm not sure we could get past his mother. She's rather . . . formidable."

Aunt Amelia nodded. "But the professor — he is right for you, isn't he? Oh Charlotte, don't try to pretend he's not."

"It doesn't matter how I feel because" — Charlotte breathed deeply — "I deceived him. When I confess the truth, he'll hate me." Her voice snagged. "I have to tell him everything and then apologize. He might forgive me because he's a good Christian, but he won't like me very much. It's such a mess . . . and it's all my fault."

"I'm so sorry," Aunt Amelia's voice soothed. She came over to her and swallowed Charlotte in a hug.

Charlotte blinked back a stream of tears. "I'd best be going." She headed for the front hallway.

On the drive back to Summerhill, she let

the tears fall until none remained. The breeze dried her damp cheeks. She had to admit she cared very much for the professor. Every time she glimpsed him, her heart fluttered.

She'd committed the unforgivable act of spying and then falling in love. Life would never be the same again.

NINETEEN

With Ruthie and Tim beside him, Daniel pushed through the waves at Summerhill's secluded beach. The young pair laughed and squealed with delight as chilly breakers smashed against them and sent them tumbling into the surf. Daniel turned sideways and splashed water at their bobbing torsos, but his heart wasn't really in the fun.

When the sun had at last split the dark skies, he'd invited the children for a swim, hoping his dark mood would lift. They ought to take advantage of their proximity to the sea while they still had the chance.

"Miss Hale's back," Ruthie called, shading her eyes against the sunshine and grinning.

Daniel looked around and spotted Charlotte kicking up sand as she approached the water. Dressed in her white shirtwaist, black skirt, and straw hat, she looked hot and agitated. Her face blazed with color. He wondered if her bright complexion came from the sun or from something else.

"I believe I'll say hello," Daniel said to his children.

Ruthie shot him a precocious grin, obviously pleased. Daniel stifled a smile as he trudged through the surf toward the shore. Ruthie and Tim followed him back, then lingered at the water's edge to build a massive sand castle — "the biggest ever!" Tim cried.

When he reached her, Charlotte handed him a towel he'd left on the sand. "Mrs. Finnegan said you and the children went for a swim. They certainly enjoy spending time with you."

The pleasure in her voice raised his spirits and sent goose bumps down his arms. He gave a sardonic smile. "If I don't find a position soon, they'll see a lot more of me."

"Surely you'll find something."

"I might have to look into fields other than teaching."

"Don't lose heart. I'm certain something wonderful will turn up. Anyone would be lucky to hire you." Her blush deepened, but she didn't avert her gaze.

Her kindness wrapped him in hope and even optimism. "Thank you for the vote of confidence."

They strolled toward the boulders that secluded the beach from the lawn, found the smoothest one, and dropped down. It didn't matter that the stone was hard and sandy. He was near enough to Charlotte to feel her shoulder brush against his and smell the faint scent of talcum powder blended with the clean aroma of Pears soap.

"How was your aunt, Charlotte?" he asked slowly. "Was she quite taken aback by the news?"

"No," she said. "Sir, there is something —"

"Please call me Daniel."

She nodded. "If you wish."

"I do. We've been formal for far too long."

She studied him for a long moment. "Daniel, if you don't think I'm too personal — I do hope you and the children can stay in Newport."

He dared to pick up her hand and hold it. "No, not at all. I want you to be personal with me, Charlotte. You must know you're so much more to me than just my children's governess."

She didn't try to slip her fingers away.

His confidence grew. "The truth is I want to remain here — with you." When her gaze met his, she was smiling — but sadness reached down into their depths. He waited for her response and hoped she wouldn't turn away or, even worse, run off.

"Daniel, I've done things you wouldn't approve of. I've made dreadful mistakes, which I regret with all my heart. Mistakes I can't easily correct." She lowered her head, yet he could tell she was blinking back tears.

He squeezed her hand, offering reassurance. "You've confessed these sins to the Lord, and He's forgiven you."

She shook her head, appearing unconvinced and uncommonly serious. "I wish it was that easy, but it's not. You'd be shocked — and disappointed — in me. I wouldn't blame you. I'm not the woman you want me to be. Or the woman you think I am." Charlotte stared at the surf, her lower lip trembling. "Under different circumstances, I'd love to get to know you better. But I have to be sensible and so do you." Her voice choked with sorrow.

"Charlotte, tell me what's bothering you. Trust me to understand."

She shook her head. "I want to tell you, but it's so hard to confess my faults — my sins. The Lord forgave me and that's a tremendous blessing and such a relief. I'm a different person than I was just a short time ago. But the effects of sin linger. I haven't been altogether honest with you about myself."

"You said you've changed and that's all that matters to me."

"But if I don't unburden myself, my sin will always stand between us, at least on my part."

For a moment he thought she'd burst into tears, but then her trembling lips curved into a sad smile.

"Please let me tell you now."

"Papa! Papa!" Tim yelled.

Reluctantly, he turned from Charlotte to gaze at his son.

"Come! Bring Miss Hale! You have to see our castle!"

Daniel turned back to Charlotte. "Please dine with me tomorrow night. We can discuss whatever is on your heart then. How does the Coastal Inn sound to you? Or perhaps another restaurant? I'd like us to spend some time together without my family around."

She hesitated so long Daniel felt sure she'd decline. He held his breath until she nodded slowly. "I must tell you certain things in private and without interruptions. So, yes, I accept your invitation."

Daniel resisted his longing to smother her in a hug. "Tomorrow at seven thirty."

Charlotte's shoulders relaxed and her lips

tilted up in a dry smile. "That is, I may go if my employer can do without me for the evening."

Daniel broadened his grin. "He thinks he might be able to get by."

"Then I shall." Her voice flowed like cream, but her smile held more than a hint of melancholy.

He couldn't imagine why she wanted to confess to him, and it wasn't necessary. Tomorrow they'd resolve all her concerns.

He glanced toward the children who were adding another level to their giant castle. Daniel eased off the boulder and took her hands in his. Gently he urged her toward him but not as near as he'd like. His heartbeat quickened. He wanted to press her against his chest and feel her softness and smell her sun-drenched skin salted with briny sea air. But he was still damp from his swim.

He leaned forward to kiss her, fully expecting her to resist. But Charlotte tilted her head back and let him touch his mouth against hers and taste the sweetness of her lips. Her gasp was barely audible, but even with the rush of the breeze and the pounding of the surf, he heard her surprised reaction. She stepped closer and brushed against the top of his damp swimsuit, obviously not concerned her cotton shirtwaist would absorb the moisture. He encircled his arms around her and gently pulled her nearer.

"I love you, Charlotte," he murmured.

She lifted her chin and searched his eyes. "I believe you do, but it wouldn't —"

He bent over and covered her mouth with his again. Enjoying the moment, he wished the sensation of holding her would never end.

Then she glanced over his shoulder, jerked away, and smoothed her skirt. "I'm afraid the children are staring at us. Please excuse me, Daniel. I must be getting back to the cottage."

Before he could object, she was gone. She strode through the soft sand and over the dunes, stepping around tall, swaying grass. With a sigh, he turned to face Ruthie and Tim. The grinning scamps shot across the beach.

"Papa, you were kissing Miss Hale! Now you have to marry her." Ruthie clapped her hands.

Tim nodded.

Daniel put up his palms. "Whoa. You're getting ahead of yourself." But he knew otherwise and from their expressions, so did they. No gentleman kissed a lady if his intentions weren't serious and honorable. Even the children understood. "Please don't tease Miss Hale or even mention — the kiss — to anyone, especially your grandmother."

"All right." Tim shrugged and then wandered off to scan the beach for shells.

"Grandmother doesn't like many people, but I'm sure she'll learn to love Miss Hale, just as we do," Ruthie said, exuding the confidence of a young girl.

"We should hope and pray she'll soften."

But Daniel didn't really believe his own words. His mother disapproved of any woman she didn't choose, and she'd especially dislike a governess joining the family. Still, though her blessing and good wishes weren't necessary, he'd try to persuade her to accept Charlotte.

Ruthie planted her fists on her straight hips. "I know the Lord wants you to marry Miss Hale. I asked Him and He said yes in my heart." Ruthie's eyes were so round and earnest Daniel had to smile and even absorb some of her optimism.

"We'll see, pumpkin." Daniel clasped his hands behind his back and gazed out to sea.

"You can't wait forever, Papa, or you'll miss the moment." Ruthie breathed out a dramatic sigh. "Remember, you're supposed to do what God wants, according to His perfect timing. And He told me His perfect timing is right now — well, not in so many words, but I got His message."

Daniel laughed. "And now I have it too. Go play before the fog rolls in." As Ruthie sprinted back to her sand castle — already dissolving into the encroaching tide — Daniel sat on the rock and ran his fingers through his windblown hair.

Ruthie was right. He should ask Charlotte to marry him. With no time to waste, he needed to propose as soon as possible and pray she'd accept an unemployed professor with no job prospects. Somehow they'd manage to get along, though without the frills his mother and children were used to.

He'd married the first time to please his mother, but now he'd choose his own wife. His union with Sarah had buried them both in misery. Mismatched, they reached out for each other, yet never touched, except physically. And that wasn't enough to satisfy either of them. But Charlotte's smile banished his resolution to remain single. She'd flung open the locked door of his heart and stepped inside, bringing sunshine and joy. Her objections didn't deter him. She admitted her affection and that's what mattered most. They'd work out their problems, large and small, and then she'd agree to his proposal. Despite her reservations, she was sure to come around.

It was well past time to close the chapter of his life with Sarah and open a new one with Charlotte.

Charlotte rushed across the lawn into the cool deserted kitchen. Voices rose and fell from the direction of the pantry. Chef Jacques was scolding one of the kitchen maids. Relieved no one was in the servants' hall, she dropped onto a ladder-back chair set around the long table. She waited for her chest to quit heaving, but she couldn't relax. She needed time alone to collect her thoughts and decipher how much Daniel's kiss had altered their relationship. They'd stepped over the line separating employee from employer. Why hadn't she pushed him away? Instead she'd reveled in his affection, *just one kiss before I say good-bye* ringing through her head. Yet she should've discouraged his advances.

She buried her head in her hands. She couldn't concentrate on anything but the kiss from the man she loved yet could never have — because of her secret and her own sinfulness. Unshed tears of regret burned her eyes. She closed them tight and recalled the taste of his lips and the scent of his sun-brushed skin. A long groan escaped from her throat.

"Now who could that be, moaning so loud?"

Charlotte startled as Mrs. Finnegan bustled into the room.

"My word, you're about to cry. Something's gone wrong, hasn't it? I'm all ears if you'd like a good talk." She squinted with sympathy as she dropped into the chair across the table.

Charlotte shook her head. Sniffing back tears, she answered, "I appreciate your concern, but I'm all right."

"A nice cold glass of lemonade might help." Mrs. Finnegan heaved herself up.

"Yes, please, if you don't mind."

Mrs. Finnegan soon returned from the kitchen with two tall glasses and sat at the table across from Charlotte. She leaned forward, her hands folded on the tablecloth. "Now tell me, what's the matter, dearie? It's the Wilmonts, isn't it? The professor wouldn't upset a soul, so it must be his mother. How are you and Mrs. Wilmont getting on?"

"She doesn't like me one bit." Heat scorched Charlotte's face as she recalled all the cutting remarks she'd endured when she really wanted to defend herself and throw her silly little doily cap at her. Or even better, strangle her with the cap's streamers.

Leaning closer, the housekeeper lowered her voice to a conspiratorial whisper. "I've worked me fingers to the bone for Mrs. Wilmont for over thirty years. And she still doesn't appreciate my efforts." She chuckled and then waved in dismissal. "But it doesn't matter one way or t'other. Wouldn't I be in sad shape if it did? She's a tough old hen, but I try not to ruffle her feathers. I do me work best I can, and mind me own business. We get along fine that way."

"You mean I shouldn't take her criticisms to heart?" Charlotte gave a lopsided smile. She couldn't imagine ignoring such a nasty lady for more than thirty years.

"I mean just that. Do your chores and don't fret if you can't please her. Some people are born complainers and won't bother to change." Mrs. Finnegan flashed crooked teeth. "Don't you know she suffered from her husband's neglect. Shameful, he was. The man never came home when he could stay away. Hoarded his money too. No wonder the missus turned bitter. He broke her heart."

"That's dreadful," Charlotte admitted with grudging sympathy. Yet an unhappy marriage didn't justify her sour disposition and mean spirit.

Mrs. Finnegan sipped her lemonade. "Mr. Wilmont owned several stove-making factories, so he was in a position to give his wife all she wanted. But he held everything back."

"He sounds like an old miser."

"That he was. He willed the business to his son, Edgar, but he neglected to leave much to the rest of the family. Of course a million or two dollars is a fortune to most folks, but to Mrs. Wilmont, it was a slap in the face. Seems the randy gentleman had a woman on the side with extravagant tastes. She squandered most of his fortune on trinkets for herself. But enough gossip." Mrs. Finnegan set her lips tight.

"I can see Mrs. Wilmont was mistreated, but still, that's no excuse for her attitude."

"Tisn't, to be sure. But it's why she's like she is. She's a hard woman to please, especially if she doesn't take to you."

The sound of footsteps in the hallway diverted Charlotte's attention. She glanced up to find the professor dressed in a fresh white shirt and tan trousers. A frown squeezed his brow until he spotted Mrs. Finnegan, then his mouth curved into a smile.

Mrs. Finnegan's cheeks puffed with pleasure. "Good afternoon, sir. Is there something I can be getting for you?"

"My mother would like a cup of tea, please."

"Yes, sir. I'll have it sent up right away." Mrs. Finnegan headed for the kitchen.

"Where are Tim and Ruthie? I ought to get them cleaned up," Charlotte said, avoiding Daniel's steady gaze. Their wet clothes would dribble sand and salt water throughout the house and give Mrs. Wilmont a good excuse to complain — not that she needed one.

"I sent them upstairs to wash," Daniel said, hovering, as if reluctant to leave.

"I'll go right up." Charlotte swallowed the last drops of her icy drink and rose. She edged around him and up the stairs, feeling the heat of his gaze until she disappeared into the cool of the stairwell.

TWENTY

The next afternoon, Daniel and his mother hosted a luncheon for the Grails and several friends. Chef Jacques outdid himself with his French specialties, but Daniel had no appetite for rich cream sauces. Later, after most of the guests departed, Jack took him aside. "Shall we talk a little business?"

Mrs. Wilmont and Mr. McClintock led Lilly into the drawing room while Daniel and Jack adjourned to the library. They puffed cigars and settled in wing chairs by a crackling fire that burned off the chill.

Jack leaned forward. "Have you considered my offer to write a column for the *Manhattan Sentinel*?"

"Yes, and I accept gladly." Daniel explained President Ralston's ultimatum and his own answer. "So far I haven't heard from any of the colleges or boys' schools I've contacted, and since I'm so late applying, I'm not optimistic."

Jack took a puff on his cigar. "Would you be interested in working for me in New York? We have positions open on either the newspaper or magazine. Or would you prefer the publishing house? All three are doing well, I'm pleased to say. I'm in dire need of management and editorial help."

Jack mentioned a salary that Daniel thought more than generous, certainly larger than he required to support his family and servants. How could he turn down Jack's offer? "I certainly do appreciate your kindness."

"But —"

"I'm a teacher. I have no experience in publishing."

Jack dismissed Daniel's doubts with a wave of his cigar. "You'll learn quickly."

"Then I accept. And thank you." Daniel nodded with as much enthusiasm as he could rally. Relief mixed with regret.

"You can begin at Jones and Jarman, my publishing house, if that appeals to you. When can you start?"

"In a few weeks, as soon as the semester ends. I'm really grateful for the opportunity, yet I'm afraid no one in the family wishes to move."

"I understand why they'd rather stay in Newport." Jack sent him a sympathetic nod.

"It's a beautiful place, though rather dreary in winter, I hear."

Daniel drummed his fingers on the arm of the chair and blew out a sigh. "That's true, but this has been our home for several years, so it's difficult to leave." Daniel hoped he didn't sound as grim as he felt.

He'd prayed — actually stormed heaven — that a position would turn up locally. But perhaps moving away was God's answer to his problem. A crucial question remained — could he convince Charlotte to come along, not as a governess, but as his wife? They'd simply have to find a way to care for her aunt and sister from afar.

After Jack and Lilly left, Daniel gathered his family, Mr. McClintock, and Charlotte into the drawing room. As he scrutinized all the anxious faces, his spirits sank.

Hands clasped behind his back, he paced between the long windows framed with velvet curtains, then halted. "I have news about our future. I've accepted a position at Jackson Grail's publishing house in New York. Unfortunately, we'll have to move to the city."

His mother's soft groan and Charlotte's sudden intake of breath made him pause. He scrutinized each unhappy face. "I'm so sorry, but I have no other choice. We'd all like to stay in Newport, myself included. But I'm afraid that's not feasible. So let's make the best of it and not complain — at least not too loudly or too long." His halfhearted stab at optimism fell flat, even to his own ears.

Glancing toward Charlotte, he noticed her normally rosy complexion had faded to white. "I hope you'll come with us. We need you." With perspiration coating his neck and face, he waited for her reply to break his heart.

"Of course I'd like to stay with you." Charlotte's voice cracked as she gazed down at her clutched hands and avoided eye contact. If she cried, he knew he'd fall apart as well. But she steadied and said, "But I can't. My aunt and my sister need me here."

"May I have a word with you — alone?" Daniel asked, heading for the hallway and ignoring his mother's *harrumph.* Even Mr. McClintock looked troubled as he reached for Vivian's hand.

Daniel heard Charlotte's footsteps as he strode down the hallway, passed through the foyer and down another hallway to the back veranda. Together they walked across the grass and out of his mother's hearing range. Charlotte hung her head and hugged her chest against the damp air. A chilly breeze wracked him with shivers as well.

Stopping by the rocks at the edge of the sea, Daniel turned to face her. He gently lifted her chin so her troubled eyes met his own. Beneath the fading afternoon sunlight, her cheeks glimmered with tears.

"Please come with us, Charlotte. I understand why you feel you should stay in Newport, but instead, perhaps you could send your family money. And of course you'd visit often. New York isn't really so far away."

She shook her head and her upswept hair loosened, freeing strands of dark silk. "It's more than just supporting Aunt Amelia and Becky. Please. I'll tell you what is holding me back . . . later."

"Tell me now," he said lowly.

"Papa!" Tim came tearing around the corner. "Why do we have to move, Papa? I want to stay here."

Charlotte gave Daniel a long look. "Later," she repeated in a whisper. And then she walked away.

That evening at seven o'clock Charlotte slipped off to her bedroom, her every nerve on edge. She searched her wardrobe for something appropriate to wear to the Coastal Inn with Daniel. She'd accepted his invitation to dine so she'd have enough privacy to confess. No one had ever invited her to a fancy dinner, so she owned nothing suitable, though funereal black might be best considering the reason she'd accepted Daniel's invitation. Charlotte sighed, wishing the whole ordeal was over and she was safely back home with Becky and Aunt Amelia.

Well, appropriate or not, she refused to wear black, for she was neither a real servant nor an elegant lady. She put on her new cream-colored blouse and peered at her reflection in the mirror above her bureau. Her aunt's lovely creation complemented her ecru skirt, her one and only dressy garment. At least she wouldn't appear shabby and cause the other diners to stare.

A knock on the door startled her. "Charlotte, it's me. Grace. Please let me in. I only have a minute."

Charlotte opened the door and Grace burst into the room.

"Oh my, don't you look grand. But that old straw hat of yours won't do. Wait here and I'll fetch my new one. I bought it at the milliners at the end of the season last year."

She rushed out and quickly returned with a flowered hat with pale blue chiffon swirling around the crown. Positioning it on

Charlotte's head, Grace examined it with a critical eye. "Perfect."

"Thank you so much." Charlotte gazed in the mirror, surprised at a reflection she hardly recognized. "I actually feel pretty." Which was not the impression she ought to convey to Daniel. She should look presentable, not fancy or too feminine.

"The entire staff knows you're going to dinner with the professor. They're all abuzz."

Charlotte winced as she pulled on her gloves. "News travels fast around Summerhill."

"Indeed, it does. One of the parlor maids overheard the professor arguing with his mother over it. But don't let Mrs. Wilmont ruin your evening. Enjoy yourself, Charlotte. Do tell me all about it when you come home."

Charlotte dropped onto her bed and let a groan escape from her lips. "I'm going to confess something important to the professor tonight. I can't talk here very freely with so many prying eyes and ears."

Grace looked at her with obvious curiosity, but she didn't ask any questions. "I'll pray everything will work out." Grace touched Charlotte's hands and squeezed tight.

"Thank you. I'll explain the entire story when I return. I'd best go now."

Taking a deep breath, Charlotte descended the front staircase and met Daniel in the foyer. Dressed in a starched white shirt with black tie and coat, he carried a silk top hat. His blue-green eyes were lit with an inner warmth that for a moment stole her breath along with her resolve. How could she hurt this wonderful man? Together they stepped outside into the glow of early evening. The carriage and coachman awaited them. Charlotte's hands perspired in her gloves as she clutched the strings of her reticule. "It's a grand evening," she rasped in an unsteady voice. Birds chirped in the gently swaying branches, waves broke against the rocks, a breeze hummed.

His eyes sparkled as he surveyed her outfit, and then a small smile broadened into a wide grin. "You look lovely."

Her cheeks flamed. "Thank you." She tried to steel herself against his compliment.

He took her by the arm and helped her down the veranda steps and into the carriage.

Ruthie and Tim appeared from around the bushes. "Enjoy your dinner." Ruthie giggled.

Charlotte and Daniel waved to his children. He leaned toward her and murmured, "I'm afraid my children are getting carried away. When I told Tim we were having dinner together, he snickered. But Ruthie jumped up and down and clapped."

Charlotte smiled. She tried to stay calm, but her nerves were prickling like porcupine quills. She'd never been to a swanky dinner with a man before. She wished he'd chosen a more informal spot where he wouldn't be recognized and where she'd feel more comfortable in her pretty but inexpensive clothing. Her mind kept straying from her upcoming task — to tell Daniel the truth. All she could think about was his arm brushing against hers and his soft voice so close to her ear. He looked cool and composed except for a trickle of moisture that formed a liquid mustache over his upper lip. He understood an employer simply didn't dine in public with his servant, but she respected him for defying snobbery. He seemed to be handling this awkward situation with great aplomb.

They kept up a steady stream of small talk until they reached the Coastal Inn, a white clapboard hotel and restaurant set behind tall hedges and shaded by towering maples. The back lawn faced the Cliff Walk and the sea. As they neared the front porch lined with a profusion of shrubs and blue hydrangeas, Charlotte's heart fluttered.

Once inside the dining room, the waiter led them to a table overlooking the back lawn bathed in gathering shadows. As she and Daniel lowered onto gilded chairs, Charlotte heard the steady hum of the cultured voices punctuated by the crackle of a fire in the fireplace. If only she could enjoy the ambiance of dancing candlelight and crystal chandeliers. Jeweled women in silks and satins might make her feel out of place ordinarily, but tonight she scarcely noticed. Instead, she focused on the man she was soon to hurt.

They ordered lobster Thermidor and other delicacies, but food didn't appeal to her. The first bites thudded to the pit of her stomach. Putting down her fork, Charlotte tried to quiet her fear. She needed to say what was on her mind and get it over with. But before she could push out even one word, Daniel leaned across the white linen tablecloth and spoke in a deliberate way that captured her attention.

"I — we — have something important to discuss." He reached across the table and covered her hand with his own.

She let his hand rest on hers for the few moments it took to compose herself. Slipping her fingers out from under his warm, gentle touch, she half smiled. "I believe you know several people in this dining room. If they see us holding hands, they might misconstrue our relationship."

His eyes lost their light for a second. "What others think doesn't matter to me. Charlotte, we haven't known each other long, but during that time we've become friends. Close friends, I hope."

"Yes, of course we're friends."

"What I'm trying to say is, how do you feel about — committing to . . . Well, the truth is I've fallen hopelessly in love with you." He reached in his pocket and produced a velvet jewelry box. "Charlotte Hale, would you do me the honor of marrying me?"

Her body froze. Daniel stared with hope gleaming in his eyes. She raised her palms to stop the flow of words before tears began to stream down her face. "I'm overcome. I didn't expect you to propose! I — I'm truly honored." She took a deep breath and glanced around, wondering if anyone was looking at them. "But we mustn't speak of marriage until I tell you something that I'm afraid will change your mind."

"What is it?" The black box lay open on the white linen tablecloth beside his plate, the diamond gleaming in the soft candle-light.

"As I've said before, I haven't been entirely truthful with you, Daniel." Charlotte took a deep breath. "I came to Summerhill to —"

His held up a gentle hand, stopping her. "Charlotte, I don't want to know. I told you before what you did in the past isn't important to me. You regret your mistakes and God forgives them. There's no need to dwell on them or reveal the details. If God has forgiven you, who am I to hold anything against you?" He shrugged and shook his head. "Don't you see? It's done. Gone. Over."

Charlotte looked away, afraid if their gazes locked she'd cry out with relief. He was such a kind man and she didn't deserve him, not by any stretch of the imagination. He accepted her unconditionally.

"No. I must tell you because — I've sinned against *you*. And you have a right to know what I did."

Daniel shook his head. "But I don't want to."

"Are you sure?" her voice squeaked. He'd handed her a reprieve. Should she take it? Confession would surely relieve her conscience, but it would wound him deeply.

Indecision gripped her mind. He was giving her an escape, but was it too easy? "How can you be so certain?"

"You can stop looking at me as if I am perfect. Far from it. If I were brave I'd ask for the particulars and let you clear your conscience. But Charlotte, I'm afraid it could gnaw at me, get in the way of . . . *us.*"

He leaned closer. "Please let me explain." His face drooped with a look of despair. "My wife Sarah had an affair with one of my friends while we were attempting to salvage our marriage. I never suspected. I believed we were making progress and we'd gradually fall in love all over again." He tapped his finger against the tablecloth. "But then she was killed in a coaching accident with that same friend. Soon after, I found her journal and began to read it."

Charlotte stifled a sharp intake of breath. She knew what was coming.

"I thought it might help me overcome my grief and bring peace to my mind. Instead, I learned of her love for another. It broke my heart that she'd deceived me."

"I'm so sorry, Daniel."

"It hurt too much to learn the truth. I was better off not knowing all the facts."

"I understand why you don't wish to hear

my confession. It surely would cause you pain." And drive a wedge between them.

He drew out a ring and reached for her hand. "So, Charlotte, will you marry me?"

"I don't know what to say," she murmured.

"Just say yes." He tried to slide the ring on her finger, but she withdrew her hand. "What's wrong?"

"I can't marry you. With all my heart, I wish I could."

"Charlotte, please reconsider. I love you and I think you love me as well."

Perhaps he'd spared her a confession, but she couldn't marry him with a weight as heavy as the guilt crushing her heart. He placed her on a pedestal. Her heart ached, but leaving him with a pleasant, if distorted, impression of her was better than confessing and bringing him only disillusionment. He refused the truth and she wouldn't force him to hear it. He was a good man, but he was only human. Hot tears stung the back of her eyes, ready to betray her confusion.

She wouldn't force him to listen, but she couldn't marry him with her conscience burdened with guilt. Besides, so many other things sought to keep them apart. "You come from a privileged family while mine is quite ordinary. No one would accept me as a suitable wife for you, and who could blame them?"

"Certainly we have differences in our backgrounds, but neither of us subscribe to such conventionalities."

Charlotte sighed. "And I won't move to New York."

She glanced away to avoid the shock and sorrow in his face — she could feel the echoes of it across the table.

"I think we ought to go," she whispered. Then a small sob escaped. "I'm sorry things can't work out between us."

"No, Charlotte, please stay. We can find a way if we try. I've prayed about it and —"

"So have I. It's no use." She rose on unsteady legs and turned away. Her throat clogged with dismay and she couldn't swallow. She didn't want Daniel to see the conflict that must be parading across her face. "I'm sorry to leave before we've had our dinner, but I must go."

As she wove around the tables toward the door, she scanned the small crowd of cheerful diners. How she envied them their gaiety.

The ride home in the buggy seemed interminable. She watched Daniel stare straight ahead, never glancing in her direction. His jaw sagged with obvious disappointment. Minutes dragged by as the horses' hooves beat against the dark dirt roads, nearly drowning out the hum of crickets and tree frogs.

TWENTY-ONE

Slouched in his buggy, Daniel watched Charlotte rush toward the servants' entrance at the rear of Summerhill. She disappeared without even a backward glance. With a weary sigh, he buried his face in his hands, blocking out the inky blue sky.

Lord, I'm not sure what exactly went wrong, but I'm beseeching You to please change her mind about marrying me. I can't imagine living without Charlotte by my side. She's everything I want and need in a wife. You brought us together, so I don't understand why You've let her turn away from me. It doesn't make any sense.

He climbed out of the carriage and watched the coachman head toward the stable. The *clip-clop* of horses' hooves soon died away. He walked past the back veranda facing the water. Pale moonlight sprinkled its glitter over the black waves edged with silver lace. The rustle of trees and the wash of the sea wrapped him with the soothing voice of night. But comfort didn't come. He stood at the edge of the lawn for several long minutes, buffeted by salt spray, chilled by the breeze and by his own dashed hopes. When he finally turned around, he looked to the veranda, wishing Charlotte would emerge through the French doors. But of course she didn't. He glanced up to her second floor bedroom. Lamplight glowed in her window, then after a while, flickered to darkness. Blank, empty windows stared down at him.

He heaved a groan as he returned to the cottage. His stomach grumbled, so he went straight to the dining room and he rang for some supper. Anything would do. He settled into a heavy upholstered chair and waited.

In a short while his mother swept in, her thin lips pursed in surprise. "Why, it's only nine o'clock. I didn't expect you home so soon. How was your dinner?"

He shrugged as a maid placed a bowl of steaming clam chowder on the table in front of him. "All right, I suppose."

"Oh? I find it strange you're hungry after dinner at the Coastal Inn. Didn't they give you enough to eat?" Cold amusement played at the corner of her mouth.

Daniel recoiled. "We didn't stay long

enough to finish our meal. We both needed to be alone, so we left early."

He took a spoonful of the rich creamy broth. "As soon as I eat a little of this, I'm adjourning for the night. But first, I'll explain what happened so you won't speculate. I asked Charlotte to marry me and she turned me down."

His mother's eyes flashed anger. "I can't believe you proposed to that woman. Whatever possessed you?"

"Love, Mother. I love Charlotte." His mother wouldn't understand. Not after what she had endured with his father.

Vivian waved her hand in dismissal. "Love? You can't possibly mean it. Charlotte Hale is completely unsuitable and you ought to know that. I'm sorry you're upset, but I expect you'll forget about her soon enough."

Unwilling to argue, he answered, "Believe whatever you wish."

"All's well that ends well, I always say." She sent him a smug smile.

Daniel winced. "You're gleeful about this, aren't you?"

She sputtered a short laugh. "Of course I am. I have your best interests at heart." Her brittle smile quickly faded to a grimace. Drawing out a tired sigh, she tilted her head back and closed her eyes for several moments.

"Aren't you feeling well?" Daniel asked, alarmed that her skin had taken on the color of cement.

A few moments later she opened her eyes and shrugged hunched, bony shoulders. "I'm exhausted, but I believe it's caused more from your recent behavior than my illness. Mooning over the hired help. It's disgraceful." Her lips thinned to an ugly gash, distorting her face.

"Yes, Mother, I know your feelings about Charlotte. But tell me, how are you feeling?"

"I do suffer from aches and pains, and now and then, a touch of angina. But it's nothing severe enough to worry about." Her voice sounded weak as she spread her fingers over the bodice of her brocade gown. She heaved for several deep breaths of air.

"Mother, are you sure you're all right? Shall I call for the doctor?" Daniel reached for her hand.

She shook her head. "Nonsense. It was only a momentary spell. I'm fine now. Just help me to bed." Her gaze focused, and her color returned, but her voice shook slightly. "Tell me. Did Charlotte explain why she refused your proposal?"

"I'd rather not go into that."

He walked his mother to her bedroom, his arm spanning her waist. She was as fragile as one of the porcelain figurines on her whatnot shelves. "Shall I ask Simone to sleep in your bedroom tonight?"

She gave a faint smile. "That's not necessary."

"All right, but please call Doctor Lowe tomorrow."

After she was settled into her four-poster bed, he headed to his own room.

He dropped into an overstuffed chair and opened his Bible. For over an hour he tried to read, but he couldn't concentrate on words that normally renewed his mind and brought him hope. And comfort. Nothing eased the sting of Charlotte's rejection or explained it.

Charlotte flung herself on her bed and sobbed until her eyes were swollen and sore. Her lies cracked her heart wide open. Much worse, she'd hurt Daniel, the man she loved. She'd thrown it all away for a dubious career at a newspaper fueled by sensationalism and character assassination. How pathetic. Sniffing, she dabbed at her burning eyelids with her handkerchief and blew her nose. All the self-pity in the world wouldn't help her situation.

She pulled her clothes out of the bureau drawers and wardrobe and tossed them into her valise, then put all of Daniel's columns into an envelope. Tomorrow she'd go home, where she could piece her life back together.

Grace came to her room just as she finished packing. Her friend's eyes grew wide as she dropped onto the bed.

"Are you leaving?" Grace tilted her head. "You've been crying. Did something dreadful happen between you and the professor?"

Charlotte pressed her lips together to keep them from trembling. "Yes. He proposed and I turned him down." She stared out the window into the dark night for several moments.

"But why?"

"I told you I'd explain the whole story and I shall." Charlotte began slowly and then let the awful truth spill out.

"Oh my," Grace murmured. She rose and looped her arm around Charlotte. "Even though it was very wrong of you to deceive the professor, the Lord forgives you."

Charlotte sighed. "I know and I'm ever so grateful for His grace and mercy. But I'm not sure Daniel would be so compassionate. And I couldn't blame him. I shall never forgive myself for my lies. They've brought such dreadful misery to him, and to me as well."

At nine o'clock she awoke with a start to a cloudy morning and a wet wind blowing through the screens. She slammed the window shut and quickly pulled on her uniform. Her foggy brain refused to think clearly and her heart weighed like a boulder in her tight chest. Memories of last night kept spinning through her mind.

Daniel had caught her off guard. She hadn't expected him to propose, though she'd encouraged his attention over the last few days. The odds of winning over his mother were next to nothing, but she'd assumed incorrectly he wouldn't marry without her blessing. She'd overestimated Mrs. Wilmont's influence on her son, or perhaps underestimated Daniel's love for a mere governess. Either way, it made little difference.

This morning she'd tell Daniel she was quitting her job and why, whether he wanted to hear it or not. Mrs. Finnegan could assist with the children until the Wilmonts hired another governess. Charlotte blew out a sigh. She shouldn't leave the family in the lurch, but she couldn't face Daniel day after day and hide the secrets of her heart. And now that she'd refused to accept his proposal . . . it was best she just be on her way. For both their sakes.

If she were a good Christian, she would've obeyed the Lord's urging to confess last evening. Instead she'd let courage slip away under the guise of saving Daniel from pain. What she'd really done was protect herself from humiliation. Then without a second thought, she'd bolted like a scared child.

She closed her bedroom door, checked on the children, and found their rooms empty. They spent considerable time in the library, so she hurried downstairs to search. Instead, she found Mrs. Finnegan supervising the parlor maids' window washing in the cavernous, yet cozy room. The smell of ammonia assailed Charlotte's nose.

"The two rapscallions are searching high and low for you," the housekeeper said as she watched the maids wipe crumbled newspaper across the glass. "Ruthie said she'd rapped on your door, but you didn't answer."

"I'm afraid I overslept. Where are they now?"

"Reading with their grandmother in the morning room." Mrs. Finnegan turned toward the young parlor maid. "More elbow grease, Maggie. And you missed a wee spot." Her thick finger pointed to a smudge.

"Well, I'm glad the children are busy. Do you know where I might find the professor?"

"I suppose he's off to class, dearie. Where else would he be going at this hour?"

"You're right. I need to give Professor Wilmont an important message."

Mrs. Finnegan tilted her head, and her crooked white bun slid even farther to the side. "Are you feeling all right? You're not looking like yourself."

"I'll admit I've been better." Charlotte headed for the door.

"Don't be running off without a bite of breakfast. How about a nice soft-boiled egg? Chef Jacques won't mind fixing something."

It was a shame that food, everyone's favorite remedy, wouldn't help, but her stomach roiled like the surf. Besides, she didn't have a moment to spare. "Not now, but thank you for thinking of me."

Heading for the front door, a sharp voice from the morning room stopped her midstep.

"Miss Hale. I wish to speak to you," Mrs. Wilmont said.

Charlotte faced the frail woman dressed in gray silk and reluctantly stepped into the room. "Yes, ma'am."

Mrs. Wilmont lifted her chin. "Come here, Charlotte. Children, please go off to the library while I have a word with your governess." Tim dashed across the room and out the door while Ruthie lingered until her grandmother waved her away. The woman turned her attention back to Charlotte with blue eyes, frozen like icebergs, yet glinting with an inner flame.

Charlotte stood before the woman, scarcely breathing. Mrs. Wilmont leaned into the tall back of the settee.

"I'll come straight to the point. My son informed me he proposed marriage and you refused. I have to admit, your answer shocked me. I'm certain he'll get over his distress in short order and get on with his life without skipping a beat. You bewitched him temporarily, but that kind of fascination can't last long. He'll be free of you in no time."

"And I'll be free of you as well," Charlotte muttered under her breath, surprised by her own rudeness, though not as repentant as she ought to be.

"I think it would be best if you left this house without delay."

Charlotte swallowed hard. She should've known dismissal was inevitable. "I'm planning to, but I'd like to talk to the professor first." She headed for the French doors. "I shall look for him at once."

Mrs. Wilmont gave her a short nod and returned to the book on her lap.

Charlotte hurried up the servant's staircase, gathered her hat and umbrella, and then hurried outside. A stiffening breeze slapped her face and whistled past her ears. Full-skirted tree branches dipped and swayed and threatened to break. Not a grand day for strolling out of doors. Overhead, the leaden sky thickened like layers of dirty cotton batting as a single raindrop splashed her nose. Charlotte increased her pace, hoping to arrive at the theology building before the sky split apart. Her booted feet barely touched the dirt road as she sprinted across the wide lawn and down Cove Road toward the campus. Once she entered the building, she paused to catch her breath and rest her pounding heart. Then she folded her umbrella, took a deep breath, and strode down the empty corridor to Daniel's office. The door stood ajar. Charlotte peeked inside. The middle-aged woman seated behind a typewriter looked up and nodded politely.

"May I help you?" the lady asked. "I'm Miss Gregory, the department secretary." Her eyes squinted, and then a pleasant smile crossed her face. "You're the Wilmonts' governess, aren't you?"

"Yes, I am. I'm looking for the professor. Do you know his whereabouts?"

Miss Gregory shook her head. "His last class ended half an hour ago, and he departed for the weekend." The secretary touched her cheek. "Wait a moment. I do believe Professor Wilmont mentioned he was speaking at a young ladies' meeting."

Charlotte's hands flew to her mouth. "Oh my goodness. I forgot all about the get-together. Do you know where it's being held?"

"No, I'm so sorry. I don't have any idea."

Charlotte groaned. "Thank you all the same, Miss Gregory. Do you happen to know where Miss — oh my, I forgot her name."

Who *was* the woman originally slated to speak at the ladies' retreat? Sykes? Simmons? Symington? That was it. "Can you tell me where Miss Symington's office is located? I'm quite sure she'll have the details."

"That I do know. Her office is at the end of the corridor, the last door on the right."

"Thank you so much." With a wave toward Daniel's secretary, Charlotte hastened down the hall.

"May I come in?" she called from Miss Symington's open doorway.

A short, plump woman of about forty beckoned Charlotte inside the empty office. She transferred a pile of books from her desk to the glass bookcase behind her desk. "Do come in. I'm Miss Symington. May I be of assistance?" Her upturned mouth softened a sagging face surrounded by a mass of graying hair scraped back in a chignon.

Relieved, Charlotte took a fortifying breath. "I hope so. I'm trying to find Professor Wilmont. I understand he's taking your place as guest speaker at a retreat . . ."

"Excuse me, but what retreat is that?" The professor wrinkled her forehead in a frown.

"The one Miss LeBeau organized." Charlotte moaned inwardly. She didn't even know the name of the group sponsoring the event, so she couldn't refresh Miss Symington's memory. "She said you were scheduled to speak, but you withdrew because your father is ill."

Miss Symington shook her head and the creases in her forehead deepened. "I'm so sorry. I don't know what you're referring to. But, thank the good Lord, my father is in perfect health."

Panic shot through Charlotte. Something

was very wrong. Or was her imagination running amok? "Maybe I've made a mistake. I apologize for bothering you."

"No bother at all," the woman replied.

Charlotte walked down the hall toward the front of the building. Missy had no reason to lie about Miss Symington unless she was playing some sort of trick. Stepping outside, Charlotte opened her umbrella. She had to find Daniel.

But where was he? Perhaps Agnes Brownington, the student she'd met near the bandstand on Sunday, had information about the retreat. Charlotte glanced from one red brick building to the next until she spotted a sign saying Dean Hall, Women's Dormitory. Once inside she asked a woman seated at the front desk for Miss Brownington. Charlotte tried not to fidget, but every second that ticked by seemed to take forever. Agnes finally arrived in the lobby and greeted her with a welcoming smile.

Dressed in a navy blue skirt and tailored white shirtwaist with a cameo at the neck, she looked every inch a scholar. "It's nice to see you again. Miss Hale, isn't it?"

"Good afternoon, Miss Brownington. I'm sorry to take you away from your studies, but I'm here on an urgent matter."

"That's perfectly all right. And please call

me Agnes. May I help you with something?"

She led Charlotte to a sitting area tucked in a corner of the large room. They lowered onto stiff chairs upholstered in a plush bottle green that matched the heavy curtains topped with tassels. Charlotte quickly asked Agnes if she knew anything about the ladies' get-together sponsored by the college prayer group.

Agnes paled as her mouth drooped open. "Missy did mention she planned to meet the professor this weekend, but she didn't give any details." Agnes raised a brow. "If she's caught she'll be in a world of trouble." Her face hardened as she stood up and paced in front of the window blurred with rain.

Charlotte was taken aback. Agnes seemed angry — but at Missy, not the professor.

"Unfortunately," Charlotte said, "if their meeting becomes public knowledge, the professor will be hurt as much as Missy."

Startled, Agnes looked skeptical. "Whatever do you mean?"

"People will misconstrue the meeting and believe the professor is to blame and Missy is the innocent victim of an older man with immoral intensions."

Agnes's hands flew to her mouth. "No, you must be mistaken. He is the most honorable person I've ever met."

"I agree, but others might not. I happen to know the *Rhode Island Reporter* is trying to discredit him. If they learn of this meeting, they'll be there to catch them together."

Agnes's skin blanched to grayish-white. "The *Rhode Island Reporter* wants to hurt Professor Wilmont? But why?"

"It's a long story. But suffice it to say, the editor of that paper wants to destroy Professor Wilmont. And he's not above conjuring up a story about Missy LeBeau in order to do it."

Agnes stopped pacing. "I didn't realize they were feuding." She crumpled into a chair opposite Charlotte, her face a picture of despair.

"Do you know where they'll meet?" Charlotte pressed. She didn't really have time to coddle the young woman.

"I think she's going to meet him at the LeBeau's cottage. I wrote down the name somewhere. Wait just a minute. I'll get it from my bedroom."

Agnes hurried off and returned quickly. With a trembling hand, she gave a scrap of paper to Charlotte. Spring Creek Lodge was written in bold, block letters — just like the message Mr. Phifer had received from his anonymous source.

Charlotte expelled a gasp. "You're the one who gave the false tip to the newspaper. Shame on you, Agnes. Whatever were you thinking?"

Agnes pulled her to the far end of the room where no one passing by could overhear. "I know I was wrong, but I wanted Miss LeBeau to leave the professor alone. I thought if she were caught in some sort of compromising situation, she'd be tossed out of the college."

"Didn't it occur to you the professor would most likely be blamed?"

Agnes covered her mouth and sniffed. "No, never. I thought everyone would know she was the one chasing after him."

"Well, you made a horrible mistake."

"Yes, I see that I did." Agnes's voice choked with sobs.

Charlotte felt a twinge of sympathy for the jealous young woman. "Where is Spring Creek Lodge located?"

"I don't know."

"I must find the professor before Mr. Phifer does."

Agnes took a handkerchief from her pocket and blew her nose. "Do you think the professor will ever forgive me?" Agnes asked, hope giving strength to her voice.

Charlotte shook her head. "Knowing him,

I think it's entirely possible." Charlotte swept out of the dormitory into the wet afternoon. She shivered. Big drops of rain pelted her as she leapt over puddles all along Cove Road. Her boots kicked up mud that soiled her cotton stockings and the hem of her skirt. Huffing and puffing from her tight corset, Charlotte ran to Summerhill until her lungs threatened to burst right through her bodice. When she finally reached the cottage, she rushed inside.

TWENTY-TWO

Charlotte found the elderly lovebirds sitting side by side on the drawing room settee, a discreet distance apart. She cleared her throat to attract their attention. Mrs. Wilmont turned her head sideways, glaring at the interruption, then looked back at her beau, Mr. McClintock. "Pardon me for a moment, Horace." She turned to her. "What is it, Charlotte? And do be quick about it."

"Excuse me, please, but do you know where Spring Creek Lodge is located?"

Daniel's mother jerked her chin upward in a regal pose worthy of Mrs. Astor. "I thought you'd have spoken to my son and would've departed by now."

Charlotte recoiled at the chill in the woman's voice. "No ma'am, as you can clearly see, I'm still here. I must speak to the professor first."

Mr. McClintock looked from one to the other as he wrung his hands. He grabbed an open box of bonbons from the marble end table and thrust it under his ladylove's nose even though it was only mid-morning. "Do have one, Vivian."

Mrs. Wilmont took two pieces and sent him a gracious smile. "Horace, Charlotte has decided to leave now that I'm feeling somewhat better. I thought she'd already be on her way home." Mrs. Wilmont twitched a smirk. "Charlotte, why don't you just leave him a note?"

"I may do that. But first, I must find that lodge."

"Well, I don't know where Spring Creek Lodge is located." She turned back to Mr. McClintock, ignoring Charlotte after one last glare.

Charlotte folded her arms across her chest. "Then I'm afraid I'll have to stay right here until Daniel returns."

Mrs. Wilmont's smirk changed to a grimace. "That surely isn't necessary. He might have left the address on his desk. You may look on your way out." Honey laced with arsenic flowed from her mouth.

"Thank you."

"By the way," she called, her reedy voice wrapping around Charlotte and bringing her to a halt, "Mr. McClintock discovered something about one of your references. Mr.

Henry Stapleton. No wonder my son couldn't locate him. The man passed away three years ago. Now tell me, how could a dead man write a recommendation?"

Charlotte felt the heat of humiliation burn her face. She knew those references would come back to haunt her. "I'm afraid I'm in too big of a hurry to explain," she tossed over her shoulder.

"I'll be sure to tell my son." Mrs. Wilmont's malicious laugh followed Charlotte down the hall as she strode to Daniel's office. *Oh Lord, I pray he left the information. I hope he's not walking right into Missy's trap. And maybe Mr. Phifer's as well. Please protect Daniel, Lord.*

Charlotte paged through a stack of test papers and student essays scattered across his desk, her hands shaky. Then on a note hidden beneath a glass paperweight, she found a few scribbled words: *Spring Creek Lodge, Bolling Hill Road — Student gathering.*

Thank You, Lord. Her relief escaped in a long sigh. Maybe she still had a chance to catch Daniel before Missy got her hands on him. Literally.

Grasping her umbrella, Charlotte rushed out the front door and onto the veranda. Rain slanted beneath the porch roof and wet the hydrangea and cedar bushes poking through the spindles.

"Hello, Miss Hale." Ruthie's girlish voice sounded thin against the splatter of raindrops on the veranda roof and the whine of the wind. "Where are you going?" Pushing back and forth on the porch glider, Ruthie held *An Old Fashioned Girl* on her lap.

Sadness washed through Charlotte. She'd sorely miss the Wilmont children. They'd grown close during their recitation of multiplication tables, piano practice, sketching, reading books, and playing croquet on the back lawn and down along the beach.

"Where are you going, Miss Hale?"

"To find your papa. And I'm in a big hurry." But she refused to be brusque with the little girl who'd befriended her. Sweetness and sass, winning qualities that defined the child.

Ruthie broke into a grin. "Whew! I was afraid you were angry at my papa."

"No, of course not. Why did you think that?"

Ruthie tilted her head, frowning. "Because you won't marry him. Last night I heard him arguing with Grandmother. Maybe I was snooping, but I wanted to know if you had a grand time at dinner." Her face clouded. "Papa said he asked you to marry him, but you turned him down."

424

Charlotte nodded. "I did say no, but for a very good reason."

"Which was what?" The little girl looked sly. "Am I being too impertinent?"

Charlotte bent down and squeezed Ruthie's hand. How do you explain a complicated situation in a few simple words? "Because we're not meant to be together." Every muscle and fiber in her body screamed her words were untrue. "I wish it was otherwise, but it isn't."

Ruthie jutted her lower lip. "Well, I've been praying about it and God told me you and Papa should marry. I asked Him directly and He said yes in my heart. You can't go against the Lord's will, can you? That would be sinful."

Charlotte didn't know whether to laugh or cry. "I promise I'll pray about it some more, but I'm afraid you misunderstood the Lord's message."

Could Daniel possibly forgive her for her deception? That seemed too much to ask. No one was that saintly, not even Daniel.

Ruthie clasped her hands. "Please, Miss Hale, pray until you hear God telling you what He told me." Ruthie's face flickered with hope. "I know Papa will make you happy. And I shall too. So will Tim if you remember he's just a little boy who says and does a lot of silly things he doesn't really mean. Even Grandmother will be nice to you."

Most definitely wishful thinking. "Sometimes we can't have what we want." Charlotte's voice choked. She cleared her throat and blinked back hot, stinging tears.

As Ruthie leaned forward the glider squeaked. "But sometimes we *can*. Please don't say no. Just get on your knees so God will know you're serious."

"I shall. But right now I must go." Overflowing with love for the little girl — and her father — Charlotte gave the youngster a tight hug and then clattered down the porch steps into the rain. She and Ruthie shared the same childish dreams and the same inability to make them come true, but the little girl clung to hope. Charlotte wished she could be as foolish.

Ruthie's voice rang out. "I'll pray for you, Miss Hale. And remember how much Papa loves you!"

Yes, Charlotte knew he did, but for how much longer?

Rain pummeled his buggy as Daniel headed at a fast clip toward Spring Creek Lodge. He pulled his derby forward to keep the light rain from his face, and squinted through spectacles rapidly fogging over. With a flick of the reins, he urged his horse to lengthen her stride down Ocean Drive. It shouldn't take long to locate the inn once he'd turned down Bolling Hill.

If only he'd declined Missy's invitation to conduct the retreat, he'd be home right now, dry and reading by a blazing fire. Or even better, convincing Charlotte to reconsider his proposal. Once she understood he'd forgive her for any indiscretion, large or small, she'd soften. Why did she want to admit every detail? He didn't wish to intrude on her privacy and embarrass her. Sometimes it was best to keep indiscretions private without alleviating some of the guilt by voicing them to another.

If only Sarah had kept her misdeeds to herself and not written a journal, he'd never had known she'd turned from him, even after their reconciliation. Of course he'd known their relationship hadn't improved as he prayed it would, but he'd never suspected she'd stopped caring altogether.

He never wanted to experience that kind of intense pain again — not that he thought Charlotte's transgressions would wound as deeply as Sarah's.

But, instead of staying at Summerhill and calming Charlotte's apprehension, he was driving down a deserted, muddy road toward a retreat he didn't want to conduct for a young lady he didn't wish to see. Yet in good conscience, he couldn't refuse anyone in spiritual need, even Missy LeBeau. If her relationship with the Lord strengthened because of something he might say, then this retreat was well worth his effort. He sighed. It was just that after last night's dinner with Charlotte, he was in no mood to present solid spiritual truths to a group of giggling college students led by the giddy Missy.

Perhaps he should've spoken to Charlotte before he departed for Spring Creek Lodge. To his regret, she didn't appear at breakfast, so he lingered until the last possible moment before leaving for his only class of the day. He'd speak to her as soon as he returned this evening. Despite the weather, he urged the horse into a fast trot. What was the matter with him? He never took his frustrations out on his driving, endangering himself and others — if there actually were others on this deserted stretch of country road. But he hadn't seen another cart or carriage. Fortunately the rain let up as he approached Bolling Hill Road, a winding lane edged with stone walls and leafy elms that arched overhead. Behind the low fences rolled green lawns and pastures veiled in mist. Hazy outlines of mansions rose behind the drizzle. Negotiating the potholes and pools of standing water, his carriage bumped along. Ten minutes later he came to a clearing with a vista of rolling meadows. A sign announced Spring Creek Lodge.

He turned down the narrow road that cut through an open field and drove until he came to a rambling cottage. It resembled an Adirondack hunting lodge with a wide porch and smoke curling from the chimney. He halted the buggy and jumped down.

Where was everyone? No other carriages parked along the muddy drive and no stable boy appeared to help with his horse. Strange. Maybe he'd arrived too early, although Miss LeBeau had said the retreat started at eleven thirty on Friday. His pocket watch read eleven forty-five. No sign of life anywhere.

As he climbed the steps to the porch, unease crawled up his back like an army of spiders. He opened the door expecting to find the innkeeper behind the front desk. Instead, he saw an enormous room paneled in rustic pine and surrounded on three sides by a balcony. No front desk and no desk clerk to welcome him. A fire roared in the fieldstone fireplace, brightening the lobby and giving off the strong wood aroma. He passed through the small vestibule into what must be the lobby, placed his book bag and valise on the floor by one of the leather sofas, and wondered what to do next.

At the sound of footsteps, he turned toward the staircase. Ah, he wasn't alone after all. He felt a surge of relief as a middle-aged maid hurried down the steps.

"Good afternoon, sir. Are you Professor Wilmont?"

"Yes, I am. Would you kindly tell Miss Le-Beau I've arrived?"

The maid nodded and climbed back up the stairs. Within a minute or two the young woman he waited for slowly glided down the steps. A sultry grin curved Missy Le-Beau's lips, unusually full and red, as if a bee had stung them. Her features looked brighter than normal. He suspected she'd painted them for emphasis. Not that such a stunning girl needed such tawdry enhancement. His voice hitched in his throat as he attempted to greet her.

Then he noticed a narrow-faced young woman with frizzy hair followed at her heels. Charlotte's cousin, Penelope. What was she doing here?

"Good afternoon, Miss LeBeau. Miss

Smith. You're Miss Hale's cousin, aren't you?"

She looked him straight in the eye and came forward, her hand outstretched. "I am, indeed, Professor. And I'm Missy Le-Beau's cousin as well. But we're related through our mothers' families. Our great-grandmothers were sisters, which makes us — well, kissin' cousins, I suppose. I'm so glad to see you once again."

"You're here for the retreat?"

"Indeed, I am. Miss LeBeau invited me even though I'm not a student at Aquid-neck or a member of her prayer group. But she thought I might benefit from your talks."

Missy's jaw tightened as she glared at the wiry woman.

"If you'll excuse me, I shall adjourn to the library for a while." Penelope strutted off.

Daniel's gaze fastened upon Missy's strange, almost seductive expression as she drew closer. She wore a low-cut gown pos-sibly appropriate for a ball, but all wrong for a ladies' retreat and immodest for any occasion. The yards and yards of shiny, champagne-gold fabric shimmered in the dim gaslight. He cleared his throat and glanced toward the door, his nearest escape route. His hands clasped behind his back, he leaned forward slightly and rocked back and forth, then stopped. He must look like a professor unnerved by a question he couldn't answer.

"Where is everyone else?" Daniel asked, glancing around the lodge as his apprehension mounted.

Missy floated toward him, her high-heeled shoes barely touching the floor. "The rest of the ladies will arrive shortly. They're waiting for the weather to clear." Her voice came in airy puffs of soft sound. Most disconcerting.

He nodded as he stepped back toward the fireplace. "That's an excellent idea." Arriving late was actually a dreadful idea. Now he was alone with a *femme fatale.* Sweat erupted on the back of his neck.

"So what shall I do until the retreat begins?" As soon as the words emerged, he recognized his *faux pas.*

Missy's eyes gleamed with unspoken answers. For a moment he feared she might suggest something entirely unsuitable. But she smiled sweetly and her eyes widened with an earnest innocence. He couldn't tell if she was sincere or playacting.

"We can stroll by the pond or . . ." she began.

He certainly didn't want Missy to entertain him. Who knew what her idea of entertainment might be, though he felt sure it wasn't the same as his. "The weather is still bad, so perhaps I should check in. I wonder where the innkeeper is. I think I'd like to go to my room." *And lock the door.* He wouldn't spend the night, though Mrs. Finnegan had packed him a bag just in case the retreat discussions ended too late for him to return home that evening. But he would appreciate the privacy of a room between sessions with the ladies.

Missy laughed. "There is no innkeeper. Spring Creek Lodge belongs to my parents. It's our summer cottage. Didn't I tell you?"

"No, you neglected to mention that very relevant fact." Maybe he should grab his valise and head home. "And where are your parents?" Upstairs, he hoped.

Lord, don't desert me now. This woman seems a bit deranged.

"They left for Greece yesterday. But don't fret. They gave me permission to hold the retreat here and explicit instructions to make you comfortable. Most of the staff is still here." She descended onto an overstuffed loveseat facing the fireplace and patted the cushion next to her. "Come sit down," she murmured in her soft-as-silk voice.

"No, I'll be quite comfortable right here."

He dropped onto the raised stone hearth. The blaze from the fire oiled his face, and he reached for his handkerchief to mop off the perspiration. "I'm sorry, Miss LeBeau, but I can't remain here, since this isn't an inn."

"Don't be silly. You won't bother the ladies and I promise we won't bother you," Missy purred.

"Naturally you understand I must return home this evening." Staying overnight with a houseful of young females would cost him his reputation. He'd always shied away from compromising situations and he wasn't going to change now. In fact, he shouldn't remain in the lodge alone with Missy for one more second.

"Of course you can stay. Our servants will watch over all of us. But if you'd prefer to return home tonight, we'll understand. While we're waiting for my prayer group, shall we take a walk? I'll show you around the grounds. They're really quite splendid, though I would've designed formal gardens, if given the choice. My father prefers nature at its most wild, as you can probably tell."

Daniel brightened. A breath of fresh air might clear his head, even if a little drizzle still lingered. "A grand idea. But first I'd like to telephone my mother. She's been ill and I need to check up on her."

A stab of irritation flashed across her face. "Of course. The telephone is in my father's study. Please follow me."

Missy led him down a hallway and opened the door to a small, dark room with a desk and bookshelves. She turned up the gaslight, pointed to the telephone, and departed. "I'll be in the main hall, Professor."

In short order, Mrs. Finnegan put his mother on the line. "Mother, how are you feeling this afternoon?"

"Much better, thank you. Doctor Lowe examined me earlier. He said I'm not out of the woods yet, but I'm doing as well as can be expected."

"That's good news." Daniel paused. "Is Charlotte close at hand? I'd like to speak to her, if you don't mind."

"Yes, I do mind, but in any case, she's not here. She left us awhile ago."

Her snicker came across loud and clear. "Now I'll have to hire another governess, someone dependable who won't walk out without notice."

"Charlotte quit? Did she explain why? Was she going back home?"

"She didn't say. As soon as you return, would you mind contacting the domestic employment agency? I'm not at death's door, but I shall require assistance for another few months, at the very least."

"Yes, of course. I've got to go. Take care of yourself." He hesitated. "Do you need me home right now? I could leave —"

"That's not necessary. Mr. McClintock is taking good care of me. Now don't worry, Daniel. I'll be fine."

"If you're sure." His mother often exaggerated her aches and pains, though he knew she still suffered from the aftereffects of her heart attack.

"I am sure. Go about your business. I'm going to play charades with Mr. McClintock and the children. They like that."

Daniel hung up the telephone and sank into a hard wooden chair set in front of Mr. LeBeau's desk. He'd hoped Charlotte would stay even though she'd turned down his marriage proposal. Yet he suspected she'd find working for him too awkward. He'd have to convince her otherwise, but the Lord had to figure out the details.

Daniel returned to the foyer and found Missy pacing in front of the fireplace, a scowl marring her normally beautiful face. "Miss LeBeau, shall we take a walk now if the weather permits?"

Instantly she flashed a wide smile. "I'd be delighted."

They stepped outside into the cool air, heavy with dampness. The clouds still hovered close to ground level, obscuring most of the lawns, woods, and bridle paths. Rain dripped from the branches of elm trees and red maples, spraying fine droplets with each breath of wind. A few leaves broke off and skittered across the grass and down the path through the deep woods.

He shivered in his lightweight summer suit and wished he'd worn thicker clothing. He'd give his last dollar to be any place but there with Missy, strolling so close he could smell her overpowering perfume. His nose twitched at the exotic odor. It reminded him of Middle Eastern dancing girls decked out in skimpy clothes and dangling gold bracelets.

Missy tugged on his arm. "Would you like to see the duck pond?"

"Certainly, if you wish." He glanced at his watch. Time dragged by.

As they started down a dirt path wide enough for only one carriage to pass through, Daniel walked slowly, unwilling to lose sight of Spring Creek Lodge and the imminent appearance of the other students.

"I'm sure the ladies will be here within the half hour, so we'll stay close by. The pond is only a short distance ahead."

Relief spurted through him. "Perhaps you should leave a note explaining you're going out for a walk."

Missy dismissed his suggestion with a shake of her head. "No, the servants will take care of them until we return. Or they can visit with my cousin Penelope." She slipped her gloved hand into his.

Snatching his fingers away, he slowly walked down the path deep into the shadows of the woods.

Twenty-Three

Charlotte sprinted toward the stables at the top of Cove Road, not caring if anyone spotted her unladylike stride. In a hurry and soon winded, she nevertheless kept up her pace until she reached the stables. Once inside she located a stable boy grooming a roan.

He looked toward her. "Can I help you, miss?"

"I'd like to take Professor Wilmont's gig, if you please." She looked around for his buggy, then realized he must have driven it to Spring Creek Lodge. "I see that it's gone. How about his other carriage?"

The blond-haired boy shook his head. "Mrs. Finnegan took it to do errands."

Charlotte groaned. "Did she say how long she'd be gone?"

"No, miss, but she usually takes her time. I'm sorry."

"Thank you all the same. I'd best be

riding a bicycle unless I want to walk."

She'd never traveled to Bolling Hill Road, but Charlotte thought she'd seen a street sign not too far from Summerhill.

"The bicycles are kept in the carriage house," he said. "But wouldn't you rather ride this horse? She's gentle."

"No, I don't ride." After Becky was thrown off their uncle's horse and paralyzed, Charlotte had never wanted to learn.

"Thank you so much." With a wave, Charlotte jogged the short distance to the carriage house, found the bicycle leaning against the back wall, and wheeled it outside. She rolled up her long skirt. If only she had more time, she'd change into her more practical split skirt. Fortunately the rain had stopped. Grasping the handlebars, she hurled upward, steadied herself, and peddled down the driveway. Pumping hard, she flew past Summerhill's entrance gate and turned onto the Ocean Drive.

Before she found Bolling Hill, the fine mist thickened to soup. She could barely read the names of the estates carved into the stone pillars by their entrances, let alone view the sweeping lawns. Even squinting she couldn't see more than a few feet beyond the front tire of her bicycle. But she rode on hoping the weather would soon improve.

She peddled on and on without spotting the sign for Bolling Hill Road. How far could it be? Panic squeezed her chest. She was lost in a sea of gray without any idea of her whereabouts.

From behind Charlotte heard the *clip-clop* of a horse. She turned her head and glimpsed the smudged outline of a horse and cart fast approaching. A young man with the smooth skin of a boy soon came into focus. Flagging him down, she stopped by the side of the road and hoped he would as well.

"Can I help you with something, miss?" He halted his horse and looked at her with curiosity.

"Yes, I do hope so. I'm looking for Spring Creek Lodge on Bolling Hill. Do you know where it is? I seem to be lost."

"You've passed the road. Turn around, go back half a mile, and take a left." He pointed to where they'd both come from.

"Thank you. I believe it's an inn owned by the LeBeau family."

The fellow scratched his brown thatch of hair. "No, miss. There's no hotels or inns on Bolling Hill. I know for a fact Spring Creek is a private residence owned by the LeBeaus. It's called a lodge because it looks like it belongs in the mountains. That's what I've been told." He nodded proudly. "I'm a gardener for Mr. Travers at Elmwood, right next door to Spring Creek."

Charlotte leaned against the handlebars to keep her legs from buckling. "Are you sure it isn't an inn?"

He pulled his cap down over his face. "Yes, miss, of course I'm sure. I work close by, now don't I?"

"I apologize. I didn't mean to question you. I'm just surprised, that's all." So Missy LeBeau had lured Daniel to her parents' summer home. A raindrop dripped off the brim of her straw boater onto her nose. "I'd better go before a downpour comes."

The young man patted the empty wooden seat beside him. "Get in. I'll take you there myself."

"Thank you kindly. I'll gladly take you up on your offer."

The gardener jumped down from the cart, tossed the bicycle in the back with a load of manure, and started off down the road. Charlotte held her nose against the stench of the fertilizer and the fellow's dirty clothes mixed with the cold, dank air blowing in from the sea. The cart jolted down the road, plunging through potholes and puddles, spewing up mud that soiled the bottom of

442

Charlotte's skirt. They travelled silently until they came upon a rutted lane separated from Bolling Hill Road by a simple iron gate set between rustic stone pillars.

The cart jerked to a halt. "Here we are, ma'am."

"Thank you so much." Charlotte stepped down into the squishy mud. Once the fellow handed her the bicycle, she rummaged through her reticule for coins.

He held up his callused hand. "No need to pay me. I'm glad to help." He tipped his cap, flicked the reins, and took off.

Charlotte surveyed the narrow road stretching beyond the Spring Creek Lodge sign. The far end vanished in a puff of fog. She pushed her bicycle through several deep puddles and then stopped for a few moments. Steadying her breathing, she propped the heavy contraption against a tree and started off on foot.

Sucking in a big gulp of air, she sloshed through the coffee-colored water. The muck oozed up to her ankles, soaked through her thick black stockings, and mired her feet. She took a tentative step, but her high-top boot refused to budge from its burial plot. Her arms swung out and windmilled, but she tottered, pitched forward, and lost her balance. Her hands sank through layers of mud. Charlotte lay still for a second, shocked by the fall. Cold water soaked her uniform, sending shivers through her body. She groaned from pain that spread from her arms to her legs. Slowly she rose, anchored her stocking foot in the mud, and then fished around the dirty water for her boot. She tried to brush the mud off her shirt and wring out her skirt, but it was hopeless. "Oh, for heaven's sakes!" she cried, looking up into the dark sky. Did God not want her to do this?

Lord, help me! I'll never get to Daniel in time to save him from Missy. And maybe Mr. Phifer. Take pity on me, Lord. You've taken me this far, please don't abandon me now.

Her heart still pumped like a steam engine, but a sudden wave of confidence propelled her forward. She'd take one small step after another, with the Lord's guidance. Although still early afternoon, the pelting rain and the clouds had darkened the day to gray dusk. A gust of cold wind whipped her wet skirt around her legs and sent shivers to her arms.

She spotted his gig in front of the lodge. No other carriages stood in the circular drive. Then off to the side of the road, hidden behind brush, she glimpsed an empty carriage, painted the same dark maroon as

Mr. Phifer's. Her heart thudded. She didn't dare guess. Perhaps her overactive imagination was playing tricks. Undoubtedly many Newporters owned similar carriages. But why was this one parked here?

Wet and shivering, Charlotte moved down the road, splashing through puddles. When she reached the darkened lodge, she waited a few moments to catch her breath. No gaslight glowed from inside. Lights ought to be burning on such a dreary day. Odd. She knocked on the carved double door, wondering what exactly she'd say once the butler opened it. No answer. She gave a few hard pounds, but still no one came. Finally she pushed open the heavy door to find a deserted lobby. No, this was the LeBeau's summer cottage, not a real lodge. So this gloomy and cavernous room was the foyer.

Where was Daniel? Or Missy?

"Professor? Miss LeBeau? Are you here?"

Charlotte stole through the room as she waited for a response.

No answer. A fire flickered behind a screen, so someone had recently been in the room. Charlotte inhaled the smell of burning wood and listened to it crackle and sizzle. From the rough paneled walls she felt the dead-eyed stares from deer and moose heads.

"May I help you, miss?" A female voice startled her. A uniformed maid came forward.

"Yes, thank you. I'm looking for Miss Le-Beau or Professor Wilmont."

"They were here a short time ago, but I believe they've gone for a walk. Would you like to wait for them here? Would you like a towel to wipe off the mud?"

"No, on both accounts, but thank you all the same. I shall go search for them."

Charlotte hurried to the porch and scanned the property for Daniel and Missy. Through the haze she thought she spied the shadow of a couple near the woods, but she couldn't be certain because the mist quickly swallowed their shapes. Charlotte rushed down the porch steps in her squishy boots and headed down the path after the pair.

Daniel strode beside Missy, sticking as far to the edge of the trail as he could. "I think we should go back. The fog is getting worse. We've already had a long enough walk."

Yet she sidled closer, chatting all the while. "Of course, but I must show you our beautiful lily pond first." Reluctantly he followed her through some low brush until they came to the small pond. Stopping, she looked into the stagnant green water and tangle of lily pads as if she were thinking hard. Then she turned to him, determination in her eyes. "I have something to tell you." She touched his arm, but he eased it away and stepped backward into the weeds.

"Can it keep for another time? We should return to the lodge. Come, you don't want a shower to ruin your lovely dress." Flounced and ruffled, she reminded him of a fancy French poodle. Daniel headed toward the cottage when he felt her iron grip.

The grit of her teeth gave way to a brittle smile. "I'm glad you approve of my dress. I had it designed with your taste in mind."

"I beg your pardon." Apprehension skidded down his spine as he stopped and stared into her glistening eyes. Had he heard correctly? Charlotte's words of warning filled his mind. She'd understood Missy's intentions weren't as harmless as he'd hoped.

"I want to look pretty for you. Aren't you pleased?" She pouted in a flirtatious way that made his summer suit heavy and hot. "You must know I care about you. Deeply. I thought my feelings were obvious, and I know you feel the same way about me."

Despite the cool breeze, sweat poured down Daniel's back and forehead. He halted and moved away from the deluded young woman. "Miss LeBeau, I'm afraid you misunderstand me. I hope I've never given you any reason to imagine I have romantic ideas because I most definitely do not. I'm your teacher, nothing more." He shook his head. "If I led you to believe otherwise, I'm terribly sorry. My interest in you is purely as a teacher and a fellow Christian. I thought you might need spiritual counseling, though I'm not here in that capacity. I merely agreed to speak at a young women's retreat."

Missy touched his arm with a hand as lethal as a burning ember. He yanked his arm away. "Stop this, Miss LeBeau."

"Surely you must want me as a woman, professor." She snuggled into his side, pressing against him.

Daniel shook his head as he took a step back toward Spring Creek. "That's ridiculous. You've made a dreadful mistake and so have I. I never should have come here."

His stomach roiled. He should have given more credence to Charlotte's warning, yet he assumed she misunderstood Missy's intentions. But Charlotte had just proven herself a shrewd woman and he'd proven himself a stupid man. Yet feigning an interest in faith still came as a surprise. "I'm afraid I must leave."

"No, please, Professor, don't go. Please forgive me. I realize my feelings shock you, but you'll grow accustomed to them if you give us a chance. I do love you with all my heart, and I know you'll learn to love me as well." She faced him, her face shining. "Don't turn from me."

He glanced toward the lodge, wishing his gig was close by. Straining his eyes, he could only make out the shadows of swaying tree branches. Then somehow she'd maneuvered in front of him and stopped his progress. Without saying a word, Missy wrapped her arms around his neck and stretched up to kiss him. He pried her arms apart. "You must stop, Miss LeBeau. This instant." He heard a note of panic in his voice he'd never heard before.

She entangled her arms around his neck once again and clamped her hands tighter, rolled up on the balls on her feet and pushed her face toward his. He recoiled, but her hands cupped the back of his head from behind and shoved it forward. Then she smashed her mouth into his and splattered him with a wet kiss.

He perceived a rustling in the woods, and then came a flash and a pop. Breaking free, Daniel wrenched his head away and glimpsed a young man with a camera running down the path toward the lodge.

"What do you think you're doing?" Daniel yelled.

The photographer was several yards ahead by the time Daniel spotted a woman coming directly at the fellow.

Charlotte?

Charlotte saw Daniel staving off Missy's advances and then Jesse Miller's camera pointed right at them. Holding up the front of her damp skirt, Charlotte sprinted toward the man she'd known from her earliest days at the *Rhode Island Reporter*. Jesse saw her coming toward him and paused before plunging into the brush. If she didn't hurry, he'd vanish into the dense woods and escape. Tomorrow's edition of the newspaper would blast a photograph of Professor Daniel Wilmont, defender of religion and morality, kissing one of his young and innocent students. Charlotte envisioned the headlines. BIBLE TEACHER CAUGHT IN THE ACT.

Spurred on by the injustice of Mr. Phifer's scheme, Charlotte plunged into the woods after Jesse. A small man with short legs, he could hardly run any faster than she could. Increasing her stride, Charlotte closed the gap between them. Her breath

450

rose from the bottom of her lungs that burned with each labored gasp. She kept running deeper and deeper into the woods.

The light grew dimmer as the foliage overhead arched to form an almost impenetrable canopy. Shards of gray light barely filtered through. Still he plunged forward. As Jesse's figure faded, Charlotte listened for the sound of his thrashing through low, tangled brush. He was probably escaping toward the carriage hidden among the trees.

Just as she thought her lungs might burst, the woods opened to a clearing by the far side of the duck pond. Now in plain sight, Jesse ran only a few feet ahead of her. With a burst of speed, Charlotte grabbed for the back of his coat and yanked him off balance. He slid on a patch of wet leaves and sprawled into thorny bushes, yelping like a hound. The camera slid from his grasp and crashed into a tree trunk. She scooped up the camera and rushed toward the water.

"Halt, Charlotte Hale." A familiar voice boomed from behind a thick oak.

Charlotte thought her heart might stop when she heard Mr. Phifer's authoritative tone. She stopped to stare at him, large and commanding like an army general, standing in his perfectly pressed business suit. "Give me that camera. It belongs to the *Rhode*

Charlotte hesitated as Mr. Phifer took a step forward and Jesse stirred. A few seconds later Daniel, followed by Missy, appeared in the clearing.

"What is going on?" Daniel demanded, his gaze sliding from Charlotte to Arnie Phifer.

Then Charlotte saw the bewilderment clouding Daniel's eyes switch to understanding and then horror. He stared at her with pain she hoped to never see. An apology caught in her throat. She hung her head until out of the corner of her eye she spotted a figure drawing closer. She gasped as Jesse lunged at her. With his arm raised in the air, he swatted the camera, but her grip was too strong to dislodge it. Spinning around she darted for the pond, Jesse at her heels. The noise of his footsteps thudded in her ear.

Charlotte swung her arm back and with all her strength hurled the camera into the middle of the water. It hit with a soft splash and sank out of sight.

"You destroyed private property," Arnie Phifer screamed, his composure gone. "How dare you do this to me, Charlotte Hale. You'll be facing charges when we return to town."

Jesse stared at his prized piece of equipment, lost forever. Missy leaned against a tree, for once silent and wringing her hands. Charlotte didn't care about the reactions of any of them except Daniel. As she turned to look at him, he turned away and started tromping through the brush toward the dirt path, his back bent and shoulders hunched. He didn't even want to look at her. Charlotte dashed after him, but Edith Ann appeared from behind a tree and grabbed her sleeve.

"You ruined everything, Charlotte. I set this up perfectly with Missy and you had to interfere."

"What do you mean?"

"I convinced Missy if we could get a photograph of her kissing Professor Wilmont, then he'd feel obligated to marry her. He wouldn't want to destroy her reputation. She would've gotten her man, and I would've had my angle on the story for Phifer. But then you had to jump in. What is wrong with you?"

Speechless, Charlotte whipped her arm away and then dashed after the professor. She caught up to him down the road, panting. "Daniel, I'm so sorry. Can we talk?" Maybe she should leave him alone until he recovered from the alarming surprise of

Arnie Phifer's plan and her part in it.

Daniel halted his long strides and faced her. "You were a part of Arnie Phifer's scheme, weren't you? Don't bother to deny it. As for talking, is there really anything to talk about?" He looked more numb than angry and his flat tone of voice reflected his shock.

"I could try to explain, but I simply have no excuse for deceiving you. I know it's a meaningless gesture, but I truly regret every moment I worked for Mr. Phifer. He sent me to Summerhill to spy on you, but I quit a few days ago. That's what I tried to explain last night."

The sadness in his eyes stabbed her with the depth of guilt she'd never felt before and hoped she never would again. She so wanted Daniel's respect — and love — and yet her shameful behavior ensured he'd never feel anything but contempt.

"Why did you conspire with Arnie Phifer?" he asked as he slowly walked toward Spring Creek Lodge, his head hanging low.

She blew out a long, dreary sigh. "I was only a typist, but he promised me advancement and a better salary if I found information to discredit you. I needed money to pay for my sister's doctor bills and the new roof. As soon as I came to know you, I began to regret my decision to take the assignment. And then, when I realized he was willing to lie, I quit my job at the *Rhode Island Reporter.* I knew I'd made a dreadful mistake. I never imagined he'd go to such lengths to ruin you."

"So this is the sin you tried to tell me about."

"Yes," she answered, her voice unsteady.

Daniel shook his head slowly as if he still couldn't quite comprehend what had just occurred. "I never once suspected you were on assignment for Arnie Phifer."

Tears streamed down Charlotte's cheeks. "I'm so sorry, Daniel. I wanted to tell you, but I didn't know how. I just couldn't find the courage."

He looked unmoved by her feeble explanation. The corners of his mouth pulled down and his turquoise eyes filled with grief.

"I feel awful about this, terribly guilty and terribly sorry." Charlotte hesitated, but she just had to ask. "Do you think you can ever find it in your heart to forgive me? I don't mean returning to where we were headed." She couldn't even utter the word *love* because now even affection was utterly impossible. "I mean just plain forgiving me."

Daniel looked like he was trying to smile, but his effort failed. "I do forgive you," he said in a monotone that belied his words. Forgiving her was one thing, but starting over was quite another. His anger and hurt wouldn't evaporate just by mouthing the words. He'd never feel the same way about her again and she couldn't blame him.

"Thank you for forgiving me," she said, choking on her tears. It was hopeless, but at least he was trying.

They reached Spring Creek Lodge and stood awkwardly by Daniel's horse and carriage. "Would you like a ride back to Summerhill?" he asked without enthusiasm.

"No thank you. I'll ride my bicycle."

He shrugged, obviously not willing to press her.

"As soon as I return to Summerhill, I'll gather my things and leave."

Standing by the gig, he seemed reluctant to depart. "I suppose you found Sarah's journal and read it."

Charlotte's face heated. "Yes, but I didn't breathe a word of it to Mr. Phifer."

Daniel sighed. "Thank you."

He sounded genuinely grateful and Charlotte felt a few moments of relief. But she still had more to explain. "When I failed to find anything dishonorable about you, Mr. Phifer sent over my so-called cousin Penelope Smith to take my place. She's actually

Edith Ann Wengle, the other woman who'd like to be a reporter."

"Thank you for that, as well. I'm certain she would've found something Phifer could have used against me even if he had to twist the truth."

"Or plant evidence," Charlotte added.

Daniel nodded. "I wouldn't put anything past him."

"Nor would I."

"By the way, I'm going to pay for the camera you threw in the pond."

She almost smiled. "You don't have to, but thank you."

"No, I shall."

He paused. "Tell me, Charlotte, was your accepting the Lord real or did you merely pretend?"

She touched his arm for only a moment. "It was real. I understood I couldn't be a part of Mr. Phifer's plan anymore, so I quit my job. But I wasn't brave enough to insist you listen to the truth. I knew you'd hate me."

"No, I could never hate you. What you did was unethical, but I do forgive you."

Whether he admitted it or not, he'd turned away from her.

Finally, to break the impasse, Charlotte spoke up. "I'm so sorry for all the pain I've caused." She stretched up and gave him a peck on the cheek. "Well, good-bye, Daniel." She spun around and rushed down the driveway toward Bolling Hill Road before Daniel had a chance to respond.

TWENTY-FOUR

Charlotte peddled back to Summerhill, exhausted from the ride. She trudged up to her bedroom, washed up, and changed into clean, dry clothes. Then she carried her valise down the back stairway.

"Mr. Grimes, would you mind calling a cab for me?" she asked the butler.

He shook his head. "Professor Wilmont insists his coachman drive you home. I'll have him bring the carriage around."

"Thank you." Too tired to argue, she went to look for Mrs. Finnegan in the housekeeper's office. She glanced up from her accounts. "Come in and sit a spell. Mrs. Wilmont told me you quit. Would you be willing to tell me why? 'Tis unexpected and unwelcome news, I might add."

"I'm sorry to leave you in the lurch with so much packing to do," Charlotte said from the doorway.

The old Irish woman shook her head.

"I've plenty of help to do the packing. When the professor came home a short time ago, I saw his chin dragging down to the floor. Would you be knowing why?"

Charlotte groaned. "Yes. I'm afraid it's all my fault."

"Do you want to tell me about it?"

Those round eyes showed so much compassion Charlotte couldn't resist. She poured out her story and Mrs. Finnegan didn't flinch.

"You did an awful thing spying for that newspaper, but you did what you thought you had to do for your family. Not that it was right, mind you. But I understand sometimes we don't live up to the high standards we set for ourselves. It was a grievous sin you committed, but you're a good girl at heart. I know you never meant harm to the poor man."

"From the beginning I had reservations about my assignment, but I ignored my conscience, and then I couldn't find the courage to confess."

"We all fail from time to time, the best of us and the worst of us. Sure, you have a right to be hard on yourself for a while, but don't stay down in the dumps too long. Tell the good Lord you're sorry for your sins. Don't dwell on your shortcomings, dearie."

"I think it'll be hard not to."

She dismissed Charlotte's attitude with a wave. "Don't indulge yourself by worrying about your failings. We all got 'em. None of us is perfect. So get on with your life and do better next time."

"You're a wise woman, Mrs. Finnegan, and I thank you for your advice. Do you think the professor will ever forgive me? He said he did, but I doubt that it's truly possible." She didn't really want to hear the truth, but her anxious question tumbled out. "I couldn't blame him for not speaking to me ever again."

She nodded. "Indeed he will forgive you after a while. First give him time to get over the hurt. When the pain subsides, he'll be wishin' you back at Summerhill."

"Are you sure?" Charlotte asked, brightening, afraid to think Mrs. Finnegan might be right.

"The poor fellow's in love with you, dearie. Can't you see that?"

"That was before he learned the truth."

"He's got a close relationship with the good Lord, so he'll pardon you, even with his heart, not just his head. I'm sure of it. Haven't I known him for most of his life?"

"I do so hope you're right."

Mrs. Finnegan put down her pen and

closed her ledger. "He's not a man to hold a grudge."

But Charlotte knew she had to return to her family and forget about the professor. She'd mucked it up, but like Mrs. Finnegan said, there was no use in dwelling on the mess she'd made.

"Where are Ruthie and Tim?" Charlotte asked.

"Playing with their little friends on Cove Road. Would you like me to run get them so you can say good-bye?"

Charlotte shook her head. "I'll leave them a note. And Grace Thompson as well."

Mrs. Finnegan handed Charlotte paper and her fountain pen. Charlotte scratched out a short explanation to the children, sealed it in an envelope, and left it with Mrs. Finnegan. She wrote a note to Grace as well. Charlotte rose, gave the housekeeper a hug, and then quickly left. She strode past the front parlor where she glimpsed Mrs. Wilmont and Mr. McClintock talking and laughing on the settee. Valise in hand, she climbed into the buggy.

From his bedroom window Daniel watched Charlotte leave Summerhill. He blew out a weary sigh. His heart ached from losing the woman he thought he loved. *Did* love. *Still* loved, despite her betrayal. He understood her dilemma. Of course, she should have rejected Arnie Phifer's scheme, but financial considerations prevailed. He sauntered down to the shore, glad to feel the cool, salty wind slap against his face. Standing on the rocks he heard footsteps and the rustle of a skirt. Ruthie halted by his side.

"Miss Hale is gone! Why did she leave us?" the little girl asked, panting from her sprint across the damp grass. She pulled on his sleeve, her way of demanding an answer.

"It was time for her to go home."

Ruthie waved a note. "Miss Hale left this for Tim and me, but she doesn't explain much."

Daniel resisted the urge to grab the letter. "She had her reasons for leaving."

Ruthie groaned. "I think she left because she feels bad about not marrying you."

Perhaps that but so much more. "We'll all miss her, pumpkin."

"Then go after her and bring her back. It's not too late."

Daniel let out a joyless laugh. "No, Ruthie. I'm letting her go."

When Charlotte returned home to Bridge Street, relief spilled through her. Her awful charade was finally over. No matter how badly everything turned out, at least she was home safe with her family, and she didn't have to pretend she was someone else. She dropped her bag at the bottom of the staircase and joined Aunt Amelia and Becky in the parlor. They both hovered around her as she spewed out her misadventure. They listened silently as her aunt poured her a cup of tea.

"I'm sorry it went so wrong," Aunt Amelia said as she sat next to Charlotte on the sofa.

In her wheelchair, Becky kept knitting, but her face drooped in a frown.

Charlotte stretched her lips into an unconvincing smile. "I might not be in high demand without a reference, but rest assured, I'll find some sort of job. We won't starve. I promise you that."

Aunt Amelia patted her on the arm. "I do admire your spunk, but you don't need to put on a brave front for us." Her hands twisted in her lap and Charlotte knew Aunt Amelia worried just as much as she did.

"I'm afraid I'm out of ideas at the moment, but Monday I'll put on my best dress and hat and go to town and find a position far superior to typing for the *Rhode Island Reporter*." Exactly what, she didn't know. But staying at home wasn't an option.

Aunt Amelia's mouth tipped upward in a

brave smile, but her eyes betrayed her fear. Without funds they couldn't pay the roofer and they'd have to go to court. Would they lose their home? No, Charlotte vowed, they'd never end up as charity cases if she had even one breath left in her body.

Sunday morning she attended the church near her home and sought the solace of the Lord. She believed He'd help her secure a job.

The next day she donned her best hat and walked to Thames Street where she'd undoubtedly find Help Wanted signs. Surely some shopkeeper needed a strong intelligent woman to sell a thimble or sweep a floor or send out an invoice.

Oh Lord, don't let me go without work, she prayed as she glanced at the storefront windows, hoping for a sign advertising a job vacancy. The dry goods store needed a shop boy, not *girl,* and the shoe shop wanted experienced help. Her feet slowed as she tired. She stopped at the grocery and purchased a bag of white corn meal for Aunt Amelia and a few mint candies for Becky before coming to the *Rhode Island Reporter.*

Out of habit she turned toward the door that led to the newspaper's second floor offices, but stopped mid-step. Her heartbeat raced at such a fast pace it almost hurt. She spun around, ready to flee from regret and hopes dashed when she remembered Mr. Phifer owed her two weeks' salary. She'd rather have a tooth pulled than face her former boss, but if she didn't insist on her just wage, he'd never pay. Sending a note would be far easier than confronting him. But ignoring a written request would be easy for him. In the end, she'd have to deal with him person to person. Charlotte took a deep breath, which failed to calm her nerves, and climbed the steps to the second floor.

She opened the door to the newsroom, glanced at her former colleagues, and tilted the corners of her mouth in a weak smile. Raised eyebrows and tentative smiles greeted her. Undoubtedly they'd all heard the story, at least Mr. Phifer's or the photographer's version. Fortunately Jesse Miller wasn't there that morning. Typewriters clicked as Charlotte approached the editor's office.

Charlotte gave a hesitant rap on the door. Holding her breath, she waited on unstable legs.

She heard a gruff call to enter but didn't move. Several seconds passed before she pushed on the door and stepped over the threshold.

"You!" he growled. "What do you want, Miss Hale? Out with it. I haven't time to waste."

Charlotte straightened and lifted her chin. "My pay. I neglected to pick it up when I quit my job."

The red in Mr. Phifer's ruddy complexion darkened to purple. "The nerve! What makes you think you deserve any pay?"

Charlotte stepped closer. "I worked hard and I deserve compensation."

"You deserve nothing," he boomed as he came around from his desk. Halting only a hair's breadth away, he towered above her.

She took a step backward, hitting her head against the hard wood. "Nevertheless, you must pay me."

"And if I don't?"

Her body melted to jelly. "I'll — I'll tell everyone I know that you refused to give me my just wages. I know quite a few Newporters, and they might not take kindly to your unfairness. They might even stop buying your newspaper."

"Get out of my office and never darken my door again." He wagged a beefy finger at Charlotte.

"I shall collect my wages from the bookkeeper right now. And don't try to stop me,

Mr. Phifer." She opened the door and stepped into the newsroom, still shocked by her own audacity. She headed for the bookkeeper's office, her heart hammering in her chest, and only started to breathe again when he didn't follow her. He was going to let her collect her salary and leave!

Five minutes later, with her money safely in her reticule, Charlotte rushed down the staircase and out into the noise and bustle of Thames Street.

Thank You, Lord. I couldn't have done that without You. She leaned against a storefront window and slowly regained her equilibrium. Without His courage she never would've demanded her salary. Feeling better, she strolled down the opposite side of Thames Street in search of a position. But at least her pay provided a short reprieve, and she was more than thankful.

A week later Daniel spent the afternoon helping Mrs. Finnegan and the children pack books from his study shelves. After emptying the top shelf, he turned to his desk. He hadn't expected to ever move from Summerhill, but he'd easily found a buyer through word of mouth. And the prospective owners were anxious to move in.

Clearing off his desk, he discovered an

envelope inscribed "Newspaper Columns." Inside he found all his writings organized with explanatory notes. Charlotte's work. He bit his lip. Her absence still stung.

His mother shuffled into the office, her hair carefully done up with her best diamond-studded pins. A long strand of pearls hung around the neck of a fancy ruffled blouse as if she expected company. She probably did. Mr. McClintock visited faithfully each day, always bearing some small gift. A book, a box of sweets, a bouquet of carnations or roses. *At least she has found love.*

"You're looking chipper today," Daniel said as he placed Charlotte's envelope in a packing crate.

"Indeed, I am. My dear friend Mr. Mc-Clintock and I are going for a carriage ride. There's nothing like bracing sea air to restore one's health."

"I couldn't agree more." He opened another drawer.

Vivian slid into the chair with the broken springs. "You need to throw away this piece of junk."

He nodded. If they were staying he'd eventually have a footman cart it up to the attic. But a move required he rid the entire house of his paraphernalia, including every "treasure" stored away. Perhaps he should have allowed Charlotte to clean it out when she first came. Or maybe her seemingly generous gesture was merely a trick to gain access to a likely hiding spot for his personal things. His chest compressed as he considered Charlotte's spying. He'd trusted her implicitly. His mother sighed, obviously reading his face. "I'm sorry to leave Newport, but I'm more than happy to leave Charlotte behind. She tried to ruin your life, Daniel."

When he'd returned home from Spring Creek Lodge, he'd told her about the incident with Missy and the photographer from the *Rhode Island Reporter.* She'd smirked as if she'd always known Charlotte's true character. Perhaps she had. Yet, despite the overwhelming evidence, he believed Charlotte's boss had misled her. And he couldn't forget how desperately she needed her salary just to survive. Now she lacked a job. He hoped she'd secure a good one quickly.

He should feel far angrier than he did, but he couldn't forget the enjoyment they'd had with the children and the lessons she'd taught him. He'd never again leave their care solely to others, not even to his mother.

"Charlotte deceived me, but she's repented, and I forgive her. At first I was angry, but after a while I realized she was trapped by her situation. She didn't want to mislead me, yet she felt she had no other choice. Eventually the Lord gave her the courage to confess."

His mother slumped in the chair, her chin resting for a moment on her tight collar. "It pains me to say it, but you're a fool, son. When will you stop trusting everyone?"

Daniel shrugged. "Probably never. But I don't want to argue about Charlotte. She's out of our lives forever, I'm afraid."

His mother's face drew in at the cheeks and fine lines seemed to have deepened overnight. Her complexion was tinged with a sickly gray. "Are you feeling well?" he asked.

She straightened her shoulders. "My energy is still low and every now and again my heart hurts. I spoke to Doctor Lowe and we agreed my little spells are nothing to worry about."

"I can fetch him right now if you wish."

"Thank you, but I don't want you to go to any trouble."

Daniel stood up. "It's no trouble, Mother."

"There's no need. Mr. McClintock will be arriving in a few minutes, and I don't want our visit spoiled by a doctor."

471

Daniel nodded, unconvinced. "Now who's the foolish one?"

She bristled. "I'm a grown woman. Don't you think I'd send for the doctor if I needed him?"

Daniel raised his palms in surrender. "Of course."

Mr. Grimes waddled into the study, an envelope in hand. "A boy delivered this from the college. President Ralston, he said."

Daniel slit open the envelope and removed a short note. *Professor Wilmont, please stop by my office at your earliest convenience.* He read it aloud to his mother. "I wonder what that's all about."

"Oh, do and go find out at once, Daniel."

As curious as his mother, Daniel washed and changed from his work clothes into a charcoal summer suit and black bowler. In half an hour he was seated in President Ralston's grand office, waiting for the academic to get to the point of the meeting. The administrator paced, bending forward, hands clasped behind his back. His furrowed forehead suggested this meeting wasn't to his liking. His heavy eyebrows twitched.

"Professor, it's come to my attention that you're an exceptionally gifted teacher. Your students give you high praise. In a word, they insist you stay at the college."

"Oh?" Daniel murmured, wondering if perhaps some of his students' parents forced President Ralston to reconsider his forced resignation.

"So, if you'd like, you may keep your position as Bible professor. And you may continue to write your column with the *Newport Gazette*."

"Just like that?" He couldn't imagine which students had become his advocates.

"Yes. I always keep an open mind and listen to all points of view."

Daniel struggled to stifle a laugh.

"Will you remain with us, Professor?"

"I shall be delighted to continue my teaching duties. May I ask who spoke up for me?"

The president shook his head. "Many of the students and their parents want you to remain here, but your strongest advocate was one of your students, Agnes Brownington."

Daniel hurried to Summerhill, bursting with his news. His mother's smile flashed genuine relief.

"Splendid," she said to Daniel. And then her gaze slid to Mr. McClintock, seated on the wicker chair beside her. "I would have missed you, Horace."

Ruthie threw her arms around Daniel and buried her head in his chest while Tim jumped and whooped like a wild man. Mrs. Finnegan hustled to the drawing room to unpack vases and figurines from the mantel and whatnot shelves.

Daniel fetched the gig and drove to Bridge Street in search of Charlotte. Surely she'd want to know about President Ralston's change of heart. He halted the gig in front of Charlotte's home and knocked at the door. While he waited, children down the block romped on the sidewalk, shouting, playing jacks, rolling hoops. Women with shopping bags and toddlers in hand greeted the little children as they passed by. These were native Newporters, whose ancestors had founded the city by the sea over two hundred and fifty years before, common people whose husbands worked hard for a living down at the docks and in the ship-yards.

The gaunt Mrs. Hillman opened the door a crack, then when she recognized him, she flung it open and stepped aside.

"Do come in, Professor Wilmont. I expect you're looking for my niece. If you'll wait in the parlor, I'll fetch her."

Daniel followed Mrs. Hillman into the

claustrophobic room, overwhelmed by carefully displayed clutter. A few family photographs lined up against the faded wallpaper, afghans draped over chairs, and a vase of yellow daisies graced the side table. He noticed the Bible he'd given Charlotte for her birthday lay beside the flowers. He stood by the fireplace, his hands shoved deep in his pockets. Every nerve in his body jangled like a sack of coins.

Charlotte entered the parlor, wariness veiling her eyes. She wore a simple violet dress, far prettier than the plain uniform his mother made her wear. "Good morning, Daniel. I didn't expect to see you again." By the edge in her voice he knew she expected an explanation. She didn't project the friendliness he'd hoped for.

"I have excellent news I want to share, but first I want to give you your pay. You left Summerhill so quickly I didn't have a chance." He handed her an envelope, but she shook her head.

"I appreciate your kindness, but I don't deserve it. Not when Mr. Phifer was paying me too. But thank you all the same. You're more than generous." She glanced at the envelope he placed on a table, but she didn't reach to pick it up.

"So, what is your good news?"

He couldn't help grinning, even though she stood there, so stiff and inhospitable. "President Ralston reinstated me, so I'll be staying in Newport."

She allowed a small smile to play on the corners of her mouth. "I'm so happy for you and your family. How did that come about?"

"Agnes Brownington and her father intervened, along with some other parents." He hoped Charlotte would cheer up at his good news, but her fingers gripped the back of an overstuffed chair and her smile remained uncertain.

"I'm thankful this worked out in the end, though I deeply regret my part in all your troubles."

"But that's all in the past now."

She shook her head. "It's not that easy to ignore betrayal. But thank you for stopping by to tell me you're staying in Newport." She started for the front hallway.

Apparently Charlotte expected him to follow. He lingered by the mantel, unwilling to leave until he said what he'd really come here to say. "Charlotte, I want you to know I hold no hard feelings toward you. We all commit sin and we all make errors in judgment. God forgives us, so we must forgive one another." He took a deep breath. "If you're willing, I hope we can begin again. We can make a fresh start and forget the past."

She shook her head. "That's not possible, Daniel. I'm so sorry."

He feared she might resist his clumsy attempt at reconciliation, but he couldn't let her turn away. "Why? I love you, Charlotte, and I thought you loved me as well."

He shouldn't have asked that question because he didn't want to hear the answer. From the dejection tugging at her mouth and dulling her eyes, Daniel knew her response wasn't the one he wished for. He wanted to take her in his arms and kiss away all her reservations. And guilt.

Her shoulders slumped. "You think you forgive me, and perhaps you really do. But you'll never forget how I betrayed you, no matter how hard you try." Her lower lip trembled as she raised her chin and stepped toward the front door.

"Maybe you'll reconsider when more time has passed." Surely she'd realize his love could fill an ocean and drown all her guilt. "You know I've forgiven you, but now you must forgive yourself."

Charlotte opened the front door and stood back to let him pass. "You're a good man, Daniel Wilmont. A godly man. And I'm sorry I caused you so much pain."

He leaned down to kiss her, but she moved to the side and gently shook her head. "I'm afraid it won't work for us."

His shoulders slumped. "It could if you'd only try to let go of your guilt. Good day, Charlotte."

"Good-bye. I'll miss you, Daniel," she whispered.

Twenty-Five

Charlotte clicked the door shut and shuffled to the parlor on wobbly legs. Collapsing into the chair by the window, she watched Daniel's buggy disappear down the street. He glanced back but didn't spot her behind the lacy curtains stirring in the morning breeze.

His buggy turned the corner and he was gone. She already missed him dreadfully. Her chest ached with thoughts of what might have been.

She'd so wanted to melt into his arms and feel his warmth surround her. She needed his strength and good sense to keep her on track, to see how her life fit into God's plan. To bring her stability. She could marry him now because he'd be staying in Newport, and most importantly, he knew of her betrayal. He forgave her, but as a good Christian, what other choice did he have? He had to disregard her transgressions or at least try to. But in his heart could he truly forget what she'd done?

She thought not. And that prevented her from acquiescing to his pleas. Nothing would erase the resentment he must feel toward her, though he'd try his best to cover it up. But she couldn't live with that.

For several minutes she let tears stream down her cheeks. Yet what was the point of pitying herself? Moping wouldn't secure her a job or pay for groceries or doctor bills.

With great effort Charlotte put on her hat, grabbed her reticule, and left for town. Her heels dragged on the dirt sidewalk as she stopped to talk to friends and acquaintances out for their morning errands to the market or dry goods store. She kept up her end of the conversation, smiled when appropriate, and tried to rid her mind of her woes. After all, she wasn't the only one with troubles. And she had to remember, hers were of her own making. She had no right to feel sorry for herself.

For three hours she searched in shops and offices for any job that would bring in money. Although she was willing to work hard for long hours, no one offered to hire her. She was either too inexperienced, too young, or of the wrong gender to suit.

On her way home Charlotte stopped by Knowles Roofing and paid the bill with her governess salary. She hated to use Daniel's money, but he'd left it for her and she needed to pay the roofer. Later, after she found a job, she'd return the sum to Daniel.

"I'm dreadfully sorry for the late payment, but this settles my account."

He took the cash and counted it. "All right. It's all here. You're lucky you gave me the money because I was about to contact my lawyer again. I can't make a living if customers refuse to pay."

Charlotte held her tongue. "I apologize for the inconvenience, Mr. Knowles. Good day."

She returned home, her feet sore and her spirit deflated. She fought back a surge of anxiety. Indulging in fear wouldn't help one bit. But prayer might.

Heavenly Father, You know my needs without my even telling You. Please provide for my family and me in the way You find best. I can't seem to manage on my own. I'm at my wits' end. Don't let us down, Lord.

Daniel drove the gig to the Coastal Inn to see Jackson Grail. He found him with his wife, Lilly, pushing the baby pram around paths that edged the back lawn of the small hotel. A sea breeze, soaked with salt and humidity, blew inland and stirred the silk ribbons on Lilly's hat. Daniel waved as the couple descended onto a wooden bench set beneath a gently swaying elm.

After greeting each other, Daniel leaned against the tree trunk. "I've good news. President Ralston reinstated me so I'll continue to teach at the college." He summarized yesterday's events, leaving out Charlotte's involvement.

"That's excellent," Jack said, "though I'm sorry you won't be coming to New York. But I suppose this is what you and your family really wanted."

"It is. But I greatly appreciate your job offer."

"You would've been a tremendous asset to Jones and Jarman. But perhaps you can still write a religion column for the *Manhattan Sentinel.* What do you say to weekly?"

Daniel nodded, again thankful for his friend's kindness. "I'd like that."

When a cool gust of wind brought a chill, Lilly bent over the baby's pram and pulled the blanket up to little Jackson's chin. Jack glanced at his infant son, obviously bursting with pride. Daniel remembered how happy and amazed he'd felt when Ruthie and Tim were little ones. And how much he wished for another child. Charlotte's child. He didn't care if it was a boy or a girl. One more or ten more.

As if he could read Daniel's thoughts, Jack tilted his head and hiked a brow. "I'd like to ask you a personal question."

Daniel nodded but braced himself.

Jack shifted on the hard bench. "Lilly and I wondered if you're interested — romantically — in your children's governess. You seem so at ease together." Jack cleared his throat. "If you care about her, then don't let her get away." He flicked an embarrassed smile and then glanced at his wife. "I had to fight for Lilly. I never gave up, even though she mistakenly thought she ought to marry someone else."

Daniel laughed. "I'm sure you made a wise decision, Mrs. Grail."

Lilly nodded as the baby mewed and slowly awoke. On her feet in an instant, she bent over her child, cooing softly. "No doubt he's hungry. If you'll excuse me, I shall go inside before he starts crying. Good seeing you again, Daniel. And do take Jack's advice."

"I know I shouldn't intrude," Jack persisted, "but I'd hate to see you lose the woman you seem to love." His voice trailed off, but he was clearly awaiting a response.

Daniel dropped on the bench beside Jack.

"I didn't realize my feelings were so obvious." He buried his head in his hands. "I've already let Charlotte get away. The situation is complicated and I don't see a happy resolution."

"Is there anything I can do to help?"

"No, I don't believe so. But thank you. I'll have to work this out for myself. Actually, it's Charlotte who must search her soul. I proposed and she turned me down."

Jack gave him a sympathetic thump on the back. "Don't give up just because she declined. Give her time."

Daniel hoped his friend was right, but he wondered if anything would alleviate the guilt Charlotte felt. He bade Jack good-bye and returned home to find his mother and Mr. McClintock on the front veranda sipping lemonade. For once Vivian flashed a grin so broad it appeared genuine. He looked closer. Though her complexion had a gray tinge he found alarming, the sparkle in her eyes made him question his observation. He'd never seen her happier. And apparently she felt well, also.

She reached over and touched Mr. McClintock's hand. "Horace and I have exciting news. We want you to be the first to know."

Mr. McClintock covered Vivian's hand

484

with his own and sat up even straighter than usual. Through a thick mustache heavily laced with silver, he quirked a self-satisfied smile. "Daniel, your mother and I are going to marry. We haven't set a date, but it will be soon if I have anything to say about it."

"Congratulations, Horace! And Mother, best wishes!"

Daniel leaned back against the veranda railing and stared at the happy couple through new eyes. He suspected the wiry little fellow, a few inches shorter than his tall, frail mother, had romantic inclinations. But after several years of courting, Daniel wasn't sure Horace would ever progress to marriage. He was an excellent catch for his difficult mother. Daniel felt sure Horace would soften her and smooth out her sharp edges. Her life with his father had been intolerable. She deserved a second chance at happiness and the Lord had given her one.

"There's no reason for us to wait. The sooner we can arrange for the ceremony, the better. It will be a simple affair with just family and friends. We'll take a trip to Boston and then I'll move into his charming home on Narragansett Avenue."

"That sounds wonderful."

Vivian nodded. "But first I'll interview

governesses. Without me here to supervise, caring for the children will be too much for Mrs. Finnegan. But don't worry, Daniel. I'll hire a capable, mature woman, not some young and flighty thing who might have designs on you."

Daniel winced. "Mother, you're totally wrong about Charlotte. Despite her mistakes, she's kind and unselfish. And if it wasn't for her, my picture would've been on the front page of the *Rhode Island Reporter* with my student Missy Le Beau. I have a lot to thank Charlotte for."

Vivian's mouth dropped open. "Grant you, she finally came to her senses, but her spying on you in your own home is unforgivable." Her face scrunched with distaste.

"She's very apologetic, Mother. And she deserves to be forgiven."

"Perhaps, but don't give her more credit than she deserves." Vivian's voice held a note of uncertainty.

"You're forgetting her good qualities. The children love her. She's playful and high spirited and —"

His mother sighed. "Yes, she was a conscientious and fun-loving governess. So perhaps she wasn't as ill-suited as I first supposed."

"Are you going to sell Summerhill or will

you keep it?" Mr. McClintock asked.

Daniel shook his head, glad for the change of topic. "I'm not sure. There's much to pray about and consider."

Two weeks later Daniel watched the whirl of wedding preparations from the sidelines. Vivian organized an intimate ceremony at the campus church with a small reception at Summerhill. She invited a few family members from Boston, neighbors, and summer friends, and hired extra help for Chef Jacques. In record time her favorite Newport dressmaker designed a simple cream gown, tasteful for a woman of her age, and galvanized an entire force of seamstresses.

Two weeks later the wedding day arrived with a burst of sunshine and cool late summer breezes. Only a few puffy clouds floated across a deep azure sky. At two o'clock Daniel walked his mother down the aisle of the campus church, grateful for her happiness. She leaned heavily on his arm, and he wondered if her nerves caused her weakness or an unfortunate resurgence of her heart problems. Her insistence on a quick wedding brooked no disagreement.

As the pastor declared the couple man and wife, Daniel prayed they'd have a joyous marriage. His mind wandered to his own life, not blessed with much happiness lately. Loneliness for Charlotte soaked his spirit, destroying the peace and joy he usually experienced. Before the altar he gave his mother to Horace and wished he and Charlotte were standing together in front of the minister pledging their own love and fidelity.

Moments later, Vivian and Horace became a newly minted couple proudly walking down the aisle to the strains of the joyous recessional. Despite her fragility and hesitant footsteps, his mother looked lovely as she beamed at her guests. Ruthie marched behind the couple, still strewing the leftover rose petals from a straw basket, tears glistening in her eyes. Tim pulled at his too tight, starched collar as he followed along with Daniel.

They returned to Summerhill, which was decorated with pink and white roses from the garden, and had a delicious luncheon with melon, soft-shelled crabs, squab, and salad, followed by ices and cake in the dining room.

Daniel would've enjoyed it, he mused, if hadn't felt so alone in the crowd.

Charlotte counted the money she had left from her last payday at the *Rhode Island*

Reporter and from Daniel. Just a few dollars remained. She had enough for a week's worth of groceries, which was more than many people had, so she ought not worry. The Lord would provide, but He couldn't tarry much longer. She needed a job.

Charlotte shoved the funds into a box on her wardrobe shelf and then collapsed in a hard chair by her bedroom window. Aunt Amelia and Becky had taken in more sewing and mending lately while she scoured all of Newport for a position.

Aunt Amelia peered into the room, a shirtwaist draped over her arm. "Would you mind running an errand? I need a spool of white thread and a packet of needles."

Charlotte rose. "I'd be glad to. And while I'm at it, I'll continue my search."

As she strode up and down Thames Street, she realized she'd inquired into every respectable store in the commercial district. The only places she hadn't considered were pubs and the wharves, which required strong young men with muscular backs and salty tongues or saucy young women able to endure their long looks and heavy flirting. She purchased her aunt's items and then turned toward home. Approaching the *Rhode Island Reporter,* she gave an inadvertent shiver.

Lord, please don't let me run in to anyone I know. Taking long strides, she quickly passed the newspaper offices and kept up her brisk pace. She glanced across the street clogged with wagons and carriages and noticed newly painted gold letters on the second story windows of one of the many brick buildings lining Thames Street. The *Newport Gazette,* Arnie Phifer's competitor.

If Daniel didn't write a column for the newspaper, she would've run to their office and applied for a position the moment she quit the *Rhode Island Reporter.* But he did work for them.

She missed Daniel, the children, and Mrs. Finnegan, though not the cranky Mrs. Wilmont. Charlotte sighed. Her optimism drained, she returned to Bridge Street without hope for the future.

Aunt Amelia poured Charlotte a cup of tea and sat beside her at the kitchen table. A stack of mail lay before them. Slowly, Charlotte opened each envelope and grimaced after scanning the contents.

"Are we falling behind on our bills?" Aunt Amelia looked up from her mending. Her long face looked so fearful, Charlotte couldn't bear to look upon her.

"Yes, but I'm sure a suitable job will come along soon." Charlotte gave a humorless laugh. "I'd like to work at the *Newport Gazette,* but that's the one business where I can't even apply."

Aunt Amelia touched her hand with sympathy. "Because of the professor?"

"Yes. Working for the same newspaper would be more than a little awkward. He doesn't go into the offices often, but when he does we'd be bound to see each other. And besides, I'm quite sure he'd object to me working there."

"You don't know that for certain. He might be more forgiving than you realize."

Charlotte laughed. "He might *say* he wouldn't mind, but of course he really would."

Squeezing Charlotte's hand, Aunt Amelia shook her head. "It's time to put aside your differences and face up to reality. We need money to pay our expenses. I'm doing my best, but sewing only brings in a little bit." She gave a weary sigh. "I'm sorry to burden you with so much responsibility."

Charlotte sipped her tea then rose from the table, anxious to try out a new plan. "I happen to have an idea for a job that may just work. If you'll excuse me, I must change my clothes and be off."

"Tell me what's bubbling in your mind," Aunt Amelia coaxed.

491

Charlotte shook her head as she headed up the stairs to her bedroom. "No. I don't want to raise your hopes. Nothing may come of it."

"Oh, do tell," Becky insisted as she wheeled into the parlor. "We can use some excitement around here. We've moped long enough."

"You'll have to wait, but not for long. I'll be back within a few hours. But truly, don't be too optimistic or you might have your hopes dashed. Say a prayer I'm doing the right thing."

Charlotte closed the door, dressed in her favorite summer outfit — a lavender blue skirt and her new shirtwaist and her best hat with a feather rising on the side. Parasol and reticule in hand, she'd hire a carriage on Thames Street. She could ill afford the luxury of traveling in such style, but neither could she ride her bicycle in the heat for several miles. She didn't wish to appear sweaty and disheveled when she arrived at Summerhill. Taking a handful of coins from her top bureau drawer, she gripped them firmly, reluctant to part with even a penny. Hard to come by, but so easy to spend.

Lord, I hope I'm doing the right thing.

Her heart twisted as the hired cab drew closer to the Wilmonts' cottage. Perhaps she should direct her driver to turn about and head back to town as quickly as his horse could gallop — before she made a fool of herself in front of Daniel, and God forbid, his dreadful mother. They slowed and rolled onto the driveway leading up to Summerhill. Charlotte's eyes widened. At least thirty or more carriages waited on the circle in front of the porch, and dozens of people dressed to the nines, along with uniformed servants, lingered around the veranda and yard. In the distance, probably from the back lawn, came the genteel sounds of a string quartet. What was going on? Curiosity grabbed hold as she climbed down from the carriage.

"Please wait. I'll not take longer than ten or fifteen minutes." Her throat dried and her body trembled. Whatever possessed her to come to Summerhill, today of all days? She must be mad. Or perhaps merely desperate.

Simone smiled from around the corner of the cottage, a silver tray in hand. Charlotte wove through the crowd and greeted Mrs. Wilmont's maid. Simone's smile looked genuine, if harried.

"What is going on?" Charlotte asked.

"A wedding. Mrs. Wilmont just married Mr. McClintock. We could have used your help. Look at me, carrying a tray like a foot-man or maid. But some of the extra help didn't appear, so Jacques needed assistance. How could I refuse my dear husband?"

"Of course you couldn't," Charlotte mumbled as she took in the crowd. Tomorrow might be a better day to speak to Daniel, though her courage could easily fail between now and then. She glanced toward her waiting carriage and retraced her steps, eager to leave. Head down, Charlotte avoided some of the curious glances from the servants.

When she reached the hired cab, the anxiety in her chest rushed out and relief filled her. The driver assisted her inside and she settled onto the seat. She'd probably find Daniel alone tomorrow in a quiet house, much more conducive to conversation. Yes, she'd return then, after praying for a courageous spirit.

Running footsteps crunched against the pebbled path and grabbed her attention. Daniel. He pulled open the carriage door and heaved himself inside. Charlotte's heart lurched as her hand thumped against her chest.

"You surprised me, Daniel. I hoped to slip away."

He slid beside her, crowding her into the

corner. Her breath felt trapped deep inside her lungs.

"I'm so glad to see you again, Charlotte. And so surprised." He took her hand in his. "Excuse me for speaking so plainly, but have you changed your mind and decided to return to Summerhill? To me?"

His turquoise eyes sparkled with hope. She couldn't bear to disappoint him, but she must. Quickly, before she lost her nerve.

"No. I've come to ask a favor."

He still smiled, but the sparkle in his eyes faded.

"I know it's audacious to request anything from you, Daniel, after the way I came into your home and deceived you. If you decline to hear me, I understand."

He squeezed her hand and waves of heat singed her heart. Her love for him hadn't diminished. She glanced toward the guests milling around the front lawn and veranda, their eyes wide with curiosity. "May we talk tomorrow when there aren't so many people about?"

"Please stay." He pressed her hand and melted her resolve.

Charlotte's voice quavered. "You ought to return to your guests. We're attracting too much attention." She slid her hand away but made no move to direct the carriage forward.

"I'll go back to the party as long as you come with me."

She strangled a bitter laugh. "I won't spoil your mother's wedding day. But please send her my best wishes."

Daniel shook his head. "I shan't leave this carriage unless you come with me. If you refuse, I'll sit here with you for the rest of the day."

Charlotte chuckled. "Daniel, think of your mother. This is *her* day."

He groaned. "All right then, come inside and wait for me. The reception will end soon and we'll have time to talk."

"But my driver —"

Daniel reached into his jacket pocket, pulled out some coins, and handed them up to him. "I'll send you home in my carriage," he said, helping her out.

"Thank you, Daniel, but I really shouldn't linger." Much as she'd like this to become a personal visit, it concerned business, nothing more.

But Daniel's crestfallen face convinced her to reconsider. Perhaps she ought to speak with him now and not delay. "Oh, all right, but I'll wait in the servants' hall."

"Please come to the reception with me, Charlotte."

She shook her head.

He shrugged, and his shoulders slumped in defeat. "As you wish. The guests are leaving, so I'll not take long."

Charlotte followed him down the driveway, then skirted around the cottage, brushing against the blue hydrangeas edging Summerhill's stone foundation. She hurried to the basement, relieved to find it empty except for a few servants scurrying around with trays laden with *petit fours* and crystal glasses brimming with champagne. The maids in their best black uniforms and spotless pinafores and caps greeted her with bright smiles and quick greetings, too busy to stop and chat. Charlotte settled into a hard chair and waited in the empty servants' hall.

Minutes ticked by. Maids and footmen carried in leftover food and dishes and the kitchen help scrubbed pots and pans. Mrs. Finnegan waddled into the kitchen, huffing from treading up and down stairs too frequently.

"Ah, you're a sight for me old eyes. What brings you back to Summerhill?" She led Charlotte into the staff dining room and soon returned with glasses of lemonade and iced *petit fours*. "We all miss you. Ruthie and Tim are cranky and running wild without your guiding hand. And the poor professor, bless his soul. He mopes around like he's lost his last friend." She cocked an eyebrow. "Perhaps he has."

Nothing slipped past Mrs. Finnegan. Charlotte stared at her hands twisting the gloves on her lap. "I miss him as well. And all of you."

Even in her absence she'd brought pain to the professor. It took time to overcome disappointment. After a while she'd fade from the forefront of his mind to a dusty back corner.

"I'm here to ask Professor Wilmont for a favor."

The housekeeper's mouth formed a downward crescent. "I hoped you'd come back to work. With Mrs. Wilmont now Mrs. McClintock, the children need a governess more than ever. And the professor, well, he needs a good woman. A wife."

A loud crash sounded in the kitchen, and Chef Jacques began to yell at someone in French. Mrs. Finnegan cocked a brow and heaved herself up. "Well, dearie, I've best go see what that's about." Mrs. Finnegan heaved to her feet with a groan. "It's the little scamps I worry about. They're missing you. My heart breaks to see them so down in the mouth."

"I miss them too." Charlotte's voice cracked.

She'd give Daniel a few more minutes before she left. But nearly a quarter hour passed before she finally decided to depart. Obviously she'd come at an inconvenient time. She scribbled a note to Daniel asking him to set a time for a meeting, if he didn't mind, and left it for him on his office desk.

Heading for the driveway, she rounded the side of Summerhill and noticed almost all the carriages had gone, including her own. Anxious to leave, she'd forgotten Daniel had promised his own buggy and driver. Then she spotted him and the newly wedded couple standing on the veranda. Mrs. McClintock clung to her husband, happiness lighting her worn face. She looked regal in her pearl gray walking suit and imposing hat, its plumes rising far above her husband's silk top hat. Charlotte stepped behind a cedar bush, not wishing to attract Mrs. McClintock's attention.

Then a gasp from the bride grabbed Charlotte's attention. Daniel's mother thrust her hand over her heart and collapsed onto the nearest wicker chair, bending over. Her breathing came in labored gasps.

Charlotte raced around the corner of the

house and up the veranda steps. "May I help?"

Daniel loosened the buttons on his mother's tight collar. "Help me get her to her bedroom." He looked toward Mr. McClintock, who stood perfectly still, as if in shock. "I think the doctor is lingering in the driveway, speaking to a couple of gentlemen. And fetch Simone too."

Daniel helped his mother rise and, step by step, led her slowly into the cottage. Her body rose and fell as she struggled to take a deep breath. Together Charlotte and Daniel helped her to her bed and covered her legs with a quilt.

"It's my heart," she said in a barely audible voice. "I fear I'm dying."

"No, Mrs. McClintock, you'll be fine. You have a long life ahead and a husband waiting for you to recover. We'll pray for you." Charlotte plumped the pillows beneath her back and head and helped to settle her on the bedspread. "Can I get you anything to ease the pain?"

"Yes, my nitroglycerin."

Daniel gave her the medication and slowly her breathing returned to normal. She dropped her hand from the bodice of her silk frock. "The pain is lessening, thank the Lord." Her voice barely rose above a whisper, but the agitation had disappeared. She closed her eyes for several seconds. When she opened them, she gazed steadily at Charlotte.

"Perhaps I should leave," Charlotte murmured. "I hope you'll be well soon, Mrs. McClintock." She stepped toward the door.

"No, please stay. I have something to say to you."

Charlotte turned around and faced her adversary who now looked so small and vulnerable lying on the large bed. "Yes, ma'am." She wondered if even in such a pitiable state the woman would criticize her for being back at Summerhill.

Mrs. McClintock motioned Daniel to leave the room. He hesitated, then quickly slipped through the doorway.

"Thank you for helping me just now. I truly thought I would die. Of course, I still might. I don't know if medicine will cure me. I'm afraid, Charlotte. But if it's my time to go to the Lord, nobody can keep me alive." A weak smile flickered at the corners of her mouth. "I don't want to meet my Maker with things left unsaid down here on earth."

Charlotte nodded, wondering where Mrs. McClintock's ramblings were leading. Charlotte drew closer to the bed.

"I — I'm sorry for being discourteous to you while you worked here. You were taking my place, and I could clearly see I wasn't needed anymore. Oh, I know you were only doing your job, but you did it all too well. I didn't want you to take over for me."

"No, you're the professor's mother. I could never take your place."

She managed a wan smile. "But he was so taken with you right from the start. I was afraid he'd want me to leave, since I'm more of a liability than an asset these days."

Charlotte took the woman's hand. "Daniel would never feel that way about you."

Mrs. McClintock nodded. "I should have known. Then when my new husband proposed, I began to understand the real meaning of love." Her eyes filled with remorse. "Charlotte, I apologize for not treating you with kindness. I know my son needs a wife by his side, but I thought only a young socialite would do. But I can see how much Daniel loves you and how lost he's been without you. Charlotte, can you find it in your heart to forgive me?"

Charlotte's throat went dry and she could barely speak. Mrs. McClintock was actually apologizing. "Yes, of course, I forgive you. The Lord has forgiven me and I must do the same." Oddly enough, she really meant

502

it. The anger she'd harbored seemed to melt away. She was amazed she could forgive Daniel's mother without hesitation and without lingering resentment. But God had changed her heart — both hers and Mrs. McClintock's.

"Thank you," Mrs. McClintock whispered and then closed her eyes.

Charlotte heard footsteps behind her. The doctor and Mr. McClintock followed Daniel over to the sleeping woman. Daniel watched her for a few moments and then quietly left the room with Charlotte close behind.

"She apologized to me," Charlotte said as they stepped into the hallway.

Daniel's face glowed with warmth and love as he took both her hands in his. A bolt of electricity shot through her from just his gentle touch, and she felt her legs grow unsteady, barely strong enough to hold her up.

"The Lord prompted her to forgive you," he said.

She gave a dry smile. "I believe that because I can't imagine your mother apologizing on her own."

Daniel moved even closer and she could smell the tang of his aftershave. "And did you forgive her? She certainly was unkind to you."

Charlotte shook her head. "Yes, I forgave her immediately. It's so very strange. I didn't even have to think about it. I just knew it was the right thing to do and I had to do it. Does that sound strange to you?"

Daniel chuckled. "No, not at all. That's how the Lord works sometimes. He helps you to become a better person than you ever thought you could be." He paused as she gazed down into her eyes. "Do you understand what forgiveness is all about now?"

"Yes, I do." She smiled at him, joy skipping across her heart.

"Do you see that because I love you, I can forgive you?" His voice was soft but urgent.

Charlotte nodded. "God forgives us and also helps us forgive others."

But she didn't have time to ponder his words because he leaned down and pressed his lips in a sweet, intense kiss that stole her breath. He embraced her with a hug, and she let herself dissolve into the heat of his arms. She'd never before felt so cherished and protected.

"I love you, Charlotte. Will you marry me?"

"Yes," she whispered without hesitation. "I love you too."

He pressed her even tighter until the door

opened and Doctor Lowe appeared. Charlotte gently pulled away, but Daniel kept her close.

The physician smiled. "Professor, I just wanted to report your mother is resting comfortably. She had a mild angina attack, but with enough rest, she should be fine."

"I'm relieved to hear that. Should she postpone her honeymoon to Boston?"

He nodded. "Yes, until she's feeling her usual self. And I'd like to examine her before she leaves. She needs to take good care of her health and avoid stress whenever possible."

"Thank you, Doctor."

They showed him to the front door and then lingered on the veranda as he departed in his buggy.

"Shall we tell the children our good news?" Daniel asked.

"We're right here, Papa." Ruthie, then Tim appeared from behind the potted palms in the far corner of the porch. When she saw Charlotte holding hands with her father, Ruthie's eyes widened. "Papa, Miss Hale, I guess the Lord has spoken, and you've both decided to finally listen. I'm so happy." She flung her arms around her father and Charlotte and let tears stream down her face.

Charlotte hugged her new family and let

the happiness she'd been unwilling to grasp pour through her.

Daniel slipped his arm around her waist. "You never told me why you came to Summerhill today."

She loved the warmth of being so close. "With all the excitement, I never got the chance. I couldn't find a job, so I decided to apply for anything available at the *Newport Gazette*. I've always wanted to become a journalist, and I'm perfectly willing to start at the bottom. I thought I should ask you if you minded."

"That's fine with me, but you won't need to work, you know."

Charlotte nodded. "But I'd very much like to. I'm used to supporting my aunt and sister. Even after we marry, I'll be responsible for them, along with Ruthie and Tim."

"In that case I shall write you a glowing recommendation," he said. "And of course, helping them will be part of my responsibility as well."

"I appreciate that, especially after all that's happened."

Ruthie clasped her hands to her chest and looked up at Daniel with pleading eyes. "Maybe Miss Hale's family can live at Summerhill with us. We have plenty of room, especially with Grandmother leaving. Oh please, Papa!"

Daniel grinned. "That's a wonderful idea. Charlotte, do you think they'd consider moving to Summerhill?"

She squeezed his hand. "You are so kind. I shall ask them, though I don't know what their answer will be."

Ruthie threw her arms around her father and Charlotte. "I knew the Lord would answer my prayers." Then she stepped away, grinning, as she and Tim headed inside the cottage to check on their grandmother.

"God's timing is perfect," Charlotte murmured. She rested her head on Daniel's broad shoulder, then after a few moments accepted the gift of his kiss and deep love, so much more than she'd ever expected. Arm in arm they strolled toward the sea. The fresh breeze wrapped them with its soft breath while sunshine beamed down from the heavens.

ACKNOWLEDGMENTS

Love on Assignment was the first novel I ever completed. Over the course of six years I wrote five different versions, two contemporary and three historical. Many giving and gifted people helped me along the way.

I'd like to thank Christy Barritt, Mary Connealy, Janet Jones Bann, Ginny Vail and Fran McNabb, all wonderful writers and fantastic friends. My Seeker sisters offered continual support and assistance to my writing journey and every day they bring love and laughter to our loop and to Seekerville. I'm especially thankful to my husband for everything he does to enable me to write. Without all his help I wouldn't find the time to type even one page. My son, Justin, and daughter, Alicia, encouraged me throughout the years to persevere and I'm so very grateful for their support.

And last but certainly not least, a heartfelt thanks to the Thomas Nelson team — editors, sales, marketing, etc. I'm especially grateful to Allen Arnold, Ami McConnell, Natalie Hanemann, Lisa Bergren, Becky Monds, and Katie Bond. Natalie and Lisa, you are both amazing editors.

And I'm most grateful to the Lord for giving me His story to tell.

READING GROUP GUIDE

1. Mr. Phifer presents Charlotte with an opportunity to further her career, but it involves compromising her integrity and secretly spying. She asks herself: "Was it really ethical to investigate an unsuspecting man, even for an admirable cause?" What do you think?

2. Charlotte is surprised by how kind Daniel Wilmont turns out to be when she interviews for the governess position. When is heeding someone's reputation important and when is it too judgmental? Have you ever made decisions about someone's character before you actually met them?

3. When Charlotte begins working for the Wilmonts, Daniel does not know his children very well. How does she help him grow closer to them? Why is she in particular so effective in helping Daniel with this?

4. Charlotte and Daniel do not always agree

on how to raise children. Charlotte believes the children should have more freedom while Daniel believes in constant supervision and guidance. Is one opinion more right than the other? Why or why not?

5. Why did Charlotte find it strange when the children and Daniel prayed for things like her hurt shoulder? Do you ever think some of your problems are too small to pray for? What does God actually tell us about prayer?

6. Mr. Phifer and Daniel are both Charlotte's bosses throughout the novel. What obstacles does having two supervisors cause for Charlotte? Have you ever tried to serve two masters? What was the outcome?

7. Several characters in the novel have difficult pasts that haunt them. How does their remembered pain affect their present-day decisions? And how do many of them decide, like Daniel does, to "shake off sad memories and concentrate on . . . life"?

8. Charlotte reads this Bible verse: "But he that doeth truth cometh to the light, that his deeds may be manifest, that they are wrought in God." What does it have to do with her story in the novel?

9. The attic at the Wilmonts' house is crowded with old, forgotten trinkets that Daniel doesn't want to let go of. What else does he not want to let go of in his own life? Is your "attic" too crowded right now? How can you clean it out, focusing on the present instead of the past?

10. Ruthie and Tim lost their mother when they were young. What stress has this put on Daniel? What struggles does a single-parent home face that one with both parents would not understand?

11. Why do think Sarah, Daniel's wife, experienced so much depression despite her wealth and societal status?

12. Sarah's journal reveals a lot about her marriage to Daniel. Was one party to blame over the other for their unhappiness? How could they both have been at fault?

13. At one point, Daniel says his work comes first in his life. How do you balance work and a family? What or who should be prioritized and when?

14. Why were Daniel's columns for the *Newport Gazette* considered so controversial in that time period? What would people reading them today think?

15. Daniel is given an ultimatum by his boss: either stop writing his newspaper

column or lose his job as a professor. What would you have done if you were Daniel? Have you ever been forced to choose between your values and your source of income?

16. Vivian Wilmont does not hide her bad opinion of Charlotte but eventually reveals the reasons for her unkindness. Were you able to understand why Mrs. Wilmont would be so protective of her son? How does her character accurately depict the complex relationship with in-laws and with mothers and sons?

17. After seeing how Missy LeBeau acted around Daniel, Charlotte asked herself, "Why was the professor so open and trusting to others, ignoring their less than honest motives?" What do you think? How do you balance trusting others too much and too little?

18. Why is Charlotte reluctant to accept Daniel's proposal? What obstacles were they facing as a couple?

19. Ruthie makes a poignant statement when she says "praying is important, but sometimes the Lord is slow in answering." How did several characters in this novel have to wait on the Lord? Do you ever feel He is slow in answering?

20. Charlotte says she often adjusts her eth-

ics according to what situation she is in. Are you more moral in some situations than in others? Do some of your high standards not apply in certain areas of your life?